FIC
WES

West, Paul

Terrestrials

$24.00

Also by Paul West

Fiction
Sporting with Amaryllis
The Tent of Orange Mist
Love's Mansion
The Women of Whitechapel and Jack the Ripper
Lord Byron's Doctor
The Place in Flowers Where Pollen Rests
The Universe, and Other Fictions
Rat Man of Paris
The Very Rich Hours of Count von Stauffenberg
Gala
Colonel Mint
Caliban's Filibuster
Bela Lugosi's White Christmas
I'm Expecting to Live Quite Soon
Alley Jaggers
Tenement of Clay

Nonfiction
My Mother's Music
A Stroke of Genius
Sheer Fiction—Volumes I, II, III
James Ensor
Portable People
Out of My Depths: A Swimmer in the Universe
Words for a Deaf Daughter
I, Said the Sparrow
The Wine of Absurdity
The Snow Leopard
The Modern Novel
Byron and the Spoiler's Art

TERRESTRIALS

A Novel

PAUL WEST

SCRIBNER

SCRIBNER
1230 Avenue of the Americas
New York, NY 10020

SCRIBNER and design are trademarks of Simon & Schuster Inc.

Portions of this novel previously appeared, in different form, in
Conjunctions, The Bookpress, and *The Literary Insomniac*,
an anthology published by Doubleday.

Designed by Colin Joh
Set in Electra

Manufactured in the United States of America

1 3 5 7 9 10 8 6 4 2

Library of Congress Cataloging-in-Publication Data
West, Paul, date.
Terrestrials : a novel / Paul West.
p.   cm.
I. Title.
PR6073.E766T47   1997
813'.54—dc21   97-20293
CIP
ISBN 0-684-80032-2

For Steve and Jeanne, with love

For Steve and Jeanne, with love.

No, never anymore, lest its mysterious fascination, whose invisible wing had brushed my heart up there, should change to unavailing regret in a man too old for its glory.

—Joseph Conrad, after his first flight

had intended to keep secret the nature of *Terrestrials* until the book's end, but worldly counsel has persuaded me otherwise. This novel is a simulation of what a book from outer space might be like (I call it *The Novel from Centaurus*, but it might just as well have come from Andromeda). So it contains quite a number of carefully worked errors, falterings, feats of valiant incomprehension. The narrator, whose name is One Eighth Humbly, has particular trouble with the concept of seasons and with that of espionage. His notion of the novel, based more on movies and TV transmissions than on literature proper, tends to be sketchy, but he has gleaned from sundry sources what the novel is like, and the form haunts him. He does his best, and he actually improves as he advances; an able stylist in the foreign idiom of English, he tries to tell the story of two aliens, pilots, whose conspicuous career at its height has been in SR-71 *Blackbird*s, the most famous spy planes of all. His story may seem derivative from all kinds of action movies, but his meditative mind proves him an original who understands psychology even if at an enormous distance.

So, then, *Terrestrials* is an overture, a puzzling out by One Eighth Humbly for *us* to puzzle out. The book ends with a recital of what he deems his weaknesses and errors, but the list is not complete. Some of his flubs are mild, as if a science student from a Russian university had enrolled at Oxford to study Greek and Latin; others are severe, as when he has enormous trouble with the word November (which, of course, is the source of the code letter N emblazoned on all U.S. aircraft). Let us say that he transmitted his manuscript at the speed of light all as a single word, which some recipient such as I has disentangled. In other words he has published his attempt, and reading it puts us in some odd positions and leads us quite a chase, as Burke said a work of art should. This is science fiction in reverse: an alien imagining how two aliens would fare while functioning as humans on Earth with no memory whatever of their life in another constellation.

The purpose of the square brackets embedded here and there in the text reveals itself toward the end.

CONTENTS

1. The Feast of Crispian
13

2. Blaue Augen
145

3. A One-Way Ticket to Palookaville
239

4. Rosebud
295

5. Shane
369

The Feast of Crispian

This day is called the feast of Crispian:
He that outlives this day, and comes safe home,
Will stand a-tiptoe when this day is named,
And rouse him at the name of Crispian.
—William Shakespeare, *Henry V, IV.iii. 40*

never having seen themselves from above, or behind, as they sat side by side in front of twin panels bristling with toggles and switches, rosy bulbs and quivering blue-metal needles, they did not know they resembled two inhuman helmets with fins. In the nineteen fifties, or even earlier, you could buy candies in the shape of these men: jelly-babies, and you popped them higgledy-piggledy into your mouth, sank teeth into several at one time, mingling raspberry, grape, honey, orange, peppermint as your saliva flowed. Or you bought plastic replicas of such men for pennies, wondering how mannequins could be manufactured at the sit, with thighs drawn up and knees bent. Then glued them, an inch high at most, into their seats in the model, usually an airplane, but sometimes a motor torpedo boat or a flame-throwing tank. The expressions never changed. The thighs and knees never unbent. The helmets never came off. It was amazing.

So too with Booth and Clegg, at eighty thousand feet over a smudged curl in the Nile west of Abu Hamed with Mount Oda behind them to the east. At three times the speed of sound they were only half an hour away from their Turkish base. Had their cockpit been open, as in the old barnstorming days, their speech would have been ripped away by the slipstream, or indeed their heads from their necks, and their blood forced back into its soft tubings even as the near-vacuum of the heterosphere invited it into the open.

Way down below them were the mother-of-pearl clouds, at over ten thousand, and the night-luminous clouds, at between forty and fifty thousand. The two men were at operational height and carried no armament. A homing missile could track and destroy them, but so far none had, this being their fifty-seventh mission over the desert and the Red Sea. They always turned back at Margherita on the equator: three thousand miles outward bound, the same back, with hardly a movement of their heads, only their hands plucking in mitts on the control column. A computer flew them while they sat as if in a doll's house with the meagerest slant windows in front of them. Outward bound, the sun on their left. Homeward on the right. It barely had time to seem to move.

Since Rupert Clegg was now an acting full colonel, they had four eagles with them in the cabin, on their epaulets, woven in wirelike braid. The airplane's name was Cyrano, for its long nose and its assignment to snoop. It was one of the best but least-known aircraft in the world: dartlike, black, rear-heavy, stuffed with cameras and sensors, its range preposterous, its potential unlimited. A titanium Gothic cathedral soaring horizontally, it had complexly tinted windows, a ground ritual that never varied. Priests in white coveralls tended it. Acolytes laden with passes and name tapes came to eye it and yearned for the day when they too could fly it. Or would be flown by it. In that cabin nothing went wrong, nothing was unforeseen. Neither Booth nor Clegg looked down at his blunt-booted foot and saw a stowaway spider glinting emerald through the visor. Neither man felt a draft, got a stiff elbow the next day from the wind coming in. No one threw up in there. Their privates were bound tight as the feet of children in ancient China. Clegg thought how Africa resembled a colossal scab, thinking back to an old Denoyer-Geppert wall map smeared with nose-bleeds. There was no relief up here, only a tinted glare. Nominally in command, by virtue of one year's seniority in the rank of colonel, Booth noted Kassala, on the edge of Ethiopia, as they overflew it on the unrolling chart in front of them, with Khartoum due west. To him, Ethiopia was shaped like an upside-down Africa, except that its western bulge was sharper, thrust like the tip of a machete into the Somali Republic.

The only sound was that of an oxygen tent, with the measured hiss and amplified suck of breathing. They said little, used an occasional expletive, mild as *Hell, look at that substrate gauge*, or murmured a name, *Massala*, or a map reference confirmed. Possessed, they skimmed southeast, parallel with the Red Sea, aimed at the Indian Ocean. The cameras and sensors functioned as and when the computers dictated, so there could be no blame. Yet semiheroic this milk run had come to be, with always the chance of a heat-homing missile impossible to elude. Not for Booth and Clegg the vision of Earth swathed in light blue haze made by the atmosphere's dispersal of light's blue component. They saw curds and whey scattered over a mottled azure flecked with pale green quadrants and oblongs, and straight lines of white as if epoxy had spilled along a seam.

Jockeys they called themselves, mock modestly, their suits vermilion, their helmets white, their mittens canary yellow, Booth tall and dark, Clegg of medium height with brownish, faintly graying hair that showed most in his sideburns.

The cooled nosecap slid out over Lake Tana, shunted it behind as Addis Ababa appeared down-range like pumice rubble dumped on a mountaintop. Booth felt an itch, really a slight induration resulting in a callus within the crack of his behind. Clegg just felt hungry and craved a smoke, he being the smoker in the pair. Alert to risk, but inured to boredom, they had only temporary thoughts and rarely remembered what they said to each other during flight. It was as if they had been anesthetized. They returned, to sip coffee, still sweat-soaked, testy with unused adrenaline, sore-eyed, and galled from the too-tight harness. Booth read a financial weekly flown in from London and printed on paper of subdued pink, while Clegg inhaled deeply his long-awaited cigarillo, sometimes tugging out from its tip a long strand of whisker inserted to hold the leaf together.

Addis past, they bore down on Lugh and Juba to the teal-blue Indian Ocean, curved round in a tight turn and came back, this time farther east so as to take them homeward along the exact line of the Red Sea's western shore. A fine day, as usual at that altitude, but dull so far. They had laughed so often at saying this, they said it no more, but it endured, like a grievance. Almost any given day in their earlier lives had been livelier than this. They longed to be novices or juniors again, and never mind the cost.

Once upon a time a red-starred MiG had jumped Clegg as he was regaining height after a successful strike on a North Vietnamese target, but for some reason the gunfire missed him, enabling him to execute a double-scissors aerobatic that put him behind and somewhat above the wildly floating other jet. He saw, and his gun camera later confirmed what he had seen, shells from his cannon hit the engine slung under the other's left wing, and explode it into flame. Across the lower half of the two concentric pink rings of the gun sight, the wing blurred as, first, a shapeless blot of smoke spewed back at him, and then, as the gun camera recorded better than his mind's eye, assumed for a moment the outline of a newborn bird, with bleached beak, bald head, and scrawny neck, all hatched out of a salmon-hued nebula. The MiG's fuselage glowed with reflected flame before it spun out of control toward the ground, which all this time had been dancing vertically on Clegg's left. Pursuing it down, wondering if he would shoot at a parachute, and then wondering why none appeared, Clegg flew too low and took antiaircraft fragments in wings, fuselage, and both feet.

Afflicted for six months with an uncoordinated double limp, he spent his time reading a fishing encyclopedia, from *Aawa*, Hawaiian name for the black-spot wrasse, to *Mako*, the open-ocean shark closely related to the white. The fledgling-shaped cloud behind the MiG did not haunt him, but it recurred: a double roundel superimposed on a winged seed, and then a bird born out of smoke, as soon gone as come. He came to depend on the image's arriving from time to time, but never evaluated it or wondered at its persistence.

Selected soon after for training as a systems reconnaissance officer, he never flew another hostile mission. SRO, said aloud, sounded like a

Japanese mispronouncing *slow*, and Clegg felt parodied in his new profession's very name.

Booth had had a genuine accident five years previously, making a normal approach to the tilting flight deck of an attack carrier. As he stove through a rainshower, into a thirty-five-knot wind, his speed was more than 130 knots, which he reduced as he neared the ramp and saw the deck drop as a heavy swell went down. So he landed too steeply. His right wheel broke off on impact with the deck. And, because of the friction, a magnesium wheel strut caught fire. An arresting cable having failed to slow him because his tail hook had given under the strain, he sped along the deck as if powered by the blinding patch of ignited magnesium itself. At that point he ejected, even as his plane pitched over the forward end of the angle deck. The canopy soared backward as he went in a shallow parabola forward at the crouch. The plane sizzle-churned into the ocean, followed by the canopy, and then Booth himself, festooned with partly opened parachutes. Only minutes later a helicopter rescue crew winched him up from the waves; he had only a broken arm and a twisted neck. Two months later, his arm was out of plaster, and soon he was flying again, with renewed elation, but gradually he began to dislike the sea, all the way from casual disaffection, as if a marriage were beginning to go sour, to mortified loathing. So he transferred to the Air Force, convinced that one who flew should join himself to the military arm that made an absolute of air, and not of what it landed on or overflew. Thus a commander, become a colonel, donned a tunic of blue and felt at home again.

Both Booth and Clegg, then, flew mentally around an incident long past: a kill and a ducking. And then their paths crossed or, as they joshed, the flight plans matched up.

On first meeting, Clegg found Booth sarcastic and imperious. A man so tall, just within the maximum for pilots, could afford a less commanding manner, or so he reasoned. While Booth found Clegg a moody starer, his hands a bit too fat, Clegg countered with affable mumbles and inaccurate quotations from the fishing encyclopedia. Booth looked away from Clegg's gaze.

So it was a standoff until they were chosen to train together, then fly together, with Booth in command. First the elementary stuff on Northrop T 38's, followed by intensive work in the simulator and five transition flights in the 71B. Clegg went on a strict diet of fish, broccoli, and fruit, and then was obliged to cut out the broccoli for steak and eggs. Cyrano crews had to eat high-protein, low-residue meals, which had been Booth's favorite all his life. Gradually, Booth's manner began to seem a natural outgrowth from his military role. The two of them even began to reminisce together in the officers' club, quaffing tomato juice from embossed silver tankards. Somehow, Clegg's punctured feet matched Booth's broken arm, and Clegg's vestigial limp with a touch of tiptoe in his heavy march echoed, to Clegg at least, the hand that could not quite touch eyebrow when Booth returned salutes. When they spoke at last of sex, Clegg confided about his divorce from an assertive, tank-trunked interior decorator with periwinkle blue eyes. All the positions are ridiculous, he said. He missed the house but not the wife. Booth, convinced that he would be insatiably faithful if he ever married, told how he missed California, reassuring himself that, in a Cyrano, he could be home in much less than two hours. He thought of California as of a woman, and all the women it contained were his, on the beach, the freeway, the campuses, in the banks and the drive-ins. He and Clegg shared an attitude to sex, not so much casual as absentminded. When making love, they thought about their flights, as if locked in some vaginal cramp of sheer aether, and, during their missions, they salted their tedium with improvisatory bordello vignettes, even to the extent of inserting the air dream into the ground dream, and vice versa, so that often they were not sure if they were dreaming of flying while they were having sex or dreaming of sex while flying, or dreaming of both while doing neither.

In the main, two kinds of boredom afflicted them, and they sometimes yearned for the open-cockpit camaraderie of World War One, when opponents waved at one another over chattering slow guns, or for the chastities of some mythic, decent marriage, in which sexuality mingled with lawn mowing and grocery shopping as just another item on a list, when the children were asleep or at least in bed. At supersonic speed, when the outside skin temperature reached over 400 degrees Fahrenheit, the Cyrano grew ten inches in length, an almost organic, human thing. They knew this and exulted, completing a lascivious thought that also included titanium's not being, as once thought, highly susceptible to lightning strikes, and high altitude flight's not being jinxed with cosmic radiation or clear-air turbulence.

All they dreaded, apart from cramp and boredom, was [solar flares,] but these happened once or twice a year at most and could be predicted. Booth murmured hello to Djibouti as they slid over its khaki splotch at a height of sixteen miles. He mentally registered at the Hotel Continental, strolled outside again to stand in one of the Roman arches and study a ferny tree slap in front of him, his only thought that, seen from offshore, Djibouti's whitewashed stone-and-mud houses and its bone-white sands made an inviting vista, whereas, ashore, you found the heat, the flies, the fleas, all merciless even when a wind came in along the mole. Clegg himself dreamed of the mal, or centaur fish, found only near coasts where the trees were so thick a cat couldn't get ashore, as Columbus once wrote in his log, little knowing that Clegg would one day clinch the entry with a horse-headed mermaid. Booth hated the sea, but it mesmerized him, while Clegg had no attitude to the sea at all except that, somewhat like Booth's California being full of women, the sea was full of fish. Two men, stranded priests of the highest technology, let their minds dawdle while their aircraft raced ahead.

Yet for both of them no dream, no matter how gorgeous or thick, altogether shut out the sense of going unheeded by civilization, by Africa, by the Cyrano itself, and of being fobbed off with a preposterous bastard role in which two men, for all of their being similar in age, bound by friendship, honored with the same ribbons on the chest, functioned as steeplejack photographers. By presidential appointment to a future that most likely would never arrive, they received hourly the images of some hundred thousand square miles of only potentially interesting terrain. And that was that. Like the rudimentary eye in science primers, they sat passively in static relationship to light, no longer caring much if the film they took back was of military significance or not. Something voyeurish jaded and sapped them. And the ecstasy of that severed-feeling euphoria of height had vanished into a humdrum servitude at the tallest desk of all. Yearning daily to be in the strike version of the Cyrano, with shorter wings, fuselage, and fin, with stubbier nose and a long posterior spike, they pondered early retirement. Fishing in Michigan, say, or playing the stock market.

Reconnaissance: the very word implied recognition, but all they felt was blind receptivity. If only, Clegg thought, [a third person] sat in here with us, behind me, or behind Booth and in front of me. If only, he thought, he were alone up here, his loneliness unmatched. His mind on the Soviet surface-to-air missile code-named Kitchen, Booth was hearing a song, "Somewhere I'll Find You," in the Cyrano's vibration, in the vibration of the instrument panel itself. Flak and cannon shell gave you a fighting chance, or even more, whereas that tufted steel dart homing after them until it struck was inescapable. He felt he was weight-lifting the Cyrano itself, all two hundred thousand pounds of it, in some Olympics of the air. Yet he had no sense of doom, impending or otherwise. On his first mission he had felt something, at any rate, an abstract qualm based on maplike vignettes of the area overflown. That damned song refused to go away.

In a frivolous moment, over steak and eggs at the officers' club, while Clegg drank a British drink called shandy, Booth dreamed up Rip Van Booth, who survived as a reconnaissance pilot for two hundred years. Told of this, Clegg choked on his drink, then hoarsely said *Before then, if ever,* which sounded to Booth like a cautious translation from the motto of some famous regiment.

The odd thing was that, the more missions they returned from, the more their careers began to resemble those of mailmen, fashion buyers, dealers in antiques, all of whom plugged on from day to day, never knowing when the ax would fall, on a snowy or a hot day, before or after a meal and the milk of magnesia, on the stairs or in traffic. Technically the missions were hazardous and the odds kept on worsening even while remaining fifty-fifty. Clegg refused to speculate, as usual, but Booth pondered the odds daily, marveling at juxtapositions of all kinds, from the permanent crease in his best pants to the map of Africa, just as permanent, that slid below them, from the knobs on the radio in his air-conditioned quarters to the toggles before him in the cockpit. Presumably, those on the ground did not mind being reconnoitered day after day, had nothing to hide, or had hidden it far too well, and a king's ransom was being squandered each time he and Clegg, or the backup team of Xavier and Young, went up. It was both humbling and ludicrous, not so much a milk run as a cream puff. Proficient at larding his boredom with color, he meticulously made the movements required during takeoff, landing and actual flight. It was enough for him to think, as he did, his brain cells were soaring over old Africa like dove-gray frogspawn rid of time.

A superb line chief groomed the Cyrano for them. There was never a walkaround inspection. The line crews wore foot muffs and used small mats when servicing the plane. An entire medical team prepped them every time. But they had both discussed, intoning the phrase softly as if it had magical properties, *break-off phenomenon*, which was the psychological feeling of being alone in space. This was their drug and their disease. The only cure was to have more of it. The lull went on, a hiatus of lulls, in which they functioned perfectly as machine-minders, good men both, high above the railroad from Djibouti to Diredawa, like a dropped strand of barbed wire. Safe in the titanium shell that was as strong as steel but lighter by far, they became somnaerialists, soothed by the same aspirin as the rest of the world, but as remote and unknown as if they had come from a different planet to look at Earth, map it, and [go back home] to drinks of molten rock and meals of fungus ingested through the pores of a Carborundum skin.

When the flame died in the left-hand turbojet, the only tangible-audible effect was that of a vibration and a hum removed. Warning lights twinkled as the computer corrected the Cyrano's left sag, but the engine stayed dead, and the altimeter began to whirl.

"Try yours," Booth told Clegg in a rehearsed whisper, and Clegg did, with a peculiar sense of being outside his own body, outside the plane itself, and looking on, as if death had already intervened. Then the other engine quit, a one in five hundred thousand chance. *Sabotage* was the word Booth mouthed as the Cyrano dropped like a forward-lunging elevator from eighty to sixty thousand feet. Try as they did, they could get nothing restarted within the accelerant whine of sixty streamlined tons beginning to steepen its dive to the desert. It was a titanium sailplane now, controllable only while going fast. Level, it would have reeled sideways and rearward into stall and spin.

Piloting as best he could, Booth with a condemned man's grin felt years younger, once again trying to land on the attack carrier, only this time he was in something gross and unwieldy, which had flown him much as Earth rotated him, and was now hauling him downward, below fifty thousand, in the same passive role. Out went the encoded Mayday signal, just the permitted once, and he heard the increasing buffet and whistle from outside, a sound coarser and more spasmodic than the rammed-home, incessant last gasp that came from the narrow front window during ordinary flight. This was an untidy noise, part of the acoustics of tumbling about. So this is override, he thought. I am pilot in command. He became dizzy and told himself to keep his head utterly still, and then he became sluggish, though calm, while something useless coursed through his brain like quicksilver: the remedy, the answer, maybe, but indecipherable. The cockpit had become full of noises, including those in his head. Why think now about the sound blood made in the aorta, picked up by an echocardiologist who did not recognize the bottled screech of a wildcat? Who was the writer who said that writing was like trying to pour butter into the ear of a wildcat? The same animal.

After Clegg ejected, he would arm the camera-sensor self-destructs and, for the second time in his life, blast forth like a seed, only today within a supersonic escape capsule with Mach 3 capability, survival gear, radio, and buoyant for water landings.

A poor-sounding *splumf* snatched Clegg upward, which was almost horizontally because the Cyrano was diving, and then out of sight. Like a mailbag collected trackside by a passing train.

Then Booth himself went, fierce inside his keyed-up lethargy, still pilot in command, wondering if it was indeed now or years ago that, in something like an old-fashioned toboggan, with rounded metal foot-ends to save his feet from the windblast, he found himself plucked horizonward, up, then at the end of a sharp parabola, down, his feet pushed up toward him as the seat thudded his rear end and, briefly, he soared butt-first, then feet-first, as the somersault took place thirty-odd thousand feet over the rusty-looking cobweb of Eritrea. Out popped the stabilizing tubes, like telescopes, to check the spin as soon as it began, and he saw the Cyrano explode far below him, in the air, though soundlessly. I am Booth, he told himself. I am alive. He had so many torn thoughts, about an explosive charge, the Cyrano, the terrain below, but not a one about Clegg, already miles away on a parabola of his own.

Something else explosive thudded against him, and like a Cartesian diver in a flask he free-fell down, throat sore from oxygen, eyes dribbling, a seepage from nowhere already forming in his shorts. He felt warmer now, after the ice-gripe in his bowels upon ejection had yielded to the warmth of the separated canopy, through whose front he saw not the dials anymore but a mountain range easily eight thousand feet high, a mottled darkness of splits and blanks into which Clegg had already descended, marooned on a sheer-sided plateau like a transplanted mesa.

It's dry, Booth thought, remotely making his own thoughts available to himself. The drogue chute opened above him, plucked invisibly, small and too small until the main canopy bloomed, apex first, followed by the skirt and shroudlines. It began as a lump, then a commotion of false peaks where high-dynamic pressures made the fabric rupture and fail. He saw two or three panels rip, perhaps even an entire gore, but he reassured himself that such mishaps were standard. Of course. The air anchor held firm while he drifted away from the mountains, down toward the desert, then below sea level into a depression made from hot salt.

It was six thirty-eight Zulu Time when the capsule, with egress window already open, clunked along the salt pans and rumbled to a dangling halt with, strange to say, the mild implosion sounds of lightbulbs smashed and, harsher without being extra loud, the noise of an old snow-shovel whose underblade has split down into a V that, through the snow, scores the concrete again and again with white lines that endure. Gruesome heat within the capsule matched the heat without.

Booth stood, then reeled as he flipped his visor only to blind himself as he saw the salt. With sunglasses on, he felt less hammered at by light, less as if he were standing on a chunk of the sun, but his skin crawled as his body tried to cool itself. He shook his head, his arms, to dislodge the enve-lope of sweat. No sound reached that silently stoked morning, in which not a bird cried, not an animal scampered. He heard the salt creak beneath him and inhaled an aroma similar to that of swampwater, only more acrid. He had always thought rock salt was brown, but this was white-silver, mottled with a pale copper-sulfate blue and in patches even glossy, the entire surface for as far as he could see split up into irregular slabs like a disintegrated mosaic. He thought of ice floes, but the mosaic came closer, and the dazzle through Polaroid lenses was as nothing against the capsule's eye-wounding giant tear next to the untidy bundle of orange laundry that was the parachute, its fabric still as the salt in that breezeless oven.

Training, Booth heard in his mind's ear. I have been trained for situations such as this. Initiative plus routine will see me through. He rummaged through the packages inside the capsule, where bread might have baked, and found a distant authoritative voice confirming his thoughts. Survival kits, it said, are carried in aircraft flying over large tracts of water, over hostile territory, or in uninhabited areas where a forced landing or ejection might occur. Here was a place that qualified on several counts. Maybe there were several kits. He was not even bruised, although a needling headache had begun and he urgently needed to urinate. In seconds the fizzy yellow splotch had dried lemon, negating his presence.

The personalized kit in his flight suit brought him back to a stronger sense of himself, who he had been and who he still was. Here were his first-aid materials, his survival booklet, his concentrated food, his water-purifying chemicals, his matches, his fish hooks, his snares, and his little plastic bags for storing water. This much, or this little, came in a waterproof wallet eight inches long, all of it designed by some passionate minifier at the Air Force College, or some Cal Tech eccentric, to keep body and soul in concert.

Yet this pocket treasure trove was nothing compared to what the capsule held, the horn of plenty's tip. This was a kit as big as his chest, holding oxygen, an inflatable life raft, a survival beacon, a life vest, a hand gun, a flare gun, a hunting knife, two quarts of water, a special knife with which to cut shroudlines, and, glory be, a Bible, as if he were in a hotel room. Suddenly he felt that something worse should have happened to him, and he remembered how the survival manual had zanily reminded readers that, in Mongolia, the dogs devour human feces, and he had idly wondered who cleaned up after the dogs.

Ah, he breathed on the compass's glass face, then spread out on a piece of chute fabric the bandages, the Band-Aids, the pack of knifeblades, the tube of antibiotic ointment, the tin of aspirins, the ammonia inhaler, the triangle bandages, and the pack of water-purification tablets. For sure he was going to be healthy now, and he almost saw himself presiding at a lonely salt-pan jamboree, troughing on soup mixes, hard candy, vitamin capsules, in a panama hat improvised according to instructions from the heavy aluminum foil the food was packed in, and otherwise intended for use in the form of ad hoc saucepans.

Dizzy again, he sipped water from a thermos, set the beacon for what it was worth below sea level, and began to do what he knew he should have done first thing. He arranged the chute's main canopy into a low tent weighted with sandbags cut from the drogue. Then he crawled underneath, came out again and dragged the capsule under the tent, where it made a broad bulge. Sitting beside it in the tent, he daubed ointment on the insect bites that had suddenly appeared on his face and arms, then checked through his heat tablets, his signalling mirror, his penlight flashlight, idly wishing he had, as astronauts had, a machete, a sea dye marker, a nylon sun-bonnet, and a bag of desalter briquets. Now, *those* . . . Wishing too for a strobe light, halazone tablets for purifying water with, he felt only a pilot in some minor league, unfussed, ill equipped, no longer related to time.

Yet he was alive and unharmed, and that facet of self-esteem cheered him no end, certain as he was to be found within the day. Already the Cyrano was overdue, and, although no helicopter from his own base could reach him, and no rescue plane land hereabouts, he could easily be snatched up on a cord attached to a helium balloon, like Jack bypassing the beanstalk. All he would have to do was inflate it, get into the harness and wait. But there was no such gear in the capsule, so they would surely drop one down to him. Out there in the bright wasteland he implored Commanding General Cyrus W. Shumacher to get off his ass and send him a gear drop. All they had to do was home in on his signal beacon, if they could pick it up at all. To or from me, he thought miserably. If they could pick me up, it would be *to* me all the way and *from* only once I was aboard, leaving my original unwanted position.

After defecating, he prepared a fire, which he lit when the coil of dung had dried out, only fifteen minutes later, light as the remnant from some indoor firework. Soon a wispy column of smoke rose from the recessed plain, its smell to him one of mingled plastic and straw. There it smoldered, stilted up on two small spurs of salt like something for ritual cremation. Half an hour later the fire was out, but the smell lingered and the blurred skein of smoke still hung in the torrid air. He had no thermometer, but he guessed the temperature at between 120 and 130. Amazed not to have popped like a balloon, he stroked his eyebrows, absently wondering why they had grown so bushy-bristly in the last few years, and certain hairs too long.

Thus far, Clegg had not even dared to move. After an endless-seeming but sunny descent during which he felt almost glad of the change in his whereabouts, as if ejection were via funicular or the gondola of an airship, he sailed in his clumsy trance past a mountain's peak, then drifted along a razor-backed ridge, thinking how humped, how rigid, how sullen and iron the planet looked. Next came a series of collisions with rock spurs projecting from a sheer wall in a high valley down which his capsule coasted, twirling and rebounding with crashes that jarred his teeth. It grew darker, at any rate greener instead of yellow or white, and the floor of what contained him stuck, then dragged along a ledge, almost halting as it settled, only to be plucked up again by a ripping wind. It resumed its ragged descent. He felt shaken about as if inside a child's transparent rattle, the only missing items being the lead shot that provided sound effects.

In roughly equal amounts the grinding and slamming went on as, unable to steer, he caromed down the valley, actually dislodging nests and birds of prey, whose understated screams he did not hear, not even when they mounted vertical onslaught on the drogue chute, clawing its fabric and dropping dung on the main canopy itself. No roller coaster had such angles. He had never felt so ballistic or known a mountain to go so far down. All he could see was Parthenon-shaped bluffs flanked by high-altitude Stonehenges, a mixture of smudged browns and white-flecked obsidian. Just as he thought a certain span of the terrain was past, it resumed lower down after another bout of jolts and hauls, as if the landscape were insisting on a limited identity with only one trick in its repertoire.

He pouted sourly. He never saw what it was the cameras uncovered, and all he could see now was a massif against whose anvil wind and gravity kept pounding him. Accustomed to the smooth sensations of flying in the Cyrano, he wished himself twelve miles higher up, sleighriding out and back in the same harness and seat as now. He was not ready for the sudden stop, which, unlike its predecessors, remained a stop and was not the prelude to yet another shuddering tumble while the chute half collapsed. Had he landed?

He glimpsed a wall of rock, haunch of something vast. On the other side was a more distant wall dropping to the valley floor, how far down he could not tell. The altimeter read 4027, but it could have stuck. Upward there was nothing but cloudless sky. Then all vision ended as the chute collapsed, enclosing him and his capsule in an orange blur that only the wind or an egress with knife could remedy. Listening to the fabric sigh and settle beyond the Plexiglas, Clegg almost gave in to levity. The scent of his sweat was that of overripe peaches. He was warm, but intolerably hungry. With the oxygen switched off, he bit into some chocolate, bitter damp stuff that clogged his teeth and made him guzzle water knowing there was only one way to fix his whereabouts, and that was to get outside and look, though the festooned chute no doubt dangled down for twenty feet, unless, beyond where it hemmed him in at the window, it had merely slumped to the ground, billowing about beyond reach. He could not be very high. How wide, then, was the shelf he was on? Going out, would he plunge a thousand feet down a sheer cliff, in a cocoon of plastic, dragging the capsule after him? Or would he lift the fabric and stride clear, down a gentle incline? Was there even a way of deciding without enormous risk? He slid the window panel open and began to use the knife, at first thinking he must not cut the chute to ribbons in case he was high up, then realizing it would never open up again, not enough to slow his fall.

Layer after layer exposed only more orange just inches from him. He found olive bird dung on the knifeblade, but could still not see beyond the fabric. The view both fore and aft was blocked as well. He listened, heard only his breath, then some shredded kind of birdcall. The shroud-lines creaked under a strain he could not identify, and an occasional click as the canopy structure did something minute according to physics.

After a while, he became reckless and sliced away madly at the chute like someone peeling an orange from within. When the knife finally seemed to move about in air, and wiggled freely, he cut out a patch and looked across about one hundred yards to a layer-cake wall of rock, golden-tawny in the sun. There was nothing in between. The view down, with his head craned out, matched that from a fairly low-flying plane. Of whitish sand, the valley floor was perhaps four or three thousand feet beneath him, shelving gently for the last thousand, but, for the upper two thousand, perpendicular slate. The capsule was on the very edge, maybe even a foot or two over it, and the chute hung uselessly down.

A sudden movement on his part and, still in the see-through cabin, he would plumbline to his death. A gust, claiming enough of the chute's area, would also send him down. At some risk, of course, he could stay put until his food gave out or he was found. He switched on his Mayday beacon, thinking he could combine shroudlines and fabric strips into a rope of sorts, but one almost a third of a mile long. Ridiculous, yet he had no climbing tools and, he began to suspect, no head for heights. Being a pilot had nothing to do with that.

Fifteen minutes later, nothing so far having budged, and with a fresh pain in his lower belly, he began to tug in the chute as best he could through the open window, afraid to hoist the lid lest it jerk him off the ledge altogether. Handful after handful, he slit it and pulled it in, hardly knowing what he did or what the next stage of the process would be. After all, to what would he fasten the one end of his makeshift rope? His hands fell still, as if severed. He had not yet found even one of the shroud lines with which to make a start.

Hyenas would not climb to him, but vultures would find him, high or low. The discomfort he now felt was a new thing, as if he had contracted slightly within his skin, in his arm the radius closer to the ulna, and in his head eye socket to eyeball. His sinuses felt smaller and fuller. His wrists seemed to articulate less completely, and his overbite was tighter. Hours were fifty-nine minutes long. There was less nitrogen to breathe. One *g* had fallen out of his name. And he could not find the flares.

Tomorrow's mission, flown by Xavier and Young, would go on as usual, while he and Booth alternately froze and boiled in the least-known of the less-known parts of Africa. Their only reason for being, his and Booth's, had been aerial, and now they were so much refuse. He yearned for the tie rack whose rotors had slowly turned his neckties for inspection and selection. Which tie went with which suit and which socks? *Went with* sounded almost sexual. Facing his walk-in closet, he used to activate the littler motor and watch his ties revolve like clusters of snakeskins whereas his half dozen suits hung still, his shorts lay flat, and his shoes aimed their planelike noses at him from a rack. That slow whirligig of draper's bliss had given way to a gradually unrolling film of Africa. All he had now was the pageant of sky and rock, the crude-looking interior of the capsule, all raw edges and uneven lines. He made ready for night, managing to cheer himself with the thought that, once on the ground, he might survive by hunting, he who had stalked deer with bow and arrows when on leave. One side of him had almost caved in while another was itching for the chance to act. Despairing of any neatness to be found at random, or by deliberate hunt, he turned to chaos after all. Ever carefully groomed and attired, he had learned early how to kill, and the horns once affixed to the front of his house, to provoke his wife's disgust, now grew from the capsule's windows, emblems of a last-ditch prowess he could hardly, however, show off on a ledge as high as this.

Clegg worked at his rope without even looking down, aware of blisters already forming on the tips of his fingers and thumbs. Above him blue sky quivered in the gash he'd made, requiring of him a mental effort that said it was the same sky he'd flown through earlier this morning. Lymph gathered in his blisters. The rope grew yards longer. He was wondering why, in extreme situations, human thought became barbaric and conjured up only violence and hate. It was the mind's way of recharging itself, a reminder not of what it feared to lose but of how not to lose it. Coughing dryly, he paused in his work for a teaspoon-sized sip of water, the taste almost that of the distilled variety. What if Booth had already been saved? Had they truly resented each other? Would he care if Booth survived? If Booth died? No, he told himself, all that is beside the point. Two men, so far two survivors. It must be so. Just the onboard computers have died.

He had an extraordinary sense of having been simplified or factorized, for the first time in years equipped with a genuine horizon. He knew now where he ended and other things, or other people, began. Parameters had come to life, that deadhead jargon word sprucing itself up. High in what he guessed was the Tegre range, he wondered how cold the night would be, how many nights he would have alone, and how to fortify himself without hymn singing, abrupt raucous shouts or biting his lips in order to taste blood. He saw himself swaddled in chute fabric, all of it yanked through the side porthole at sunset and pushed out again at dawn, so as not to freeze, any more than to swelter. In more ways than one, he needed the parachute, and he knew he would soon be wrapping himself for the night in yards of daisy-chained rope, no longer a fabric at all, until there was length enough to send his flashlit helmet down. Or even himself, which meant going down before his strength and wits gave out. So he should work all through the night. If he went too soon, his descent would end in a long drop. Was it better to go at full strength down an unfinished rope than at one fourth strength down one that reached all the way to the ground? Other pairings occurred to him, such as half strength down a half rope, the one criterion being the maximum drop he could survive. Sixty feet or fifty.

It all depended on what he wanted to do once he was down, whether to walk to death in the desert, as would be easy, or to die broken-legged at the mountain's foot.

In a daze he began to work again, cutting fabric and twisting it as if making firelighters from newspaper. Then he tied the ends together. After an hour, although he still had not laid hand on a line, he saw one coming up toward him, and at his feet he had a fifteen-foot daisy chain of orange loops, useless no doubt, but a promise to himself that he would not let himself die. Clegg inhaled deeply, ready to greet the first of his last few days, and his eyes closed, excluding the ripe light cast by the chute.

The sun was almost overhead, its blot a vague ivory beyond the illuminated orange of his roof. He felt oddly Arabian, tented in mid-desert, or like Aladdin's genie in the lamp, at the beck and call of someone, some power, other than the one that said every officer and man must carry on a string around his neck an identity disk showing rank and number, and in the right-hand skirt pocket of his coat a first field dressing. He felt obsolete, one of the walking wounded from another era, vaguely remembering the command that, in action against a civilized enemy, no one other than a stretcher bearer was to carry a wounded man to the rear, unless ordered to.

Now, where had that come from? Which war? Which manual? He was almost a connoisseur of military handbooks, as of books about fishing, but the sources of his quotations usually eluded him. What he liked in the military manuals was the hard-and-fast rule that, although he was reading about it, he did not have to obey.

Now, for the first time since ejecting, he wondered about Booth, well aware that he who bales out second bales out lower down. Or almost always. He might be dead, trapped in the Cyrano and burned, or unconscious only fifty yards away, or a hundred miles off, having drifted through a sandstorm. It was no use worrying about Booth, though, when a Clegg marooned at high altitude. Again he set to work on the makeshift rope, doubting its strength, still ignorant of anything to attach it to, and sure it would never be long enough. What his hands were doing was as symbolic as pragmatic. Paid out far enough, to flutter a couple of hundred yards over the heads of passersby, the line might save him, especially if to the lower end he tied his helmet, which would clang like an empty bucket. A flashlight inside it might draw attention during the hours of darkness.

He almost cheered up, he who had lined the moats of his boyhood sandcastles with aluminum foil taken in a roll to the New Jersey or Virginia shore as part of his holiday gear. So provident a mind, he thought, should be able to descend a few thousand feet without disaster. He twisted and tied, twisted with gasps and tied with his breath held, exuberant when a length of shroudline came into his hands, manfully resigned when it was the fabric's turn again. When everything had been used, he still would have fifty feet of high-strength fishing line from his survival packs. Then he thought about the chance of a skyhook recovery and rejoiced, in his mind's eye already in the harness and inflating the balloon from the helium modules. He sat with the wind at his back and waited for the plane's yoke to snag the line and waft him away. The rest was easy. Good Samaritans aboard the plane winched him up the open rear-loading ramp and so inside. A thermos of hot coffee was in his hands before he could mumble windblown thanks.

Now some power restored him to the high ledge. Like General Edward Pakenham, the chivalrous one, killed at the Battle of New Orleans, he would be shipped home in a keg of rum. He stirred from that heroic dream. Perhaps the chute would cushion his fall, and he should not be reducing it to a rope at all. Lunging sideways, as he might have done an hour earlier, he went nowhere, held by his shoulder straps, which he then released. Again he heaved to the right, but the capsule did not even rock. After ten minutes he knew how firmly based he was, released the hatch up into the chute, and for the first time stood. Only one layer covered him and he soon slashed it through. He gasped at the openness of everything and burst into a fit of sneezing. Had he, up to now, been in shock? He would never know, but he could see there was nothing to anchor his improvised rope, and the capsule itself was too light. All of a sudden he felt, as never before, a doomed exhilaration. There was no way down, at least not under his own steam, yet the fact did not unnerve him, and he wondered why. Up here the air was half-crystalline. The wind dabbed at him, the sound of everything was plucked away. It was an aerial plateau preliminary to death, where a man collected his thoughts uninterrupted save by eagles, or tumbleweeds of cumulus. He would by all means let his helmet down with the flashlight inside, but he had already adjusted to its never being found or seen, except by archaeologists years from now. Alone to the end, he would study each moment with infatuated glee, as a gift or a truce, and in the end consent. That way he had more poise than if he were to fall from a rope that broke or came adrift when he was halfway down.

With binoculars he swept the distance on all three sides, the fourth to the west being the cliff face. North was a corrugated granite barricade rising to twelve or fifteen thousand feet. East was the sable blank of the desert, waxing white in mirages above and below the horizon. Nothing moved. To the south he saw only more desert, gruesome silver nitrate plains with an occasional wink of unusually intense reflection from what he guessed was quartz, or a flake of metal. Not that he knew, or was even thinking along those lines, but one of those flashes was from Booth's shaving mirror of high-sheen steel, suspended on a cord from two knives driven into the salt upon which Booth had spread a three-foot patch of silver foil, shiny side up.

To Booth the effect was one of scintillation, at which he chose not to look, but which he varied by tugging gently at a second, longer, stiffer cord fed into the shelter where he sat on a cushion of his folded-up flying suit. Hoping it would be seen, but without so much thinking of Clegg, he just sat there savoring the quality of silence. He could have been a boy at camp again, snug in the open, in a stealthy torpor, or seeming to wheel with Earth as the June sky stayed put. There were so many stars they must have been sprayed on the firmament.

The heat squeezed him until he shivered in a lethal-feeling reflex, his eye sockets full of silver milled coins. Dry as his mouth had been before, it now contained a leathery fungus. Aircrews, he remembered, soon learn the value of fresh meat. Anything that crawls, walks, swims, or flies is fair game. Insects cooked until crisp have a high fat content, and from larger game everything should be consumed, including bones, blood, and intestines. Yes, he remembered, new cadets were escorted into the mountains by upperclassmen and left to find their own way back, but given a small ration box, one cake of compressed meat, and a live rabbit.

Again he opened his mouth beneath a hollow stem held vertical until the water droplet fell. Back at the academy he had eaten himself sick, in a weary rage. Tonight, however, as his training prescribed, his shelter would be a paratepee with lighted candle inside, easily visible from the air. Had he, that second, gone outside into the blistering fug, he might have seen the flash of binoculars twenty miles away as Clegg swung them up and down. But Cadet Booth was already gone, back in the days when he made his first meal of earthworms chopped, not so much grilled as fried, with dandelion-leaf garnish. The taste was neutral though tainted with soil, as sometimes with freshwater fish.

Younger than ever now, he was at the microscope, holding his breath over a slide of his own ejaculate, in which tadpoles mingled freely among long fibers of something else. It was like seeing for the first time, like having eaten grapes only to notice how the grape stalks, denuded of fruit, became tiny knife rests.

Who am I? he wondered in the paratepee. I weigh 186 pounds, have gray eyes with a hazel cast, and I once read, for a bet, Boethius's *Consolation of Philosophy*. Ten pages learned by heart, as a cadet. Now long forgotten. I know who I am, I am death warmed up.

As the sun swung, without its heat varying in the least, he tried to remember what to do to stay alive. Keep his head clear, if nothing else. Do that. And never mind what night-prowling ghouls roamed through it. The universe was his oyster after all, if only he could make himself believe it.

By nightfall, after passing through virtually none of this mental to and fro of Clegg's, Booth had somehow gone beyond a fatigue entitling him to sleep. Stifling in his makeshift tent, he had begun to brood on the upas tree, deadly and legendary, under whose branches ancient travelers contracted terminal inertia. All he lacked was the tree itself. The sore in his rear end had grown tenderer. His ill-knitted arm ached as if the air were damp. His eyes grated against what felt like wisps of wool. An incongruous day, it had been an eon compressed. With better luck, they would have been partaking of another low-residue lunch by now. So, he told himself. The night will be Ethiopian, not Arabian. Dozing, without having checked even his sidearm, he saw how he would look if he died in the night and were found before desert scavengers had ripped him apart. Straight as an Indian, six feet two in his stocking feet, his frame padded with limber muscle suggestive of undue strength. His bones and joints were large, his mouth wide, his irregular teeth uncapped. Too tired to wince, he let himself float away again, then abruptly shook himself and went outside.

He had heard a scamper, a rustle, a click. He had heard all the noises possible, and he heard them again. What he saw was a prancing rocking horse with outrageous arms uplifted to seize a big shrimp halted in its tracks. If not arms, they were antennae. The horse had what seemed four testicles, dangling criss-cross. The sky had frozen solid.

He had seen this constellation before, but not from here, and agreed with textbook assertions that Centaurus was one of the most splendid of sky sights, half man, half horse, commonly delineated with four feet deep in the Milky Way, the forelegs unbent and splayed, the rear legs larger and angled at the knees. The body was a right-angled triangle from whose apex sprang the parallelogram of the torso, topped by a rhomboid head round which those arms or those antennae waved, in static assault on Lupus, less a wolf than a prawn or crayfish. For the first time in hours he felt at home. Clearly one creature dominated the other and might only just have made the final leap that put it within killing range, the victim having halted in midstep. Yet what drew him most and held him, out there at 14 degrees north on the salt, wool-gathering his way through the night sky, was what he knew about the star called Alpha, the nearest to Earth of the bright stars, and a superb red-yellow binary. He thanked the academy for celestial navigation. Alpha was the predator's most forward foot.

There was as yet no moon, but the salt had a wan refulgence, a visual coolness that seemed to infect the atmosphere itself. For the first time since the flameout, Booth found he could breathe easily; the temperature had fallen from 120 to 85. Insensible of Earth's wheeling, he studied the Centaur and the Wolf with renewed attention. Now he saw the fat rear empennage of the Cyrano. The four shimmering testicles were cameras or sensors. Down he swooped on Lupus, filming it to death as it declined to budge.

He tried to sleep, but he could neither drowse nor float. Trying to sleep tired him even more, but it was another hour before he succumbed and knew nothing as, encircling his tent at a distance of a dozen yards, a group of whispering shapes armed with six-foot poles took up stance, one-legged as herons against the salt, one foot propped heel-up against the other, the long poles used for support. All they wore was a turban, ragged sackcloth, and leather sandals with upcurled sides and toes. As Booth had suspected, he had landed on a dried-up lake, into which the rains leached salt from the surrounding hills. Evaporation did the rest, leaving slabs of salt that these men mined both day and night. Compared with Clegg, still plaiting rope and unable to see Centaurus through the gash in the roof, Booth was badly off, hemmed in to the west by Clegg's mountains, to the north and east by the mountains of Eritrea. South lay the desert, direction from which no help could come, except such as the ferocious tribe of the Afar might devise, than which death itself was better. In short, his radio beacon reached no one friendly, just as Clegg's, aimed in vain through rock, northward, at the Dahlak Archipelago, Cyprus and Turkey. The downward sweeping audio tone of the emergency transmitter was reaching no one at all three times a second, a dumb voice amid a heap of wreckage.

Prodded hard in the belly, Booth butted his head forward, saw the long poles and the fierce men holding them, crouched intimately round him under the scorched-smelling fabric. Light poured in, faint ocher in color, and from the distance a screech of contending birds began and died away. His throat was thick and stiff, so instead of trying to speak he mustered an awkward grin that seemed to anger several of them, who lunged forward to test his muscles and urged him to stand by tugging his ears.

Not far away, and no time at all as the Cyrano flew, Clegg worked at his rope without even looking, sensible of blisters already forming on the tips of his fingers and thumbs. Over him, blue sky quivered in the gash he had made, requiring of him a different image (though he did not call it that) readily supplied from the harbor at Djibouti where, in a shack assembled on the side of a wrecked steamer, he squatted behind an old cotton sheet nailed to the frame to shut out south, and two crude sets of steps conducting from the floor of his hovel to the convex plates of the vessel's flank, on which he walked at peril. Telephone wires linked by two sagging posts ran behind him along the quay, sometimes seeming to hum, and, seen from the harbor's other side, gave him parallel slash-parentheses, a cross at either end on which to be exposed to public taunt once the rickety diagonal braces that held up the shanty had failed. Coiled round an upright, a towel was a boa constrictor; a barrel oven, his *moufa*, crammed with fire, baked the dough plastered on its sides, like a vision of scalded pig. His mind roamed back to other enclosures, such as the beloved maroon caboose stationed in the outsize yard of the old family house, both a paneled study and (up three cast-iron footrests) a low-ceilinged sleeping quarter unspeakably peaceful among the maples and pines. A small refrigerator droned and an intercom to the house kept him in touch or (when he unclipped one battery terminal) not.

Lining up to enter the narrowest of his capillaries, his red corpuscles kept rebounding, or seven in ten did, instead of three. The gas bloating his stomach seemed to push upward against his heart, setting it aflutter. His sternum ached. That g had fallen out of his name, or even the one vowel. Cleg or Clgg, he had begun to exaggerate, or so he told himself mirthlessly, trying to attune himself to a situation (yes, it was that prosaic thing, a situation) extreme as to kind, banal as to outcome. For years now, he had held on to a battered dictionary whose title had extended over two pages, though the left-hand one was missing, so he called the big book [the *Onary*,] having thrown *Dicti* to the winds. He had no faith in the signal beacon; he had looked at the mountains. Where were his flares, then? Aloud he said, "How come we don't get flares?" Unless Booth had them (Clegg was wrong in this). Conceivably, reconnaissance pilots had fairweather friends only; once down, you were not supposed to advertise your presence, even with the wreckage of your jet not far away, making a liar of you as you hid your dust. No one would come looking, not through an airspace no one should have been crossing in the first place, even if only to invigilate installations that should not have been on the ground either. *Expendable* was the word.

He felt excreted. Preposterous as it seemed, two men who, only hours before, had sat in a multibillion-dollar aircraft consecrated to the hush-hush inspection ritual of the century were now just so much disregarded waste. Their only reason for being had been aerial, their only use had consisted in their being in the right place, and aground they signified only twin absences to be remedied. Did that therefore mean all their expensive training was a write-off too? He would have thought the military husbanded its investments better, not out of concern for the individuals involved but for the sake of economy. It was no thought to linger on, not when, as things were turning out, it was likely to be one of his penultimate ones.

There was one chance only: tomorrow, as Xavier and Young flew a second Cyrano over the same route (their whole vocation one of endless duplication), their beacons might reach the onboard computer, which then would take a fix. A decision would then ensue whether or not to mount a rescue mission, contrary to protocol, on behalf of two outcasts who, officially speaking, were not even there, any more than mercenaries who tended bioblitz-viralfare installations and remote-control missile silos. Since the enemy had not yet fired upon a single Cyrano, they might not mind a rescue mission. By the same token, though, leaving Cyrano alone was the only concession you could expect. Already the wreckage would be underground, being dismantled and explored by experts who combined the delicacy of stamp collectors with the self-righteousness of the Inquisition. At dawn the manhunt would begin with pink-and-white-sprayed helicopters moving south-north to scout for parachutes and tune in to unexpected signals. Meanwhile, Clegg half froze and Booth, ringed in by a dozen human salt-herons dressed in sackcloth, dreamed of an eviscerated camel trying to register in the Hotel Continental, Djibouti. Prodded hard in the belly, Booth jackknifed up, saw the long irregular poles and the fierce men holding them, crouched around him under the scorched-smelling fabric of the tent. When they spoke incomprehensibly, he tried out his rudimentary French *(je suis où?)*, not pronouncing the second *s*, rightly or wrongly he didn't care; but it was no use, no one laughed or even seemed to listen. Instead they made a shambles of his equipment, clinching their explorations with the chute, which they bundled up and then slashed into strips with gigantic double-edged, broad-bladed knives bared from long angular flat scabbards worn across the pubic area. Each man wound a length around his lower part with arrogant dignity, then swung another over his shoulder. They seized his revolver even as he cowered from the blast of direct heat, and urged him to accompany them. Several of them, he saw, had teeth filed into points, like human bats, and he shivered. Refusing to let him drink from his canteen, which they also commandeered, they shoved him before them across the salt toward an area that looked excavated. Weary of being prodded by their stout poles, he made as if to hasten, but a pole at once tripped him, making him gash his knee: a poor start, considering what followed. Not that they killed him, which he expected them to, or tortured him; they put him to work, prying up enormous slabs of solid salt from the bed of the lake. Almost at breaking point, the poles never gave, though Booth's arms felt unhinged at shoulder and elbow after only a few minutes' labor. Too dry even to gasp, he heaved away at the slabs while others trimmed the edges of some into flagstone shapes and a couple of the youngest-looking loaded mules and camels. A hundred yards away, black silhouettes of animals shuffled to and fro at what he supposed was a water hole, but he could no longer see what others could, and he knew only from memory that the salt slabs were buff or verdigris in places and the ground beneath them a pale granular brown.

For miles the blinding white surface waited to be broken up, as if all of Africa had been spread with icing. One of his captors said something to him with a comprehensive sweep of a badly scarred arm, but Booth could only nod, whisper his name to himself. The heat increased, yet no one drank. Needles drilled into his forehead. Salt of his own sweat caked his face. Both hands bled, then stung unbearably as he strove on; all he had to do was pause and one of them pricked him with a swordpoint from behind, the weird thing being that they seemed to have no sense of incongruity, having accepted him from the sky, on the salt, as just another pair of hands, a victim-captive, yes, but more useful than exotic, more of a routine hack than a god out of the machinery. He had been traded in, all the way across the centuries, from supersonic flight to the sons of Ham: a changeling at risk. Rumor had it that these people, so fierce to look at, were genial at heart; they were certainly not genial to look at, so maybe they were fierce through and through. Yet, rather than cruel, they seemed almost maniacal about work and having him do his share. Toward sunset a group of them finished loading the mules and camels and then set off at a slow, time-abolishing gait. The rest trudged a few hundred yards to a huddle of square salt igloos in which, presumably, they passed the nights. Booth could not decide whether they lived here permanently or whether this was just a labor settlement. Motioned into one of the igloos, he stooped and shuffled in, or rather he bent lower from the near-crouch he could not straighten from. His entire body blurted with pain, and he took the proffered hunk of bread, the goatskin of water, without gesture or facial shift, his mind weirdly on the open shelves of an empty refrigerator's freezer compartment, newly defrosted, with the motor's purr newly unhindered and a crisp white nap starting to form on the zinc. He cursed the heat, the indoors fug, the lack of light to read faces by.

When his neighbor shoved bread or water at him, he took it, a mere phage in the gloom. When someone broke wind, he half assumed it was himself. Only yesterday he had been streaking over Africa, sixteen miles high, at over two thousand miles an hour, almost freed from human restriction, a halcyon outsider, and here he was, primitivized beyond belief, a cipher in a chain gang, among folk who had only enough imagination to put him to work. From what he had heard of civilized men gone ape, or native, the process was gradual, entailing a whole series of inconspicuous surrenders under gruesome pressure, but these pitiable salt miners were not even trying to break him. Like children interrupted at play, they had fitted him into their game, not resentfully or exuberantly, but with economical dispatch, and not a word exchanged. Over and over it he went, as if constant review would break some spell. So long as he pondered it thus, he told himself, and kept trying to analyze what was happening, he would remain himself, more or less, not a colonel or a technological man, but Beauregard Booth who hated the sea, habitually read financial papers flown in from London, and had a small boil in the cleft of his rear. Yet, overpowering that image of himself, the retinal one of the day just over crammed his head with light, and once again three or four of them, knees bent and shoulders quivering with the strain, pried up the outsize white scabs, their bleached barkless poles like the prongs of a deformed fork upon which the miners looked ready to impale themselves, two prongs per man. Their grunting seemed to come from the cracking salt itself, and they seemed mere marionettes of the crust, eager and automatic creatures as fixed in role and stance as the Centaur and the Wolf had been in that previous incarnation of his last night, when hell was still optional, and the star called Alpha Centauri had seemed hearteningly close. Why then did he feel something had now been proved?

Years ago, to settle perplexities that had usurped his mind for far too long, he had summed up for himself as follows: Imagine yourself behaving toward those near and dear to you as the [universe,] so-called, deals with the race at large, doling out cancer of the face to your mother, say, and celiac deficiency to your wife, so that the one's face falls away from her in tatters and the other's belly bloats with gluten, and her feces, always causing prolapse of the rectum, are white. From the impossibility, for him as for most, of such conduct, he deduced as follows: We are not evolution, we only move through it while it moves, unconscionably purposeful, through us. Atrocities he had ruled out, along with other random quirks of will, whereas the refusal of human cells to renew again after, what was it, twenty-six renewals, was nothing to do with will at all, but was rather the state of the art under the heading of Evolution. Yet, he wondered back then, wasn't there too a state of the art under the heading of Will? Only a hairsplitter, he decided, would vindicate atrocity as necessary to evolution or condemn disease and death as acts of will. There was a difference: for some of their cells, men and women were responsible, and for some, not, at least not yet. Headily grateful for the little cottage industries of his entire body (all those organs, well behaving), he halted discussion with himself and summed up the [universe] as the overbearingness that includes us in. As here. It was like being dragged back into the universe through a crystal of salt, after feeling exempt, then irrelevant, then bored. God, he thought, we were like medieval monks in the Cyrano, and *this* is the Renaissance. Is Clegg too reinvolved, or is he dead?

The goatskin water tasted foul, not salty as it might have been, but of rancid shellfish and weird, reconstituted dry peas. The bread, at some stage between soggy and moldy, found its way into the spaces between his teeth and his cheeks, making him mentally nod in the direction of chipmunks, but he scooped it back with his ruined fingers and it went down as paste. He asked for more water, able only to grunt and point, but whatever his companions saw or heard, they ignored him, and his throat stayed as it was, texture of cactus. Having considered making a run for the doorway, he rejected the idea: where could he go? His emergency kit was gone; the pockets of his coveralls were empty; the orange chute was no longer spread out as a landmark. Odd choice as it had to be, between raving helpless through the salt wastes and biding his time wordless among demonic-looking miners, he chose, anxious to sleep, which he soon did, where he lay, on sacks and rags, but not before noticing how one of their number had blocked the door hole with a slab of salt. Lulling himself with fantasies of Inuit life (except all day not a woman had appeared, or anyone female-looking), he soon was able to ignore his sweat as it ran nonstop, even when he lay utterly still. In a cocoon of bad air, bubbling phlegmy coughs, and stoked-up heat, he slept just under six hours, almost enough. And then the workday began, without drink or food, greeting or explanation, a gigantic red wash of dawn on one horizon, a Prussian blue sky above them, quickening by the second, and in all directions the salt's iridescent duck-egg blue fading into eye-scalding ivory as the sun rose. Gruffly, one of the miners handed Booth the sunglasses taken from him yesterday, still intact except for the lenses, which had been struck out. He put them on, a reflex, then felt securer merely from the weight on the bridge of his nose, like a bird yearning for its cage.

Again they denied him water (he having begged for it with a cupping motion of his hand before his mouth) and handed him two stout, irregular poles with which, no doubt about it, he was to heave and shove. Hiccupping, he tried to hold his breath, but only managed to cough. There was sketchy blood in what he spat, he could not imagine why, and a red film in front of his eyes, but that was perhaps only the sun climbing. The work went on, stultifyingly gross, not so much a chore as an attack on geology itself. To peel up the surface of the entire depression would take years, by which time it would have renewed itself throughout, and he, Booth, would be buried under it, if the miners had even that much finesse. On he toiled in empty sunglasses, now clad in his shorts only, his feet swathed in triangle bandages he had found slung away by his captors.

Clegg had slept fitfully, the ad hoc rope between his fingers, its length by now some sixty feet, and strong enough to hold him. Cached is how he felt, or secreted, stashed, and bound to be collected later. He was going to be called for by someone as yet unknown. He thought of his mother, years ago, curled on a sofa like a meek pygmy, seeking comfort on the spinning planet with a cherry or mint bonbon dissolving in her cheek. He had never felt so close to her since, as a child, he had licked out the mixing basin and the wooden spoon after she made vanilla cake. Untheological in the extreme, he nonetheless voiced a prayer after he woke up for the fifth time with just a few stars quivering over him in the gash and the rest of his context a faintly moonlit purple.

Our help in ages past, he said, if not exactly a prayer, then a fervent wish, uttered maybe to some mirror image of himself, an Ancient of Days who supervised an hourglass. It would be days before he could even attempt the descent, but he had enough provisions to see him through to then. Thereafter, though, would be a different tale, and only a quick rescue would save him. Booth, he felt sure, was better off, had more than all the necessary smarts, so he stopped thinking about him, and, just before dawn, when Booth was starting work, he began a two-hour stint that extended his rope by forty feet. He still, however, had found nothing to hang it from, and he had no means of nailing into the rock face. All he heard was a fairly distant sound of birds and his own breath, a bisected-sounding wheeze that fluffed his eyelashes as he looked down at what his hands accomplished, lost in an African belfry repairing frayed bellropes. Not that he disliked enclosures: caboose, cockpit, the hunter's blind, all pleased him to death; he might even have relished Booth's salt igloo for an hour or two. What he hated, though, was the prospect of people's knowing something about him that he didn't: the fact of his death, and a death in ridiculous circumstances at that. Dead in his descent capsule, with enough rope to get him down but nothing to fasten it to, that was ignominious, whereas dead at ground level, from dehydration and hunger, that was at least half decent. Astonished to find himself hypothesizing in such detail, he vowed eventually to ransack the mountain face for some kind of hitching post, even if doing so entailed death by initiative instead of death by inertia. If, as he had heard, London's pigeons actually made use of the city's underground trains, getting on at Blackfriars and hopping out at Charing Cross, or wherever, depending on where and when the pickings above or below ground were best, then he could surely extricate himself from this hermitage on a ledge. *The bearer of a flag of truce,* he quoted, *also the trumpeter, bugler, or drummer, the flag-bearer and the interpreter may, for instance, be blindfolded.* No: that would come later, his memory was ahead of him, and would have done better to have lobbed up something relevant to imprisonment in the field. Thus, *Soldiers not in disguise who have penetrated into an enemy's country to obtain information are not considered spies. To this class belong, likewise, individuals sent in balloons, airships, and airplanes to deliver dispatches. . . .* This was neutral territory anyway, or ostensibly so. Yet savages unacquainted with the Field Service Regulations, from an antiquated text he was involuntarily quoting, might shoot first, or worse. He was lucky, perhaps, not to have taken a round through the skull even as high as this. Or a shell. Bombs even. Napalm. Were they to furnish him with a printed postcard (the fastest means of correspondence in this zone of war), he would choose his words and phrases carefully, heeding all injunctions (Nothing is to be written on this except the date and signature of the sender / Sentences not required may be erased / If anything else is added the postcard will be destroyed). *I am quite well,* the first line said; he let it stand, then deleted the next one about having been admitted to hospital, but kept the third: *Sick and am going on well.* As for *Wounded and am going on well,* he crossed it out, as he did *I am being sent to base* and the next two: *I have received your letter/telegram/parcel,* and *Letter follows.* But he felt the last one—*I have received no letter from you/lately/for a long time*—generically applied, and let it speak for him, not least to his gifted sister who shuttled between Cooperstown and California, her purse full of undiscarded keys. Twittering dawn brought him a visitor, a vulture, which, after darting its head through the side hole, seemed to propel the beak toward him along the runway of its neck, bringing him an aroma of carrion even as the bird hissed. It was a smell of decayed liver and hot rubber, causing his gorge not so much to rise as to retreat and shrink. He fired and missed. The vulture had already retracted its neck and head and was now crashing about against the fabric outside. Then there was silence marred only by the buzzing of insects. Falconoid, thought Clegg, wide awake: that's what the vulture is, yet also, it's—a hairless erection. That echo of his hunting days had heartened him fractionally, had given him back a measure of self-esteem: he could still *do* things, and he would do them again when the vulture (or vultures) checked him out later on. Not with finesse would he do it, but with all his heart. He would draw the fabric blind and, when the tips of claws or beaks came through, shoot point-blank at the shadow. How responsibly he was thinking, he could not tell; thought of some kind was going on, of course, but its caliber stayed hidden, as in all self-describing systems. He longed for John Brown's warm sunshine in the country of peace, but knew he had to get from second to second without wavering, whereas getting from hour to hour was a triumph of nonimagination, and to sit still as the days moved past him, with his stomach churning, was so close to mysticism that he knew he would have to become one of the elect. Or not survive. A shabby elect, of course, paramilitary and passive, but also fabulous, the envy of high school boys, a Polaroid angel. Hearing of someone promoted to one-star general, Clegg had exclaimed, and then again when his interlocutor added, "And after three failures too." Vitriolic, Clegg had said, "How lucky. They usually insist on four or five." That was in the dark ages of his career, when he was a captain, eager to function cleanly but unable to quit his loathing of fools.

He was thin and brittle-looking then, a starer but not so moody a one as now, and briefly assigned to a munitions depot in middle New York State, where he inspected nonstop, daily, nightly, with and without warning, in his sleep and sleepwalking, always to no purpose. After a year of that, nuclear warheads were as commonplace to him as his tie rack and the venison he culled from the section of the state park the military had cordoned off. Rupert they had called him until he began to insist on Clegg (just and only that) after a visit by British NATO officers who surnamed one another as if referring to herbs, gasteropods, or defunct polities: "Ah, Fogg! Whitmarsh, old boy, it's Ponsonby!" Wowed thus into shedding his first name, he soon became Clegg even to himself, not least in the most casual spells of daydreaming. Whereas most folk do not name themselves, or even get as far as "I," when self-communing, Clegg did, thus achieving a complex interior status: he was impersonally formal, verging perhaps on the autistic, and he was somehow dramatic as well, as when, instead of vaguely participating as the toothbrush stroked his teeth, he made a point of thinking, "Clegg brushes his teeth." It was as if, from the hinterland of personality, he seized new instances of initiative. So his life, since he became a senior captain and an acting major, had doubled. On he lived with, in parallel, inside his head, a homemade movie devoted to addictive vignettes of Clegg. No wonder that now, in spite of heat, loneliness, trauma, cold, the imminence of death, he was still, with his mind's voice, doing commentary on himself, thus: *Stranded several thousand feet up, in the mountains of Ethiopia, and eager to descend, Clegg busily twists a makeshift rope.*

At times he used the continuous present, which gave an extra sense of immersion in his own unendingness (*Clegg is twisting a rope*). Other times he used the perfect (*Clegg twisted a rope*), which made him feel like someone narrated and therefore in someone else's hands, not responsible for what happened. This odd, self-aimed ventriloquism had begun, perhaps, when as a boy he had imagined himself outperforming famous names on football or baseball grounds, and simulating crowd applause with hoarse breaths into the cranny of his hand. In this way, to tumultuous homage, he hit a hundred home runs one-handedly and made touchdowns with everyone, players and spectators, looking the wrong way. But, naturally enough, the radio and TV commentators observed him: *Clegg seems hardly to look*, they would rave, *but that old one-handed swat has done it again. The ball has gone over the crowd, out of the stadium, into Flushing Bay!* Or, winterwise: *Clegg is doing push-ups on the line and still nobody has even seen him! His eleventh touchdown today!* Such fantasy soon became epical, and his military career inevitable. So, now, all of a sudden forced into an extreme emergency, he kept himself calm by narrating to himself. Horror could not scare him, nor boredom dull, nor anxiety sap. Everything he could tell himself about himself was of interest, and therefore life-enhancing. Jules Verne could not have entertained him more than Clegg entertained himself. An oral pendant to his predicament, he found that the act of describing converted a zero activity into a something one. What wasn't worth knowing when unverbalized was almost appetizing when told. He could not figure out why, but was happy to protect his sanity thus, or at least, less spectacular, his presence of mind. Which was just as well: his distress beacon was no longer transmitting, although it had functioned long enough to provide a fix. The battery was dead, as in Booth's too. Both men were out of range, except to unfriendly forces, and it was only a matter of time before discovery, although spotting in mountainous terrain was a hit-or-miss affair (and Clegg was almost hidden by the overhanging cliff), and the salt miners were a law unto themselves, as befitted their tribe, among whom hardly anyone in his right mind ventured to go.

As Booth soon saw, while Clegg narrated his head off at altitude, his own troubles had only just begun. Indeed, one zany part of his mind informed him, the Almighty works miracles not in order to supply what is missing in nature, but just to vary the fabric a bit. A savage-looking posse had arrived, smothered in banderillas, carrying up-to-date-looking rifles, and clad in cast-off military battledress as ragged as grimy. The territorial gestapo, Booth decided, observing how the miners let themselves be stared down, almost as a team caught red-handed, and then made submissive gestures with shoulders and feet (one shoulder hunched up to the neck as if to shield it, one foot gently stroking the top of the other from ankle joint to toe). Such truculent faces he had never seen, blurred as his vision was. Abruptly they seized one of the miners, who resisted not a jot but began to shake in wide-eyed palsy. All work on the salt ended. The leader, a touchy-looking six-footer with a crude-cropped Afro and a skimpy beard along the rim of his chin, motioned at Booth. At once they felt him over, as before, but in more detail, his hair, his calves, his privates, even his tongue and teeth with his mouth forced open. Testing Booth's flesh between finger and thumb, first that under his chin, then the small collop at his hip, the leader grunted a few words.

Everyone formed a hollow square, and Booth found himself tugged into one of the lines. Then the prisoner, flanked by two of the new arrivals, walked to and fro like a frogmarched epileptic while the other two chattered affably across him as he turned this way or that. Once, twice, three times, the trio crossed the open square, almost like German university professors taking a postprandial stroll in Göttingen. Then, after a few yards of the fourth sortie, the man on the captive's left paused, pinched the side of the man's chest as if to emphasize a point or gain attention, and, as the wretch turned with his head canted somewhat sideways, the third man with a curt swing of his arm cut through the neck, from the tensed muscles on the one side to the relaxed muscles on the other, with a broadsword such as Booth had noticed yesterday. A viscous sigh came from the onlookers. With a reverse lop the executioner freed the head from the still erect trunk, whence blood pumped in a drinking-fountain curve. Booth reeled, gagging, unable to vomit, but they caught him by his sun-sore arms and held him up.

Perhaps he was next, but that was wrong, the grisly ceremony was over. The visitors went, leading their camels. The head and trunk lay where they had fallen. But, before leaving, the leader had the miners take off their festoons of parachute fabric, which, rolled into a lump, went onto the back of a camel, intended for who knew what reckoning or auto-da-fé. Feeling lucky to be alive and unaccused, Booth began to worry at speed. What were they saving him for? Something worse than beheading? Were they truly so little concerned with him, or just lulling him until they were ready to perform? He saw his entire emergency kit disappear with them across the salt, even as he heaved with his two poles at yet another slab, but all he felt just now was nauseated relief, being as yet unmutilated, even though his hide felt like that of a roasted pig. What had the dead man done? There was no way to find out. Thievery? Adultery? Or had it been done just to keep the others in their place? Blind with sweat, harassed by flies that favored his nostrils and eyelids, half swooning from the heat and the pain in his blistered palms, he tried to concentrate on the work at hand. He could hardly see, but after several decisive blinks he caught a glimpse of the surface, mottled like Styrofoam and nothing like ice. Four men, heaving with the standard two poles apiece, managed to dislodge all but the very biggest blocks. Had the salt deposit not split apart from the colossal heat, there would have been the extra chore of cutting through to a depth of four or five inches, no doubt with axes, at the kneel. He shuddered, longing for water, and even tablets of salt. As he leaned on the straighter of his two poles, the others rebuked him in guttural polysyllables, their faces rigid and burnished. They might have been chastising a dog.

When, he wondered, did the rains come, the rains that flooded the lake and brought the salt down from the surrounding hills. A white man could lose his life here without enough sense to realize the fact. What would a loud scream accomplish? Or a sit-down strike? Or a solid faint? They would wait him out, then shove him back to work, or lift him by the ears again into his position on the salt face. Or cut his throat while he lay unconscious. Dazzled and numbed as he was, he clung to the notion that, if he could only be more alert, he would find the answer to all the things that puzzled him. He could just walk away, past the halved corpse, toward the slate-blue mountains. Failing that, he could kill all twelve (or eleven) miners with his Luger, if only he could retrieve it. Or beat their heads in with his pole. Ridiculous. And bribery was out, he had nothing left to bargain with. All that remained to him was adjustment, waiting it out; but, deprived of water, he would not last more than another day, not in such conditions as these. Then he would be of no use to anyone, and someone else would have to do his day's work for him. Therefore, he decided, they would irrigate him soon, prosaic slavedrivers that they were.

He was right; after two hours more, by which time his heart was thunder-fluttering, with several beats missed, they passed him the goatskin as if oiling a hinge. His shorts were stuck to him, dried on like plaster of Paris. Blobs of mucus dried out on his upper lip where they had lodged on the way down. Some crust rimmed his eyes and his mouth was clogged with foam. Turning away from them to relieve his bladder, and half amused at being so coy, he found the flap of his shorts pasted shut with sweat and salt. Next he saw his hands, as if they were in some exhibit, two mangled snails, blotted with red and encased in transparent-looking pouches that were sun and friction blisters the size of radishes. And some taboo in him kept him from touching his penis with such hands, as if they might transfer the insult downward, then reinfect him from the core up. He braced his legs apart, relaxed his sphincter muscle almost like a child wetting the bed in a dream, and let the fluid run down his leg. It cooled and tickled him while, deep in the back of his mind, he reasserted the facts of his name, his rank, his height, his weight, his injuries. Then the miners grouped around him, one with the severed head on one of the poles, a joke presumably, yet one at which they did not smile. All the man did was to flip the head away from him with a bunting motion and point the smeared end of the pole at Booth, urging him back to work. Already his leg felt dry, though now the hair on it was taut. He coughed, gestured for water, got none, and hobbled back to where his poles lay on the salt, crutches themselves arthritic.

He had virtually no shadow, which seemed appropriate to his condition and was surely prophetic. In other words, he had already begun construing the sun's random effects. The severed head haunted him, or the severed neck, he hardly knew how to refer to it. Either of the arteries, he heard from some distant clinic where the light was not from the sun, supplying blood to the head: carotid, on each side of the neck. Snipped like tulip stems. With such people, his chances would never be anything less than zero. And that went for either group, the miners, who saw him only as a contraption handily delivered to produce so many foot-pounds of effort, and the others, the gestapo or vigilantes, who would remove him from salt labor only to subject him to something else and unspeakably worse. Licking Booth salt from his lips, he felt frail as crystal, longing all over again for high-altitude flight, for ejection, for boredom even. All he could look forward to was a hunk of bread and five or six hours' sleep. He soon found a new trick to play, skimming each successive slab with half-closed eyes to produce beyond it an oasis, a mirage of lemonade and chlorine-blue water, in which cocktail islands awaited him: circlets of leather-upholstered seats that seemed to float like dinghies under a glass cupola, upon which late-evening rain made moiré patterns, all bleb and dribble and spot.

Then the slab fell forward, every time exposing the foothills fifty miles away, like the dorsal tectonics of some elongated sunning pachyderm. This, he tartly advised himself, was he-man country, the only good thing about it being that, so far, every yahoo had not acquired a portable radio. He longed, ferociously, for the crammed, chaotic buses of the Port Authority that shuttled you from terminal to terminal at Kennedy Airport, for the airless heat in the lofts of a million American houses, for his childhood fist plunged into the hot fluff at the center of a new-baked loaf. Sure enough, his mind had flickered briefly to life, countering the present mess with peripheral evasions that just managed to work, and for which he was snidely grateful. On the bread all of a sudden thrust at him, he almost choked. Yet he whispered a belated token thank-you to the incurious retreating back of the donor. Squatting, he rubbed saliva-wet crust on the surface of the salt and tried the taste, vaguely remembering the salt his body had to have. It was not so much salty as acrid, not so much acrid as even caustic. Look on the bright side, he told himself, they do not have fishes to go with their loaves, they are religious fanatics in nothing they do, they are minimal men such as philosophers prate about, they have reduced living to terms the actuaries cannot imagine. I am more than earning my keep, anyway, I am entitled to be cheerful; they might not be feeding me at all. He again tried talking to them, making crude signs for baby, airplane, woman, gun, and swim. An ebony glaze met his gestures, not so much as if he had not spoken or moved, but rather as if speech or gesture of any kind were invalid here, where a silver-white metallic element, which was the base of soda, consorted with a compound of chlorine, thus creating an underfoot monolith too hard to lie on, too bright and beautiful to be looked at, and too brittle to be incised with letters, faces or symbols. The salt refused them. Yet the humidity was low, a thought that kept Booth from a gibbering fit, even though his back and left side were covered with hives that itched and crawled. At least, when it was free from mucus, his nose had air to breathe, instead of steam, but air so hot it felt like invisible fire or mustard gas.

Around and around his mind went as he labored, trying to cook up something to be glad about. He vowed to walk over to the watering hole where the camels and mules remained. A couple of hundred yards away, it was an abstract destination only, could not be smelled or properly seen. Maybe they would kill him just for attempting it, or just watch him trudge there and back without responding in any way at all.

High above him in the sun, a rich thrumming sound of accelerating tur-bines came and went, as if a jet had dived and shallowly pulled out in some aerobatic routine. Again Booth heard it, an aerial signature exotic enough to take him the next forty yards past the dead trunk and the head, to where the salt carapace ended, giving way to something like petrified suede, which he realized was only salt in an older layer. A commotion of iridescent-bellied flies accompanied him, making him tingle whenever they touched and, when he was not scratching himself, flail at them as they came to his face point-blank. No one accosted him or fired off a warning round. Knee-deep in the mud at the pool's edge, he shoved at a mule and lay on his back until he had coated everything but his face. The dankness, reek-ing of dung, was a joy; there he lay, watched by a haughty camel or two, a full fifteen minutes, not just cooling himself but setting his ravaged skin to rest. When he got up he could hardly stand for the suction of the mud, and he at length walked away slop-heavy and mud-caked, making no effort to clean himself up. He hardly felt the flies or the sun, but, as the afternoon wore on, and the mud dried out, he felt enclosed in chain mail, a daubed knight; but the others, unflagging in their incuriosity, eyed him not at all, and so made him feel natural, part of the scenery. Flakes dropped away from him, but most of the mud remained, which meant just enough of his pores were open to the air, just enough of him was shielded from the sun. As his shadow lengthened, he stared into it, as if tuning in to a friend; again he went to the watering hole to submerge himself, first defecating with some discomfort at its perimeter as the animals did. After rinsing his smeared shorts in twelve inches of muddy water, he slid them on over the shimmering milk-chocolate surface of his limbs and walked back erect to where his two poles awaited him. Flecked with mud, his empty sunglasses glinted like parts of a head prosthesis. Exhausted, but less feverish in his mind, he went slow with the slabs, but the others left him alone, neither barking rebukes nor goading him with shoves.

If only a dinner in a motel followed, all this might be tolerable; but the prospect of another night in a salt igloo mortified him, his only problem being where else to sleep and on what. A chill coursed along the marrow of his arms, as if his mud sheath for the first time kept the heat out. Deserts grew cold at night, he knew, but this one seemed to break the rule. Or was it hot only inside the stinking igloo? Tonight, if at all possible, he would find out, maybe even study the Centaur and the Wolf as they rose and fell, more human than the beings they hovered over. Looking past the limb of the sun, where incinerative core yielded to the halo of crisp flash, he kept his gaze steady and let his eyes begin to burn, hum with the white that stoked the world, hydrogen into helium, easily said, not so easily done, at any rate not by anyone on the rowdy planet. Aware of having rather more mental spunk than earlier today, he thanked mud and the bread that had come unexpected. A beheaded man lying there was a poor emblem, but he would serve when the Centaur, commemorating Cheiron, tutor to Jason of the Argonauts, was invisible. And when the Centaur showed, the corpse would not. It made for a balanced world, crude but cogent. For an instant, Booth sensed he was getting his bearings, equivalent he supposed to someone on the guillotine, an actual Frenchman, he had forgotten who, twisting his head around to look up at the released blade that for some reason had stuck and, in the few accidental seconds remaining to him, managing to relish the way the blade bisected a blue sky flecked with lambswool cumulus. No, it was not quite that, of course not. Here, at rude minimum admittedly, there was enough to apply his mind to: a routine, a community, a substance worthy of contemplation. Oh, it was not what the old ads for jobs used to say (three square meals and found), but it was more than nada, it was superabundantly in excess of that. Never had he felt so far from the trophies of high culture arrived at random, spermicidal jelly, the big bowel movements of gourmets in the dying cities of North America, pigmen astride sows with aerosol cans of pheromones. It was as if civilization, like an event, were over, and you could go home, ticket stub in hand. Not that he was giving up the arrogance of intellect for an Oriental submissiveness; not quite. He was contracting himself, shrinking himself, dealing with fewer phenomena, readier to lie awake naked in a ploughed field for a week than to dream of a long sleep among kings. Reality had made his imagination stammer, as did the vultures flocking around the dead man's head and trunk, trailing ribbons of viscera after them and tossing them up for ease of eating: loops rather than strands, coils rather than loops. The gristly necks appalled him, even at a distance, making him forget he used to be a man of needle-point reflexes, keen mind, and ebullient heart. It came to this in the end. Odd, though, how his mind got grandiose in such circumstances as these, when he would have expected the mental equivalent of monosyllabic surrender.

Looking about him in one of the increasingly long rests he had begun to take, and went unpunished for, he scanned the stark horizon, letting the mauve hills come into his mind much as he had let other images enter it when flying, not to relieve his boredom but to domesticate the almost obstetric clinical white of the land, against which his fellow miners were licorice black. A gigantic sand dollar, imperfectly round, had become his only context, on whose surface he was a malformed bead. Thoughts of ice fields, atolls, and rolling acres of seabed sand occurred, but he rejected them, amazed to have even that much control over his mental processes. He was fighting back. Salt, he told himself, was a pyramid-shaped crystal, at least if unmachined, so this was a plain of tiny pyramids comparable, in its vast intricacy, to the universe itself, and forever doing preposterous things with light, which it fractured and made bounce, taxing the viewer with rainbow mirages and a combustive shimmer that outdid all the chrome on all the cars ever made. To look was rash: the eye felt scalded, and things not far away, such as camels and outcrops of rock, were silhouettes only, like herds observed on snow from twelve miles up. His main concern, to survive, was yielding to knowledge and speculation, but perhaps the only way to survive was to keep the brain cells pulsing, if pulse was what they really did. On, then. Flog gumption's horse. He still had not lost the conviction that he would somehow get back to Turkey, to narrate his adventure over lamb chops and steins of imported beer, and this altered somewhat his view of what his eyes brought in: booty for later relishing, an experience he would eventually say he would not like to have missed.

Whereas, assuming he would be dead in a few days' time, he felt oddly disobliged, sure that thrilling perceptions meant nothing in their own right, were not worth having, were merely exercise for the instruments of sense. In theory the difference that should have appealed to him was that between having perceptions and having none, something to do with an old chestnut about life's being a gift. Yet, since it had no prospects, the gift was worthless; in other words, landscape fed him by an apparatus that would soon be defunct and had no appeal at all. A weird thought, it implied that, because all human apparatus will eventually become defunct, nothing is ever worth attending to, ever. Mumbling mentally, he could only conclude that experience in the raw was as nothing whereas experience recollected was almost everything, saturated as it was with words and comparisons, *made over*, as it were. On a scale of two or three days, there was no time in which to anticipate the joys of recollection, while over a lifetime, whose quotient remained inscrutable but was taken for granted, the question hardly ever came up, even at sixty, say. From this point forward, Booth looked hard in his every perception for the attitude that rejected phenomena per se because there would be no future to savor them in. He failed to find it, though, and this proved to him his hunch that he would survive to brood on it all, oh, on a patio in Arizona with peanuts in a glass bowl in front of him, or skiing at Gstaad with a hare-lipped Romanian nurse whose body he had never seen the likes of. The imminently doomed man's perceptions were dead. That was it. You always knew. And the key to the whole enigma was something abstract and often mistaken: the presumption that you, unlike others, would survive, all predicated on the suave dream that life does not bring us into being in order to waste us. Concerning individuals *en masse* the dream held up, but not concerning one individual at a time. Half dizzy with pondering meant to be accurate but grown woolly, Booth groped for summation and in the end said, to no one, the future is the present's frame; we want the future not for itself, but only to be retrospective in; I am alive only if I know I am going to live. But it still felt wrong, he knew not why, and he put the thought away, angrily noting that none of this would have come up if he had been working on an ordinary salt-evaporation bed, in a panama hat and wielding a rake according to strict shifts.

Instead, here he was, giving off a midden stench in the armpit of Africa. His fellow miners were still busy, toiling with the minimum of groan and talk. Was there, he wondered, an o'clock relevant to now. Five or six perhaps. It was the onset of evening, of course, with the sun low but still severe. A fit of colonel's anger ran through him: they had wrecked his emergency kits, and all he had left were the triangle bandages on his feet, now heavy with filth. But no watch, no compass, no gun, no map, no signal, no chute, no medicine. He still wore the frames of his sunglasses, more out of elegiac rectitude than anything else. This night, come what may, he was going to sleep in the open, with his two stout staves to guard him. No more of the salt oven, no more claustrophobia; if they wanted him to work, they must let him sleep. Let them guard him if they so desired, or even tie him up. He need not have worried; they were more fastidious than he gave them credit for; he smelled so bad they declined even to eat alongside him, but tossed the goatskin from a distance with exquisite aversion that broke into a short laugh, the first he had seen. The bread came along the same parabola. Idly brushing his hand against his scalp, he felt corrugations and scrolls, firm and rough, as if his skull had rippled up and frozen. No, it was his hair, hardened by the sun at work on the mud-slick top. Wondering how he looked, he peered into a shiny flat of salt, but saw nothing, only his laurel-wreathed silhouette, at which he gaped, distracted from that blurred sight only by a glint of metal. One of the miners had a rifle alongside him where he sat, the barrel canted at a varying diagonal, the combination as impressive to Booth as an electrified fence. At what distance would the man shoot? Somewhere beyond the water hole, obviously. Booth knew there was going to be no rescue helicopter, but just maybe a bombing mission to blow them all to bits, unless of course the other side found him first, in which case he would soon be having his first serious encounter with hypodermically elicited truth.

Devouring his bread, he practiced saying his name, an aside to crumbs, then emptied his mouth and proclaimed Beauregard Booth to the assembled company, the landscape, the violet sky. A waste of energy. And he knew that, if he said his name aloud a hundred times, it would begin to sound unfamiliar, as when you stare incessantly at a word. Fixing on the *oo* sound in Booth, he mouthed it silently again and again as the salt plain reacquired its pastel blues and the igloos began to look less like sugar cubes than derelict refrigerators. The world of tints had come back into its own. Isaac Newton had ousted Apollo once more. Even the vultures looked milder, just a clutter of bird life rather than a complex climbing plant, a parliament of hosepiped beaks that did awful things to the organs you cherished most. He looked away, marvelling how he stood there like an habitué, as if something proprietorial had entered him; not so much proud of his desert as inclined to take it on trust as a going concern. All he heard was the vultures' bickering hiss, monotonous jogtrot chatter from the miners, a camel blurt or two, nothing from the mules. No wind, no plane. The insects had formed a silent smoke cloud over the corpse, ovipositors no doubt at the ready, braving the vultures in the interests of the future; no, they were safe as houses, vultures did not eat flies. Perverse, he strolled over to the body, one pole in hand, with which to beat off the birds. A small light industry was under way with the trunk, like a long squashed fruit, at the center of it. Not a bird was idle. There must have been twenty, probing and tugging. He wondered why vultures, rather than hyenas or jackals, had arrived first, the answer no doubt being that animal life rarely ventured into the salt depression. In any case, birds traveled more easily above it than any quadruped upon it.

Flailing at the mass of birds, maiming a few in the first seconds, he seemed to be thrashing the trunk itself, but it was only a layer of feathers and gristle. The vultures flew or trotted away to a safe distance, a dozen yards, to wait out the intrusion, and he took his first close look at what remained. Had there been no limbs, he would not have known what he was looking at. As for the head, it looked empty, an incomplete model almost skeletal except for gashed flesh that dangled almost free. Only the hair survived, an evocative tod, too luxuriant a growth for the remnant it crowned. Alas, poor Yorick, he recollected haphazardly, but he had never known this man and he still had no idea what his offense had been. A stench of decomposing potatoes made him bend his nose a little with his clay-thick hand. Again he slammed a questing vulture as it planed toward him; in his day he had felled bats from behind with a squash racquet. He was adapting, he told himself, to African life, he the Jason of the computer console, and he wondered, in savage afterthought, if Clegg were doing half as well wherever *he* was. With his pole he shoved the ruined head toward the trunk, sensible of some maltreated passion for order, an officerly aplomb not valid here, but still a form of comfort. In a local sense, the vultures were even tidier than he, just waiting the chance to do their job. He ambled away, pole on shoulder, its end messed with feathers and blood. The corpse was still clad in its original rags, but the vultures had jerked the fabric aside in order to bare the vulnerable zones. Charnel, Booth thought: from carnal, meaning of the flesh.

Then he realized it was getting dark. The splotch of the trunk was already vague, the moon was edging up, Centaurus would follow, and Booth promised himself another night under the stars, astonished at being so sedate, or if not sedate then composed, in what he had only just now called a charnel house. Clearly his officer's training had begun to pay off. He had been trained for this. Of course, they would guard him, no doubt taking turns; in fact, they must have guarded him in the salt igloo, so the idea was not new to them. Against the chance of his escaping, he suspected, was the smell he gave off, which meant they would station him downwind and where he was visible. But there was no wind and they might not care how he smelled so long as he was visible. His mind was buckling and slithering, using the right concepts no doubt, without quite making them dovetail into sense. The problem was how to ask them anything, they who answered his laborious sign language with scowls, then a rude finger pointing into the mouth of an igloo. He was not to sleep in the open at all, and the lunatic notion arrived that, shoving the salt-block across the doorway each night, he and the miners were like self-made resurrectioneers, faking a miracle each morning.

As things turned out, though, the night was warmer than usual, and Booth, too fatigued to reckon every consequence, plodded away from the igloo to where the dead trunk lay, free of vultures but quick still with flies, and flipped it over on its front, which made a faint, damp slither as of wrung-out laundry set down. He felt at the torso's back. It was reasonably intact, and then he realized that he had done this with his hands even though he had a pole with him. It was more fitting, he self-approvingly decided: if you are going to use the scavenged trunk of a beheaded fellow human as a bolster, don't move it with a stick, be human and tender. Watched by one of the miners just outside a doorway, rifle in hand, Booth lay down and eased his head back; the trunk propped him up at almost a reading angle. But Centaurus lay in the other half of the sky, southward, whereas he had been facing north, whence he initially had come. So he switched sides, resting his nape on one of the surviving bits of cloth, ordering his nose to calm down as the rotten-potato smell began to sharpen and multiply. Centaurus shone clear, or at least it did once Booth had mentally connected star to star to make the big triangle again of the man-horse's pelvis, the two rhombuses that were chest and head. Then the legs, the front ones reaching up to the triangle's right angle, at lower left, from the blatant pair of stars, Alpha and Beta, the one white, the other ruddy, Beta's name Agena or Hadar, Alpha's (at least to air navigators such as himself) Rigil Kent. The very names calmed him as he stretched out, somewhat tense, on his salt mattress and what he vaguely thought of as his cannibal pillow. With a delicious shiver, he recognized how well he was remembering in the midst of experiences he had never had before and had never expected. Nothing in the sky moved, but he was conscious of the star diagram's even wheel past him, ice-age slow, gradually moving sideways and down to go behind him, behind the planet itself, but not for hours yet, Centaurus being only just past the meridian, with Lupus bang upon it. Some renegade portion of his memory told him Centaurus was something he'd seen before, only differently. How could that be?

He watched the rifleman watch him in the gloom, in fact he alternated celestial and prudent gazes, nodding abruptly down from the prancing duo in the heavens to the inert, knees-up figure in front of the silver-hued igloo twenty yards away. From the sublime to the iniquitous, he thought, knowing he would soon be asleep in spite of everything. A buzzing drift took him in its stride. Centaurus and Lupus fanned lazily down-sky.

Dreaming appropriately of eighteen-inch African rats, flesh-eating ants, and hyraxes whose bloodcurdling screams erupted from the mass of bougainvillea that grew from Clegg's mouth, Booth awoke to barks and a rifle shot. Teeth and a cold muzzle grazed his leg, a pale yellow form yelped twice and spun somersaulting away from close to his head, interchanging shapes hovered about him: eyes, jaws, and he leaped to his feet as a second shot cracked through the night. Ringed by hesitant jackals, he groped for his pole and swung wildly, then again, both times missing. As his eyes cleared he saw a mouth, an open dark bag rimmed with fangs, and rammed the pole's end into it, deep down into some soft stuff, then twisted it sharply to the right, forcing the animal onto its side as it gave out, in choked blurts, the hyrax-type screams he'd heard while sleeping. Shoving even harder, he sent the pole a couple of feet into the body, next with all his strength heaving the thing erect as blood spilled down the pole from the nosedown jackal's chops. Another shot sounded and zipped into the barely moving carcass he still brandished in midair even while his throbbing head split wide open and just before he let the animal slide off. The last jackal had gone after hovering around him with truculent scampers this way and that, pretending to advance, then backing up only to nose forward more boldly from another direction. Giddy, he walked toward the miners, lined up as if waiting to be selected from, and was amazed when the one with the rifle gave him a fractional grin, but less amazed when several of them, then the one with the rifle, motioned him inside. He was glad to enter, but it was a full hour before he got to sleep again, his limbs atremble, his head sore to the touch, the hives itching nonstop. The last sound he heard was that of the rifle being reloaded, whether against jackals or himself he did not know or care.

As he trailed off, he had a thought he determined not to lose, namely that the miners were all of them malefactors at hard labor, yet in some kind of open prison, perhaps awaiting execution at the whim of the itinerant camel-caravan gestapo he had already seen in action, who no doubt even hauled unfortunates away from sleep to behead them in the moonlight. Vaguely he felt a bond he had not felt with them before, he the political prisoner, they the doomed. No one seemed to care how he smelled, being unquestionably ripe themselves, though Booth was the only one there caked with sulfurous mud. If the jackals had returned in the small hours, there was no way of knowing. Booth had heard no more shots. When he woke and looked out, having overslept, he saw vultures galore, cloaking the trunk, almost unified into one big black mantle save for an extruded naked neck, a wing uplifted for poise. Light-headed, he went toward the heaving mass to retrieve his pole and, unable to resist, thrashed it down hard into the oblivious, functionary backs of the birds, producing a short-lived squawk made individual by one bird that, with mashed eye and ripped-off wing, thrust its beak back into the body cavity, impelled by something stronger than pain. Some of the stench had gone by now, as had much of the two dead jackals, not so much dismembered animals, or even wet mounds of sundered guts, as a reliquary done in fur and bone, set amid magenta gouache on the hot salt's disk. How fast Africa consumed its fauna. The thought took him to the igloo again, where bread and a goatskin of water awaited him, like room service, just inside the doorway, underneath a saddle-shaped wedge of salt that reminded him of diagrams illustrating a universe of negative curvature.

Ravenous, he took his breakfast within the shade of the doorway's over-hang, chastened to see the others already at work in the broiling sun, lift-ing tabletop-sized slabs of salt. Surely another caravan was due: no, the camels and mules at the watering hole would carry out the new-trimmed lumps, but who would come to lead them? All the miners did was to mine, unlikely to be promoted or, indeed, allowed to live out the year. Perhaps, even, an execution took place each time the salt moved out. Doomed thus, *he* would have risked stealing a camel or even walking across the salt to the foothills. No, he decided, the miners weren't working on the desert's death row, they were a select band only one of whom (if *of* them at all) had gone astray, like himself, an odd man out, which could surely mean, then, that his own would be the next head to fall. Who, with any reflexes at all, could not respond to having his side pinched, thus taut-ening up the other side of his neck for the blade? Booth resolved never to flinch when pinched. Once in Australia he had watched flying foxes— fruit-eating bats—grapple across a forest floor, walking as it were on the tips of their wings. Ungainly, at the prostrate crouch, they had reminded him of crippled Masters of Arts, in long black gowns that had baggy sleeves, scrambling on hands and knees to some unstated destination, sweetness or light.

So, now, he crossed the space between igloo and work area grudgingly, at the mental crouch, hunchbacked for the nonce, on the one hand at uncanny peace with the landscape, the work, the lurid rankness of his body, on the other hand mortally ill at ease about the next salt caravan, indeed about anyone who came next: the headsman or *carnifex*, who in Latin "made you meat." He shuddered as he thrust his two poles' ends under a slab already levered partway up by two of the miners. This was no way to be spending his last few hours. Better to get his hands on the rifle and take things as they came: kill, threaten, decamp, hunt, bushwhack, and in general get the hell out, in all the senses of that lordly phrase. And maybe even look for Clegg.

No longer stolidly narrating himself into and out of sportscast epics, Clegg yielded again to the miseries of enclosure, knotting his makeshift rope, of course, but in his mind going through the motions of the hobbyist or handyman. He remade the thief-proof milk-bottle box of twelve years ago, the slit prong that squeezed last remnants from a toothpaste tube, and he lingered on happy glimpses of himself knelt on a sawing horse as he cut down-grain along a broad piece of wood or, with left hand curled horizontally around the nose of a smoothing plane and the right clamped on its rear's top, fetched spiral tongues of shavings up through its maw from the surface. The jack plane was the long one, usually made of beech, used for large work, whereas the smoothing plane was smaller and used for finishing off to a dead level. Both these planes were wooden. Religiously he rubbed both with linseed oil to reduce friction on the sole. Someone, not in his right mind, had done something similar with this mountain. There was no purchase, no grain. Or did he mean the Plexiglas of the canopy, that flawless emergency bubble? He caught himself half hoping the moment would never come when he had enough rope to descend with. Not that he wanted to stay, but he wanted out only a fraction more than he didn't, and that fraction was eroding minute by minute. Initiative, the Excalibur of the officer class, had drained out of him, leaving only a homely vignette of a plump-handed man with razor-parted oiled hair in the fastness of his garage, sighting along a piece of two-by-four as he held a square against it to test the right angle after planing. A square was essential for testing work of all kinds, and in the same category came ruler and pencil. A folding boxwood rule was popular as it could be kept in the pocket and not get lost among shavings on the floor. Any kind of pencil would serve, but not one too soft. A mallet, of course, you couldn't do without. . . . He would think about the mallet later, it was no use inventorying his toolbox all at once, not under circumstances such as these, grievous and worsening.

Try as he did, he could not piece together the vulture's face, *the* vulture's or any's. Patches of white, red, and black swam across his mind's eye: like *muscae volitantes*, a term he had once looked up after straining too hard to defecate, after a long flight that included midair refueling, and the little black flies, or dots, had done squadron drill for several minutes right there before him. The vulture's head and neck stayed fragmented, a bony dagger point, a section of bristly tubing, an eye like a wound with a small black olive embedded in it. Clegg groaned, torn by the longing for design in things, a design *to* things. A death should have some symmetry to it, as when the unopened chute plumed behind you while you fell at so many feet per second per second, or when your jet sheared sideways in ever-smaller downward helices as gravity exerted increasing control over it and your trapped legs. Whereas this stint of solitary in a bottle on a perch was neither dignified nor final, not even as dignified as the steel body sheath his father had been obliged to wear after an operation for a perforated ulcer (otherwise his belly fell halfway to his knees), and not as final as the divorce that had deprived him of the house he doted on. Surely, at the end, the pieces of the jigsaw should come together, the bulges going exactly into the slots, click-click, as bullets into the chamber. On the face of it, his predicament was weird enough to be a final one, but it lacked severity and gruesomeness, might just as readily fit someone's notion of the hilarious. Like certain foods in jars, he was perishable; like a botanical specimen he was under glass; like Eichmann, on show behind bulletproof glass, but only vultures came to see.

Once he had tried to explain to his sister, with the aid of a Mercator map of the world, where he was going. She had heard him out civilly enough, but all through had tapped her foot and oscillated her body to some operatic aria, throbbing nonstop in her head, not only as if he were not really there but also as if she resented being polite to his ghost. Perhaps this, then, on the map of Ethiopia, might win her attention, posthumously, and she would say *Gee*, something as compressed and pregnant as that. His pulse was sprinting, his forehead chafed from nonstop perspiring. One ear, the weak one, popped and faintly twanged, while the other did nothing at all. Both his eyes ached, not as muscles did, but with a needling, dead-center pang that evoked tiny fragments of fish hook. To make water outside, he had only to crouch sideways, which he had done twice, but he could also stand and aim the stream upward as if to defy the vultures, waving his penis's little neck at theirs. His bowels, when the time came, he would move into a piece of chute fabric easily slung out.

Half grinning, he realized he had evolved routines for daily living, but not for surviving or dying. No hand would hold his, no person become the last (and actually discoverable) image on his retinas, which would only have to be submerged, still within the removed eyes, in a bath of alum. If only he were found in time. After a day's delay the image for chemical reasons would have faded, so, yes, they must find him at once, so that the image of his murderer would be plain in either eye for them to read, according to the method of Giraud-Teulon he once had read about in Jules Verne. They would see an eagle, or vultures, *they* no doubt including the immortal Booth who had a knack of getting his way even with death. Yet Clegg was more offended than panicky, more put out than overcome. It was just his pattern complex, he told himself relentlessly. Millions had died untidily, unfittingly, uncannily, and no amount of postmortem ritual had made any difference to the how of it. Why should one therefore debate the quality of one's last moment, when consciousness went poof? There was no moment after the final one in which to savor the quality of the final one, good, indifferent, or bad. Yet Clegg, plying his fingers to make the rope, drove again and again at this invisible point between the here-and-now and the hereafter. It quivered like a dot of dew, refusing to be quizzed, bourgeois because it was a trillionfold, unique because not a single report had come in concerning it, the reconnaissance pilots had failed to photograph it. Two old expressions, *time out of mind* and *not long for this world*, locked horns in his head, and the stalemate went on. Yes: time was made of mind, yet the mind could not encompass it by sheer thought. Yes: not long for this world meant he would soon die, but also that, by the standards of this world, this universe, human extent was mighty short. Life was a spasm of life plus an eternity of deadness.

Something, he was sure, must come of such basic pondering, and he wondered why the old gladiatorial farewell, *nos morituri*, et cetera, entailed a salute from those about to die rather than a ribald finger stuck erect. Clegg palmed his genitals, eased the sit of them in his sweat-stiffened underwear, and began to work again at his rope, almost as if doodling with a vine. Soon, he knew, he would scream, his eyes would gush blood, his innards unstintingly relieve themselves, his brain fill with water, his bones' marrow pall into a slime. Clegg would become unclogged, prior to taxidermy. A tiny defeatist's smile greeted this sally, he had always thought taxidermy was a skin infection one caught in limousines. The disease one caught in the mountains of Ethiopia was a palsy of the skull otherwise known as indignation, from which one never recovered even if rescued. *Our father which art,* he said aloud in his huff, *in place, and on form, and up to scratch, and under the impression that we like it, think again. I too have been a carpenter. I know.* He gave up. Clegg had two sides, the finicky perfectionist and the woodsman-hunter. Perhaps they belonged together, the first honing the atavist in him, the second alerting the carpenter-handyman to nature's random untidiness. At any rate, they intersected, made an angle, and for a brief time his wife, rigged out in black velvet, hard riding helmet, blue velvet jacket, and cream corduroy pants, made a triangle of him, especially when he watched her show jumping, her buttocks flung high above the saddle, making him smile greedily at her cloaca hoist high before the multitude, even though sheathed in fabric.

The day soon came when he did not desire her unless he had recently observed her executing a jump, which in turn made for logistical problems in their daily schedules. After that, she took to frequenting bars in her riding habit, thus acquiring some reputation for being lesbian, which in part she was.

While training, Clegg had expected air combat to be neat, a matter of diagrams and clear-cut trajectories. But dogfights were chaotic, as he discovered early, beginning with formation flight, then atomized fast all over the sky. Looking for permanence and fixity, he might have turned to star maps, which he, like Booth, was obliged to peruse for navigational purposes; but he did not, instead running down and almost memorizing an item altogether more epic, at least as he saw it, while Booth took his pleasure from maps of the heavens and the Earth. What Clegg fixed on was the Battle of Britain, before his time but definitive of panache and guts. Daily, almost, he restaged the massive air encounter of September 15, 1940, in which the RAF's Hurricanes and Spitfires shot down 185 German planes. That was the nub of it, but he held a continuum of that entire crucial summer in reserve, like some Macy's variant of the Palladium, the statue of Pallas, which, itself preserved, preserved Troy as well. It was not a battle shrouded in the majestic and dreadful smoke of a land bombardment, with guns detonating, shells flashing, and inverse landslides of erupting soil. There was neither noise nor commotion, only a design of crisp white vapor trails, gradually blurring in form and number, etched by tiny specks that scintillated in the virtually unclouded skies of what everyone agreed was an otherwise perfect summer for cricket, boating, tennis and picnics. Only rarely did the sound of battle reach the watcher-connoisseurs below: machine-gun fire, like the rattle made by a stick run along a stretch of iron railings, but only in the next street, or, almost ill-manneredly from the background of engine mutter, a fierce quickening bleat as a crippled bomber fell, faster and faster while its unsynchronized motors raced against gravity's pull, or raced low for the other shore of the Channel with fighters on its tail. Sometimes watchers, on office-block roofs or lodged in the keeps of ancient castles, saw the blue field whiten with parachutes.

Meantime the ground received its debris, still emblazoned with swastika and black cross, or, less often, red-white-and-blue roundels, the red disk central. Battalions of infantry guarded all that fell, until inventory could be taken, maybe years later, when the derelict fuselages had filled with rabbits, mice, and grass. For a year, Clegg might have lived in one, undisturbed and minimally serene. The September battle he doted on happened within an aerial cube eighty miles long, forty broad, and about six high. In this space, between noon and half past, as many as two hundred individual combats took place, some of these extending into pursuits as far as the French coast. Alone in a Hurricane, rather than in the more glamorous, elliptical-winged Spitfire thirty miles an hour faster, Clegg recalled how the dawn mist had cleared by eight o'clock, revealing light cumulus at between two and three thousand feet, which generated a few local showers. The wind came from the west, shifting northward as the day went on. After nine, enemy patrols appeared in the Thames Estuary and between Lympne and Dungeness, harbingers of the first wave, which arrived just after 11:30, consisting of almost three hundred planes, crossing the British coast at three principal points, Ramsgate, Dover-Folkstone, and near Dungeness. Their principal objective London, they flew at altitudes between fifteen and twenty-six thousand feet, black hobnails at the head of elongated streamers of frosty vapor, the white lines of which made Clegg a rope long enough to shimmy down from London to Nice, whereas all he wanted was descent from three thousand, not from his Hurricane, but his capsule. Of the two, the Cyrano had the more vulture-like beak, the Hurricane the longer flotation time.

His belly grumbling, Clegg looked upward through the gash in the orange fabric and identified Heinkel 111k Mark V low-wing, all-metal, twin-engined cantilever monoplanes en route to Addis Ababa, much farther south, unmolested by vultures until he opened fire at a range of two hundred yards, closing to fifty. But the forty yards or so of makeshift rope impeded him as he reached back and forth in the cockpit, one loop round his neck, another round his left arm, so that he tugged at his throat when he moved his wrist, a parody of the wholly articulated human. Up into the orange-rimmed slot he peered, not so much orange as cadmium, its exact hue quite invisible as she soared above the saddle when the horse's rear legs flicked high so as not to catch the topmost bar of the facsimile gate. He had spent hours ogling that puckered little eyehole, in the raw, glans too bloat to enter, no matter what lubricant she came up with, though thinner candidates had managed it, she maliciously told him, in the old days, before Clegg. Blunt-nosed as a Dornier 215 or a Junkers 88, or sleek-pointed as a Heinkel, he could make no headway at all in that direction, a mission that others had flown into that apricot-hued desert, at whatever speed. Firing his eight machine guns forward, outside the airscrew disk, he downed vultures galore before the deployed squadrons floated out of sight en route for the fighter aerodromes of Biggin Hill, Croydon, and Northolt, which they bombed solidly for half an hour, as in several movies Clegg had contemptuously watched on the late-late show at his most insomniac, while a captain. He laughed aloud. The bits of his world were coming together slowly, as if underwater, and he longed once more to be vacuuming the swimming pool, aiming the brush at a brown patch of algae that refraction of the vacuum tube put out of reach, but he allowed for that, as for wind drift, and wiped it out in one sweep.

At first, the suddenness of the pain that started in his chest like a tiny hand grenade going off seemed only insolent, something he did not need and therefore could not possibly have. Something grated on his heart, not a stab so much as a clawing interference, making him catch and hold his breath, shoving a couple of fingers deep into the muscle between two ribs as if to push the pain away, into another part of his body. It went, then whisked itself back, first skimming the sore point, then bearing minutely down upon it with an accuracy so taut that he exclaimed in an indignant gasp, discovering in that instant Clegg the neural automaton who, in the next interval, frantically reviewed the possibilities, from indigestion to heart attack, wondering if his last medical had been a sham or if the pain was in the external muscle only. Shocked, he found himself envisioning it as a trapped bubble, a raspberry made of lead, a dandelion seed made of crystal, something incorrigibly alien implanted in him by the commotion of a long fall from where the sky had virtually no air at all. Embolism, he thought, an embolism not of coming up too fast but of coming down, hypothesis he at once dismissed as silly, but here he still was, alone in the mountains, mustering a smooth bedside manner at his own imminent death, and obliged to diagnose insult added to injury. It was a rippling pain, by no means steady or always in the same spot, its motion taking it at least a quarter of an inch this way and that. He took a deep breath, which hurt him fiercely; he thumped his chest, which had no effect at all; he raised his arms with elbows higher than his shoulders, trying to free the acid bubble, but it held its ground, waiting for him to resume a normal position before prodding him again. Next he tried mental feedback, addressing it direct, O bubble, please go away, I have enough to put up with; but it stayed, five minutes, ten, fifteen, a little stranger compact of neuralgia and heart-burn, and Clegg began to bribe it, vowing pell-mell, yes, I will mess my pants, I will leap to my death from this ledge, I will believe in the Lord, I will remarry the woman I loathe, I will enter a monastery.

Nothing altered, and Clegg, whose visual imagination always out-stripped his vocabulary, began to entertain a vision of himself as a weirdly elongated near-skeleton, thinned out into the proportions of a wire figure made of pipe cleaners or plaster of Paris, armless, eyeless, buttockless, penisless, his feet in the act of dissolving into a fine clay, his face at a fluid droop that took the nose down to the bottom of his jaw, and there he stood, at emaciated attention, legs gruesomely long, his waist a mere twist of newspaper, his expression one of submissive imbecility in which an earthworm had somehow developed a rudimentary, down-pointing beak, he was no more human than that, waiting only to be eaten, or swatted, or trodden into nitrate. Then he burped, as if back to life, a sound as critical and moving to him as a child's first wail, spanked upside down or not, whether a parboiled red (as indeed he had been at birth, though hardly anyone remembered) or flavid with corrigible jaundice. Now the pain dislodged itself, moved several inches upward, making him lean forward in order to swing the contents of his chest fractionally outward, in fact nursing his wind up and inducing a second, longer burp that cleared away the hurt into the open, hot air inside the capsule.

The smile his face then relaxed into was a smile of Lazarus, his features regrouping themselves as if drawn up by a magnet, his body flesh reassembling itself out of nowhere, from close at hand and the remotest perimeters of the Galaxy, and his eyes beginning to register all over again the mess he was in, and he was so glad to be registering even that. I have just had a token death, I have just had a dress rehearsal, he told himself, faintly adding the fact that a heart attack here would have something almost decorative about it, a slice of overkill providing pathologists-to-come with a mid-dissection joke. Infantile in his delight, he stuffed a chunk of the makeshift rope between his teeth and bit down hard, loving the peculiar vinyl-canvas aroma and sizzling his spit against the ultrasmooth weave that had floated him he had forgotten how many thousand feet down, into Africa. He spat it out and coughed. There was work to be done, whole days of it, and not doing it meant certain death, whereas doing it meant just the slightest variation in that certainty, a housefly's wing added to the scales of fate. So he began to narrate, in that hoarse, cozily aloof *victor ludorum* idiom he had acquired over the years, positing a Clegg who, once again, had come through, matted with sweat and half blind with Herculean zeal, but nonetheless there, on top and in command, doing it, only undoing it to do it better than humankind had ever seen. *Yes, yes, it is clear now, Clegg has tamed the pain in his chest, he is no longer the ashen man of twenty minutes ago, and now he is fighting back—no, he has already fought back and is blazing a trail straight to his goal. The man has triumphed once again, as ever over wounds, insults, bad luck and careless navigation. The rope has begun to grow again: he ties, he knots, he reaches for another piece, which he twists and fastens to the last one, he might be finding his way out of a maze, his breathing is heavy, his hands are slick with blood, his lips are caked with salt, but here he comes, foot after foot, he leaps, he swerves, he scores, he scores again!* Banal, trumped up, and merely percussive in its sequentiality, Clegg's ventriloquial obbligato, fed into the dummy of himself, took him almost gaily through the next hour. He was working well, with an inspired dexterity befitting a Guatemalan rug weaver, his mind shut against the ghastly echelon of the next hour, followed by the next ten hours, and then the next day and its own successor, the point being that somewhere in this inevitable doldrum something major would have to be done: go down, one way or another, not leaping or arranging an accident that dislodged the capsule, but becoming his own boss and entering a realm in which no excuses, no bungles, no shirkings, had a place; an heroic destiny awaited him, or at any rate a bit of good exercise after which he might eventually get a lemonade, if lucky, or a decent burial, if not. Failing everything, there would always be the vultures, the jackals, the sun and the insects; he would not go unrecognized, and the same was true even if he stayed at three thousand feet, where in his ruptured Plexiglas cocoon he would not be immune for long.

Half reassured that, wherever he was, there would always be a force field of the natural around him, of both photosynthesis and manure, he worked with a will, not quite realizing that his most recent thought had come to him from Booth, not direct of course, but out of those long conversations over shandy and sandwiches in the officers' club; it had been a Booth-type thought, such as Clegg had never arrived at in the years previous to their meeting, whether he fished or broke horses (a sideline at which he had excelled), stalked deer with his bow, or carpentered exquisite footstools from lovingly sanded beechwood. Only too ready to acknowledge Booth's status as a man of ideas, as a more completely technological (or technocratic) man than himself, Clegg had often wondered what it was, then, that he himself was special for; his senses were not acuter than Booth's; his mind was less adapted to what was abstract; his capacity for command was less robust; his sense of wonder was more homespun; so the answer was perhaps that he was special for nothing at all, and his mission in life was to furnish a background against which the Booths could become conspicuous, a conclusion he found both degrading and too easy, so what was it, *what was Cleggness?* What he next thought (and he had thought this next on scores of occasions, forever galloping down the same axiom-lined avenue of self-debate) made him laugh aloud, and the least he had ever done on reaching this point was to smile.

He, Clegg, was *kind*, that was it, it was as simple and as ordinary as that; his big-headedness was one of size only, and his big incisors embodied nothing of his character. Pale and something of a night person, compared to ruddy-faced Booth who faded out after an early dinner, he still hankered after the kits he had spent much of his boyhood on and, deep down, remained the peaceable, somewhat introverted lonely builder of things, his favorite expression By Jiminy! indicative of good-natured adaptability that sometimes extended into heartiness, when he slapped people's backs and showed them what a good listener he could be. In contrast, Booth was more clinical, more deliberate, less capable of losing himself in some physical activity. Clegg warmed to this favorable portrait painting of himself, already aware that, in this bout of analytical self-regard, he was trespassing into Booth's own territory. What lingered was the day when he and Booth had compiled lists of their favorite words, at least their favorite ten, and he, Clegg, had come up with *flank, sludge, wench, slut, festive,* and *mother,* among his ten, while Booth had, somewhat circumspectly, listed *quaint, hydrogen, sylvan, mordant, contraption,* and *Nunki* (the name of some star). He could not remember the other words, his or Booth's, but he felt these few retrieved did fairly well at expressing the difference between them: he, for instance, liked Rachmaninoff and Elgar, whereas Booth went for Hindemith and Bruckner, a more astonishing thought than the difference between them musically being the fact that they had both spent so much time listening to music, the answer being so much time to kill, or to bring back to life. Even Clegg, who was not a connoisseur, knew you did not have to be one in order to type the individual who liked what he liked as compared with one who liked what Booth did; it was evident, perhaps with some overlap, and with the august presences of Samuel Barber and Aaron Copland in between, what the difference was, but it would never be enough to say that small-toothed, rosy-cheeked Booth was more cerebral than he, it was more a matter of Booth's almost reflex assumption that he was a finer-fibred entity than Clegg, or any Clegglike person, and that was that, yet the man did it without the least arrogance, more like gold shaking silver's hand, or the sun the moon's.

Unoffended after the first few months, in which Booth seemed to be exercising a commander's hauteur without actually being in charge, at least then, Clegg had grown to enjoy this almost mineral beauty of Booth, the beauty of him being that you could never imagine him dead, as you could, Clegg could, imagine so many others. Booth had something of the Cyrano's titanium in himself, something already dead and therefore in a mighty technical sense immortal; you could not preview cancer withering and stunting him, or his heart bursting with an attack, or his physique surrendering to a stroke, or even an air crash rending and incinerating him, no. At his best, Clegg decided, Booth was as fresh as dew and invulnerable as a star map, as much at home in the universe as hydrogen itself, one of his favorite words, whereas he, Clegg, at times had to beat a retreat and shield, if not his heart, his overexpressive face. There was no chance that Booth was not alive, not so much surviving as transforming emergency into the most desirable state yet known, much to be sought and hymned in afteryears. And that helped. Convinced that Booth was thriving, he could predicate his own responses on that almost abstract exemption of his fellow pilot, by no means deciding that a Clegg had to perish for a Booth to live, or that Booth always got the better odds, but certainly steering his emotional course by that point, and lumping together in one overblown but timely concept the notions of twin, reprieve, and flight plan. Clegg had a good reason to go down: Booth could be found, and indeed Booth might this very second be en route to him, with hot coffee, a change of underwear, and a can of dry-roasted mixed nuts. Preposterously homesick, Clegg yearned to hear a train, a dog, a toilet in midflush.

Truth told, Booth was by no means so fortunate or such a paragon of rescuing finesse, having mounted a mule only to be hauled off by a couple of the salt miners, one of whom he then shoved into the mud at the watering hole. With his pole taken from him, he tried to land a punch on at least one of the glowering faces, but they grabbed him and spreadeagled him, stripped off his befouled shorts, and, with what struck him as gratuitous intimacy, touched the end of the rifle's barrel to his anus. At the second not so gentle shove, he felt the foresight bite him, as if the weapon itself were giving an organic threat. The shot, if one came, would bury itself in his lacerated tripes, with no wound visible. He waited, then realized he had been yelling a series of okays. They let him up, and he was on the point of congratulating himself when a pole caught him horizontally across the mouth, cracking a few teeth and drawing instant blood. Reeling backward with face numbed, he skidded into the mud and went full length down, even now neither mocked nor rethreatened by these wooden and puritanical people who might just have been chastising a member of their dreary family. He had been bared, prodded, and then struck, not for trying to get away but for wasting part of the working day, that must surely be it. They meant him no harm, and no good, but wanted him to do his share. Anything so crass and routine he had not met since his schooldays, and now his mouth was full of blood and mud, he farted a liquid, he could not blink the pus from his left eye, and his teeth had new, rough contours.

In effect they had just removed a day from the few days left to him. They were peeling him away from himself by punitive subtraction. An awful shiver, beginning at his toes, worked zigzag through him until his scalp ran hot, and he knew he would have to find something to hold to, something light-years beyond all this, something that was wry and supreme and appetizing, a cracked grail, a shit-soiled golden fleece, a sneeze while licking Florence Nightingale's untried twat, in other words a map reference for pain. And how easily it came, an almost esoteric reference, a bit of world history foreshortened into closet drama; it took him by surprise, arriving upon him not out of the desert or the mountains, out of aerial lore or the science of photography, or via Clegg, California, and *The Financial Times* of London, but, like a shawl of pictograms from Mexico, the man who guarded Trotsky. In this way he extended almost immeasurably his range of comfort and escape, nourished by the blood-knot of a vicarious life lived out in hectic circumstances, and where Clegg's refighting of the Battle of Britain took him beyond the mountains into the muted blues of an English sky, if anything making him lonelier than ever in the cockpit of his Hurricane fighter, while making him heroic, Booth entered a new society on the famous Avenue Viena at Coyoacán on the outskirts of Mexico City.

Was Clegg fortified or enfeebled? Should he have turned instead to a fantasy about Mount Everest, a sailor marooned, or someone buried alive? Should the man trapped alone seek analogies or contrasts, assuming the former will teach him how better to cope with his emergency and the latter how to transcend it mentally? Does your Crusoe dream of, or dream up, the swarming streets of London? It must be remembered that all Clegg needed was a mental scenario to soothe him while he worked hour after hour at the mindless chore of making his rope; none of the great ropemakers of history occurred to him, in any case, so the least that can be said is that he filled his mind and nourished his heart, whereas Booth, having tried to fight and get away, became something of a static guard to himself, as [Harold Robins to Trotsky] in the fourth year of Mexican exile, 1939. Epitome of the well-informed, even well-read and literate, military man, Booth had most of the facts at his disposal, not because he ever thought he would need them for a purpose such as this, but because in the old days he had wanted to find things out. He had in no sense lived by Trotsky as Clegg had, for years, lived by the Battle of Britain. The one was exploiting the fruits of his leisure hours, the other was intensifying the myth he already lived by. Yet, strangely and no doubt ironically, their remedial dreams were only three weeks apart in 1940, the day of the ice pick being August 20th, the day of the salient battle over southern England September 15th.

Images of violence, both, of course, through which Booth failed to save Trotsky from Mercader the assassin and Clegg succeeded in saving England from the Luftwaffe. Booth had never heard, from Clegg or anyone else, about this private heraldic dream, and Clegg had never heard Booth discuss Trotsky, his life or his death, so the dreams went unshared, and only a third party, privy at one time to both men's heads, could relish the coincidence not only of heraldic heroism, but also of closeness together in time, like an assignation unknowingly kept by two men who, only so recently side by side in the cockpit of the Cyrano, now seemed continents apart and equally doomed, yet astonishingly enough living out their last days (as they plausibly assumed) under an alias, or aliases, several decades old. Although not much to live by, it was almost enough, though by some standards the consequences it led to were terrible in the extreme, more terrible than being marooned at three thousand feet or being held laborer-captive below sea level. The ice pick and the Luftwaffe are merely ways into the puzzle of their fates, the external emblems of what became mazes of displacement, horrors beyond horror, but also, since nothing in this life is all in one category, exquisite spirals beyond the here and now into a sky out past the sky of 1940 and a split head not Trotsky's. Two men, removed from their own time, reenter history through becoming involved in events that, in either case, changed the course of world events: an invasion held off, a revolution delayed. Clegg, now in the cabin of his Hurricane, now on the sweet velvet lawn of the ground, roared his own applause; Booth, wearing a suit with vest but with his shirt collar open, stood at Trotsky's door, revolver in hand, and heard the surf of history seething in the Mexican breeze.

When the execution team reappeared at first light, Booth decided his end was near; he could not see clearly, he could not rightly breathe, he could not spit, and his entire body hurt as if it had been rubbed raw with an ice made from salt. Two of them came straight for him where he crouched in the doorway of an igloo and hauled him to his feet, made him stumble to the headless cadaver. So, then, this would be it, they would give him an object lesson, then dispatch him at the march, neatly beheading him as he flinched one way or the other when the swordless one of the two nipped his side between finger and thumb. Did Trotsky's scalp tingle an instant before the ice pick sank home, when the fragilest tip of the point first grazed his skin? He did not have time to pursue the speculation; once again, he realized, he was not the condemned man, he was the sexton, and not much asked of him at that. What they had him do was hack a trench a foot deep in the salt with an iron rod provided for just this purpose, and drag the dead trunk into it (by now less a human corpse than a bloodsodden scarecrow with, of all grotesque things, a walnut of dried dung attached to the exposed white of its pelvis). Booth did as commanded, then dragged a slab of salt over the remains, his still vestigially neat mind already wondering about the head. What would they do with that? He found out. They gave it to him, motioning that he must keep it with him. But how? Under his arm, they informed him by ramming the hairy, slotted, bird-scratched turnip into place and shoving him away from them into a reel at the end of which he fell full length. Lifting him, they breathed into his face, a stench of lilies mixed with weeks-old cauliflower, making him gag, which impressed them not at all. There he stood, like a parody of some inmate from the Tower of London, except that the head beneath his arm was not his own, that was evident, that was good, that was unspeakably vile.

"Trotsky," he said, at once; out of some indomitable perversity of being the only civilized man in the vicinity, he would call the head that, what better head could a man want in a mess such as this? They stared at him when he spoke the one word, half inclined to lambast him with his own pole, and one of them waved it threateningly, only in the end to hand it to him with an oddly aspirated grunt. Clearly he was to work one-handed from now on, a standing symbol of who knew what, with against his left biceps a ragged head reeking of sulfur. What if he dropped it or changed arms? He might get away with it once the overseer-executioners had gone, if in fact they left at all; but now, he took every care, zanily imagining his own head under the arm of one of the miners, and all of history over for him while the salt went on being mined. Back to work he went, lopsided but eager to please, glad to have found the name Trotsky for what he ported, a head from Halloween, rough as a cow's tongue or moistened wool.

I am dying, Clegg told himself, of manual fatigue. Looking at the last few yards of rope, he saw how the orange had turned maroon with the blood from his fingers, and he wondered what the next color would be, blue for no boy, pink for no girl, black for moribundity. He still had nowhere near enough to begin his descent with, at the most a hundred yards, although there seemed still acres and acres of parachute outside, awaiting its turn to be spun. He had forgotten to eat, and now he no longer wanted to, perhaps afraid the bubble of dyspepsia would reassert itself in his body cavity, waxing bigger than the bubble he sat in, half attentive to the rhythmic pluck-scratch of the insects, the hiss of the regularly returning vultures, who had obviously underestimated his powers of survival, and the drained-sounding suck of the African mountain wind, evocative to him of wind tunnels in which, now, he sat inside a model being tested for airworthiness. Peering up through the gash for Heinkels or Dorniers, he saw nothing at all, no enemy, no friend, and felt suddenly glad to be alone at such an altitude with eight machine guns and a capacity for 335 miles an hour. The antenna was behind him, just beyond his eyes' reach, twanged by gusts, and, farther back, the unretractable tail wheel on its rigid stem like a two-dimensional berry beneath the big fat fin. How he longed to cry Tally-ho! instead of, as he watched blank patch of sky succeed blank patch of sky, By Jiminy. Then he realized nothing could be above him, he was up-sun, and the enemy was down below, so he doubled his speed, twisting and tying fabric into rope at almost seven hundred miles an hour, plying and rotating his hands like a madman in a seizure.

Now the wind sliced past at a scream, all the relevant quotation from manuals he knew by heart blew away, and he went from Dungeness on the coast to Tilbury at the mouth of the Thames Estuary in a golden flash, not so much flying as shouting himself along toward the desired 738 miles an hour, speed at which he would be flying faster than his shout, as in the Cyrano, in the good old days, before he was called upon to play Houdini to no audience save his own mediocre future, a delegation of vultures, and insects that he could not name even as they dug under his skin to lay eggs and so, at some not too distant date, take him over altogether. He itched, he sweated, he wept from eye strain and frustration, vainly trying to calculate how many days' weaving he had yet to come, little knowing that he had at least another week to do, provided he maintained his recent pace and was still determined to make a rope long enough to go all the way down: no jumping the last twenty yards or so, but always letting his helmet down, with flashlight inside it, once the rope was more than halfway done. Letting his mind be lax, he partly abolished time, filling his mind's eye with a relief map of the First Phase of Göring's Bid for Total Victory, covering a huge chunk of southern England, from Oxford in the top left-hand corner to Martlesham in the top right-hand one, from Bournemouth in the bottom left to Boulogne in the bottom right. A triangle marked the fighter stations, a ring the areas already attacked, and a little rectangle enclosing six model ships represented convoys.

Yet his mind's eye kept on lapsing, at the mercy of the pain in his hands, the encrusted-looking blubber where his finger ends still were, the searing headache no aspirin had killed, the amputated-feeling cramp in his upper back. Battle of Britain or no, the enemy was one thought, coming and going like a lethal squadron: granted that the rope be long enough, in the fulness of time, what would be left of him to go down it? Clegg dodged the thought, but it stayed on his tail, even when he took a deep breath and worked his hands for all they were worth. *Something* was going downhill, someone was losing heart (as if you could, he told himself, but if you did would it wobble over and out, plop down the mountainside, and dry out in the sun?). His heart toiled on, which he knew because he was still alive enough to listen for it.

Booth was trying not to catch sight of the empty eye sockets as he leaned sideways the better to work his salt-mining arm. No, not empty, he told himself, unable not to look, there are little shreds of what looks like fishing bait.

Clegg was dumping yards of completed rope beneath him, festooning his boots with it, then dragging more of it, with a heave that made his hands blaze, into the capsule from outside, gently marveling how hot it felt from the sun of whatever time of day it was. He had forgotten to wind his watch, and he wondered, in a dim and distant way, why they were not equipped with watches that self-wound.

Or self-wounded, he bitterly punned, waning Clegg who asked himself if anyone witnessing him would feel sorry for him or just write him off as another military fanatic.

Booth dropped his pole to catch a bath-sponge-sized hunk of bread tossed to him by a miner. The overseers had gone, at least were nowhere to be seen.

Our help in ages past, Clegg was murmuring. What if it breaks when I let it down? Make it good in every joint.

Trotsky smells viler than he did, Booth thought, for a few seconds holding his breath and still trying to masticate dried-out bread.

Clegg cried out a series of hellos.

Booth stuffed the unwanted bit of bread into Trotsky's eye.

Clegg, having received an answer of sorts, mentally damned all vultures who hissed as if trying to catch his attention in the dark.

Booth, squatting to relieve himself as usual by the mud of the watering hole, eased his shorts down with one hand and brought the dead head round to face him with the other. He blew a balloon of air and that was all.

Clegg spent a whole minute licking his hands' blood.

Then their respective days gained momentum again, Booth setting to work with renewed zeal born of delight at his recent reprieve, Clegg resting one hand while he used his teeth to anchor the fabric he was twisting. Booth yearned for a sandstorm, even a storm of salt. Clegg, feeling the capsule rock and shudder, prayed that no wind should rise to fell him from his perch. Unseen by either, a commercial jetliner somewhat off-course left a narrow contrail that cast its own shadow against a patch of cloud at whose edge the black trail ended sharp. There was nothing else to be seen, by Booth whose neck was too tired for him to look up, by Clegg whose quadrant of sky did not include the jet's path. Those who kept the miners in order, dealing out life and death to them, had once again departed with a new caravan of salt. Two visits, Booth was musing, but only one beheading: the situation could be worse.

Vexed at himself to be so hopelessly yearning, Clegg longed for warm milk, fresh bread, for Vaseline and any pair of gloves. Now one of his ears had blocked up and failed to pop. For some reason telling himself, apropos of nothing, that there is no word in the Gaelic that has quite the urgency of *mañana*, Booth explained the thought as a gesture to the minimum life, such as this, lived out of time. Trotsky appointed him chief of the guard but became angry when he enlarged the lookout holes to command a wider area. Vandal, the great man called him, and he filled them in himself, he, big-browed and shaggy-mustached Leon Trotsky, whom Booth alias Harold Robins called a vandal in turn. They gave each other hell. Now Booth was loading the head's eyeholes with mud, giving them a look of statuary unearthed after centuries; but still the ruined maw gaped at him, as if in disgusted rebuke because he had finally eaten the bit of bread he had cached in the eye socket before filling it with mud. Clegg was tasting nothing at all, not even the K ration he had just consumed. More frantic than before, having in a fit of clearheadedness just managed to calculate the time required to finish the rope, he wondered if he needed to twist the fabric and decided yes, he should, it was no use having the thing split halfway or wherever. Listening to the sounds of his labor, from percussive gasp to the slight, rodent noise the fabric made between his hands, he willed aero-engines, Rolls-Royce mainly, to blot out everything as they dived and zoomed, fed on the best octane, and at times comically backfired in the middle of a cloud. To date he had shot nothing down, but he had not been trying. Now the twists became the stick, he squeezed the gun button, the spray of lead flung itself far forward, trapped a Dornier in its shower and sent it twirling down. Score one, Clegg noted wildly as his capsule heaved in what seemed an increasing wind that smelled of goats or lions, honey and dung. They were hatching miracles down on Earth.

Trotsky was laying down the law to Booth, insisting that visitors should not be searched, that the house was already too much of a fortification, blocking out his view of Mexico City's two magnificent mountains. It was bizarre to have a head talking to you from under your arm, calling you Harold into the bargain, but Booth played along, only somewhat missing the scrunched-up fierceness of the face behind the pince-nez and the full mustache. Levering up his umpteenth slab of salt, and once again wondering at the total incuriosity of the miners, he could not fathom his value to them, especially now his workload had been halved, indeed cut by more than half; he could do much less with one arm than a half. He was off-balance, he was preoccupied with the head, after all, at least until he decided he no longer was, and that was now. Down fell the head named Trotsky, like a heavy lettuce moist and black, and no one moved. Then the miner with the rifle (usually the same one, he decided, and no doubt the best shot) waved at him to pick up what belonged to him, but Booth stood his ground, tightening his entire jaw until it ached, ramming his bandage-clad feet hard into the ungiving salt, daring the sun to blind him as he flung his head back to bellow a parade-ground command. "Ah-ten-Hut," he actually cried, only it came out as a frayed whisper. The shot missed him, was meant to, and he caught the head by its hair and restored it to its place under his arm, where it made a minor squelching sound, surely not the bone giving already, but perhaps an effect of air in the gaping mouth. No doubt of it, the miners had plenty of ammunition, there had been no need to fire at him.

To test them further, he stumbled with his carrion to where the salt slab imperfectly covered the corpse, and lowered the head gently until it sat still after slightly wobbling. No shot came, but the rifle barrel again motioned him to resume normal functioning. On the way back to his work site, he told the Trotsky head about his troubles, the whole thing being, he stressed, rather more pointless than death itself, only to realize he was addressing the very man who, on May 24, 1940, had survived the first attempt on his life when a gang of Stalinist painters had broken into the house and deluged Trotsky's bedroom with machine-gun fire. He had survived unscathed, awakened by the first shots, and had looked into the yard, where he saw a Mexican policeman. It was all, Booth told the head, the work of the secret police. Soon after, the head of it, Salazar, came to apologize to Trotsky on the orders of President Cárdenas. The idea, he seemed to hear the head's blank mouth asserting, was to kill Trotsky and leave the guards alive after the example of *Macbeth*. The bastards, Booth said, being Harold Robins, only to be told not to use bad language or slang. Again he looked down at the head beneath his arm, wondering at its first survival, and at his own.

Not altogether strangely, the things Booth and Clegg dreamed about could not fill their present lives, or the living deaths that their present lives were. The function of a talisman is to protect and preserve, not to provide total distraction, but both men, in their quite different ways, tried to stretch the parallel dream into becoming their entire context, Booth trying to shut out the miners by concentrating on the head he kept on calling Trotsky, in the vocative of the mind's ear, Clegg averting his gaze from his busy hands to the bit of sky that soared above him, and in which he patrolled the south coast of England. No good: the present had too strong a hold on them through skin and nerves, not to mention such miscellaneous things as the perforate nostrils of vultures and the long legs of the Abyssinian red jackal. Yet here, by virtue of what each did next, the two men parted company, if that is not too ironic a figure for men already apart. Having noticed the iron bar was still on the ground where he had dropped it after hacking out the shallow grave, Booth with a sauntering limp went casually toward it, picked it up and, dismissing a reckless impulse to charge the miners with it, jammed the head on its sharp end. Then he advanced toward them brandishing Trotsky-on-a-stick, abuzz with flies of all sizes, the sound akin to that of a minor electrical appliance. As he expected, no one so much as moved, or laughed, or cursed. Scalding air billowed around them, making the hives along Booth's sides and back tingle as if abraded. He walked away, found a crevice in the salt and stabbed the iron bar in as far as he could. The head fell. He restored it, but the rough end of the severed spine grazed his thumb, making him shiver; the moment in his dream, when the ice pick sank home, had yet to happen, and he was saving it, having not the faintest idea what he would think of then. Half a dozen rapid-fire rifle shots ended his reverie as the bullets hissed into the head on the pole. He had been warned once again. The rifleman was a good shot, and Booth would never get farther away from him than the head was now.

As if articulately commanded to do so, he uprooted Trotsky and made his painful way back to where he had been working one-handedly. The rifleman came over and took the iron bar. The head sat on the salt and Booth made no move to pick it up and reinstall it beneath his arm. It seemed the miners did not care what he did with it, their only desire being that he work, preferably with both arms, which meant they disagreed with the orders of their superiors. Booth went along, determined to wait it out, the only thing he could do, keenly aware of two things, namely that he would soon be in the hands of enemy intelligence (indeed, should be already), and that his Trotsky scenario would divert him at best, a toy, a back-of-mind metaphor, able neither to preclude nor to occlude. His fate was his fate, even if that was an old-fashioned way of putting it. And the miners, whatever their thought processes might be, knew it. The abyss that started at the top of his hair stayed put.

Clegg's dream died piecemeal from the pain in his fingers and wrists, he having almost decided it was not humanly possible to make a rope that long in so short a time with the hands he had. Cavorting about the sky of 1940 was one thing, both fun and grandeur, but you could do it only if conditions were right and the holy cluster of cells that was you and nobody else cooperated. In his case they were staging a protest: his nose had begun to bleed, his hearing had dwindled into a weird series of echoes, and his feet were numb. If he had thought it through, he would never have done it, but he did it with mixed impetuosity and reflex pique. He stood up and almost fainted, breathing deep while the pain surged and began to subside, as if his feet and shins had been electrified. Recalled in tatters, an inscription on a plaque presented to him many years ago gave him something to fix on, even though he could hardly figure out what it meant, from *his untiring good efforts, his unselfish service in* to *Beta Theta of Pi Delta Alpha . . . this plaque.* Yet the near-gibberish worked almost as an emetic, bringing bile into his mouth and the back of his nose. How it stung. He was breathing through his mouth only, his nose was thick with crusted blood, his reawakened feet burned in his boots. He tried to look down, past the piled-up fabric of the chute, but it bulged out too far, without however cutting off his view of the length and breadth of the valley on either side, flashing ocher and green, colors he did not recall having seen when he last inspected it. Like some dancer gathering in the folds of an outsize skirt, he tried pulling the fabric toward him, his idea being to stack it on top of the capsule so as to look right down. He badly wanted to see what precise thing lay between him and the ground. Suddenly the thought came that he could go down now, on the rope already made, taking with him enough fabric to make it longer once he found a ledge, another ledge, to rest on. No: he could release the rope he already had and use it again, use it in stages. He did not need three thousand feet of it, only, say, five hundred reusable six times over, but that meant he would have to toss it loose, from beneath, and reattach it, six times over. The chances against that were colossal. With wincing slowness, and almost in symbolic gesture, he fished out the rope he already had, tied his helmet to it, and let it out over the piled-up chute. This he did for a couple of minutes, when there was no more rope to go, and he listened for the clank of the helmet against rock, but he heard nothing at all, only from higher up a strange aural combination of squawks, slithers, rattles, and the lethargic beating of capacious wings. Eagles, he hastily thought, looking up at the zenith to no avail; the rock face cut off his gaze. Deciding he was lucky to be here at all, and doubly lucky not to have been blown off, he pulled the rope toward him, but it would not come. The helmet, meant to sound out the vertical terrain, must have snagged on something a few hundred feet below him. Now he made the rope ripple and flex, trying to unstick it, but it would not come, nor had it come ten minutes later as he alternately tugged and waggled it, weeping from desperation.

It had to come up; otherwise he would have to begin again or risk going down. Over he leaned, praying tinily that he would not dislodge the capsule and its sheath of fabric, but he did, a fact that only a midget part of his brain took in as, with a muffled gravel-grinding lurch, the whole thing wobbled, jerked toward the cliff as he tried to right it with a huge body swing, and then keeled over in reciprocal motion over the edge and off, with Clegg half in, half out, the loop of the rope still round his wrist. He almost fell out as the capsule inverted itself, but it as soon righted and gave him a chance to fall back inside as it tumbled along the rock face rather than off it down. Knowing he would hardly survive the drop, he wondered why he was not already knocked senseless. His mind was trying to cope with going around and around, with irregular crashes and different parts of his body being jammed against the sharp interior skeleton of the capsule, so he was late in realizing that motion had ceased and silence had begun again, apart from a few showers of stones and soil coming in at his face.

Was he down? Was this the bottom?

He could not believe it, and he was right.

The capsule had suspended itself by the parachute lines from a spur about halfway down, the result being that it dangled free in space with the main part of the canopy above it, resting on top of the lines that held it up. Looking up he could see the spur's underside, the lines curling up and over it, the orange cluster of fabric above that, and now no sky at all. Oddly enough, the rope was still his, its loop coiled around his wrist, which meant that the helmet was out there somewhere still, and maybe free. He pulled, and the rope began to move, so he hauled it in knot by knot, little aware of a face pouring blood and a loose, plucking sense of flotation in the region of his collarbone. In came the helmet like a bathysphere fished up from the depths, little the worse for wear, and he moved to pat it, with a dithering mumble, but halted in midgesture; his collarbone was surely broken, but not his wrist. He wrote right-handed anyway. He could weave rope still, the question being how far down he was. All he could think of, as his punished body paid him out in mingled stabs of pain and bouts of unrhythmical aching, was that the distance down was less, he could not have fallen up. The world made a sense of sorts, after all.

Perhaps he fainted then. At least, his mind roamed free and off, scandalously neglecting the urgencies of the at-hand, going liquid when it should have mobilized itself into a crisp instrument that knew not only what to do next but also what to do an hour after that. Not an imaginative man, certainly not to Booth's degree, Clegg nonetheless found silly thoughts arriving when least opportune, of the Hanging Gardens of Babylon and brave adventurers wafting in balloon-suspended gondolas over the Alps. His body felt more like [inert cargo] than like the masterpiece of evolution, fuller of soft wet ship's rope than of bone, less like a colonel's than like offal. It would not go, it had not been wound up since the last time it ran, it flopped. Haven't I, he dismally queried, been shot in the legs and feet? Was it a MiG? Did I crash? Am I in the hospital again? Gradually the off-red mist receded and he was able to take stock of his new setting, no longer static but subject to constant motion as the down-valley wind twirled the capsule this way and that, occasionally thumping it against the rock face itself.

It was almost as if he had just made another descent by parachute, from nowhere to nowhere, demoted like a seed from an altitude not quite known to one he could only guess at, and still alive. For a moment, happy on his needle point of survival, Clegg mustered his gumption, instructed himself to break down the happening into its component parts instead of responding with a big emotional surge to a crude overview. Faintly suspecting he had heard that kind of language during reconnaissance training, he began to ponder item by item the latest installment of his coming to Earth.

Fairly soon the lines would fray and snap; he did not have forever in which to make rope or decide his next step. Urgency turned his dried-out mouth sour.

How high was he now? He would have to recalculate the odds against the final jump, for instance, and, while in the act of thinking that, he realized he could hardly release the capsule before the lines gave. Nor should he want to, or should he? Could he survive yet another fall, perhaps one not so far? He doubted it.

Down in the valley it was darker, but maybe that was the approaching night, which he was going to have to spend floating in air like a plant in a pot. He managed to take some water, once he had found the thermos.

Another question confronted him: what, if anything, had fallen out during the tumble? He would have to take inventory of what the capsule held. He offered his face upward to the ocher light, knowing the parachute had not functioned as a parachute and never would again. Its presence above him atop the spur was merely emblematic.

Once again he lowered his helmet, this time with the flashlight inside in the On position; it would last until dawn for sure, and he might never need it again if he handled himself sanely tomorrow. Gradually he became used to the creaking noises, the strict grinding noises of the cords, the click-tink as the capsule metal cooled. If this was luck, he liked it: from ledge to spur to what? Very much hoping the third in the series would be terra firma, and with no more bones broken, he tried to sit comfortably, the thing that bothered him being not the pain, or the prospect of it (his collarbone was not hurting that much), but the decreased chance of being inefficient. Should he sleep or make rope? Doing the latter would ensure the former, he decided, and at once began to work with what was left, enough fabric for maybe thirty feet more, and then he would have to haul some down from on top of the spur, twenty feet above him, which he felt was like doing push-ups in hot volcanic lava. Was the capsule stable? He should have thought his next move through and through, but he was too tired; he did a little jump, bouncing his rear on his seat, then stood up and did the same again, this time with all his weight on the tinny floor. The capsule did not fall, making instead a noise somewhere between that of a gong and a heavy empty bucket set down on a bare wood floor. He gasped with pain, clapped one arm across his chest to support the broken bone, but only made himself feel worse, so he sat again, bemused, unsure whether to feel glad or furious. After all, if he had not landed on the ledge in the first place, he would have been home and free by now. Well, almost; the whole thing was one fluke after another, the odds against it being unthinkable. He twisted up the remaining fabric into rope, tied the addition to the rope already paid out over the rim of the side window, tied the end twice around his waist, in a painful maneuver, and slid out the extra length. Down below, the helmet clanked as it descended a little farther, its flashlight a dirty yellow in the amber of the valley afternoon, but destined for brightness in a matter of hours. Clegg slept in fits that got shorter as the pain between his shoulder and the bottom of his throat increased, but it was as if someone else were doing his sleeping for him, taking the benefit, which he felt not at all while undergoing all the pain.

Sensing daft flutters in his head, Booth looked up from the salt to where the head rested on a crude plinth and tried to fit the name Trotsky onto it, but in vain: the head and the name were separate whereas, only an hour ago, they had been one and the same, and he had been Harold Robins, the miners the Stalinist painters come to machine-gun Trotsky where he slept on the Avenue Viena. Sometimes the mind just did not take advantage of the passive materials at hand, and sometimes the passive materials changed nature and took advantage of the mind, as if a life belt took you down with it, a parachute caught fire as soon as you opened it up, a rifle backfired into your skull. To punish him, the miners had not passed him either bread or water when they themselves took both; Booth had motioned for some with no result except that the rifleman with an imperious flapping motion of the barrel sent him back. It was clear that one did not waste time by fussing with severed heads on iron bars.

A craving for conversation asserted itself; he had for too long played snakes and ladders with his erratic mental flux. All here was physical: salt, poles, trunks, heads, bread, water, igloo, rifle, jackals, vultures, mud, mules, camels, and he began to hate with renewed intensity the sturdy but mindless fresco they composed, an about-face from what he used to feel when, sick of windmilling thoughts, he doted on things physical from vulvas to cigars. I am brimming over mentally, he decided; perhaps that is the first phase of an interrogational stratagem already under way for days.

He was being left out here to cook in hot storage until they were ready for him. The vigilantes who rode through at intervals were merely a front and perhaps even the miners were not as innocently pragmatic as they looked. Amazed to be so analytical in spite of the heat, the nonstop assorted ills of his body, the lack of any nourishment save the most elemental, he concluded that at saturation point the creature you are either quits or finds a new plateau from which to view the world. So far, of course, no one had tortured him or done him injury, all they had done having been to overwork him and threaten him, possibly the prelude to an onslaught more vicious and concentrated, but nothing to get suicidal about. The curare-loaded pin, easily sprung from the rim of his identity disk, had not even entered his thoughts until now. There his death in seconds dangled, a few inches below his Adam's apple, and he wondered why they had not taken it along with everything else. Whoever was running the operation was not that knowledgeable, unless not taking it from him was a masterstroke of duplicity, the only catch being the chance that they did not want him alive anyway. Booth felt amiably betrayed, pawn in a game being played according to spasmodic rules, if any, and he longed for clarification. Ah, that might be it: they wanted to whet his appetite for clarification until he would do just about anything to obtain it.

Their adored Cyrano was wreckage and dust. There would be no reassembling of it in some museum or in an underground hangar, with each feature labeled like a hunting trophy, and then, a few years hence, the first pseudo-Cyrano competing with the original, which by then, by the standards of his own side, would be obsolescent. One thing he could do, though, and that was to steal a look inside the other igloos. He almost grinned, as he heaved what he hoped was the final slab of the day, at the thought of discovering therein a telephone, a high-powered radio, even radar. Skeletons would not surprise him, nor rotting heads, muzzled dogs, the furled-up flags of half the nations in Africa. If no one made a move to stop him, he could assume there was nothing worth finding, and if they did, it was not certain proof, but it would be a sign worth acting upon. Yet when?

No time like the present, he told himself, wryly adding that in this place every time was like the present; the phases of time were indistinguishable, he himself having been responsible for most of the breaks in the monotony. Ambling toward the mud at the water hole, he made a circuitous return, arriving at the first igloo unshot at and therefore almost exhilarated. Involuntarily adjusting the sit on his nose of his lensless sunglasses, he leaned into the gloom of the interior, after a few seconds registering nothing save a clump of sacking, an old gasoline can that held water, and a candle stuck to the salt with a congealed pool of wax. The orange thing he saw was a foot-square piece of parachute fabric, illicit of course, and cached from the vigilantes, but to what end? Souvenir? He could hardly think of the miners as going in for anything as frivolous as souvenirs; so far below the minimums, they had no culture save sleep. Identical on the outside, the next igloo was a shock; when he peered in, something moved, [maybe an animal,] certainly not a phantom, far gone as Booth was with heat exhaustion. He looked back out, saw the miners observing him with what he judged to be no more than casual disdain, no rifle aimed his way. Again he looked into the brown darkness, heeding the stench hardly at all. Something moved, not far, and on the floor, rolling rather than advancing, making the sounds of slobber rather than of dog or goat. His vision improved and he saw a face, its cheek flat on the salt floor, looking not at him but past him, with wild-eyed aloofness. A child? A dwarf? Neither, he reckoned, but some chronically sick old man. The deformed eyes were level with the huge nostrils. The face and feet were gnarled, yet the popped-out eyes seemed young, the bubbles of spittle that the mouth blew were infantile, in effect at least. Then he saw that the creature had no arms but little streamlined fins that it moved compactly whereas the legs, quite short, did not move at all. He heard only the sound of gently seething spit, the urgent intake of air into the nostrils, the slight chafe of the trunk as it maneuvered this way and that on the black-looking salt. The word *leper* formed itself, but this was no leper, the nonarms told him that, not having rotted away but never having been.

So! The exclamation formed mentally but never reached his lips. Someone was hauling him backward into the light. Two of them in fact, looking neither angry nor sad, but just urging him away, back to the work site. Released, he pointed at the doorway into the igloo, but they made no gesture whatever, not that they were any of them dumb, he had heard them jabbering among themselves. Odd, there were no women here, but at least one ruined creature of indeterminate age, a pariah maybe, made to live out here where so-called civilized behavior was a mere rumor. So, then, were all the miners outcasts? Why had one of them been beheaded? At this rate, even while the mystery increased, he would never know. There were no explanations, there was no interchange. Vainly trying to add things up, he resumed work, as did the miners, but he could not resist deriding the spectacle he made in his mind of supercivilized man trying to make sense of random phenomena, as if the keenest solecism of all were to be meaningless. At first thought, his circumstances were primitive, but only if you saw them incuriously, the salt in fact being worth a year of scrutiny, the physiognomy and mores of the miners worth another year, not to mention the sun's diurnal blare. It was no good saying such things as *crude*, *unevolved, below minimum*, facile labels all in the presence of a highly specialized society given over to several arcane purposes. Locked up for a year with a chunk of salt, or with one of the miners, or with the pitiful creature in the second hovel, he would learn what he otherwise would never be obliged to: textures within textures; one black face's range of expressive mobility; a human also-ran's gamut of leers and blanks, even the quality of that spit. In his time he had seen a pair of European brown bears ride piggyback on a motorcycle. He knew the humble barnacle was solitary in its youth but became gregarious with age, seeking out colonies of its peers. At night a male toad called to a female by croaking, which swelled its throat and so formed a pale balloon for her to navigate by. He tried never to close his mind, but to leave it ajar at least, never demanding much of phenomena until he had pored over them, tilting them this way and that, fondling and probing them. Nature was full of arrangements that made expedient sense, although sometimes not: certain ants refused to drag away a dead wasp by anything but a certain antenna. By and large, though, there was a scheme, could he but find it, and human behavior was full of arrangements too, as here, and it was no use playing astronomer with what went on, doing the terrestrial equivalent of linking up the dots and drawing lines that simulated this or that shape, a centaur in Centaurus, a wolf in Lupus. Somehow he had to define what was going on only in its own terms, superimposing nothing, wanting nothing that was not present among the givens. And that was a chore of specificity; merely to say, without flaw and omission, what confronted his senses, was an almost impossible assignment. Yet here he was, without having dissected the evidence, already forcing interpretations upon the miners' doings, as if to make sense would enable him to die happily.

It was no use, he could not help it, he who knew beauty itself was arbitrary, that a cancer cell espied under the microscope could yield an accidental artifact of uncommon visual appeal. A dull gray sky, properly apprehended, was just as beautiful as a rosy sunset, as was a mushroom cloud of radioactive dust. All that was needed was a thorough recognition of what was present, there being nothing in the cosmos unworthy of being admired. You had only to provide yourself with the right frame of mind. All this he devoutly nodded at, but he could not practice it in the officers' club, or California, or at eighty thousand feet in the Cyrano, so why should he expect to do it here, degraded and converted into a cipher of hard labor? The answer, he decided, was that the copious and profound attentiveness he envisioned conflicted always with the will, and of will he had his fair share. It was preposterous to be below sea level in Africa, maybe in the last few days of his life, and splitting hairs with himself as if his life depended on *that*. Torn thus between the role of perfect observership and the urge to preserve himself, he opted for the latter, yet miserably sensible of having sold out to an inferior cause, his mind aflow with the tatters of arguments unconducted and qualifiers gone to waste. To succeed, you rammed through phenomena and cooperated with them only when you had to; it was the excrescence's view of the core, like it or not.

He did not like it, nor did he like having come up with the story of Trotsky as something to lift his mind, only to keep on forgetting about it.

When would they come again, on camels, with mules, faces and hands dyed with shoeblack, in their turbaned heads the name of the next victim for the headsman? It would be better to be gone, but there was nowhere to go, at least where an armored car disguised as a Red Cross ambulance could not ferret him out, behind a crag of salt or prone in a shallow pit. Trying to laugh, at the enigmas of now and the horrors in prospect, Booth managed only a dry gibbering noise, even as he took the bread and water proffered him. He knew that laughter was a sudden sense of the superb, the criterion being superiority to one's previous self or to others, even if the fancied improvement were bogus. The effect was tonic. It promoted you out. You looked at your mess and henceforth commanded it. The superego donned its crown.

The rest of his day is not worth describing; he achieved, as rarely, a mental halt to match his physical quietus, the two halves of his being like two broomsticks held end to end, with no give, no play, hardly any contact at all. His ending thought had to do with the creature in the second igloo, whom he intended to revisit when the chance presented itself, which meant when he presented it to himself.

As for poorly sleeping Clegg, in a snooze in which he dreamed he kept awakening from a sound sleep, he fidgeted his way toward dawn, certain he was being weighed in the balance while he dangled from the spur, while his flashlit helmet dangled in turn beneath him, attracting no one.

This same Clegg, who already felt sensitized in those areas of his body where vultures would gouge and clip the flesh away, as if two dozen lozenge-shaped sites of scar tissue had begun to crawl, was the same who had dragged a dead deer to the concrete pad of the barbecue and sawed off its head, vowing in his loudest huckster's voice that he would pitch it into the live coals, yes, you bitch, this is the golden fleece, this is the Medusa's head, this is what in your nightmares you find nuzzling its blubbery way up between your legs, where even rats and skinks and carrion-sucking blueflies would not dare to go, that journey having been his legal right, his optional torture, part of the trouble having been the caustic nature of her syrup, partly slime of snailtrack, partly the liquefaction of a thousand stinging jellyfish, from which his member emerged bleeding and abraded as if after tiny flogging, some of those ulcers never having healed despite antibiotics and the subtlest versions of cortisone, thank the Lord for foreskins, otherwise he would not have been able to walk at all even when proudly bearing the standard of stars and stripes with an eagle hugging the spike, and even so a little wince left, another wince right, that had been his locomotion for too many years, long before the shrapnel in his feet, and a nickname had come and gone, Tenderfoot, awful emblem of her nocturnal proximity as well as a mild augury of what he came to think of as his main accident, but they could have been unkinder by calling him Clogg, evocative of the wooden sabot his head was fast becoming, or Clagg, fellow-traveling limey slang for clay or dung, it mattered little which substance he was mired in, any one of them would do, his domestic life having exploded one bright December morning when he marched through every room in the house with the horns of a water buffalo fastened to his head, making the appropriate sounds, swam a circuit of the pool to keep the comparison accurate, and then entered the house again, the bedroom into which she had retreated in incredulous disgust, and charged the bed she hid in, his buffalo bellow setting the grackles and jays in the trees outside into an original frenzy, but not the pillows and mattress that accepted his horn thrusts with a material equanimity she could not muster, especially when the feebly mounted horn brushed her thighs and he cried *"Cornada!"* appealing for a stretcher, an ambulance, giving up the charade only to tend the monster headache that followed, the first of many that took him into remote corners of the property they owned, the paneled maroon-painted caboose, the bottom of the plungehole in the pool beneath whose wobbly wooden deck lived a whole zoo of chipmunks, mice, toads, and garter snakes, even the furnace room, where he figured out ways to blow up the entire establishment with an ordinary but ill-proportioned mixture of gas and air, none of this coming to pass except in his mind, where the doomsday weapon detonated daily, the fuse for the most part bourbon acting upon overpunished brain cells, which had the weird result of superimposing a new headache on the old one, a layer cake of what he fancily called migraines although he never had optical disturbances, the cure certainly not the diabolical sandwich he one day made and actually conned her into eating, after two days of petty hunting and scouring the yard, the filler just a mincemeat verging on pâté of frog, toad, chipmunk, snake and bits of cricket, dragonfly, snail, sowbug, ant, and, bristly as a fireplace brush, one milkweed tussock moth caterpillar, none of this a planned recipe, anymore than her comment that it tasted something like groundhog, which she had eaten as a girl in Louisiana, the truth being, as he told her, that she still ate as a girl, which was also how she thought, his final retort among a hundred similar ones being, I decline to be marinated anymore in the likes of you, or something like it, and he was gone into Asia to fly and kill, but in his own mind more like the good man retreating into the wilderness to meet his maker, come what may, while she for the first few months waited it out with a shabby fox fur round her neck, too many beads, too much mascara, too much gin but not enough for her, and then it was over, he was wounded, God had paid him back, and she could blithely unseat him from her life, as legally as greedily, tell the Salvation Army truck to come get his possessions, the tables with animal legs, the plaques with manure-smelling horns, the fishing poles, the arrows and the rainbow-painted bow she had never been able to bend, even the fisherman's encyclopedia, its vital pages marked with feathers or bits of line and smudged with blood from having been with him at the lakes competitions.

In order to keep herself from writing him in the future, she made herself write him almost daily, the mind-blunting repetitions of which chore drove her also to sending him her favorite quotes, she having nothing to say, whereas the voice of the ages went on and on, forever wise and affable, all the way from know thyself to a thin man inside every fat one, his response to this semipersonal deluge being to mail her in flimsy prestamped aerograms bits of the fishing encyclopedia, which he knew pretty much by heart as far as he had read, anyway, *Aawa* to *Mako*, thus counterdeluging her with all manner of data she did not want and could not use, from the deeply indented snout of the cownose ray to the wet fly known as female beaverkill (this sent her not without malice), as far back as Adirondack Guideboat, a famous double-ended lightweight sportsman's rowboat of the past that once dominated the landings of upper New York State resorts, as far forward as the first-class Asiatic gamefish called mahseer, to be caught mainly on spoons and plugs with fairly heavy spinning or bait-casting tackle, his point being that he knew it backward, always remembering what he read and only reading what he already knew by heart, which explained his buying in the course of his military career at least three copies of the same encyclopedia and his never advancing beyond Mako, the open-ocean shark whose color is a striking cobalt to bluish gray, in fresh specimens at least, another reason for his nonadvance being addiction to, among other things, the Battle of Britain, painting kits that enabled him to copy old masters with almost grotesque competence, and books of military protocol, these preferably obsolete, his ultimate objective being a life that had its solaces forever on either side, he could not always put it well, it was too intimate a thing, but he meant he had the things that cheered him embedded in the soil of his head, growing there and thriving and flowering, an internal garden of prophylactic inscriptions, whether about fish or painting or courts martial, into which enclosure the intermittent violence and scapegrace mayhem of his flying career could not reach, and not even the scattered mind that resulted from tours of duty all over the world, adding up to a cosmopolitan posy, the upshot being that he had a mind within a mind, as he once phrased it when high on scotch, not his usual tipple, a circus minimus within the circus maximus, after which they lugged him off to bed, a motion that fetched bile into his mouth and past his lips onto his best-looking terracotta tie, chosen after stealthy consultation of his tie rack's harmony chart, what they failed to understand to just about the same extent as his sister being his vision, never worded, of a chariot race in an outer circuit paralleled by a similar chariot race in an inner circuit, a very simple symbolism but sufficient for Clegg, who just knew he would die if all the pressures and percussions of his outer life got through unstrained and unpurged into that final resting place his photographic memory was, so that what he held on to might have seemed, to any mental trespasser, denuded or woefully attenuated, a life factorized or castrated, less something to remember than something to pump water into, or fertilizer, spray with malathion, drench with cupboard love, but certainly not leave as such, an as such that the uncomprehending sons of bitches who spilled scotch on his tie could not even get to first base on, their lives being outside-inward, his own being inside-outward, hell, that was no fucking way to formulate it, what he really meant was simplicity itself, in its unstained underpants, while he sifted what went inside his head to stay, because what stayed took root and therefore had to be something he could live with, so after a dozen years at this he had a mental version of perfect squadron drill, every move according to the book and perfectly executed, the leftovers having been dumped, well, not quite outside, but into a sort of septic tank within the mind, where motion was limited, the sun never shone, and what was vile inevitably broke itself down into what had no smell at all, some of this having come from Napoleon himself, who said the mind must be like a chest of drawers so that you could ignore the contents of the drawers closed, some of it from Grandfather Josiah Cornelius Clegg, who died at ninety-seven, having kept himself young by diligently forgetting each day as it passed and starting each new one fresh, a six-foot perpetual tadpole of a man whom Clegg adored, had gotten his first taste of fishing from, and how to use a saw, a smoothing plane, an awl, lore never to be forgotten, not even in the jungles of Viet Nam when a pebble amid the mind's flux and the uproar of high explosive was as manna within a hamburger bun, Clegg himself being quite certain he survived because of what he learnedly called mnesiac hygiene, unpracticed by the majority, but essential counterpoint to the rocket's red glare, by which Clegg actually advanced to the point of deciding I have finally learned how to live, it is an esthetics of give and take, it takes very little, but that little within you has to be your Stonehenge Parthenon, no matter whose lives it costs excepting your own, it just has to be as constant during your lifetime as the genetic code seems to be, like the seasons, the heart, otherwise kaplooey, your life is as good as over, there is no return game, the mind happens to be like a private swimming pool, pale blue water if you keep it clean, green if you let the algae pile up, the most fruitful and soothing thing in the world being to plug in the vacuum cleaner, with its variable 360-degree brush head, and float it gently over the bottom surface, three or eight feet deep, like someone divining for water or uranium, wiping a six-inch-wide band clear with each motion, with the towering pole above or behind you, unimmersed, flicking trees or providing itinerant monarch butterflies en route to Florida for the winter with a resting place in sunlight, better than cold and stiff in a tree for the night, their orange and black reminiscent of golden trout, *Salmo agua-bonito,* what a lovely name, it loses its colors if you rear it at low altitudes, but not the monarch, who might be glad to see you ridding the pool of algae, better than the so-called guardian, flying saucer crammed with chlorine cachous, that tours around the rectangle suffusing the pale blue water with dissolving white powder, your arms get tired of course, but a full season's vacuuming develops the bicepses, correct as to plural I try to be, the worst part being the murk that gathers inside the wrinkles where the vinyl has glitched a bit in settling to contour, the next worst part being the dust suspension the act of vacuuming always creates, taking a day to settle again, just like life, you can't move dirt without disturbing some you cannot move, a most peculiar thought for one who carried with him on reconnaissance flights the touch of curare that will end him in a few seconds, no questions asked, no orders given, it being quite up to him whether or not to use the infernal thing, like Cleopatra with her asp, your mind in extremis fixed on images of home, that very pool whose skimmers filled with frogs and little rodents, bees and spiders, most of them dead when you tapped the basket against a tree, but as often as not a frog escaping flip-sprint into the grass again, unless very unlucky and being sucked along the underground pipe into the filter itself, where air is not, not even for misnavigating frogs, whose limbs, ah, perhaps seen from the rear while bouncing above a horse's saddle might have more appeal, whereas those of the giraffe are truly sexual, full of a highstrung twitching lasciviousness born of life conducted among tall trees, at which thought he was once more vacuuming with a pole at least fifteen feet long, wide enough to touch bottom halfway across at the deep end, one of the bizarre sensations he had being that he was poling an invisible barge in slow motion through ultramarine lotions where no fish swam, the water making an occasional sucking clonk as he pushed the brush deeper and the metal pole filled up to water level, only to empty itself again as he lifted the pole upward, but that sound was much fainter, easily fainter than the woodpecker wholeheartedly hacking a gash in some tree or even the cross planks above the fake Oriental garden out front, how it battered its beak at the wood, its voice when scared off a loud *peenk*, its vice must have been solitary, like the man vacuuming the pool, shifting all that muck into the sand filter, whence, during backwash, it poured out on to the rough grass in the rear of the house, not that he thought about the suspended particles when he ventured in, his slight bloat enlarged by the blue shallows but made lighter as well, the vinyl smooth to the soles of his feet like bosom skin spread out and oiled for nonresistance, and once graced with his medals tossed into the deep end so that, according to the pool manual, he could test the water's cleanness, his technique a variant of the one that says you should be able to tell which side up a dime is on the pool bottom, the chore in this instance easier because the medals were bigger than dimes, he having thrown them in out of some forgotten pique, either to show her how little he cared, or how little she, who in fact, this being earlier than the phase in which he sported horns, dived in and brought them back to him, dried them off and polished them with a metal restorer containing acid that could have seared her hands, a poignant thought whose neck he wrung, exclaiming By Jiminy, the nipples of her tits are rough, as if piranhas have been nursing on her, so he had her supple them with Vaseline nightly while watching television, a sensation she grew so to like that it occupied her in the day as well, whenever the impulse took her, comfortable in a soft chair shaped like a toadstool and tweaking what might have been invisible knitting while the caustic sap drooled from her, to no purpose, since he had refused to be anymore marinated in all that, the need to get out and fly at something exceeding the speed of a shout for help being paramount, backed by an optional need to kill or strafe as the mood took him, not that the majesty of flight escaped him, but it was only a characteristic of flight, one of his maxims, borrowed, being that he who collects enough chamberpots will not eventually find the holy grail but will have a lot of chamberpots to choose from, such the cast of his mind, practical in a hobbyist's way, romantic only through formulas, religious only in the fashion of one who relishes the outdoor life, his temple a tent, his altar a frying pan over a pinecone fire, his sacrament an eviscerated salmon, none of him outright vicious, none of him outright amiable, enough of him patriotic and loyal to secure him a reconnaissance job, the qualities needed being nerve, stolidity, and low paranoia when confronted by superhuman machines, so he qualified easily, though he chafed alongside Booth the intellectual, the officer-class technocrat, two years in the Ivy (Brown) before transferring to the Navy, where he was needed more, whereas Clegg had often wondered if he himself had ever been needed at all, something optional and refusable about him being evident in his face, at which he had spent so many hours peering, wondering if his eyes were not too bulbous, too often rotated themselves upward as if to examine an invisible passing aircraft, and gave a mild hint of never being able to rotate down again, to the mediocre plateau of ordinary folk, not that they worried half so much as he about the ample convexities of his cheeks evocative of certain overfed clerics, or the straight fleshy nose that someone had pinched hard on either side so as to force the flesh upward, thus making the nose fatter the higher up it went, a silly-looking tuber above the curlicued pout of his mouth tucked neatly into the mound of his jaw, whose lines were only a little more visible than they weren't, although he rejoiced at the inordinate length between his nose and the top of his upper lip, emblematic he had heard of sagacity and grit, the only flaw in his makeup being his earlobes, which jutted out and tapered like the toes of Oxford fronts, a characteristic he somehow knew denoted unreliability, thus making him an officer who was wisely fickle, or bravely mercurial, and so what, I'll suck my navel, Clegg, no one is perfect and few are even gloriously above average, but Booth had only muttered, not being that much interested in Clegg's estimate of his own officerly qualities, an attitude that drove Clegg even further into himself, tormenting himself from then on with his grotesque and unseemly resemblance to one Count Tommaso Inghirami, an early-sixteenth-century secretary to the Lateran Council as painted by Raphael in 1512, chubby in olive-eyed aloofness inside a loose-fitting red skullcap, his entire mien one of upholstered sanctimoniousness somewhat at odds with his insistent personality, a bun face, a bulb face, an inflated and mushroomy face, a night-polyp of a face, a face as slithery as an eyeball, and that was when he looked at the painting of the count right way up, the mouth-drying horror of it showing only when it was upside-down, and then it was a belly with two gigantic, widely spaced olive testicles at the groin, from which sprouted, thick to thin, the nasal erection all the way to the rosebud mouth of his navel, the only difference being that the count was ruddy, rather like Booth, whereas Clegg was a nocturnal pale creature whitest in the face, that belly never exposed to sunlight, not even right way up when it was almost a face again, and he thanked God, Raphael and the count he never saw himself wrong way up in the mirror, which meant that he avoided fun houses like the plague, certain that, inverted, his true belly would pour down into his belly of a face, double-paunching him until his chops burst, a loathsome event that might happen during aerobatics, when looping the loop, say, or during a stall, which explains to some extent why Clegg restricted himself during air combat to certain maneuvers only, but which does not explain how he survived, a man with an aversion to being inverted, whether in his own plane or in a capsule rolling down a mountainside, the fact being that he was very expert indeed at those aerial motions he permitted himself, perhaps even fooling enemy pilots by not looping when he should have, and so forth, so that he shot them down from the midst of an expectation unfulfilled, he, Clegg, who prided himself on his kindness but who, for private reasons akin to avoidance of nightmare, broke the rules of the game, becoming not quite an ace yet good enough not to be trifled with at combat altitude, even when the mouth-puckering bile filled the space in front of his teeth and his liver slid out of its site, all he had to do being to aim and fire, the other veered away disintegrating, not as if Clegg were an angel of death but as if he were its inspector general, actually in the course of combat having managed to do a commentary on himself, in the vivid present, hushed into the back of his mouth and nestling behind his nose, thus making himself epic on the spot, never mind what happened during the dogfight of the moment, whether he missed or spun out, took metal fragments or nearly swooned, never mind which assorted sensations he recalled later on, from the frozen cramp of his upper brain to the blurts of pain in his knees, from violent earache to the slight numbing of his finger ends, none of this of course during the Battle of Britain, when the auspices of heroism were untainted and gorgeously heraldic, permitting him to ask Booth offhand giant questions, Shall we pop up and kibosh a few Huns?, to which the other's answer was the propeller churn of his Spitfire to Clegg's thundering Hurricane, a Rolls-Royce noise appropriate to updated Knights of the Round Table, the table being deep underground in the Operations Room unfindable in the countryside of Kent, on whose crowded top disks and counters and actual models of planes represented men and aircraft in the abstractest manner possible excepting that of curt numerals, there being no little wooden movable chess piece that stood for ripped lung, demolished heart, intestine scissored through by tracer bullets, an eye flopped down the cheek in the upstairs cold where blood froze like the water slicked onto their hair by early-morning schoolboys in Maine, wanting to look smart, or like the spit that made a cracking sound even before it completed its parabola from mouth to ground, all from Clegg's childhood and the childhood protracted into his thirties, he who had walked a whole day with an apple between his thighs, had for a dare kept a squirrel in his bed nightlong, had enclosed a whole frog with his heaving mouth, stood at attention in the forest for an hour with a sprig of viper's bugloss in his dangling penis, eaten bedstraw, gromwell and the wandlike stems of blue toadflax, discovering the textures of a world he could not even name, an act of omission he later made up for by learning the fancy names of fisherman's lures, dry flies called White Wulff and Spirit of Pittsford Mills, nymphs called Leadwinged Coachman and Zug Bug, scores of them, all contrived by obscure, taciturn men in dingy sheds across the breadth of America, fiddling with feathers, fibers, olive dubbing and tying silk, merely to trap a fish, not so different from air combat, except in the one you cast a bait while in the other you came cleaving down from out of the sun, if you knew what you were doing, and zapped the fish into the lower depths, at random destroying the pilot's pancreas, his rib cage, his kidneys, none of which you saw, thanks to the thickness of flying suits and G suits in later years, it was a serene way of making a living until the day came when your own intestines flowed green into your lap while you plunged downward inside an arrow of smoke, blinded and broken, yet wearing the perfunctory dun blue winding sheet with brief honor.

Clegg smiled a little mouth-pulse, heaving on a globe of air that would not ascend from his chest, most of him given over to an image of autumn that was the swimming pool closed for the season, like an outsize lifeboat beyond the main window, covered with a rectangular blue vinyl sheet held down by vinyl bags filled with water, these like dead porpoises or seals arranged along the sheet's edge, some frozen in the act of rearing up, others prone as if bleeding quietly away while the middle of the sheet filled with rain and leaves, sipped at by rodents and reconnoitered by hopeful crows and, on one occasion, lain on by Clegg himself, undulating as if on a water bed, a bottle of bourbon in one hand, a shotgun in the other, which he fired at random into the stark black tracery of the trees above him, consoled so long as the rounds hit Earth's atmosphere, while his wife awaited him in the house, certain one of the rounds would blast through the picture window and spray her with buckshot, but no, all he ever did on that day was to light a big cigar and leave a smoke ring behind him like a retreating octopus, once, twice, three times, all without a word, as if the smoke said something final and thorough, his only conversation with her having been to say how the water-filled floats out on the covered pool resembled scalded and shaven blue pigs, not what he had been thinking at all, one of his habits being never to tell her what was in his mind, but to invent things to tell her misleadingly, so that she should never again know him or ever come near his conclusion that ignorance was when you got hold of the wrong end of the stick, or did not know which end was which, or did not even know that a stick had two ends, at length hitting yourself very hard as a result, this to be followed by other bits of marginal wisdom, from how to treat the contact dermatitis produced by poison ivy (after washing the area, apply the sap of the jewelweed) to Gordon of Khartoum's maxim that every man has a final weapon, his life, a weapon that Clegg had always been expecting to have to use, but not dangling in a basket from a crag in Africa, with no one watching. Once, he had seen a bird of fire hatch from an exploding plane, something than which his own passing would be even more vivid.

Notions of heroism had not occurred to Booth at all. Wanting answers and having none, he had resolved to create a few. It had not taken long. Here he was, in the faint light of dawn, threatening to crush the skull of the creature he had kidnapped from the second salt igloo. There had been no guard, no one inside, not even the man with the rifle to intercept him as he made his way in the darkness to the watering hole to await daylight. Of course they could see him as, first, he raised aloft the pathetic deformed body and made as if to brandish it as its blurred wail hit the semicrystalline air. Neither the miner with the rifle, nor the others, appeared to care, turning away to begin work with their poles. Booth had expected a warning shot at least, or a sudden scurry that buffeted his skull and took his trophy from him. The body weighed nothing, as if made of French bread, but it reeked, something like bananas mixed with tar, and the wail changed to a bubble-blowing seethe, then back to a wail. He decided to wash the creature off, as much for something to do rather than out of kindness, but when he sloshed water at its chest and face, with fairly gentle scooping motions, it let out a howl, or what would have been if it had had volume; instead, he heard an indignant, throaty moan and saw the bulb eyes redden and strain. If this was a shape visible in the night sky, like the Centaur and the Wolf, he had yet to find it. A sudden miserable sense of everything's being undeveloped came home to him: nothing he did had any consequences; nothing seemed to intersect with anything else, and yet here they went in for beheadings about which there was no language to inquire in.

So he began to walk, the creature clasped against his chest like a long cushion, the overall agony of his own body now incorporated into his shadow. He had so many hurts he almost had none. Reaching a slight eminence, a bunker of salt, he stood on its crest as if to dare the two who watched him, then shuffled down the other side only to confront the beheading team twenty yards away, arranged in line abreast in front of him, as if at a parade. With ghoulish abandon, he advanced and began, as best he could, what with his burden and his half-numb feet, to inspect the camels, the mules, the tatterdemalion battle dress they wore. No one moved. He saw flashes of orange parachute fabric. Sword handles glinted in the sun. An automatic weapon clicked. Flies toured around his head, darting and floating until he felt enclosed in gauze. Now they moved into a circle, hemming him in, and he began to formulate just a few words, *This is it, this is going to be it,* but all they did was to haul the creature from him and right before his eyes begin to unwrap it, exposing first the weird rough neck, the surface like a bird's nest, the sweat-glistening chest with two inverted nipples erect as if tugged out between forefinger and thumb, then the belly like a little black melon from which a good three inches of umbilical cord dangled like something a vulture had only half engorged, followed by the genitals, those of a young man except that there were no testicles at all, just a bush of rough black hair and the warped candle of the penis. Huff-puff-sizzle went the creature's mouth as its eyes roamed and groped, hardly aware of what was taking place, even when a stately conversation began, with one man indicating certain features of the shockingly deformed young man: the elegant smooth fairings where the arms should have emerged from the shoulders, the tapered wispy legs that did not move but like two rubber parsnips lolled down from the reverential horizontal at which they held the trunk. It might have been a medical lecture, with patient and students; the spoken tones were those of authoritative definition followed by those of convinced murmur, with nothing exclaimed or guffawed, nothing queried, nothing added. Now they looked at the head, surely outsize inside its tumbleweed of hair, opening their hands wide as if to measure at a distance, and then spanning the distance between the eyes and from eyes to mouth, which was an insucked white wound rather than anything with lips.

Booth gasped as someone dragged a swordpoint from the top of his shoulder all the way to his hip. Now they held him and scored him back and front for the operation that would render him without arms, just like the creature. He felt blood seeping freely down him, but was afraid to move. When they laughed, he tried to laugh with them, but his lips were glued tight. For sure, they were going to lop and trim him, then do something awful to the muscles of his legs, force his balls back up into the body cavity, stab his nipples with some gruesome awl they no doubt had with them for occasions such as these. Instead (and it was the insteads that had begun to sicken him), they made him hold the naked body once again and motioned him back to the water hole, bade him go on with the bathing procedure, even as the buttocks squirted a noxious yellow gruel whose fumes made him heave. Education through degradation, he thought, as in the death camps. Oh for a bit of language to ask things in, to be answered. Washing away, he felt the water half soothing him, with one part of his brain wondering why they allowed this pollution of the water hole, then realizing that this was no worse than bathing himself and rolling in the mud.

Yet not a single thought of suicide crossed his mind; the death pin in his identity disk did not apply. He was too busy anyway, commanded now to wrap the entire body in a large sheet of parachute fabric handed him with scrupulous accuracy. Now he was to carry the orange roll, with the big head at one end and the tapered small dead feet at the other, back to where he came from, but where it seemed he was no longer to mine salt. Escorted to the same igloo he had invaded in the night, he found himself being urged inside with his freight, without a rough word spoken, without a single shove. Within, he sat by the now silent body on the ground, vainly trying to connect this creature with the man beheaded only so recently (the father? the mutilator? the tormentor?), but found nothing to satisfy him on the level of sense. Once a pilot, then a miner, and now a custodian, he was going up in the world, would be a tutor next and then a privy counselor to the local gestapo, as he still thought of them as being. It would be better, though, if he could devise a name for the creature, for whom "it" was clearly inadequate, as "Trotsky" had been for the head, which he seemed not to have handled in a hundred years. He fed, this time on fresh bread and, it could not be but it was, wine, both passed to him with almost civil smoothness by a ferocious-looking fellow with badly chopped short hair and a prominent, snakelike vein at either temple, the eyes unwavering as coal.

Weird images assailed him of camels at rest, with the gross flap of the nose and the bulging outcrop of the forehead thrust toward him for approval. Now he was drinking goat's milk, culled from where he had no idea. He was cleaning his teeth with a frayed stick passed in to him by a hand whose owner he did not see. The fearful heat was no different; his limbs ached just as much; and he was no better off, militarily or mentally, than before. Yet something cheered him, not surely the new role of custodian-nurse to the armless ballsless one, but perhaps the mere change of rhythm, his absence from the salt, his no longer having poles to wield. Resolving to name his charge, even if only to boast in later years about having done so, he reviewed appropriate names, unsticking his lips to say them aloud in that fetid small oven, his pilot's brain fetching up for scrutiny place-names along the Red Sea coast maybe fifty miles to the east: Massawa, Mersa Fatma, Edd, Bellul, Assab, Djibouti (ah! the hotel), and then he stopped, knowing he had said the one that served; there was no need to travel down into the Gulf of Aden just for the sake of names. [Mersa Fatma] it would have to be, never mind what it meant locally; in another fix he would have called him Rigel Kent or Poindexter and have done with it, but need consumed him. There on the salt floor, rolled up like an orange carpet with a bush at one extremity and two narrow wedge-shaped feet at the other, Mersa Fatma, so-called, lay motionless, never to walk or talk, never to lend a hand or embrace his keeper, but soon perhaps to have a ring put through his septum, a couple of carved wooden testicles bound to him with leather thongs much as, back in civilization, shoelaces ended in little leather acorns. Booth began to drift, the wine had dazed him, and even as he began to slump sideways he knew he had guessed the truth about his situation: the man beheaded had been from a rival tribe, serving out his time until execution, while the wretched Mersa

Fatma was a victim of radiation poisoning, maybe from the disaster at Semipalatinsk, in which the Russkies had deliberately exposed an entire population to fallout just for information's sake. Now, he supposed, knowing too little about the scandal, they were exporting the deformed as cheap labor. Why then were there not dozens of Mersa Fatmas in the area, superholy sports of nature except to the Russians? Aghast at finally beginning to make sense of things, he allowed the drowsiness full sway over him, keeling over when a song formed on his lips but failed to come.

In an overwater luxury jet a Teutonic hostess seized the lever moored like a big key in the door and wound it through 180 degrees to the position marked Open, then spread her arms to grip the two handles that enabled her to free the door, twist it sideways and toss it out, after which she tugged a cable that unfurled the plastic escape chute and vanished down it as if descending into a swimming pool, her hands held high from her right-angled arms. *Too soon,* said Booth to her retreating back, and she began again, this time sliding an entire window inward and then out so as to step with one groomed stockinged leg onto the wing before slithering off it over the rear flap. Still too soon, he said, having her stare avidly with parted lips at the oxygen mask as it dropped from the overhead rack into position in front of her face, then reach up as if palping an afterbirth, only to thrust the plastic cup over her mouth and nose, the sling over her head, inhaling deeply as if gratified by the latest in venereal machines. Where, he wondered, were the *balsas salvavidas?* Life rafts? In the igloos there was no emergency door but one, no window to unstick, no oxygen mask, no facilities at all. A slab shut out the light, making him a prisoner all over again, but at least one high on wine and goat's milk, with Mersa Fatma for company, and no more of that stinking head he'd misnamed Trotsky, no more slabs to heave with poles, no more jackals and vultures. An image from long ago, when he was first captured, now stood a heron in front of him against the setting sun: a weary salt miner, resting one leg by propping its foot against the inside of the opposite thigh, while leaning on his pole, remained that bird for six hours while Booth slept, his dreams excluding Clegg, his scabs hardening, his head beginning to ache with the alcohol, his sunglasses' frames still on his nose. Once again he was born jaundiced, grew up small-toothed, became ruddy-faced and switched from Navy to Air Force after crash-landing in the sea off the deck of an attack carrier, vaguely puzzled why the igloos had been so close to where his capsule landed, and wondering if his capsule were still there, or was the hostess still jammed in her seat inhaling contraband oxygen while everyone else escaped aboard a *balsa salvavida?* When he woke, he thought he was dead, in a tomb or a very hot morgue.

It was still dark, as he ascertained by peering through the crack between slab and wall, so why had he awakened? Heaving with his shoulder budged the slab of salt not an inch; it must have taken several of them to shove it into position. Therefore, he concluded, they still regarded him as a captive, and he wondered why he had not tried to move it, or slabs like it, before, he who had heaved many a one out there in the sun with his two poles. As far as he could tell, Mersa Fatma was asleep, but there was no way of being sure, in the darkness, and with a creature whose waking day drifted between vegetal stoicism and drooling indignation. He could not even make out the cylinder of orange fabric in which his companion slept and would go on living since he had no way of freeing himself from it. Booth sighed in the act of shaking his head, alert enough to his own behavior to wonder if people only shook their heads in the daylight, but discerning in his mind's eye a drawing by Vesalius of a skeleton, with both elbows on a tomb, looking at a skull, its own head or skull propped up like a bored schoolboy's on the back of the left hand. From one point of view, this was no life for an Air Force colonel who had recently ejected from something as valuable as the Cyrano, but from another point of view it was the best education in the world, or in the desert at least: his experience (as the personnel evaluation dossiers said) was broadening, indeed it had begun to burst at the seams, indeed it had no seams, in fact no longer felt like an *it*. It—he got no further with the thought, self-contradictory as it was; rifle fire had begun outside, first a couple of shots, then a fusillade with what sounded like half a dozen rifles at least, followed by scattered yelling and commotion. He could see nothing through the crack, but he instinctively began to grope about the floor for some weapon. Nothing came to hand. A stray round hit the slab and pinged away, then another, and he had the zany thought that he was in some Maginot Line of his own, invulnerable to bullets until several people hauled the slab away.

Over on the other side of the igloo, Mersa Fatma had begun to gibber faintly, and then he began to cough, as if buried under mucus. Booth crawled over to him and felt at his mouth, patted the cheek as if to reassure, and felt an irresistible desire to empty his bladder, which he did by kneeling at the door and directing the stream into the crack beneath the slab. Amazed to be relieving himself thus at the height of some presumed attack, he once again noted abstractly that his experience was widening all the time, thanks this time to the wine and the milk. Then he returned to Mersa Fatma, foolishly felt for a hand to hold, and settled for a gentle pressure on the brow. The coughing ceased and became a gentle pulsing of spittle.

For what must have been fifteen minutes he crouched there while gun-fire continued outside, although there seemed to be much less shouting. When urgent voices sounded at the door and the slab began to lean sideways, admitting a feeble azure light, he crouched as low as he could, not knowing what would be next. But it was miners with poles, *his* people as he astonishingly found himself thinking, all grins and jabber. Never had he felt such a need of an interpreter, but their gestures to him to come outside and look were explicit enough. At first he could see little except the gleaming salt, the watering hole, the dwindling purple of the distant mountains, but as his eyes adjusted he saw bodies on the salt, one of the miners carefully stacking rifles, and several of the others honing or wiping off their enormous knives on bits of orange fabric, with which he, Booth, had supplied them. If they had been attacked, how had they come through so well, having as he had supposed only one rifle among them? The answer was not far to seek.

Erect against one of the other igloos stood two of the local gestapo, as he had called them, automatic weapons in hand, at the ready. Two more, similarly armed, were strolling back from some perimeter inspection. Not far away, one of the miners was kneeling to carve away at one of the bodies, rising to brandish what might have been a handful of sweetbread, but this was no thymus gland of an animal, it was genitals, sloppy in a new autonomy as the fellow fluttered them like a handkerchief. A small cheer arose, more of a vocal nod than an actual celebration, and Booth felt nauseated, finally aware that the people he was among were not only fierce, but precisely those who collected such trophies and, when they died, were allotted heaps of rocks, each rock denoting an enemy slaughtered, his genitals taken as a matter of routine. Involuntarily cupping his own with one hand, he set them laughing; they thought he had made a joke, but they didn't look fierce at all. No, he had simply grown used to them, they looked baroquely savage in the eye-scalding light of the new day.

That breakfast should follow such events was preposterous, but it did, though the usual meager fare of bread and water. Motioned to force-feed Mersa Fatma, he obliged as best he could, making a paste of the two constituents and easing the wads into what seemed a willing enough mouth. Then he poured a little water onto the bottom palate, looking at the miners, who had lifted Mersa Fatma out into the late dawn, to see if he was doing right. They nodded him on to further efforts, making no effort to assist, so he propped up the head on a piece of salt while the rest of the body remained in the orange wrapper. Mersa Fatma burped, once, twice.

Then he writhed, wetting himself, which seemed to offend no one at all. Then he moaned until Booth made him another wad of bread paste and stuffed it home. Tentatively he said the name aloud just to see what would happen, but the two miners remaining to supervise him merely pointed north and nodded. It was not much, but it was communication; his map reading had finally paid off, he knew where he was, he had known all along, but he had not expected to see, as he now did, a row of beheaded corpses, naked and very black, laid out on the salt, with vultures already hovering, settling, moving in for a fine fat feast. Something nagged at him: was this just another bout of tribal warfare, or was Mersa Fatma somehow involved? He marveled at the ease with which he thought the name, applied it, whereas calling the severed head Trotsky had been a pretentious bagatelle. Amazed at himself—scarred, scabbed, enclosed in wizened mud, racked with bone and muscle aches, forever having headaches and spells of dizziness, itching with hives, burned raw even under the mud by the sun, bleary-eyed and half dead from hunger—he had somehow found within himself the means of going through the motions. A piece of him had clicked. How could it be? It was as if some blueprint deep inside him had taken over even while the rest of him was wasting away. Some filament that could not snap had gone on burning when everything else had quit, or almost had. And it was not training, or presence of mind, or stoicism, but something like a reflex enabling him to assume positions, make up his mind, do as he was told: not much, but the vital minimum in this place of the blighting salt. Half inclined to pat himself on the back, he looked right up at the sky, now a dense trembling blue, yearning for a jet to pass over, never mind how high, like a schoolchild wanting a reward for having worked hard. Only vultures came, which made him look back at the bodies on the ground, like burned-black carcasses of hogs, or waterskins made from skins of hogs: a wretched, vilely static sight. Apparently none of the other tribe (as he supposed it was) had survived for execution. A hundred yards away, as if patrolling an invisible herd, the outriders of this group nibbled their way across the salt on camels, driving his mind into hopeless questioning about the source of their arms, the reason for their superior paramilitary status (no salt miners they), and how he or Mersa Fatma fitted into the local war.

He would not have been surprised to see an armored car roll over the horizon, or parachutists drop from the skies, or helicopter gunships lumbering low to wipe them out, but nothing added itself to what was already an atrocity scene. One of the outriders came to collect the rifles of those killed, which included at least one miner, perhaps even two (there seemed fewer of them at the work site), so it was clear that the group's, or tribe's, labors were divided: the miners mined, but used weapons when attacked, while the outriders otherwise known as the gestapo carried weapons all the time and also ferried the salt, maintaining the peace as they did so, as well as carting away the personal effects of all downed fliers. He seemed to have been promoted from miner to custodian, as he had already decided, but there was something else involved in his new role: more than custodian, he was nurse and votary (he winced inwardly at this latter thought), useful because so ill equipped for anything else. All he had to do was do his chores and bide his time. He suddenly realized there were no more than half a dozen bodies on the salt, there was no telling how many of the others had fled and were still, presumably, in the vicinity, although the entire region offered no cover at all beyond a few knolls of twisted lava.

Stop assuming, he told himself; you don't have all the facts. Maybe the other tribe only wants the water hole. They cannot want the salt, because they could help themselves. There is nothing else for free.

Partly satisfied with such an exhortative explanation, he went to inspect the chopped red liver of the bodies, feeling curiously indifferent, and then returned to Mersa Fatma, picked him up like a child in swaddling clothes and carted him over to the carnage, at which they all laughed, no doubt finding the combination wry. Yes, Booth told himself, remembering a bit of Vesalius, *For the semen and for the urine there arises a common channel which is led slightly downward and again bends back upward. . . .* All he saw was wrecked circuitry congealed and ahum with flies. The vultures kept their distance, certain of the meal, and no doubt jackals were already on the way. He felt like someone who has been denied the chance to dream, even about Vesalius's notion of a strong vessel like a worm growing in the rearward region of the testis. Had the other tribe, he thought without warning, come for *him?* If so, he had been royally defended. Or was he just irrelevant after all?

In those few moments, something came loose in his mind, something delicate came free, like a note played on the extreme right-hand end of the pianoforte keyboard, its sound a forlorn hollow *plink* fusing submission with a wind chime that might have occurred on Mars, making him sure he was feeling something for the first time, something between intricate poignancy and brittle insignificance, here in the blazing salt desert an icicle of bittersweet faintheartedness, unprecedented in a man such as himself, as burly in intellect as in physical daring, as handy with ideas as with a jet airplane, the sum of the sound being the utter helplessness of mind vis-à-vis not only his present situation but also his future, which he now recognized was to attend Mersa Fatma unendingly, to dab him and mop him, to lift him and carry him, to keep him company night and day, with never a word uttered, never a gesture exchanged, the poor devil blinking blinks he did not know were blinks, soiling at regular intervals a winding sheet of orange parachute fabric of whose nature he had not the merest conception, yet continuing to be in spite of everything, less an identity than a specimen of the process called existence, like a beautifully shaped honeycomb of scar tissue, plonked onto the salt by some erring master sculptor, Tuareg or Bedouin, armed with only the most superficial knowledge of the human form. The saddest thing of all, Booth decided, looking down, was not that Mersa Fatma had been mutilated, oh no, but that he had been exported, and here he was, blank, inert, and wholly unbiddable, but also an absolute without cowardice, ambition, or self-concern, a human terminus in a human frame, a human inaugural in his very infancy (he could not "speak"), and Booth entered upon a train of ideas that took him from Saint Booth to Satan Booth, from nurse to inquisitor, from asking why, or why me, to the final silly tinkle of what was random, the joke being that a billion-dollar airplane had delivered him from sixteen miles high to become slave, servitor, laborer, and camp clown, whom no one came to see although the vigilantes on the camels checked him out from time to time, which did not exactly make for a thriving social life, the minuses including his Porsche, his books, his electronic gadgets, his salary, his vitamin pills, his bath and his shave, oh the deductions were endless, and he began to wonder if, as he had heard, the stripped man loses layers of thought, as it were dethinking himself until, in the end, he has reduced himself below even the level of his captors, the cause being some civilized propensity for overload, for making a good job perfect, thus converting himself into a subsavage, yet oddly enough retaining sufficient *nous* to diagnose the fact without any more being able to do anything about it, that bit of mind bouncing about like a solitary pinball in the empty machine of the body, a cranial vestige disappearing long before he was exhumed by Danish archaeologists of the next century, quaffing lager while poring over photocopies of U.S. Air Force records, who could only jest about his having been marooned on the salt, conceivably beheaded or made to have sexual relations with a subhuman before being castrated, blinded, and eaten alive by cannibals and buzzards mingling unresentfully together since there was so much of him to get at, the buzzards not wanting his sweet brains, the men not wanting his sweetbreads, the flies using all of him that remained as a day nursery and incubator, Colonel Usable, he, a space-age Crusoe to be written up by stylists, and written down by mere communicators, commemorated in a little clanking symphony by the Roy Harris of 1995, commemorated in a prize for survival techniques at the Air Force College, or, most gruesome thought of all, personified in a statue of salt installed in a quiet arbor of the base for birds to shit on and passing aircrew to strike matches against, and he shivered along his entire living length under the milk-clotted Wedgwood sky, abruptly beginning to flex his neck by describing with his head the letters of his name, his full name, the *B* taking it from slumped-on-chest all the way to erect and then rightward in two connected loops, this followed by the *E*, the *A*, the *U*, his neck muscles making audible cracks by the time he reached his original surname, especially when he shifted from rightward to leftward, describing the *R* and the *D* backward, so to speak, and resolving to embark on lowercase after finishing with the capitals, the one thing he had not bargained for being Mersa Fatma's pathetic attempt to do likewise, there on the salt, managing only to wobble his head a bit in the one plane allotted him, and to jut his chin a bit, roll his tongue as if savoring an invisible Popsicle, scrunch up his cheeks in slow-motion squints that sometimes excluded Booth, sometimes not, it depended where the eyes had rolled to, a derivative behavior that Booth found awful, as if he were some macrocosm and Mersa Fatma the minor version, a concept he junked as fast as he conceived it, because, as any fool could see, the so-called macrocosm had little in common with the microcosm, the universe with mankind, a cosmos was not a person, a firmament was not a fellah, and the net result of all this exertion was that Booth's neck felt lissom and whippy, whereas Mersa Fatma seemed to have yanked something out of place, which fact he signalled by hoarse hiccups there on the salt, flicking his head sideways as if trapped in some horizontal St. Vitus' dance checked only when Booth, despairing of a remedy, took off his lensless sunglasses and adjusted them over Mersa Fatma's eyes and bridge of nose, like fine brass tracery on the black udder of some unnamed desert mammal, stilling him at once, which meant that again, through his weird aural swap of outward noise for cerebral quiet, Booth heard at a distance the wan, cowed *plink* of the right-hand piano key, whose exact sonic quality he could not define, unless it were a finger idly flicking the toy piano of a dying child (but he found that too luscious an account), or the one key being used with Dresden china delicacy as a tapper for Morse code, or failing that an epitome of everything forlorn, ripe in a pious fragility, hoping not to die but with its little finger saying it might not mind.

Dangling in midair, Clegg decided it was permissible to lose hope, perhaps that was the way to get through what was left. He reckoned he had almost enough rope to descend with, but he no longer felt any urgency about the move. Sipping and nibbling, he became accustomed to the grievous sway of his capsule, half convinced he was inside a lightbulb that would fry him when the power came on. To see how it sounded, he let out a stagy, neat whine, and then another; given enough time, he decided, he could become perfect in the art of it, a whiner beyond compare, whereas his true nature, he knew, was to make an oafish shout that sent his own timidity packing as, on many an occasion, he had dismissed this or that segment of the Luftwaffe. He now remembered the Battle of Britain better than his own actual life, except that his daydream had of course been part of it anyway. The ghost of a policy wafted through his aching head: maybe, if you thought forward, expecting nothing, it would be easy to die, and what that entailed was neither hoping nor not hoping, but rather being the impartial witness of his cells' continued self-maintenance. Just the sort of idea he would have stolen from Booth, who was so adept at wriggling mentally into and out of predicaments, with a phrase, a glib summation: Absence of evidence isn't evidence of absence, or did it begin the other way around, his very ribs seemed to be palpitating. Was Booth dead? Was that why his mental set kept on coming through, as if Booth had already died Clegg's death for him? So that Clegg-death, when it came, would be just as trivial as adding a final domino to a sequence in which no one had been much interested in the first place. He dreamed that Booth had been set on fire, made into charcoal-colored sludge, and his eyes burned at the thought. It was strange and offensive how, for reasons unknown, Booth made the right thing happen, and, even when he did not, it happened on his behalf, thus shutting out a decision that would have been wrong, shifty, or inelegant.

Their reciprocities were skewed.

Now Clegg had outlived Booth and was the senior man. One was always senior to someone dead, provided one was alive.

Booth could not, Clegg reasoned, have dreamed up the death of a Clegg, it would have been beneath him, whereas here he was, morbidly presuming, the ridiculous fact being that even when he dreamed Booth's death it felt as if he were dreaming the next act of his life instead.

In fact, Booth knew Clegg was still alive but he did not know how he knew that; if he saluted, Clegg somewhere in the mountainous distance would reciprocate, whereas in the normal course of things Clegg, the junior man, should initiate the salute, the formalization of a gesture that showed the open hand held no weapon.

Now, how come, Booth asked himself, I assume he's in the mountains? Why not below sea level, on the salt, like me? No, I'm right, he ejected over hills, he went out first.

So how come, maundered Clegg, I feel so miserable? The rivalry is over. I don't miss it. If he were alive, he would surely have come for me by now, with stretcher, morphine, and a cigar in that goddamn slack mouth of his; I was always wondering what had last been in it.

Now Booth, his mind a crust of snot, forgot Clegg just at the moment Clegg decided *The shit is alive, he's just holding off to see if I'll break.*

Then Clegg felt ashamed even as Booth cast him a brief thought running: He has the power of all stolid men to endure while the flashy, fly-by-night Booth quit.

Clegg, furiously piddling his pants, called out for anyone to come and get him, he was sick of being unneeded.

Booth rocked Mersa Fatma in his arms, aware of a new odor, that of brine and saddle soap, coming from the region of the teeth.

The only Clegg in those mountains gave up the ghost, then recalled it in a fury.

Brimming with a new sense of power that was only a last-ditch perversity, Booth thrust a finger down Mersa Fatma's throat.

Clegg said a viscous hallelujah to the rock.

Booth wiped the other's bile off his fingers.

Clegg sneered at the god in the echo.

Booth licked his fingers clean.

Clegg in his gondola ate nylon.

Booth on the salt retched.

Clegg slung his helmet out again.

Booth sang "Annie Laurie."

Clegg licked blood off his wrists.

Booth tickled Mersa Fatma.

Clegg longed for salmon.

Booth closed one eye.

Clegg said something he didn't understand: a vocal heave.

Booth heard jets.

Clegg heard

Booth hearing

Cyrano,

Cyr-an-o, like that,

and each began to live a bit, apart from the other as Lupus from Centaurus (those neighbors) or chinook salmon from sockeye (those siblings), two men side by side in dereliction, each assured his last ooze would be mighty royal, Booth a prince of pus, Clegg a pauper of perlon, one down, the other up, saluting one another across a sloping distance, their history having almost been over but, because not over, bound to continue (there is little rising action with fallen men), their two lives once again open to interference, Booth even more senior while yet a poor misfit dunce of a thing scrabbling away on the salt, Clegg a more senior junior while yet a poor misfit frozen aerialist like a winged seed unsown. As unalike, to the careful eye, as two peas.

When Clegg heard what sounded like a harvesting machine, he blearily enjoyed it as yet another illusion, to be savored in the gathering arithmetic of dementia. Next would come an ocean liner, a fishing fleet from the Florida Keys, the angel Gabriel complete with laser and doomsday book. How strange, he thought, that the world is coming here to me: if you wait long enough, it all happens. And he hummed a little, made double turle and Stu Apt Improved Blood knots without even looking, as if in the middle of an exhausting fishing trip, his mind on how the ground would feel against his feet when he finally got down. It was only by chance that he looked up, through the rent in the fabric that was his roof, and saw dangling above him, like a piece of masonry fallen but coming no lower, a bulbous tire attached to a pair of struts, all three black in silhouette. The capsule was shuddering, a big blast of air was fanning down, the mechanical uproar stayed constant. No illusion could be this loud, this forceful, and if a helicopter had not arrived he had no idea what it could be. Impulsively, he swung open the side door and let out all the rope he had, determined to make an heroic gesture, even if it seemed decorative at best, and swung his legs out so that they rested on the clumped fabric that had fallen down from the spur above, blocking his view. What a grotesque position: instead of tapering away from the sheer side of the mountain, the spur fattened up like a wedge, which meant that looking up from inside the capsule gave a better view than he had now, looking up past its outside camber. He could no longer see the tire or the struts, but the roar continued. Following the shroudlines as they came together and then went over the top of the spur, upon which the remains of the parachute had flopped, he decided to risk yet another gesture. Making certain the end of the rope was triple tied to the mooring ring in the capsule's floor, he tugged and tugged, his collarbone halving the effort and making him almost faint with pain. Again he dragged at the orange rope and, when it did not give, he took as firm a grip as he could, spun a loop around one ankle, thrust that leg into the open void, and, screaming aloud as the broken collarbone grated not only in his chest but all through his back, slithered out on his rear, as carefully as he could bringing his other leg around and setting the sole of the foot on the top of his other ankle. There he swung, panting, a new darkness rushing through his brain, with a view up and down the valley but in one of the other directions only the flank of the capsule and in the other the fallen panel of the fabric. It was much farther down than he had thought, and his grit-filled eyes traced the rope's line until it lost color well above the bottom of the valley. It might have been five hundred feet short, as good as five miles. He could not hear anything for the motor's roar, not his helmet clanking or his own breath, by now a stammer of gasps. It was no time to stage a self-aggrandizing commentary, it was a time to go on down or clamber back into the capsule, the latter perhaps the more difficult. So down he tried to go, one foot curbing the loop on the ankle beneath it, but letting it slide, while his hands worked down the rope in grab-sized spans. It would have been easy without the broken bone, which flashed and bit with his every move and, when it did not either flash or bite, droned a hole just above his heart. In two minutes he descended only a yard, and after half an hour he would have fallen into the abyss, his hands unable to exert themselves more and his feet numb from noncirculation. As if his mind were an anvil and he were thinking with only the pointed part that jutted out, he wondered why the helicopter had not moved, deciding in the end that they could see only the parachute on the spur, but nothing of what dangled beneath. If he managed to get down another fifteen feet, he would be able to look up around the other side of the fallen fabric and see what was going on, so he hastened his descent, actually slithering several feet under almost complete control. Expecting the capsule to topple off the ledge any moment, and cursing himself for not staying put, he worried his way down while looking up, knowing the thing would brain him if it fell, then drag him down with it, a Jack with no Jill, well past where his helmet dangled against the rock below. His life seemed to have been slow-motion zero since, oh, a week ago, whereas other people had interesting lively lives, taking trains and growing vegetables and fishing the Finger Lakes. Everything he did was a scramble or a sit-down crisis; there were puzzles, but no solutions; there were pieces to work with, but no triumph in completing the chore. It all led to the same dead end. Almost tempted to let go and plummet to the valley floor, he looked up at the fabric still impeding his view, then slid the rest of the way, a good dozen feet, arrived panting at exactly the point he had chosen, and with one hand lifted the bottom of the screen. The giant rotors were still there, the airwash cooled him, there were helmeted faces looking down, seemingly without seeing him, but the chopper had no markings on its side. Then he saw the floppy ladder snaking down toward him, afloat in the down-gale, an irresistible invitation, but from whom? The question detained him less than a few seconds as he chose rescue over an ungainly dive to the bottom; all he had to do was seize a rung and be winched up, that much he knew. He would not have to climb. Some bird whizzed past his face, attempting, he thought, an ablative peck even as he reached one hand out and then, as the ladder sank, a foot. Bisected now between ladder and his homemade rope, he felt the twin energies of the two systems, the ladder that ended abruptly at his feet, the rope that trailed away into nothingness where his helmet banged. He saw hands gesticulating from above, mouths rapidly changing shape, but to no purpose, not until he saw what his swing to the ladder had done to the capsule. Swiftly, and starting a blurt of terrible pain all through his chest, he flung his other hand to the ladder (a cool rubbery substance), and swept the rope from his foot, as the capsule with an inverted soaring motion bundled against the fabric on its way down and, like something a conjuror had delivered, flashed from the bottom of the orange screen on its way to the ground, a crash he never even heard as the ladder began to lift, with his feet on different rungs, such had been his haste, and his hands too far apart, one holding a rung, the other the right-hand structural member at least a foot below, in a crouch that favored his broken collarbone. Up he went, like a trapped insect lifted from the surface of a swimming pool by the long-armed skimmer, crouched in such a way that he seemed to be shrinking from punishment, the down-draft, or the sun. He scrambled over the rim into what seemed a doctor's office, populated not with uniformed airmen but two men in white coats with incongruous-looking crash helmets on their heads. They spoke English but they were not American. They offered him coffee (the coffee he had dreamed of incessantly) and then, what he had not anticipated, a cake of meaty-tasting bran. Then a cigarette lettered in Cyrillic, with a long filter tube that had nothing inside. Faintly acknowledging the fact that the other side had him now, he felt as uninvolved with them as with the intending brides and grooms portrayed and described in the *Sunday Times* social columns. Enemy, no; different, yes, but all heeding the same laws of aerodynamics, the same geography, the same certainty of death. Not exactly jovial, they were affable. One did a makeshift setting of his collarbone with splints and bandages from a locker, explaining in good but British-sounding English that a more suitable dressing would follow when they landed. *Dressing?* Wrong word, Clegg thought bemusedly. *Would follow?* That wasn't how to say it at all. *Landed?* Idiomatic, but where? They gave him nothing for the pain, however, and the helicopter's motion from air pocket to air pocket made him wince, and he tried to keep his mind on their faces, but these were bland and blank, the faces of functionaries. There was not a weapon in sight. He reached for his long-forgotten sidearm, but it was gone. The outside of the ship was pale blue: no insignia. The inside was drab green, the lettering on the instruments and panels in Cyrillic or Arabic, he could see that much without even leaning to look. No questions, no threats. All of a sudden he wondered if Booth was aboard as well. No, only the two-man crew, the two men in white coats with business suits underneath, and one other clad in a fur hat and what resembled a uniform except that the buttons were leather and the shoes were suede. Haunted by the image of himself clambering up the ladder, *no,* stuck fast on it, as the Cyrano capsule thundered down only inches past him, he felt sick, not from pain or the helicopter's rambling lurches, but from suddenly realizing how close he had come to joining his helmet and the capsule. Too much had intersected for him to feel that this one bit of experience, his rescue, had come clean away from what had hemmed it in. But rescued he was, his only remaining duty having to do with name, rank, serial number and, if he chose, the cyanide pin in the disk round his neck, but that was gone too, so they knew who he was and that he could do nothing reckless, not even jump out since the door was slid shut. He now had what he had dreamed of in the capsule, getting ready to die: an utterly undivinable future, with no clues, no guidelines, no map. He was theirs completely, with no phrase book provided, no introduction made, and as yet nothing asked of him. Nothing fierce in their demeanor put him off, nothing meek in his incited them to try his mettle. For now, only a voluptuous lull during which he savored once again the presence of the human race, he the specimen, they the collectors. Doing the dishes when living alone, he used to stand the glasses on a doubled square of kitchen paper towel, noticing the next day how the wet rings had dried into circular ribs that bulged through on the bottom side, strengthening the towel so much it did not even flap, but like some ribbed wing cruised ahead of him in the air, not moving, not curling over either. Strong through being impressed, he told himself giddily, as a composite image of his specialized world hovered in his mind as if in farewell: the fishing encyclopedia, the name Rupert jettisoned long ago, his bows and arrows, his daughter with her drawerful of keys to locks that no longer existed, his redness at birth, the bigness of his head, the nickname Tenderfoot, the firebird that sprang from the MiG when he shot it down, space jargon such as "break-off phenomenon," ancient military manuals that covered such matters as Hints for the Use of Soldiers Proceeding to India and Bayonet Fighting for Competitions, plus cigarillos, the caboose, mnesiac hygiene, the Battle of Britain, all the self-commentaries on Clegg the consummate athlete, who prided himself on being kind but wished his eyes were not so large and did not roam upward. He had not realized his life had been so rich, nor did he relish thinking of it as if it were already over and done with, he who had strolled through the empty house at night with a tall drink in his hand, and the ice cubes tinkling against the glass had sounded like a very distant train's bell clanging through the American language.

Can, he worried, they smell the mess in my shorts? They will be thinking: hm, some officer, he has shit himself already, and we have not even begun. At any rate, his life had opened up; it was a new blank in which they were no doubt going to write. Peering out, he saw blockish towers in spacious but demolished courtyards. They were not very high, then, above the sand, but he knew that at first, for about ten minutes, the helicopter had climbed. He just did not remember coming down again, but descend they must have, while he was lost in some enervated anticlimactic dream. Odd things combined. He smelled talc. His collarbone was pulsing. He felt as full as if he had eaten a several-course meal. Music in the helicopter's harsh chatter might have been Elgar's *Wand of Youth*, a thought that made him grin at being so cultured an aviator; but many aviators were, it was the long loneliness that drove them to it. Truth told, he felt like a snubbed tourist, willing to ingratiate himself with the natives without bending over backward. He should not, he knew, have relished feeling so much of a civilian, freed of secrets and duties, salutes and rosters, but part of his mind felt frisky as a linnet, part of it booming with a bell tolled underwater, which was the pain of his collarbone, which was also what he now regarded as his *wound*, a follow-up to the shrapnel in his feet. Come what may, he knew he was going to be well, take a holiday, phone room service, fall in love, go to symphony concerts when they played none of that twelve-tone manure, take out subscriptions to all the hunting and fishing magazines there were, and purchase the latest edition of the fishing encyclopedia in order to read onward from MAKO (*Isurus oxyrhinchus*) to—where would it end?—ZEBRAFISH or ZEBRA TROUT, there could surely be nothing beyond that. Handed a wet napkin, he wondered why, but wiped his face with it anyway, which befouled it crimson; his face had been covered with blood, like his hands, and he handed the napkin apologetically back. They cared how he looked, that was promising. But maybe there would be cameras awaiting him, they did not want him to look beaten up. In no time they would retrieve the capsule and ferret out its secrets; it was after all part of the Cyrano's cockpit, indeed the only part of the plane intact, except for Booth's own. Dismally grinning, he remembered how, years ago, a Soviet Foxbat flown to Japan by a defector had been found to be made of steel and therefore almost an antique, not the least weird feature being its lack of an ejection seat. Therefore even the capsule of a Cyrano would be to them like something from Ali Baba's cave. Smirking, he thought how the Foxbat could sustain high speed and altitude for only about ten minutes before running out of fuel while the Cyrano got its longest range (never published and unthinkably huge) at top speed and highest altitude. So Foxbats could only reconnoiter in short dashes while the Cyrano could safely overfly any country in the world, excepting maybe two. Sadly, all they had to do was inject him with one of several fluids and the lowdown on the Cyrano would be theirs, without fuss or intimidation, the only catch being that he did not know the maximum range, a fact they would soon recognize. The rest of the avionics, though, was self-evident, wasn't it? No, range was not avionics, and how come he did not know the maximum range? Surely that was a significant fact about a Cyrano pilot, not enough wedded to his machine to care how far it would travel when pushed. He knew that Booth would know, Booth whose facial and bodily angularity seemed more in tune with the plane itself, and he at once found himself wishing they would soon capture Booth as well, which would save him, Clegg, an awful lot of trouble, a thought he was keenly ashamed of although he went on thinking it all the same. Booth was the kind of man of whom one said, the only man who could have caught it hit it. Trapped in a capsule on a ledge, and then dangling in midair, he would have found a way out instead of waiting to be collected like outgoing mail in a rural post box with its red metal flag erect at the beckon. It was the difference between a man whose ambition was to be great and a man whose longing was to be at home, the only thing that amazed Clegg being how long he had coped fairly efficiently with a military career and how long Booth had soldiered without ever quite achieving greatness. A flaw in their luck must have caused it, matched by the good luck, at least in his own case, which had kept him competent in a job he perhaps did not belong in at all. Yet the last thing he trusted in was his luck, in both senses, after all else failed, and yet it was the one thing he shrank from trusting. Life was very muddled because it was so many other things as well. The helicopter was preparing to land, ducking its nose and carving downward at a sharp, nongliding angle that made Clegg grateful he had never settled for aircraft without wings. All he could see was a rocky hillside with one or two overhangs like the ledge on which he had been marooned. The helicopter flew straight into a tunnel cut into the rock face and landed in a gigantic chamber faced with black glass and alive with neon light. It was as if they had strayed into an updated pyramid complete with galleries, wells and antechambers to immortality. Clegg's helpless mind shifted to bats, from fierce miniature faces to bats with tall noses like pudenda and long slanting ears like outsize human fingernails, bats with stinglike tails and bats without, all dropping dung over the centuries on boxes that held kings. It was no place to go fishing or hunting in, and then he recognized that *he* was the prey. Instead of hunting him down, though, in a simplified maze appropriate to a white rat, they did something unexpected.

Ushered into a paneled room somewhat like a study, except there were no books, he found himself being seated at a table set for dinner, complete with white linen cloth and what he guessed was bone china. Music came from speakers he could not see (Rachmaninoff perhaps) and a waiter in white jacket trimmed with gold entered and lit two candles. Sipping water from an elegantly stemmed wineglass, without for an instant questioning its chemistry, Clegg mused on his bizarre fate: from the Cyrano to being marooned to luxury living inside a mountain. But perhaps this was standard for prisoners arriving with broken collarbones, and he suddenly felt a wave of hate crest through him as he reviewed their priorities: gastronomy before first aid. He need not have worried. Two male nurses escorted him to an oval room where, after being x-rayed against a screen like a stained-glass window, his arm was lifted, his collarbone was set, and he saw himself in a mirror with his elbow up and his hand frozen at the beginning of a karate chop, in which lopsided attitude he would spend the next weeks, if he survived that long, and surely they were not going to waste medical care on a doomed man, although it was not unknown. If they didn't kill him, he'd recover soon, he was suddenly sure of that as of a transmission picked up by a tiny radio in his ear. He would soon be back to tennis, golf, all that elegant time-wasting stuff, living a different life.

What was different here, around the oval room, was that the aides or guards, whatever they were, spoke with too much timbre and no elocution; he couldn't understand them. What they said sounded like Gaelic, but why? Had their tongues been chopped out, or what? The makeshift dressing given him aboard the helicopter had been more comfortable, but he ignored the discomfort and concentrated on his setting, back now, and alone, in the paneled dining room, still music-filled. He welcomed the thought that this was the procedure preceding all interrogations, not so much to soften him up as to distract him, and no doubt in some instances to narcotize him too. After leathery soup, which made him cough it was so fresh-from-the-tureen hot, and a slice of smoked salmon berthed on lettuce, he wondered what the waiter would bring in next, a course or the first interrogator. It was chopped steak, with mashed potatoes and French beans, airline fare, almost, except the portions were large. Wine he declined one-handedly while resolving to deny himself something in the interests of not falling hook, line and sinker for such blandishments, which he realized was irrational in the extreme: anything they wanted to get into his system was no doubt already there by now. The dessert was a rainbow-colored sherbet that made his teeth ache, it was so cold. Puzzled why they had not offered him a bath before letting him eat in his filth amid such finery, he attributed the move to compassion, as he almost always did, being not without it himself, and sat with his coffee admiring the groomed veneer of the wooden walls. Rachmaninoff (if he) gave way to Glazunov perhaps, he could not be sure, and he began to doze in spite of himself, only to be courteously escorted to, of all things, a sauna, in whose plunge he just dangled his legs. His shoulder throbbed. Thus far, as he recalled, no one had spoken to him since the helicopter landed; the waiter had merely proffered the bottle of wine, a man in a white coat had positioned his arm for X rays and setting, while another had guided him to the sauna with manual motions, and no one else had done anything at all. In fact, he was not accustomed to conversation, his vocal cords having all but frozen up during the last few days, as they sometimes did after he had been concentrating hard on some problem. As he dressed, not in his own clothes, which had vanished, but in a one-sleeved medium gray jumpsuit provided by unseen hands, he rallied his defenses as best he could, at the same time unable to believe he knew anything vital. He just did not want to be bothered, he wanted to sleep, and he recalled letters from Tulsa, Oklahoma, that friends had received, reading, "Use this prayer sheet to tell me about the [miracle] you need. Send it to me right away because I want to get serious with God for your needs." Amused with himself for remembering something so fatuous, he nonetheless wished for the miracle of sleep, even there in the paneled room, in the easy chair with the little hinged stabilizer that lifted his feet level with his hips.

Standing alongside Clegg in the black glass underground hangar, Booth tried to rid his mind of a crusader image, but the chain mail kept his body and neck enclosed, the broadsword stood at the ready, the shield decorated with cross and dagger did not budge, and the shallow metal cone on his head got tighter and tighter. His top right eyelid twitched, perhaps from too much coffee, perhaps from living on a schedule that had no days and no nights. Clegg seemed exultant, said he was going to wear all his neckties at the same time. The big helicopter made not a sound, but it shone and it dominated them, a tranquillized mammoth insect whose mighty flapping would soon begin again. There was no sign of Mersa Fatma, but there must have been a dozen guards, in white smocks like strayed chemists. The smell of aviation fuel, keen and rather sickly, wafted to and fro on the currents of the air-conditioning. It was like being at a mechanical wake, with everyone trying to see how slowly things could be done. They had both had solid breakfasts, taken together in a canteen that reeked of new paint. Toast and some kind of sausage had stirred their spirits at the same time as taking the edge off both of them.

"We're being moved, I think," Booth had said, not quite awake. "Maybe we don't need to try to escape after all. Or maybe now more than ever."

"I wouldn't mind staying on," Clegg said with weary gravity. He looks dreadful, Booth thought: the skin of his face is paper-frail, the rings under his eyes have been scored in with sharp charcoal, his eyes are streaked with the sort of red you find in sunsets. He did not look so good himself, he knew, with cracked lips, at least five cold sores, his nose still raw from the sun, and several of his teeth still splintered along the biting edges. An hour's prudent dentistry would have worked wonders. Booth found much of the recent past, vivid and horrendous as it had been, disappearing already, perhaps because he was emptying his mind to accommodate the next crisis. "Save your misplaced humanitarianism," he told Clegg, "for yourself. The Corps doesn't need us. Now, what is that smell, something like leaf mold?"

A small door had opened in the far corner and three men came in sideways, then advanced abreast, or rather two of them carried something in a deep capacious canvas bag fitted with loops that went over their shoulders. All Booth could see was a lolling head, sunglasses, haywire hair, and he found himself wondering how the Danakil could get their hands on sedative and hypnotic drugs. Were they supertechnologists in disguise? The two men carrying Mersa Fatma as if he were a golf bag came right up to Booth and Clegg and stood, expressionless. "What now?" Booth asked one of them, but received no sign whatever that he had spoken. "Who the hell?" Clegg whispered. The only sound was that of Mersa Fatma's impeded breathing, urgent as if he had been exercising. He smelled of disinfectant and his face was wet with sweat even in the artificial chill of the hangar.

Then part of the ceiling slid away and hot sunlight blotted out the neon; Mersa Fatma began to moan and to wrinkle his nose at the same time as a pilot appeared, also led by two men, his mouth taped and his hands cuffed in front of him. When he drew level with them, he nodded, at which Mersa Fatma began to do neck exercises like a statue in a sheath. "I'm sorry," Booth said to Clegg, "I didn't think it would end like this. I take it we are all going somewhere together?" The pilot shook his head, gave a suffocated pout, and moved his linked wrists upward as if to clinch the point. The tape across his mouth was flesh colored, reaching to the angle of his jaw on either side.

Clegg grunted something about home sweet home (or Soon See Home), Booth gave a look so complex that it stayed in Clegg's mind for the next hour, imposed upon all the other looks he saw Booth produce. It was a look that said, as it were in a deployed babble, This is too unceremonious, too taciturn, a parting, with our best arias unsung, our deepest confidences unexchanged, our minds unmatched. The pilot's leathery cheeks held firm, and his eyes seemed to pulse, not with tears, but as if breathing his last. Behind the tape affixed across his mouth, something moved, not moving mouthlike but as if the whole head were trying to come to a point. Then they belted Mersa Fatma three ways into a rear seat, the rotors began to churn, and the machine lifted into a vault of combusting sunlight. It was midday, Booth said. "Why not," Clegg answered, and said not another word until they landed.

Now Booth groaned as the helicopter sank toward what clearly was the salt desert all over again: igloos, the watering hole, camels, mules and more humans than he had ever seen in his own time there. He tousled Mersa Fatma's hair as two guards lifted him out, then lowered him to waiting hands on the salt. Enigmatic cargo offloaded, thought Booth. Now we will never understand about him. Perhaps we [know him already] and should recognize him, but I'm damned if I do. All the same, he had an uneasy sense of something's having flashed in front of him, then gone forever, to his eternal cost. Forces unknown were trying to manipulate him. It was as if creatures from different worlds, contrasting dimensions, were trying to have their way with him, perhaps even to drive his mind asunder. Clegg was waving good-bye with the hand at the end of his injured arm. Baffled and exasperated, Booth gave a military cough and tried to stand, but a guard shoved him down again. The pilot was on the salt, being led by guards toward a circle of blacks clad in orange fabric. Mersa Fatma was [nowhere to be seen,] but Booth's view was impeded by his guards. The pilot vanished into the throng, then reappeared in the center of the circle, flanked by two gigantic strongmen who walked him this way and that, appearing to converse even though, as best Booth could make out, the tape was still over the pilot's mouth. At that point, Booth's mind froze, although he said something to Clegg who, in a horrorstruck lunge, bumped his face against the window. Down below, something traditional and baleful happened again as a new crew plucked Booth and Clegg sideways from it.

At about one thousand feet they banked and picked up a fresh heading. "They—they," Clegg stammered.

"I know," Booth said, "it's happened before." He craned his neck for a view of something, but all had gone, and the most he saw was black scud on the receding salt, and then only a buff plateau like a prehistoric earthwork etched with dotlike beakprints.

An hour later they were flying over fishermen cleaning their nets, the ocher dome of some tomb or temple, and what Clegg, the fisherman, recognized as *sambuks*, built of teak and rigged like cutters, their decks glazed with light that came, he said, from being coated with fish oil against the sun. How quickly he has adjusted, Booth thought, whereas I, I have no stomach at all. The helicopter hovered over a freighter and a dhow, then set down on the very end of the mole in what was surely the harbor at Djibouti, well away from the warehouses and wharves. The exchange took twenty minutes, Booth and Clegg for a tall fair youth with a scarred, even burned face, who gave them not a glance as he walked past them at the halfway point between the car he came from and the waiting helicopter. I have never learned, or learned to live with, the fact, Booth groaned, that experience ends when it ends, ragged and messy. And he felt even worse when all that happened was a transfer to the best hotel in town, where he and Clegg received a thorough medical, which resulted in Clegg's arm having to be reset and Booth's being told the boil in his rear end needed surgery, the sooner the better. Under the anesthetic, Booth talked repeatedly about a ladder and Clegg recited garbled bits of an Anglo-Saxon epic poem. Debriefing, back in Turkey, took almost a month, and much of what they said elicited only a polite skepticism to which they soon became inured, able to talk to each other at least with a measure of understanding, verging on affection, as is common with survivors.

"The open sea at last," said Clegg, not having relished the torrid delay on the Bosphorus. His white-sheathed arm hailed the sun lolling in the south across miles of shot-silk Aegean.

"You *could* cover your arm," Booth told him from the wheelchair he did not now quite need but used when on deck, almost as a vehicle of honor. His teeth had been fixed.

"I am drying it out, it always feels damp."

"You could cover it with the sleeve of your sweater rolled down."

"Don't fuss, Booth, for God's sake don't fuss. Let me enjoy the ocean."

"How green and open it is, almost like flying at high altitude."

"Never again. What will you do?" Clegg rolled his sweater sleeve halfway, making a white and dark gray contrast.

"Breathe deeply and slowly for a whole year."

"We fouled up. Funny thing, though, while it was all going on I never had any sense of doing the wrong thing, of not going by the book. Is *that* 'Lack of Moral Fiber'?"

Slyly bitter, Booth sighed. "Ah, the book. Who ever went by the book?"

"Protestants do."

"I mean military."

"But," said Clegg, "we were never *very* military, were we now?" He tugged the sleeve down all the way to the wrist.

"Look at the sun, it nearly did us in." Booth never looked at the sun now without a slight shiver of homage.

"It will in the end, it can't help doing that."

"You look like that statue of Poseidon somewhere in Sweden. Its arm sticks up just like yours, and a fountain plays over it."

"Then," said Clegg morosely, "I may have a future after all, as a decoration in some public park, somewhere in Albany maybe."

"They won't be naming any constellations after us."

"Or streets."

"Or latrines in foreign theaters of war."

"Not even that. Hell," Clegg exclaimed, "look at that sky!" It was the unquenchable superthick lazurite of an angel's eyes.

"Bluest blue," crooned Booth unself-consciously. "It goes everywhere. It doesn't stop."

"It's radiant," Clegg told him shyly.

"It sure is. It has no opinions."

"None of *us*, anyway."

"No, it has no opinions of anybody. It just is."

"And it goes on is-ing itself. Can you," Clegg teasingly asked him, "say that?"

"You just did and the sky didn't mind."

"It goes on and out, and then around." Clegg sighed the sigh of the fisherman with no pole, no catch.

"I just might go into advertising," Booth said apropos of nothing. "There might be a place."

"Things will always need advertising, they never let things look after themselves."

"Always a sell," said Booth. "What a swell afternoon."

"We've weeks of this to come. Know what?"

Booth looked blandly away and asked what.

"I'm going to read the fishing encyclopedia cover to cover. Just that." Clegg near-giggled.

"The long way home."

"The rest cure."

"The well-known tonic of the ocean voyage."

"Port outward, starboard home," Clegg mused.

"*Posh*," Booth crowed. "It's what the British used to say about their ocean voyages to India. It meant that a good berth keeps you away from the sun."

"Just what we could have used," Clegg murmured. "On the left of the ship when you were going eastward, and on the right when going westward. You would always be facing north."

"And we, right now," Booth told him, "are facing south, but our cabins are on the right and we're sailing westward. Very posh indeed!"

"Did we," Clegg wondered, "deserve it?"

"Maybe not, but it's like the last favor."

"Before the pension." Clegg gave a dry-lipped whistle.

"Just like a dream," Booth said, spacing the words out to match. "Were you scared?"

"Back there? I mean up there?"

"Both."

"I was more scared in the mountains than in the underground installation."

"And I in the desert. *I* chopped salt for a week. It seems like a week." Booth mined salt with his hands.

"I thought I was dead, I really did, but I didn't think I'd done anything wrong. How could I?"

Booth nodded and stared through the rail down at the ocean scudding by. "Quite a few knots."

"Less than the old days!" Clegg's good arm flew in a vague parabola.

"It's tempting," Booth told him quietly. "You could go all the way back to the cabins, get up speed and shoot yourself clean out of your chair into the sea."

"*You* could," said Clegg, making a pretense of affront. "I didn't mean anybody else."

"You'd pull me out."

No he wouldn't, Clegg told him curtly. With his arm . . .

"But you otherwise would," Booth insisted. "It would be your duty. As second-in-command."

"Of what?"

"Good question. Anyway, you're famous among the tribes back there."

"In a pig's eye I am."

"All things considered," Booth said, fingering his jaw as if testing the tan of his skin, "I'm none the better for any of it. It's as if somebody else lived that piece of my life for me and, in doing so, screwed up the rest of it. We didn't even make the newspapers." He took a cup.

"Not in a big way," Clegg corrected him. "There was one story."

"Yeah," Booth scowled, "they called it a malfunction."

"It sure malfunctioned us."

"For keeps," Booth snapped. "You don't want that kind of thing in the middle of your career."

"Or ever. It stops you dead."

"We survived, that's something." Booth drank all of his bouillon and slung the cup into the sea. There was no splash.

"One cup missing," Clegg chanted.

"Fucking cup," Booth snarled, then cracked a smile as he heard himself. "I was glad to discover the opposite sex again, even in the hospital."

"You always are," Clegg said dreamily. "Will we write each other over the years?"

"You bet," Booth told him crisply. "It's a deal. And maybe get drunk together, real smashed, in Cincinnati, halfway across the country."

"Chicago maybe, at the Palmer House," said Clegg from an opulent dream of deep leather chairs and twilit bars.

"Wherever." He no longer wanted to be great, only to feel so.

"You're on," Clegg said, relieved to be at home *somewhere*, even on an ocean liner inexplicably named *Mazzaroth*.

"No more Cyrano," moaned Booth.

"Already," Clegg told him, "there's a Mark Four. It was faster by fifty knots. I guess it still is."

"What a kite!"

"What a prang!"

"They no longer need us," Booth said faintly.

"*Want* is more like it." Clegg sounded euphoric.

"Good-bye, Africa," Booth said.

"No more mountains," said Clegg.

"Case closed."

"Dumb."

The steamer veered left just east of the Dardanelles and aimed its bow at the sun for half an hour as if heeding evidence of things not seen. The part of Booth that had always felt aloof from this planet now sensed that, in Mersa Fatma, it had witnessed one of Earth's holy [icons,] though for the life of him Booth couldn't see why, and Clegg had never been privy.

The slow blundering boat from Turkey to London, then from Southampton all the way to Newport News, was bad enough, even though both Booth and Clegg healed en route, chafing at every stop. Yet why complain when all they were on the way to, they assumed, was months of interrogation, by who knew whom? Sure, Clegg thought, it will be the holy army of infant inquisitors: clean-cut, blazered and flanneled young Americans mostly in glasses, with faint tans and beautifully tooled shoes, probably Rhodes Scholars, mellow fellows, brilliant and athletic and invincibly patriotic, even to Cecil Rhodes's pernicious vision of South Africa. All called Vince. They would all be young majors, Clegg decided. More than half of them queer, thought Booth. Give me the Danakili any day. No, he went on, these fellows lived on the base, to make or break the careers of officers much more active than themselves. Consecrated to the notion that brainpower mattered more than heroism, they sat in judgment after asking and listening, their hearts in it little, their hands accustomed to paperwork, their worst wound a paper cut. They would be just the sort of young Turks you thought the United State no longer had. In would march the Alphas, worn down by combat or extortionate orders, and out they would go, sucked dry, glad to go to pasture, as if their sperm had fired backward. What was the name of that damned disease? It was like an old phrase once heard in the boxing profession: you better get some extinction on your punches, or else. These were the boylike providers of Or Else.

A carpet knight, Clegg was calling himself, resolved to do himself proud, whatever they did to him next with needles or electric shock. No, they were just needling him, that was all. The way to do it, retaining as much self-control as possible, was compose an imaginary love letter to some woman, a love letter to an imaginary woman. So as to give nothing away. Yet what was a carpet knight? Entire areas of recollection were floating away from him like rafts, then heaving into view again, blistering with their Technicolor. A carpet knight, O my beloved, Clegg was murmuring, is a man devoted to pleasure and idleness: a Me. In the early days of the Jamestown colony, dearest, most of the settlers were carpet knights with neither the wit nor the will to get by in the wilderness. *Kär-pat-nīt/n.* Where had he seen it printed thus? They have injected me at least once, he told her, making words come to mind that he had never used, might never need again: *bonkers, owlish, flabbergast, dumbfound,* coming from all over the world, but basically harmless like obsessive malaprops. I address them with a surreptitious hoarseness of my own invention, mingling a fanged whistle into it. You know how it goes on TV, when the announcer yells out the name of the boxing referee and the poor guy hangs his head, amazed to be singled out as if he were a third contestant. Well, they try me out with little hints dropped to see if memory will latch onto them and blow everything. All they learn is that my tones have a lilt, I make the vowels loll in my throat, saying only a hello that sprawls out in the air, elongated and cozy, revealing my easy good nature. If I am only a little friendly about nothing, my heaven-sent one, they will let me go, they will find out nothing at all, not even my longing to know what the torrent lily is, I having heard the phrase so often without ever looking it up, or my yearning for a 1949 Mooney Mite, advertised at twelve and a half thousand dollars, serious inquiries only, 812-268-0924. New prop. 1023 total time. 210 hours since overhaul. Rebuilt in 1980 with Stits cover, always hangared. What a beauty: sold by now; I should have grabbed it when I could, and then I could have gone places waddling and ogling. What they need to know is not about the Mooney Mite, that peacetime bird, but about where I am from; yet what comes to mind lies between them and me.

How like judges in ermine, I tell them, my beloved, are gravestones in the snow. Gorillas have oozy, tarry faces, oozy tar for faces. After his wife died, the king who built the Taj Mahal for her went in there alone and came out a week later, shrunken and white-haired. That is how love can take you, my gorgeous perfect one. If I do this for a year, you will be born, you will appear in the flesh.

What have I learned, beloved?

Only that, no matter how hard they press you, never mind how honeyseductive the entreaties of the questioner (who loves me almost as much as I you), there is no getting past the portcullis of amour. Each time they come near to fishing something drastic out of me, the shimmering veil of your exotic presence gets in the way, as if we were all trapped in a poem by Shelley, and, oh, the radiance, the fog of the stained glass of your adored form, throws their minds out of focus. I hope you understand what I am saying: verbalized love cocoons me, even though you never were, we never met. It is, perhaps, like [loving God,] and being a mystic sheathed in piety even while going to the stake and being burned. The more I intensify this lovingness of the mind, the less they get out of me. They hear my answers, but don't understand the adoration.

The other veil or baffle, less hectic but just as ravishing, is my love of the air, of air's craft, such as the Mooney Mite, about which they need to know nothing. I am going to get through this, simulating, marshalling my fervors.

Yes, I tell my questioner, weeklong I write a letter to my beloved. I sing my tribute to the air and its occupants. Your flesh feels like fever, my revered one, your hands tremble among the hooks and your eyes blaze like incinerated zinc. Your hair swirls up crisp and crackling under the comb.

What he heard next had genuine stage quality, from opera or symphony concert, propelled down a long trumpet by lungs paid a goodish paycheck. He had heard it before, but translated into a cry in the night, or a disemboweled shriek from over the toast and marmalade of the breakfast table, or the cut throat coughing its last under the railroad bridge as yet another Ripper got to work. It was akin to the stiff-upper-lipped gabble of the airman in trouble, up in the high clouds with a halted engine gathering snowflakes, but using the radio to joke about the weather, not wishing to sound panicky: "You got a little old snowman, sir, up here, about to turn blue. I am a glider, sir, descending through seven." Clegg had heard himself sound like this, pleading, joshing, hoping for vectors to somewhere safe, frightened yet unable to fix on his fear, instead, in some abstracted oblivion, trying to recall ancient names for modern acids, vitriol for sulfuric, aqua fortis for nitric — now, what was hydrochloric? And what was Aqua Regia?

Then he heard Barney Booth, hectoring him about his, Booth's, still being pilot in command, whatever else had taken place. "You still gotta empty the honey bucket, Rupe." Clegg turned his inner ears away and fixed on the apparition he adored.

Yes, my angel, he said inside himself, that's the clue. I can't tell if they are using liquid or electricity. It squirts through me, turning me inside out, making my babble, my shriek, into theirs. They own me, right now. They tell me what they want and only a little renegade bit of Lieutenant Colonel Clegg's brain resists, tells them to shove off. Can they be using one of the old acids? Is that why the liquid hurts so much, making me quiver and slaver? Why bother, he wondered. If they keep this up for a month, they will find out everything; but isn't everything easily found in some aeronautical encyclopedia? Surely they will be doing these things to Booth as well, wherever he is, but he will hold out longer, being senior. The hero-worshipping part of Clegg took over, convincing him that, whatever he said, however he resisted, Booth would go one better, Barney Booth, the arch-hero.

In that case, he decided, all I have to do is convince them I know nothing, somehow tilt their attention to him. He would persuade them he was too junior to have any top-secret information at his disposal. He just flew, he did not think. The trouble was that Clegg enjoyed inventing his ghost woman, his shuntling beloved, even if, at first, she only came through to him as a toe, an ankle, velvet to his touch, supple even as he peered at it by the caustic light of his overtaxed brain.

Gorgeous one, he whispered, but found that crass.

Exquisite one, he tried next, but found that fussy.

Beauty of beauties came next, yet he dismissed that as derivative; if he was going to resist his interrogators, he would need someone, some eternal feminine new-minted and unique. No formulas, then, and none of those automatic, grandiose Latin-American *piropos*. In the end she would tease him, laugh at him, for trying too hard not to divulge things that, sooner or later, both he and Booth would know in common—there was only one answer to the really tough questions hurled at them in manicured British, not American English, but a somewhat sappy silken variety. His interrogators had been expensively well bred. Well educated, then. His problem now was to get her, still nameless, edging into the light out of a mythic darkness in which Cleopatra and Eve mingled. She would have all the best of them all, but in no way resemble any. And, being a potent image, she would remain real for ages, long after these agonizing interviews were over and he was repatriated—oh blessed word, evoking half-gallon two percent milk, cable TV, automatic garage doors, and whistling microwaves. In other words, Clegg, the somewhat sentimental materialist, was attempting something outlandish, not so much stealing fire from the gods as love-calling the blessed damozel out from the sex dens of prehistory: a chore for which he was not properly trained.

Only under circumstances such as these would he have attempted it, but desperation had made a savvy artful dodger out of him, boosting him to a metaphysical plane he hardly ever occupied. The very metal in his feet became the batteries of his inspiration. He became creative. In his mind's eye he reached out for a ringing telephone only to set his hand on hers, stationed there in the trembling vacuum sponsored by his delirium. Try again, Clegg, he said. That will never do: too routine. This time, in the very act of refusing their question about somewhere in Turkey, he uttered one of his few bits of Turkish—*bur ev*, meaning the house—and with his as yet intact fingers began tracing her outline, full-body, on a nearby plank to which he had been manacled. A few hooded men uninvolved in the interrogation stood watching him, copying his drawing on yellow pads. As soon as his hands stopped moving, they left, arguing fiercely.

Now a detail or two came through, began arbitrarily to form. She was dressed in soft crimson with, about her waist, a burly golden chain. Feetless and faceless, she seemed to float, not ethereal at all but almost zoftig: a well-fed woman evicted from his dreams, and almost enough to sap the interrogators' fluids of their magic. Now she drifted away, a torso flaring on takeoff, wafting ever higher until he could see her no longer and returned his mind to the pain, if pain it was; rather, it was a needling intrusion probing more and more finely the farther it went, leaving behind it on his synapses flecks of merest mousedirt, fractionally just enough to produce an ache that, combined with a thousand other aches, created an expert pang of compliance. He wanted to betray himself to get it over with, but the memory of his lady—wench, damozel, bint, goddess, angel, fairy queen, whatever she was—kept him straight, saved him at the last moment. The babble that had begun to be the harbinger of truth became prefix to obsession. Just a body in crimson, she saved him again from their clever askings, and he wondered how much longer the interrogation would go on, and slapped himself with the answer: until he learned to love the whole of humankind.

Obliged to fabricate her, he spilled over with delight.

Resigned to losing her, he cast about frantically for other ways of parrying his questioners. Perhaps they would take him for a madman and, like American Indians of old, let him go free as one helplessly involved with some supernatural dimension where ordinary braves did not belong. Who, then, in history, he asked himself, did this kind of thing and got away with it? Who supped this kind of junk and went back home to his toys? He knew no history, but could not rid himself of the notion that several senior men had exercised mind over body, imagination over absence, to superlative effect.

It had been less exalted men, but who? He dropped the matter, with all his force trying to summon her back against the next squirt of the drug, against which, he had heard, normal steady men stabbed a providentially found nail deep into their palm, or a shard of glass. This was no doubt harder; Booth would have done fine with nail or glass, but he would never have chosen this way. Clegg could not resist condemning himself for choosing the way of voluptuous weakness rather than that recommended by the military manual of covert operations, which expressed the priorities as curare, pain, abuse. He had lost his pill, chosen against pain, and was keeping oral abuse heaped upon the interrogator for last. Then they would kill him out of hand.

All he could marvel at was this sprig of womanhood arising from the core of his resistance: an unreliable phantom, to be sure, since she wafted to and fro, but she had certainly been in evidence, as lawyers said, and she would surely come back, with sausage or revolver in hand, eager to see justice done. There was a sweet style and a harsh style, as among the old Italian poets, and hers was the former.

Surely, he rebuked himself, only a pedant would want to know her name. You don't call her up by name; she arrives to greet your wanting. She is a flame, not a walking folder. All the same, something in him never eradicated wanted her named, not as a means of identifying and retrieving her among the fugitive hordes of mystifying beings, but for neatness. And, under such duress as needle and fluid put upon him, he came up with names of no great dignity:

Could she then be called Aqua Regia? [Royal Water?]

It wasn't bad. But what about her being a Marge, as from Margaret? Or a Marg with a hard *g*?

Royal Water was more like it, though he disliked its regal sound, which Ethel Dredge, say, lacked. Perhaps he could fight acid with acid. All he knew was that, according to what survived of his meticulously kept calendar, it was spring back home. The temperature sign outside the A & P would already have scrambled its numbers into something that resembled Japanese, and the small woodpeckers with a red head-flash would be staking out territory by hammering their beaks against the metal signs on stanchions at roadside.

Now he noticed that two of his interrogators, the young one with the sardonic lisp and the older one with almost no forehead at all (his hair grew so far forward), correctly addressed him as Colonel, a civil convenience invented by the British, Clegg thought; they called an air vice-marshal an air marshal, so life was full of empty little promotions that gave you the sound of eminent futurity. He wondered what ranks these interrogators were accustomed to dealing with and how their sense of protocol went. It was well known that the most punctilious inquisitors were the most fiendish, as if amenity sanctioned savagery. So far savagery had been that of the needle, into the vein rather beneath the fingernail or into the eyeball; but you never knew. The trick, he assumed, was that while you were building your internal antianswering device you did not lull yourself into thinking these questioners were honorable men. Perhaps they were making fun of him, aping the Creator who, when he made the first zebra, knew it had no hope of behaving as anything else. So, when they injected him, Clegg, they knew he had no chance of being anyone, anything, they didn't want him to be. He was will-less. Or so they thought, having no inkling of Clegg's phantom woman who already, in the tender tantrums he forced from her, had appeared to him with his heart in her hand, rippling and contorting, telling him to eat it raw and become immortal. Like a wild card in a sedate game of poker, this image both encouraged him and daunted him, making him believe he would have to lose his life to survive the interrogation. In which case it was hardly worth conjuring her up out of nowhere. He might as well agree to die and have done with it, answering or refusing; even if he answered, he suspected, they would shoot him out of hand anyway.

Would Booth handle things differently? Was that what Booth, some-where, perhaps in the next room, was doing? Had he already finished, his corpse dumped among the rotting figs and the putrid rice? Clegg aban-doned that line of conjecture and addressed himself once more to the cre-ation of his salvatory lady, to the fleshing out of that ankle, that tentative toe. She must have a leg or two, and all the rest, importuning him in the very act of saving him through grace. Why had he thought *grace*? Perhaps he meant graciousness, not gracefulness. It was certainly not a religious act he was performing; seen in the round, full length, she would resemble no saint, no angel. A whore-savior was more like it.

At least he thought that, all the preceding matter having occupied a mere five minutes of his interrogation, until a blazing cloud hovered in front of him, like an airplane on fire and ready to plunge, but hovering in that compromise of forward motion unfinished and gravity so far cheated. The cloud *he* had not come up with, yet he felt an unusual urge to eat it, biting through fire as in some circus test. Then it was gone. The ankle and the toe replaced it, the red robe hovered above them, empty and starched. This was the end of the future, Clegg thought; his evasions had failed, and his tombstone would say only "Thick lips and a peaceful demeanor." One of those who had committed *huggee*, the political form of scrupulosity, or *pusillanimata*, otherwise called spiritual debility, Clegg marveled at the terms that came to mind to describe what ailed him. From Booth? From the military? Never. Actually, he had thought he wasn't doing too badly, having disdained all questions about the Cyrano and its performance, and with a spiritual bodyguard to his credit, at least in part. Here he was going downhill, after surviving in the desert, almost as if he had forgotten to be brave, rather than being frightened of being so. For what was bravery but an abstract design you forced the body into, heedless of consequences? Not fear but oblivion sapped him.

In that case, he commanded himself, all you have to do is tell yourself what to do. Don't blanch. Don't funk it. *Remember* to bring her back; you are going to need her. And more of her arrived than ever before, except for her face, blank as a muffin, with neat designated bosom (nothing swollen) and satisfactory legs, a skimpy rear. She had the kind of figure that zoftig women aspire to, and are tormented with by advertisers. It all made sense. He was far from being lustful. It wasn't that kind of situation at all, and she was going to be more of a tourist guide than a whore, more a good-conduct bridesmaid than a lewd chatterbox from a 900 number. Clegg spruced himself up mentally and, after taking stock of her, decided how to use her best, talking about her as if she were the Cyrano itself, explaining how she was put together and weaving into that palaver some time-honored jokes from the Air Force: How do you design a wing that will not tear off? Go to the toilet roll, observe, and then perforate the wing root, for never has toilet roll sheet torn away yet. They let it pass, knowing he had to sprinkle a little buffo into his stuff about streamlining, air brakes and waste gates. Everything he said they took on trust, even as he ogled his Aqua Regia by truth-serum light, no nail in his palm, no shard of glass.

"So, Colonel Clegg," said the younger, "you can attain astronaut altitude?"

"She sees the curvature of the earth," he answered, blathering in a dream, "and the air is mauve."

"And there is only one of you."

"She is the only one of her kind, newly invented."

"We are all friends here," the one with the low hair said.

"That being so," Clegg retorted, "what's this new tradition of interrogating a friendly officer just back from a severe ordeal? If that's the new friendship, the latest in collegiality, I'll join another air force pronto. You guys have something on your shoulders. Not a chip, but a timberland."

"The Clegg sarcasm again," said low-hair.

"The very same, sir." Clegg occasionally in his checkered career made minimal concessions to those in power, but he never let it go too far. He greased his rapier, that was all.

They began again but he somehow contrived not to hear them, stuffing his ears with visuals, closing his eyes with tactiles, in a word using synesthesia against them like a man inspired. Beyond the rank of captain, he thought, nobody deserved to be treated like this. It was so Japanese, the nation who actually evolved for young officers the exact degree a bow should be at: 20 degrees for a distant how-do-you-do?, 30 for bowing to a senior officer, and 45 degrees for an apology. In a way, he supposed, officers committing hara-kiri were executing the supreme bow, no more, no less.

They redosed him, and his Aqua Regia began to falter, to diminish; she beckoned to him in panic with disappearing hands, a ghost in whom nobody believed enough. At all costs he must get her back, willing her until his skull ached, but trapped now within a poisonous nimbus she could not cross. With a flash of disintegrating crimson she was gone, levitating away into the muggy air of midday. Meals and times and bowel movements no longer figured in his world. He was merely a hunk of physical potential, a remnant of himself, answering now with nervous promptness, using words such as *fabric* and *noseplate* and *gear* with fuzzy aplomb, hardly aware of what he meant, but determined to confuse, dragging a metaphor from corsetry or maquillage to make an aeronautical point, beginning with *tail* and ending with *flair*, which he wanted them to read as *flare*.

It was not enough, though. They took his ambivalences with a smile, recognizing a private lingo without realizing there was an entity or effigy behind it, sponsoring and shaping it. He wanted to do more, but finished by making motions with his hands, almost in parody of fighter pilots' night at the pub, all hands gesturing amid the smoke the maneuvers that had saved the day, from the Hun in the sun to being at thirty thousand feet with nothing on the clock. Again they humored him, eager for the tiniest seed of data: anything he might let slip while he grumbled, They have the wreck of the plane, why don't they look?

Proud of himself in his jumbled state for having let slip something so trivial as their high-protein breakfasts, Clegg began to allow his mind afield, mentioning Upper Heyford and Glastonbury in England (where they were *not* based), and the radar-jamming capacity of a plane other than the Cyrano. Piqued with him, or perhaps as part of a carefully devised plan, his interrogators told him Booth was in the next room. What was the outside body temperature of the Cyrano at cruise speed? If he refused to say, they would chop off one of Booth's fingers. Pausing, debating, then plunging, he said what it was not and heard the smack of the ax, the howl of pain. Strangely enough, he felt more relief that Booth was near than he felt guilt at causing his mutilation. Did he believe them? Cut off mine, he said. Or show me Booth. No, they said, we will ask you several more direct questions, and when Colonel Booth runs out of fingers, we will remove one of your hands. Through a narcotic mist he heard this, knowing he would have to think now that they had become impatient with him. He cried out to Booth, but to no avail, though he discovered the room's echo. It was cool in here because it was underground. When Clegg gave another fake answer about the Cyrano, he again heard the smack of the ax, the muffled cry. Now he decided to answer seriously, but about the Raven, a smaller aircraft. Dizzy and clouded, he nonetheless felt able to scramble the facts, introducing his captors to a plane already known about. How much did they know about the top-secret Skunk Works where the Cyrano was designed and built?

Wherever Aqua Regia had receded to, she was no longer responding; she could not be summoned up, by either cry or prayer. Anything but this. Another life. A life of sorts.

* * *

With or without Booth, whom they surely had not mangled in the other room. One peep and he would feel better. He hated this quivering dizziness that weakened his knees and made his ears buzz. He kept groping for something from another magazine (Clegg was nothing if not a riffler of pages, a connoisseur of nattily described lives), an article about British universities, or rather Oxford and Cambridge, where, he'd read, a student had a tutor who was his accomplice, his coach, his ally, against the examiners, whom he did not get to know unless they gathered in plenary session after the student had performed brilliantly in the examinations. How different, he thought, from our own almost incestuous system in which your teacher is your examiner. Now, is that how I see Booth? Is he the teacher who examines me, or is he my coach against the examiners? Does he want me to make full colonel, as I now never will? He could not sort it out, having always found Booth imperious and cool—a glacial ally at best—whereas he should have been brotherly and genial. When you fly with someone, Clegg said aloud, you do not necessarily become bosom friends. Then, to himself, I wonder what grade I am going to get. Who grades *him*? After all this. We both get F, we both flunk, and even now they are probably devising a way of abolishing us, wiping us out as if we were tactless entries in the *Soviet Encyclopedia*.

Any minute now, they are going to show me Booth's ruined hand, or roll his head from out of a plastic garbage sack. Never, they would save him for more adroit maneuvers. They are far from done with us. This is only the overture to a butcher's night out. The truth drug has failed, hasn't it? Or is the drug making me feel all these things? You think you're fooling them, but you're not. Gentlemen, I confess: all my life I could never remember the two main things about the sound barrier. So I wrote them on a little card and carried it everywhere, even on missions. One: Compressibility. Two: Inertia coupling. Name six blues other than Prussian or navy. Forest. Space. Madonna. Linden. Gulf. Bay. Thus the updated extravaganza of an interior decorator.

He was really cooking now, a picaro of tangents willing to take them anywhere for the price of a finger. When he got really old, able just to potter about in a small apartment in Santa Monica or Santa Barbara, he would tear up his paper plates into tiny pieces, tossing them into the garbage as confetti, eager to reduce to the minimum the signs of his presence on Earth. Out of shame. Or, having become fond of the strip of emery board he filed his nails with, he would go on using it until there was nothing abrasive about it, just a little rough curlicue here and there, and it would take him days, then weeks, then months, to file his nails, quite obliterating his other activities. What a way out: the saint of buff. Even Udet killed himself, after a distinguished career. Others did not, but did they feel the shame? Sensing he had power over his captors, Clegg wanted this part of his ordeal to be over with, not even thinking this was the last act of his career. Always he thought, at the very end someone would pluck him out burning: a dramatic, fancy phrase, but one indicative of faith, perhaps in Allah, who was responsible for everything. And when, if you happened to be a Muslim, you said "Allah willing," you meant that Allah took a declared, vital interest in you and actually made a decision about you. Nothing flukey here, taking you at random as in the temples of Las Vegas, but a probing, inquisitive deity, deciding the best thing for you and utterly impervious to pleas. Did he really want something so stern? So *ad hominem?* He was proud of his spotty Latin, no use to him at Mecca, of course.

If he got out of this mess, he promised to grovel and pray, to be a decent man to all men. Even life of the most reduced or median kind had some merit now as the huge fan of fear began to cool him down, readying him for the decision about Booth's next finger. Clegg had heard that senior officers, before being promoted, were led to a room where, in a hole in the wall, sat the back of a human head. If you refused to fire a pistol into the head when ordered, you failed, you were retired as deficient in officerly qualities, not allowed even to go back to what you had been doing in your mediocre, unbutcherly way. And now this. He would have preferred condemned tennis, in which you played with two kinds of balls: routine, and those loaded with explosive.

What made him more or less happy was how his fuzzy mind brought back to him the events of every day. He was accustomed, when not flying, to finding he could not remember something he knew well. The word or name just wouldn't come, and now, through sheer willpower, he had brought about the same thing under interrogation. Or he *thought* it wouldn't come. Perhaps, though, he was babbling vital names and facts without knowing it; the lips that seemed still to him were moving fast. What he wanted was paralysis of spontaneous reference: not to know what he knew, hiding it like a black sheep on a starry night. Never again was he going to know what he had known; maybe his brain was permanently injured by, how many, at least three injections. The drug interfered with his mental visor; but, unless he was wholly unhinged, he could tell if what he said was fact or fiction. The problem was to know if he knew all he was saying.

To focus his thoughts, he raised one hand and made a mock aircraft with his fingers, extending them close together with his thumb at right angles to his palm to do duty for a wing. Wasn't there, he remembered with a wry pout, a German plane in World War Two, a Blohm und Voss with only one wing, or rather with a wing on only one side? It *flew*. It worked. Almost anything was possible. Then he glided the hand forward, suddenly dropping middle finger to simulate an undercarriage dangling at right angles to his palm. He tried to close his fore- and fourth finger over the gap, but failed to make the fingers meet. His interrogators frowned, but took it in as an image of possible use. Down it flew, approaching an invisible runway. He even made the whining sound of jets spooling down and landed the plane on his thigh. There: something demonstrated, something won. Some time wasted, at least. Then he sent it straight up like a Harrier jet in vertical takeoff, the jet engines whining again, the gear at the correct altitude flipping up into the fuselage of his other fingers. Now he flew his hand again, in devout mockery of what he gave his life to. He was being brave, or so he thought, *seeming* to communicate, especially when he began to do his hoarsest, most uncouth whistles, suggesting a blasé pilot at the controls, no doubt with cigar and white silk scarf, finding his chore far too easy, amusing himself with one of those tuneless, unconstructive whistles that high-geared sensibilities utter during boredom. In part it was a whistle of the relative wind, so-called, as it hit the leading edge of his hand's wing; in part it was the sound of the wind finding gaps in the leaky cockpit cover. In part it was the whistle of the totally abstracted man happy in his work.

Yet it was no doubt not enough for them, so, on a sudden inspiration, he began to recite for them something he had culled from a specialized magazine. Sapphire fibers, he told them, were the coming thing. Airplanes were already built of them. "Ceramic science," he blurted out. "They use a composite made of sapphire fibers in a nickel aluminide intermetallic matrix for future fabrication of turbine engine compressors. There! And exhaust nozzles. Tough at low temperatures. Why, ladies all over the planet will be trading in their engagement rings just to give supersonic airplanes the shove they need." He had really told them something this time: easily worth two fingers. Now they would put Booth's fingers back. If they had really cut them off.

"Actually," he added, "most of the aircraft we're supposed to have flown are being dismantled for museums." They watched him with incredulous contempt, wondering if he was worth persisting with. He had told them he was Steve Ishmael, but they knew who he was, even when he said he was Nat Gonella and Woody Hirdhitze, or simply Recon to his friends. It all went by them, providential fluff from a man who, did they but know, collected pieces of his hair in an envelope when he did a trim, hoping one day to construct a hairpiece against future need. Clegg peered ahead with big round blue eyes that looked as if they needed restraining.

After some haggling, they decided to let him come out of it and rest. They already knew most of what he might have told them, and now they were beginning to collect about him the kinds of data only a novelist would need. Given a small shiny brown cigar case, he smiled, opened it, found two fingers, failed to recognize them, and told them to take him to the room where you had to memorize the patterns of a tiger. He had had enough, given away too much, and confirmed their notion of his moral fiber. Clegg, they found, was a softie, easily manipulated and terminally used up, having achieved nothing very much save many repetitions of the same role. Unpromotable. Demotable. Ripe for disposal. He should have been ushered out of the Air Force years ago but had stayed on as some kind of remittance man, a feather not so much in someone's cap as up someone's ass.

Booth was already asleep, his first dream some infernal whirligig of memory trying not to remember itself, like a stick bilking the rocket that made it soar. He wanted, of all things, to be back among the Danakili miners, at sea on the salt like them, and no longer in command of anything, not even of his huge scarred hands. Even now, in spite of his poor performance, a plan was going forward; someone had found something for him to do, appropriate to his skills and his sentimental leanings. There would be no hurry. He would be told to take his time, to go as slowly as the Cyrano went fast. In other words, an embarrassment was going to be put to eminent use. Clegg's guess about the tiger, or his brave petition about it, had not been that far off the mark, but there would be no tiger, nothing that live, only a colicky peace.

When a man changes from hero to research animal, it is better that he not know about it, otherwise he will play up to the magnifying lens, fawn on the fabricators of squared-paper curves, and in general corrupt himself by trying to please. Heroes build themselves of sterner stuff, making of their very intractability a virtue; lenses, curves, and concepts of pleasantness follow in their wake, mere additives to the spectacle of moral and physical splendor. In the old days, interrogators and assessors said among themselves, Booth and Clegg had a touch of the wunderkind, when they were less than human, more than red in tooth and claw: *asking for it*, as someone said, and thrilled when they got it, bloodied face, punished bowels, broken limbs. It was not that they had, since then, done anything wrong. The Cyrano had only itself to blame and the Cold War, or the absence of it, whose fault was that? Hardly theirs. Yet, although the conflict had abated, the imperial mood had far from waned, and the apparatus of truculent deviousness had not been dismantled. Simply, Booth and Clegg had had bad luck, an event attributable to metal fatigue and improper maintenance: an enigma their masters wanted to make sense of.

Hence the rigmaroles, disguised as debriefing (a word that Clegg smiled at because it evoked more the panty raid than a serious collection of military facts). What both men wanted most was to talk to each other again, to thrash things out or to reminisce within safety's silken rope. Vaguely, Clegg knew he wanted to read again, something obviously Hemingwayan, about horses tromping through deep snow, all done in simple words that horses understood; Booth, far from done with, though no more expected to yield anything valuable than Clegg did, fancied something strict and bold, perhaps a four-mile run, or a hundred push-ups, wholly unaware that Clegg had now begun to worry about selling him down the river, letting all his fingers go even at the expense of his own hand. The question had not come up of Booth's being executed, not quite, but he knew he would have allowed it to happen. He would have gone on refusing, dodging the drug's effects, until there was nothing for it: to convince him to speak, they would have rolled Booth's head along the rug toward him, out of that see-through plastic garbage bag, and then he would have told, even remembering what he had never known, hysterically spilling his all and its hinterland just to keep a head on his shoulders. Wouldn't he? If the case of the two fingers meant anything, the answer was yes; his senior colleague was expendable after, for so long, being quite otherwise. In those days, Booth would have gone to the block without demur, happy to go down without a fight other than the one with his own emotions and nerves. The role of hero was quite open to him and he knew how to assume it—without too much pondering. Perhaps the Danakili had knocked the metaphysical stuffing out of him. His old taste for sulfur and fire had deserted him, much as someone grows tired of lobster.

Yet Clegg wondered if his own so-called heroism had merely turned inside out, assuming a more callous form, an audacity from which goodness of heart had been sucked. Perhaps letting Booth's fingers be removed one by one was an act of courage in a new octave, still within the category of what many other men (or women) would not dare to do, yet of refined flagrance not like the predictable old deeds. Surely it took guts to make such a thing happen, and not so much indifference to your fellow officer as an algebraic rather than arithmetical view of pain, humiliation, and death.

So Clegg ruminated, coming down from the drug, in yet another room of epic anonymity in Virginia, land of aromatic earth and ruddy faces. Not that eager to reason things through, he nonetheless kept his mind open to some appetizing, vivid explanation from which he emerged either guiltless or newly purified, at last behaving like his own man, no longer a formula-spouting subordinate, nobody's pussy anymore. He was worth huge dark orchestral chords, oxen beheaded, calves roasted. He fretted, though, wondering why now, after all those years, he had graduated from spontaneous (although querulous) courage to something like the Romantic view of selfishness. To come down so far in the world usually demanded a huge excuse, but he had none save inertia, worry, middle age. Again and again he reversed the deal, wondering what Booth would have done for or against *him*; would he have betrayed *him*, let him go bleeding down the chute like a young, disreputable heifer, or what? Certainly to a senior a junior was expendable, but there was also another angle: a senior was responsible for his men, his man, *his people*, and there was an almost holy bond obliging him to put himself last, whether it cost him his life, his fingers, a hand, or not.

Somewhere in Booth's brain there was an inscription like an old cave painting that told him what to do, requiring that he never be in doubt. Clegg knew no such thing, having learned heroism rather than having it sprout from between his shoulder blades like a bulletproof vine. It was a big difference, he thought, having perhaps to do with testosterone. Certain men marched in front of others, and nobody questioned their precedence. Marching in front was how they got their kicks, born to dominate as they were. Therefore, Clegg thought (shuddering at the effrontery of his logic), those to whom it did not come naturally to lead were entitled to less than honorable maneuvers just to keep themselves brave. How was that for speciousness? He was not sure, but he knew that within his skull he had a machine that would serve his backsliding and eventually convert it into a diadem of sullen pride. In one of his poorest moments, he had almost caught sight of himself saying *To hell with him*, I am drugged to the hilt, I have no idea what I am doing or saying, so *let* them chop his finger off, his head. I am not any longer my brother's keeper or his kennel, his blanket, his yes-man. It had gone something like that. Had he been a student of classics rather than a riffler of magazines, he would have seen how, like a hero of the French playwright Corneille, he confused the spectator by multiplying the obstacles he had to overcome. Yearning for an intellectual passion that blazed and burned, Clegg ended up with self-serving excuses—he admitted as much—but excuses to which he was entitled. He had not signed on to be perfect. And, taking those appallingly difficult ground-school examinations that admitted him to the Cyrano's cockpit, he had construed the resultant headaches as badges of honor, like old-style German fencing scars. He too had been at Göttingen in the olden days and bared his cheek to the blade. Would he ever, he wondered, have been such a killer of men as the renowned Winston Churchill, that unbridled amateur strategist? What was a Clegg to a record such as that? Sir Winston Clegg. He smiled: it had a rococo sound, it almost worked on the plane of dignity and fame; if only he had been a painter, school of Marrakech.

He saw it now, who these fledgling interrogators were, with their giggly high Rhodes Scholar voices, their squeaks of wit and fitful pinches at one another's rears. They were experts on classical philology, knew ancient battles by heart on Crete and at Brundisium, and had studied economics as a sly aside. They perpetuated one another like an arcane civil service. They were supposed to absorb a tradition of natural vitality and civilized ease, but they ended up despising the Cleggs and the Booths who got out there and did the dirty work, put their lives on the line and returned the worse for wear, scarred and spoiled, no longer fit for arduous duty. These were the *perfesser smarts*, as Clegg dubbed them, young and frivolous until fifty, the equivalent in other professions of the senior-juniors, brought onto the strength because they were gushily nice and knew what to do at a military cocktail party. Clegg longed to parachute a dozen of them down to the Danakili salt miners, by them to be processed and matured, and then, if they were lucky, debriefed: in other words, on their return, they would suffer the indignity of having their shorts pulled down and their penises painted red. Something like that. It was almost a class aversion that he felt. These were the wimps who evaded the draft, owned real estate in Canada or Bermuda, and jerked off into condoms while listening to Ravel's *Bolero*. Not that Clegg was uneducated, or undereducated; it was just that he had taken courses in military history (modern), recent literature, and celestial navigation, in the end accumulating a hodgepodge that qualified him only as an aspirant. One day, he had always vowed, he would dust the musical appreciation off his transcript and hit the books for several years, doing the serious stuff from business administration to phenomenology, and then become president or dean of a small college on the theory that men of action move easily into positions of administrative power.

Fresh from the lions' den, Daniel was the just the man to run a cathouse—Clegg laughed at that one, wondering how esoteric his wit was and if it would pass muster among the Rhodes suits who really ran the military with here a giggle, there a sneer. Did he really care? Other countries called these people, collectively, Intelligence, a berserk personification if ever he'd seen one, as if there were other collectives called Memory, Taste, and Jubilation. One day he would examine his decorations and medals to see what they really stood for: where he had been and what he had done, wondering if his exploits were worth, oh, fifty extra A's in whatever subjects. Yes, he told himself, after my F in ass-licking and my D in obsequiousness, I had no hope, and here they are, these bastards, grooming themselves as courtiers, that's what, while we do the honors on the field of blood. Boy, am I a vet and proud of it. I could eat ten of these needleshovers for breakfast and still have room for a pan-fried hypocrite.

This was what he called his Hamlet feeling, not that he was well versed in Shakespeare, but he knew more than enough about the reputation of the Bard's plays to get by, always able in a difficult conversation to retreat while executing a true slice from the *esprit d'escalier*: "Yes, but think how in the old days, *Hamlet* occasioned much more comment than *Titus Andronicus*," and he was gone before they knew if he meant the play or the man in either case. He had discovered that, if you spoke only of eponymous works (*Adam Bede, David Copperfield*), people had to apply themselves to what you said with double fervor. It was a way of moving on, leaving behind you a thicket of dubiety as rank as marsh gas. So he had had his social triumphs too: not many, but enough for him to linger on in the small hours over his favored whiskey medley: scotch mixed with bourbon, no ice. This belt soon floored him, but not before he had reviewed his bons mots of the day or evening and found them adequate for a man whose education was a shallow miscellany—just enough, as he liked to say, to keep a dying man cheerful as he looked back on his biography, especially if he was drowning. Why he himself had not been assigned to Intelligence, he had no idea. Perhaps, in the military, if you opted for one big thing, such as copilot of the Cyrano, you couldn't have another; that was as much as they could extend you. Besides, they had shaped your mind for so long, they wanted a return on their investment.

None of the courtiers so much as dirtied his hands on an airplane, and, it was said, they used sugar tongs to hold themselves at urinals, which of course had led to a whole range of in-jokes about tweezers and fire tongs. Clegg might have enjoyed being privy to such banter, he thought, which was the true humor of the Bantu. But he had never heard the jokes. It was like his knowledge of Shakespeare, always at second hand. There were just too many societies from which he had been excluded, so, in a way, piloting the Cyrano was ideal for him: just what a foolhardy recluse, as some called him, required, believing everything that Booth told him, except that Booth was no courtier either, and certainly no reader of plays and books. These things Booth left for the afterlife, for armchairs on the rim of hell, knowing that by then there would be no temptation to try out in life what he had picked up from a book. By then the die would be cast. Not so, Clegg had once told him. "It's all shadowboxing, Colonel. I heard about this Dante feller who arranged everybody on this or that level in hell or paradise, like a grocer stocking his shelves. Now, who the hell was Dante to know who belonged where? What right had he? All the same, it's a darned good way of letting your friends know what you think of them. He lined up the dead as well according to how he felt about them, and they were in no position to argue. It must be wonderful to tidy up the universe like that and kind of exempt yourself from having to be anywhere at all. Is that how it feels to run the Pentagon?"

Booth had yawned, but that was his way of showing ravenous interest, and many had been put off by it. Clegg knew about an awful lot of stuff, he had thought; he is a prince of the secondhand, all of which worries him to death, and then he flies wonky. Clegg would never fly the Cyrano again, but he did not wish to. What he wanted, most of all, was the scales to fall from his eyes and show him what was really going on: not the usual old pretense, but some new fakery worse than ever. What did they want and why? What had the needle wielders been trying to prove? If *he*'d been running things, he would have shipped Booth and him to some sanatorium in Wyoming under assumed names. He stopped. Maybe this *was* a sanatorium in Wyoming, and he was Jenkins, Booth was Smith. It could be as ludicrous as that. How, he wondered in a half-quoting self-mesmeric mode, can the person in a closed system verify anything about it? The spirochete in the bloodstream could consult only the local, the internal, railroad timetable; there were no excursion trains out of the body. That was almost it. Ever since the Cold War ended, the élan vital had gone out of everything and nobody knew what to do with his or her suspicion.

Booth was the Californian, of course, but Clegg was more of a Californian man than Booth would ever be; part of him warmed to the notions of surf, sun, mysticism, and erotic driving, whereas Booth had actually left the Navy because it trafficked with the sea, in which he had had one accident. Clegg was the average sensual man, in some ways as ordinary as a cop with raincoat bunched behind him above his clasped hands or a drummer in a band, engaged in what looked like a nonstop mix minus the bowl. So it was not surprising that Clegg, whose emotions had always remained accessible to him, should generate enough internal zest to create an Aqua Regia. And then, having an Aqua Regia generated even more internal heat. He could not lose, although he had no idea how ghostly beings regulated their comings and goings; he just knew that, out of the stress and pressure, certain hypersensitive beings could transpose part of themselves into a counseling entity akin to the Angels of Mons, who appeared above the contending armies in World War One. If someone had told him these angels, so-called, were manifestations of the deity upset, he would have scoffed, but he went on half believing in the power of even an electromagnetic chauvinist to project altruistic traits and eventually marshall them into a persona of sorts. Fantastic as it seemed, it also struck him as plausible, no doubt because he attended so much to feeling, to emotion, and claimed always that what mattered most about people was not their ideas or their schemes, their labels and catchwords, but their passions. From these passions a sentient human could make all manner of things: literature, music, painting, even science. What shaped personality, he had convinced himself, was how a person felt, and grappling with surging emotions for seventy-odd years impressed him as a major assignment. Maybe he was too emotional to be an officer or a soldier, but his career was over now, a plaything for lisping courtiers who blew their brilliant brains out from the bestial pressure of it all.

Nagging at himself, he kept asking what had caused Booth and Clegg to lose face when their Cyrano malfunctioned, as if they two were to blame. A piece was missing from that puzzle and always would be. They deserved sympathy rather than obloquy, he thought, and could easily be put back to service again after some R and R, a few sessions of head-shrinking, several special doses of the secret military drug called perlopi-caine that spruced men up and helped them regain their combat fiber. Or it was just that, absent the Cold War, reconnaissance pilots were no longer needed and would be put out to pasture, to impregnate each other (Clegg's grudging laugh) or their neglected wives. He didn't believe a word of this; it was likelier that redundant pilots would become stooges for courtiers or drab meteorites chained to desks. He foresaw a future of acquiescence, tedium, and reversion to one's previous rank (in his case major). What he heard next was a mode of keening, an internal whining that gained impetus and volume, then burst forth from his mouth after the long journey up through bile, becoming a flower of song. He had long felt the impulse to sing, nothing fancy, but an aria, perhaps, in Italian, no more than a few seconds, yet evincing in a little blush of recitative his unmellowed fury. Was it the equivalent of primal scream, someone thrashing a mattress with a tennis racket? He had to let it out, and out it came, purged and trenchant, from the mouth of one who had never sung and might never sing again. There was no audience for this freak, but he saw himself in the mirror, mouth wide as if being strangled, eyes bulbous with blood. He was straining, with shoulders incorrectly hunched up, but nonetheless pumping out the sound like someone threatened with death if he didn't vent all his emotion in thirty seconds and a hundred syllables. It was melismatic, meaning he did not sing in words; he bellowed phonemes that sounded like words but were really meaning's cousins, bare as quoits, inscrutable as coals. Literally, he had burst into song, although much of him was left behind; he had not burst altogether, just his heart, used in the metaphorical sense.

The sensation of doing this gratified Clegg and made him feel he had gotten away with a major transgression. Free of coercive chemicals, he felt some shunt within him that, whenever it had happened before, he called his heart coming free or his coming free in his mind or even walking on air. If death were akin to this, he would gladly die, poleaxed by gossamer levitation. In another mood, he would have ascribed the whole sensation to having a good burp, but he was far from such mundanity now, gliding away from the hovel of his prosaic self, with the Taj Mahal of his self-esteem booked full. Now he was a general, one of the greatest minds known to compilers of history books, willing to stand and be admired by millions. Why, he had fallen to Earth from a high purple vacuum, and all in one piece; he had even been proved to be a loyal, decent, worthy man, apart from a few moments' backsliding in the business of Booth's fingers. Was he a courtier in the making? See, he was a courtier made, a person who spoke so precisely and with such a keen sense of oral ordonnance that his listeners could see where the punctuation went. Yet all this concocted splendor came only from his having been able to sing, after a lifetime's silence. Life had wrung this voluntary from him with such finality he hoped he would never have to sing again.

But words began to come, summoned by the occasion, taking him to a lyrical level he had never known. They had not done this to him; he was doing it to himself, inducing melodic mutations that consorted well with the dramatic image he had of himself being ferried to an island by two men in black duffel coats, both plying their oars gently while singing in grave bass voices of his elegant integrity; he was dead, and they were going to lay him to rest, but not before he sang to them once more, light as a fir cone, quiet as soot. On they glided toward the island, and at last Clegg burst into song once more, recalling the beautiful body of Alcibiades rotted by a three-day fever, his entrails in plain view. Clegg felt moved as never before. A sunflower was choking him.

Now fond Clegg, as he sometimes called himself, began to speculate; as the drug wore off, he came into a clarity of mind hitherto unknown to him. He saw through everything, nodding amply that indeed there would be newer Detroits, other Chicagos. It was just possible that the government—the military—were phasing out the Cyrano and might be looking to sell the plane, secondhand, to a friendly buyer such as the United Kingdom, from whom, long ago, the U.S. had bought the Canberra bomber they then redesigned, actually equipping it with long thin wings, then with even longer and thinner ones so that it too might double as a reconnaissance plane at extraordinary altitudes. He wondered what the British would want to peer at from such a height, but he could see what certain other nations might do with such an aircraft—Canberra, Cyrano—in their hands. He shook his head, paying lip service to the notion that something was afoot. The Pentagon didn't want bad publicity about the Cyrano, not while a deal was being cooked. That must be it, he decided, it couldn't be anything else. But couldn't they put us out to grass without this palaver, all this interrogational howdydo? He put it all down to the fact that courtiers must play, flashing their *summa cum laudes* like plumes, wetting their shorts at the prospect of making a couple of live he-men squirm.

Once he had known a Phi Beta Kappa man who, in company, when ushering people about, as he liked to do, bowing and mincing, fished out his Phi Beta Kappa key and pretended to open doors with it, as indeed he metaphorically speaking could. Clegg doted on these rituals from the meritocracy: maneuvers of a kind denied a mere lieutenant-colonel. He too would have enjoyed [walking on water] before an invited audience, and he cherished every medal and badge that came his way, exposing them on his chest in the exact right order, then restoring them to the display case in his room at the officers' club. A sash, a seal, a coat of arms, would have suited Clegg all the way, even an honorary degree from an unknown university; he had studied such matters and coveted an honorary degree from the University of Istanbul—cape of golden satin with a gold neck chain. How strange for an almost compulsive hero to crave such baubles, to remind him how well he had done in his profession, how little he had lost face. He wanted to be one and three quarters himself, especially in the orbit of Booth, to whom honors came like homing doves, only to be stashed in a dusty cupboard among the rejected mouthwashes, the freebie razors with permanent blade and deadly shaving angle, the Lilliputian toothpastes in the one-shot tubes. Booth blazed anew each day, always starting from scratch, but Clegg's way was the quiet accumulation of talismans and good luck. He could contemplate tomorrow only if yesterday had paid off. So he was less an opportunist than Booth, more of a self-watcher, more than a little haunted by something so prosaic as a Japanese postcard crammed with pagodas and archways, drastically slanted trees, and imposing pavilions. *Kyoto* the legend said in English, but Clegg hunted through all the crisscross bramble of black on khaki to find, tucked away near the top above some triangular bushes, a pale brown sun like a dying cell or a roundel from a crashed plane: no wider than a cross-section of a knitting needle, but his own confetto, emblem of a life constrained and taut.

His day would come, he was sure, but it would come in camouflage colors. Here his mind leaped, reminding him that something seen from above over the sea should be marine blue whereas something seen from below against the sky should be gray and azure. It all depended whether the camouflage was meant to fool you or to get your attention. When ecstasy at last found him, if it had not already (and he thought it had not), it would require of him the trained eye of the naturalist, asking him to discern it amid a background of earth colors intensely affecting it like the Kyoto sun.

As he recovered and rationality, the past, balance and authentic self came back to him along with a hundred other privileges and standbys, Clegg felt newborn. Never would he go that way again, no matter what they squirted into him. A nail or a shard of glass in the palm would do the job. Why, he had been playing into their hands, greasing their palms.

The room in which he found himself wasn't that bad: not a hovel, but a brightly lit tank that tapered from a good ten feet at one end to only a couple of feet at the other: a horizontal wedge with bleached-looking furniture of a color that might have graced a starlet's boudoir. At the far end, the low one, he saw a quite wide bed on which he longed to sleep; what he did not see was food or drink, and he longed for breakfast, ham with eggs over easy, plus strong sweet tea, more than sleep. Seeing a bell-push, he tried it, but no one came, though he imagined Phi Beta Kappas convulsed with mirth next door, incredulous that he should think the place a hotel. So he pressed again and, glory be, someone came with meager rations: a glass of skim milk and a chicken sandwich not exactly fresh with the bread curling upward as if part of a pagoda roof. No doubt already licked and spittled by the boys next door.

The phrase that came to him, as the formal-looking waiter in white jacket with rose buttons left, came from a Thelonious Monk piece; was its title, in fact. "Well, you needn't," a catchy amputation of utterance, had always struck him as the perfect riposte, blending obtuse refusal with raw finality. This was how Clegg longed to speak, without going to speech classes; but there was more to his fondness than that. He liked the way someone such as Monk took a familiar phrase and tore it out of a million contexts, to head a piece of music that had nothing to do with it. So the listener such as he, Clegg, had to imagine both the context—the other words uttered—and what conceivably the music might be saying. With such radical economy and imperious mystification he had whiled away many hours, convinced that was truly the way the universe was. It was no use fighting against it. You had to school yourself to function in the presence of enigma, and this he had tried to do during the wacky interrogation itself. Thus he was able, now, to satisfy the mystified part of him that asked where they had contrived to get those two fingers, human and fresh. From up one another's assholes, it was clear. That was all he needed to say to himself; his knowledge of the senior-juniors told him the rest. He and Booth were in the hands of naifs, as was the whole U.S.A., who used taxpayers' money like spray paint and turned foreign policy into a new kind of bobby-soxing. Damn them all, he muttered, for a dried-out sandwich among other things. Next to come would be a month-old newspaper, an airline toiletries kit with things missing, and a hot face cloth from hours ago. He was not going anywhere, but he wanted the amenities of travel.

Often spoken of, even to his face, as having an attitude, Clegg wondered at the phrase, deciding it had more precision than the mock-idea behind it. Who did *not* have an attitude? If it meant he stood up for himself, then very well, it was on the ball; he was never a patsy, not even to Booth, who was his superior only in rank. Weary, Clegg scooched into the low part of his living quarters and tried to sleep, but found only a rapid movie of recent events whizzing past his mind's eye, making no sense, not even stirring memory or desire. He longed for something unprecedented: a unicorn committing sodomy on a person in a full body cast, say, but he felt his mind flagging, able to come up with only the category and one or two stray examples culled from the rag-and-bone shop his mind had become. Whatever he thought of, he would rue it, he knew. If only he had a remote to spin through channels with, summoning up and dismissing one image after another, like a god in the heyday of his power.

Who am I, he whispered. Am I among the great aviators of history? Mitchell, Doolittle, St.-Exupéry, Lindbergh, Bong, Alcock, Brown, Hoover? The notion was fatuous, though he felt closer to Hoover than to the rest, Hoover with handlebar mustache and elegant sombrero, who flew a twin-engined Commander to a full stop with both engines out. Hoover wore a tie to all his exhibition flights; to hide the vomit, he said.

That was what endeared him to Clegg. Hoover was a high-octane fellow creature, latterly tormented by the boorocrats of the Federal Aviation Authority merely for having grown older.

Now the red domina he called Aqua Regia came back, making him think of all the reds there were, at least those in his head, from vermilion to cochineal, from carmine to crimson, rose to blood. The trouble was, at the moment, she undulated in the spectrum, never at any given time showing the whole of herself, and darkening or lightening in hue at whim. Reaching forward, he plunged his hand clean through her midriff, sensing nothing at all: no body, no innards, no backbone. She hardly flinched, but her face aged and grew young in an instant, almost as if trying to settle on one that suited him. There she wafted and billowed, a robe in a draft, resisting him and egging him on, making him wish himself both older and younger at the same time, any age at all that enabled him to make contact. If she were a projection of his own mind, he had little say over her movements. If not, the sooner she vanished the better; he wasn't up to extra demands today, he had overflowed already, making a fool of himself in front of the Rhodes boys. In all the crises of his life so far, she had never appeared, and he wondered what precise combination of events brought her out of the bottle. He was not even sure if she fortified or weakened him; all he knew was that, when she had a face, she turned it upon him with august beneficence, making an enterprising boy of him again who built balsa gliders and flew them with success. Under her spell he grew young again.

Children with freshly washed hair would come and in the gentlest fashion request him to go with them to his death: it was time, sir. We have found that people will go peacefully if a child invites them, whereas wild horses cannot move them to such an end. Such conductings he found alien to the child's lifestyle, but he could see perdurable tact in the routine, the strength in merely inviting rather than in a severe command military style. So be it, he would go when invited. Perhaps Aqua Regia, this figurine of curvy photons, was his inviter, saying little, but ultimately there to suck him back into the maelstrom he came out of. As he vaguely recalled from his not wholly misspent reading years, the noble, dogged apparitions in old medieval poems were never original speakers, but flawless mouthpieces given a script and an infallible sense of destiny. That was all. Hence Aqua Regia's insubstantial cavorts, there to remind him how fleeting and filmy were all human antics: best to give up the ones he still retained, let them go the way of all the rest as so much behavioral detritus.

"In the old days, ma'am," he began with a somewhat heroic lilt, "long before your time, with the B-26's, torpedoes were slung underneath. The drop speed of a B-26 was two-twenty-five miles per hour, whereas you weren't supposed to launch an MK 13 torpedo at anything over a hundred and sixty. No wonder the torpedoes bounced back off the sea into the air and briefly flew alongside the bomber in formation. Those were the days."

"Don't be callow, Clegg," she snapped. "You can't fool us with ancient anecdotes. Now, take my hand, and let's get about our business."

But take her hand he could not. It was not there. Nor had it ever been. She was handless and feetless, so he tagged on to her sash and hoped for the best, nauseated by the weird aerodynamics of her sway, from lurch to chandelle, in which latter figure she stove along at great speed then shot at right angles upward, trailing him behind on the sash. He was going to his death, he just knew it, and the Furies in the back room had tossed in the aerodynamics just to make him feel at home, like a torpedo.

Then it was over. He was standing sedately in his tapered chamber with Aqua Regia, his solace figment, purring alongside him within a pink smoke turned to textile, urging him not to shy away or to hang back, but from death or sleep he couldn't tell. "I have come to mellow you," she sighed, "and then to make you mine. Be brave, good colonel."

Being brave, or attempting to be so without exhortations from Booth, was difficult, but he thought again of the two fingers, now easily getting them into focus as further toys of the boy brainstrust, culled from morgue or operating room, best classed as medical waste unless reattached. They had been cut off the hand of a thief, Clegg decided; one such as he or Booth, overflying other countries and stealing their most secret view of themselves, had snapped shots a thousandfold. It was a view of themselves these countries hardly ever had, certainly not the general populace, and never would because the worn-out Cyranos would never be sold to them. We snapped them when they weren't looking, he decided; no wonder we lose a finger now and then.

Aqua Regia was fading again, perhaps because the image of two fingers was not catalytic, and Clegg braced himself for extra loneliness, wishing with all his heart he could go up in a Cyrano again. Flameouts were so rare it was a sin to penalize pilots subjected to them, but that appeared to be the way things were going to go: first humiliate, then demote. Unless that was a thing done only to lieutenant-colonels, colonel in name only, in truth glorified majors. All his endearments came back to him, ideal for winning Aqua Regia over, no matter how thin she had become: angel, darling, dearest, treasure, beloved, even swan and peach, but never honey or sweetheart as too profane, too vulgar. She was gone, with the amazed air left tingling behind her, no doubt while she ministered, as her wont no doubt was, to some other military casualty or his fingers. Maybe there was a way, next time, of incorporating her into his body: sucking her in and installing her like a decal on his pericardium where nobody could get at her, and she would become the keeper of the gate, the phantom of the viscera, cooling and soothing, making all those innards behave even under severe duress. He had heard that unborn children got to know their mothers' voices thanks to the double tympany of lungs, perhaps acquiring a few words or some tendentious torso rhythms, so why, once she came aboard, not tune in to her as she monitored and calmed him, using a language filched from Mercury or Alpha Centauri? Yes, she would take up residence and cling to him as a leech to an orange, resisting all other claimants, even averting compassion from the two fingers, instead teaching Clegg's erratic heart to beat normally again, bestowing on him a mental flower each time it missed a beat, or beat too often, determined to make a regular man of him so that he would never again have to say the word *palpitation*, which God help him he linked with cowardice and fear. Clegg believed all men were cowards and that courage consisted in staring cowardice down, ending it by outfacing it. You did not go to officers' training school to make your mind go blank; you went to learn how to resist the weak side of your nature, becoming brave because you had refused to allow cowardice—fear, shyness, whatever—to unman you. In time you became a regular warrior because you fed your willpower as if it were a tiger lily, and that was all. So long as the mind remained alive, it could resist unworthy behavior, even under torture. Nifty theory, Clegg thought, but I would have told them nothing and let them amputate all of him, then kill him. I really would, palpitations and all, and he would have been proud of me, taking the initiative like that with his own life without so much as consulting him. I would have gone too far, Colonel, I would have gobbled up your future just like that.

Could anyone, he wondered, live with other men on such a basis, feeding with them day to day while each knew the other was expendable and had tacitly given the other rights over his mortality? It didn't make civilian sense, but it was the soldierly way, fused with the rigmarole of salutes, saying *sir*, wearing badges of rank, and using such resonant words as *captain, major, colonel*, each of which suggested more than anyone remembered, a lieutenant, for example, being one who *held a certain place*. These thinly disguised hierarchies used to please him, but he realized he and Booth had gone beyond protocol and become impersonal servers of the same destiny, more committed to it than to each other, or to anyone else. This touch of the superman or transcendent monomaniac worried him, yet never enough to make him pack up boots and saddle and head for the nearest YMCA, motel with monthly rates, or beach cabaña with a cold six-pack inside. Once Clegg had found even keel as high-altitude pilot, a part of him never came down with the Cyrano but stayed lofted, an aerial synecdoche of self that he kept free of mundane temptations. Even the basics such as oxygen and nitrogen he found spurious, wanting that separated part of him to stay stranded, at bay, barely alive until called upon to perform some final service. No doubt policemen, paratroopers, and commandos felt the same way, the point being (he surmised) that you could never, at short notice, conscript part of yourself from its everyday ways into doing heroic duty. There was never enough time, anyway, and impromptu heroism usually went wrong. The only way was to keep this holy-ghost-type piece of yourself up where it could hardly breathe, and use it on demand, never explaining or guiding, but letting it loose in an instant like some Pavlov dog. Be prepared, he always told himself, and he was, he had been.

Where had he read the saying that a man should hope to betray his country rather than his friend? With him, it had always been the other way, and he would phrase it—he would phrase it with debonair severity— I hope I would just manage to betray my friend before my country. Oh, I'd agonize, but in the outcome I'd have my priorities straight, wouldn't I? He tried to imagine situations in which he would sell his country down the river, and there were too many. The answer seemed to be, then, he was not that devoted to Booth, for as soon as he thought of a loved one the whole notion of heroic sacrifice of a colleague went out the window. This was a highly theoretical and heretical idea of loyalty he was messing around with, indicative (he berated himself) of instability in the one and only Clegg, playing both ends against the middle. Why was he no braver than he was? Why was he so little, in a radical way, attached to Booth? It was nothing to fuss about, though, as the question would never arise; indeed, he and Booth might never meet again, sequestered three thousand miles apart in different arms of something like the witness protection program, with not so much as a postcard permitted in between, no phone calls, not even a go-between taking the one some oranges, bringing to the other a small bottle of Armagnac. That would be best, Clegg thought. Could he have let me down in the same way? He doubted it, though the most acute test of the hypothesis would have been in the Hanoi Hilton, epitome of the worst and final resting place, with nary a quarter given and no broken bones repaired. That hellhole would have taught them the truth about each other rather than this trumped-up charade of the boy-courtiers, all parchment and tweed.

Now he stopped. Such self-onslaught used to be called the agenbite of inwit, or the gnawing of remorse, and he hectored himself never to do it again, not even to prove to himself what a pencilneck he was.

Blaue Augen

t was the same old voice, bravado mingled with imperious reserve. Into his tank burst Booth, in an old green jumpsuit, accompanied by several of the young interrogators, jostling to be nearest him. "You got these old boys wrong, Clegg," the voice said. "They been through all kind of arduous training, pain and everything. You shouldn't go putting them down like that."

"Like what? So there you are."

"I been listening, Rupe. You been talking aloud again when I was right next door with these young clevers. Thank the lord we are in the clear or they would have fixed us toe to head. I have been overhearing you."

"If I'd known," Clegg said, letting his statement trail away.

"No, no, we want the real man. Together again, Clegg!"

"On the whole," Clegg answered, "I wish I'd stayed in the Danakili desert. At least you knew what was going on."

"You knew at least what was going on," Booth corrected.

It might have been a tree talking. Booth the survivor was harder to take than Booth the victim, and he had all fingers intact. Why was he using that spurious Texas accent? Where had he been? How come he was this well connected? Perhaps he was one of those special men the military called darklight leaders whose role was never clear but whose impact was unmistakable; everyone took them seriously and salaamed before snapping up into a stiffer brace than had been seen since Eisenhower visited West Point. Darklight leaders skipped ranks in the promotion rigmarole, soaring from lieutenant to major, from major to general, although such was the speed of their trajectory that no one heeded the emblems on their epaulets: always something flowering on that eminence, people said, he'll go clean through the roof. Usually, though, darklight leaders did not wear badges of rank but white coveralls with small rosettes on their lapels as if something or other of the Légion d'honneur. Booth was exotic, all right. Clegg felt the old rush of resentment and uncurbed fellow feeling; he wanted to tell Barney everything, be guys together, get smashed with him on European beer, knowing that when two American men go out to get plastered together they are entering upon a ritual of suicide. It may not seem so, since the whole episode smothers itself with bonhomie and hail-fellow-well-met candor, but it is two guys tasting death together under the auspices of quaff. Never again would Clegg go drinking with Booth. They had had their brush with death and it had left one of them stained, death had, death the old lurkster, the smiler with the knife.

"No more desert sand for me," Booth sighed, beginning to hum Sigmund Romberg.

"And no more salt," Clegg added. "Why so much quizzing on our return? Repatriation, or whatever it was?"

"Oh," Booth explained, "they like to find out what you don't know you know. That's all. They're quite nice really, fit to take home to Mary Jane Rottencrotch. Boylike, but they're as old as spawning salmon, Clegg my boy. They have been around, reading maps, peering at operations, listening at keyholes. I'd call them the cream of human milk. Get to know them, you'll want to marry one."

"You always were so straight," Clegg told him, recalling how he had always felt happiest with Booth when he sat behind him in the Cyrano, talking on the intercom to the back of his head. There was something he wanted to make clear, something about being captured and maltreated, then released and sent home, but none of it added up to a question other than "Why am I so baffled? Has something really gone wrong or is the whole business over? I don't even want to know what's going to happen to us. I want to go back to a normal life, read the newspapers, do some channel surfing, get my stomach back in tune." Booth was welcome to his esoteric games; he needed them whereas Clegg was an old Victorian, not eminent maybe but anxious to feel that, at the heart of things, a [heart beat] just like his own (or better than his; his next visit to the flight surgeon would put paid to him). They could take from him whatever they wanted, as with Captain Dreyfus, just so long as they showed him no more chopped fingers and did not bust his loyalty. When your own put you on the rack, you felt as if life had never been worth living. You should not have been born. He never again wanted to feel that twisted, with the feelings heaving out of him like mutant phlegm, choking him and making him retch. So much for what was called disingenuousness; Clegg's anger soared away, then turned back upon him, funking its logical target. Could it be that Booth had been putting him on, just to flaunt his superiority? Friends, as Clegg saw it, did not sharpen their edges on each other, they stood back to back in battle and felled all before them, at the last turning to enfold each other in a fraternal clasp. Clegg smirked a little at the grandiosity of his notion, knowing that life was not like that, but certain he could just about live it that way—the heroic outline amid the hurly-burly of daily scuffle—if he put his mind to it. Alas, his recent life had made a virtual automaton of each man, a machine-minder behind a machine-minder, nothing like two knights on one charger riding into the thick of the battle, eyes becreamed with conjunctivitis, loins rotten with the pox, hands deeply seamed from too much sword work without gauntlets, teeth loose and deciduous from simple lack of hygiene, their skin scrofulous, their feet a paddyfield of boils and blisters. Yet on they galloped to the next affray. Two men, with half a thought between them, Booth its dynamo, Clegg its lover.

Now they showed Clegg where he had been incarcerated: no prison at all, but a punitive motel with exquisitely landscaped grounds, somewhere between tropical and finicky. There was even a pool ("Acid, concentrated," Booth joshed, "so be careful"). The familiar patriotic stench of burned franks wafted on the afternoon breeze, making Clegg look eagerly for the national flag over the cupola on the main building. Life here could be good, even salacious, he thought, and the food would be a riot. Here the boy-interrogators troughed on sugar, in both their drinks and their franks, and Booth, clearly, dominated the bar at night, regaling his boys with war stories, peace stories, and stories of monstrous diseases evaded, caught, and bested. Perhaps we will never move on from here, Clegg thought. Maybe there is even a flying club around the corner with some Tiger Moth to toy with. We could age gracefully. The instant Booth left his side, he began thinking grandly of their days to come, but as soon as Booth returned he stoked up his anger again and yearned for a sea voyage to push him overboard. Early spring, Clegg decided. I did not know I had any seasons left. Soon the heat will be intolerable. Oh for the arctic bars of yesteryear, when you dried out in five minutes cold and had to curl up the collar of your jacket to keep out the frost when it was 98 degrees outdoors. Those were the days, before boys were boys.

Now, Clegg knew that, confronted with inscrutable Booth and his boy sophists, he was in much the bind of a nineteenth-century surgeon peering into the body cavity by the light of a solitary candle, hardly able even to distinguish the slippery from the matte, the bulbous from the suety veiled. It was no use wondering. Cut deep and be damned, wondering why Booth, good pilot that he was, prospered so well in his profession and had what Latin Americans called the *enchufés*, the connections political, military, and social. He would have thought Booth too churlish, too vain, to win people over, but he did it with superlative disdain, as if acquaintances were mirrors and he saw himself with delight reflected back at him. Clegg had never had that much confidence; had he ever risen to such a level of humbug he would have rued it. Indeed, that must be how Booth saw him, not as a clone even though he, Clegg, was a good pilot, but rather as a penis of homage that swelled and rose, not in the auto-nomic surges of night when men all across America lusted and broke the postage-stamp edging their shrinks had told them to fix around their tools, but in raw adulation. That was Clegg, the suppurating groveler chiding himself on an off day, a day so bad he wished he had slept through it in a liquor stupor. Multiply that by 365 and you were really in trouble.

In their ascendant years, Booth had always reassured Clegg that he, Clegg, was a lion, his favorite lion, and should never doubt himself, must always assume he had been put on Earth to achieve a certain honored goal. The trick, he said, was to invent your own confidence and, when things seemed to be going against you, create the hypothesis of your own supremacy and live it out, deflected by nothing, almost as if being brave were a reflex common as peristalsis or breathing. In this way, Clegg had managed to outdo himself, never flinching, but in the process becoming more Boothlike than he wanted to be. It was not a matter of changing his personality, though he could have done that too, but of adjusting how the light shone on him, canting his head or shoulder this way or that to achieve the winner's stance, or even, also of the winner, that measured superior smile, really an effect of clenching his teeth a little tighter than usual. This he called the Booth pout, to himself of course, saving it for awkward interviews and after-the-fact laurels, as if to suggest a man so brave and fierce he could hardly open his mouth, or one whose utter-ances were so brave and fierce et cetera he dare not let them out into the air. Demeanor was everything to Clegg, who had never before teaming with Booth known what may broadly be called the aspects of the hero. This was why busts, whether of Julius Caesar or Napoleon, attracted him to an unusual degree, not so much ordaining how a Colonel Clegg should look as opening wide in the private amphitheater of his soul a whole range of imposingness. A little arrogance from here, a jut of the jaw from there, and Clegg found a face he could look at without wincing. Was it the face of a winner? To be sure, and a winner who, if he felt the urge, could abolish the game.

"Ever a lion," Booth said in a rumbly whisper.

"Yes sir, Colonel." Clegg said it without listening, and then had to won-der what indeed he *had* said. Speech with him was fast becoming like cave painting, silent and dim, with grope and scratch his main modus, as if nobody would see what he had said for a million years. He paid minimum lip service to what others said. Besides, events of the past few months had hardly readied him for social intercourse even of the highly circumscribed variety assigned to soldiers. The other part of his being, the nonsoldierly, craved for outlet, but got none and remained stuck with introverted sign language nobody could see. Yes, he thought, life of late is like a postage-due-begging letter; you don't know whom to refuse first. Booth in his brand-new crewcut seemed to have changed little, more lined, less patient, the rest of him trapped in unreadable stereotypicality as if put together from a kit. No errors in that wholesome face, nothing betrayed. It could go to a funeral or a wedding with no change in expression. It did not respond to extremes. Nor, mused Clegg as he mock-punched his colonel in the midriff to demonstrate collegiality, cosurvivorship, was it responding to the aftermath. It did not smile, but, if you were quick, it flickered, achieving the tiniest augment in severity amid which an infant smile died smothered. It was a fast, knowing face, best heeded in the same way you heeded question marks, traffic signs, menu explanations. Clegg had learned long ago to tune in to something behind the face, its thermostat or its metronome, knowing that there, under the surface, lay the clues to deportment, strategy, guile. He didn't always read his Booth aright, but something guided him; indeed, he could often construe the mysterion by watching his hands, which often gave the game away, sometimes mimicking the action to be performed: wringing, fisting, unraveling, stroking, counting, conducting. Such was the key to a mood, but only an aerial intimate could deduce the full complement of what made Booth tick, or what he was making tick that instant. If Booth had been that easily deciphered, Clegg would have found him boring long ago.

Yet what should one make of a subordinate who finds fascinating beyond measure the man who gives him orders? Is there not in such doting scruple something slavish? Should not the one who obeys look away and get on with things? He should not linger, marveling at the intellect behind the imperative, which could well be an order that sent him to his death, no demur permitted. This holy bond was what the military was for. The military was what this holy bond was for. There were jobs you volunteered to do, and jobs imposed upon you. Truth told, Clegg was fascinated by the death-dealing quality of language, the word that became the protocol for death or being maimed. There was a gap between commander and commanded and it was full of succulent, violet, harmless words in which you were measured up and found adequate. Do it. Yessir. And that was your head blown off, your leg severed, with not a sigh in protest although you were allowed to scream later on. The truth of their life together as Cyrano pilots was monotony. Hardly ever had Booth required anything of Clegg not specified beforehand in mission orders. Their lives had gone forth before them, as it were, and the risk taking happened all the time. There was never a moment, at that altitude, at that speed, over that terrain, their lives were not in jeopardy. The snag was that, when the everyday was potentially disastrous, what did they do for kicks? What beyond risk was there? Praying to God to smite them arbitrarily down for their disciplined effrontery? They would never have done that. Well, what then? They had never figured it out, though breaking down and weeping in front of a Giacometti statue might have come close, or going quietly off their rockers during some Mahler.

They were together again, Booth having already seized some kind of ascendancy but subjecting Clegg to arbitrary blood and thunder, an acte gratuit approaching auto-da-fé? Simply to assert himself? Or in preparation for something far more dastardly intended not just to humiliate or distress but to open wide the Chaliapin of pain, just because Clegg was Clegg and Booth had the rank to maim him. There were limits, though, and Clegg adored the one in which an officer, even at gross personal risk, had to look after his people as if he were running a golf club or a car pool. Given that, who would treat him badly? Well, Booth had, and Booth had much support, enough to indulge in malevolent paternalism. Clegg decided to evolve some means of self-defense, but what? He might take to spouting military regulations (the Regs), so as constantly to remind Booth of his higher responsibilities. He could quit the military—all right so long as Booth remained behind. Or he could demand a posting to a different arm of the service: a lectureship, maybe, with a good deep library to peck at. Life was not over, it was just under grotesque attack.

Clegg dimly recalled a poem in which the old gods were lying around and moaning as the new gods took over, unable to do anything against the takeover. That was how he felt, but was Booth also one of the old gods or one of the new? With such notions he tortured himself to no gain.

The two of them were unlikely ever again to saunter together through some sleazy part of Istanbul, bar crawling or brothel sampling, buying all kinds of doodads—shish kebab skewers, martini stirrers, hand-carved meerschaum pipes, attar of rose, filmy scarves—they later reviewed at a café table by matchlight and usually dumped in the Bosphorus with a faint curse. Clegg remembered the scenes of their roamings: being greased down with sewing machine oil in one hovel before the possibly terminal encounter with Madame Bnarski, the growling whore; another time locked with Booth in a room that contained several fowls, a puppy, and one lamb, make of the menagerie what they could; or in a cistern that was a room—you opened the door and faced a five-foot-high wall, over which you climbed into a depth of four feet, on the surface of which floated paper plates, condoms, tampons, little abstract curlicues of dental floss, sheets of newspaper. Entering these places was an attempt to go beyond what they had already known and become accustomed to. Clegg, in his semiliterate way, had found that grammar (or vocabulary) did not permit you to say ["enthuse"] which only a god could do. The word meant capture by a god, so obviously you could not do it to yourself. Perhaps the two of them were looking for *enthusiasm* then, offering themselves up for seizure, and they would be ravished by delight when the godhead grabbed them and dislocated their lives forever. But, the farther they went in their *nostalgie de la boue*, so-called, the farther they realized they would have to go. All extremes turned out to be provisional. It was astounding how much the body could stomach, at least in the interests of an experience so outrageous that no one else could share it, excepting Booth, excepting Clegg.

"You know what it is," Booth once said. "It's the pagan form of prayer. It's the heathen way of bending the knee."

"Nah," Clegg retorted, "it's enthusiasm, that's what. Waiting to be clipped off because we can't find anything better to do with ourselves. People with proper jobs don't go looking for trouble. They have it on their hands."

"Then I'm more mystical than you," Booth snapped.

"No," Clegg parried. "You're more like yourself than *I* am like you, that's all. We're better off sixteen miles high, where there aren't as many distractions. If we really meant it, we'd go out, get AIDS without really trying that hard, and take the consequences. What we're after is a cozy finis."

"Eff that," Booth said, haughty and dismissive. "You know that old shit about the icelike flame, flaming with it. Well, that's what it's about." Once again he had uttered something that began like a question but ended up as a querulous absolute, a statement not to be brooked. Clegg winced and wished for a less intractable partner. Booth was always right, which was to say he did not qualify as a discussant. He knew how to obey and how to dominate. That was all. And he expected others to be the same.

Predictably, men who flew a witchdoctored aircraft that did New York–London in two hours became impatient with routine gratifications and veered toward sadism and necrophilia, aching for the forbidden, the unspeakable. It was their form of poetry, whereas the average sensual man would want nothing more startling than New York to London in two hours, depending of course on how much he wanted London. Men habituated to sideways-looking radar or computerized threat libraries needed remarkable toys, and, once they retired from active duty, preposterous compensations. Or they would go batty, unless, as Clegg said more than once, they hit on things untried: archaeology, philately, knitting. All very well to say such things, Booth had told him, but there was what he called the arcane criterion to be reckoned with. Whatever they went to had to be Promethean, even the music they listened to: rock that ruined the neo-cortex, painting that blinded as the sun did; dances that crippled you for-ever with one leg hopelessly locked in its socket, the head irreversibly craned backward. Drugs awaited them, though they had tried them early in their careers, with varying effects. Drugs were too much what other folk were doing; there was a snobbish element in their cravings, though both men tended to think of humiliation as the key to the next wonder of their world. What had happened in Africa attuned them, in different ways, to the possibilities of an afterlife lived now, Clegg's somewhat sentimental, Booth's august. The trouble was, Clegg decided, after the flameout and all that ensued he and Booth approached the same problem from incom-patible angles. Gone the days of bluff bonhomie, quasi-brotherly alliance. They had grown, nay jutted, away from each other, maturing exceptions to each other's rules.

"There was this guy," Booth said, for once resorting to what he had read, "in some movie, who played sax and blew so hard at a door it would split and fall, at least in his imagination. He wanted like hell for it to open and show him what was there. Well, it's that kind of feeling I have, and I have no sax."

Clegg had seen it too, but it was too long a film for him and he had walked out after an hour of it. He preferred TV, especially the kind he saw back in the States, *Unsolved Mysteries* most of all (adequately mingling mayhem with family reunions, though he many a time wondered if all those missing siblings and children really wanted to be reinvolved with their families after, in some cases, having managed fifty years without them. Who wanted to be dragged out of happy obscurity down into the fold again, hugged by the fat and the tainted?). The program was not avail-able in Turkey, though; very little was. He had, however, once bought and then refrained from reading a novel called *Memed My Hawk*, Turkish done into English. He thought the title must have mesmerized him. "Yeah," he sighed, "that guy huffed and puffed to blow the door down. He thought God was behind it, with some secret in his belly button."

"You don't say," Booth sneered. "With a sax."

"Better an ax than a sax." Clegg giggled.

"Leave doors alone," Booth told him.

"Well, I am not a door man. A skin man, a quim man, and sometimes a liquor man."

Booth rebuked him with a sickened grin. It was no use talking about such things, citing the classics on heroism: brave Japanese, brave anti-

Nazis, brave Serbs. They all made him sick because they had political intentions whereas he and Clegg were—what would he call them?—technocratic hedonists. What an awful mouthful. Couldn't he put it better than that? Okay: they were the virtuosos of the industrial revolution. That was better. They aimed upward and looked downward, murmuring *Man is magnificent.* Oh for their apprentice years at Groom Lake, learning the Cyrano, being the envy of all, having passed those dreadful examinations, gotten accustomed to being in space suits just like astronauts. Was it astronauts they had wanted to be instead of pilots, moving into a different ball game that made them more passive, more passengers than savants-in-command? Jesuitic to a fault, he tried to distinguish between flying the Cyrano (being flown by it) and what the astronauts did, and arrived at the dismal conclusion that the contrast wasn't great. Both roles demanded a lot of quiet sitting down. Then he remembered something taken for granted and so set aside: the fuel that burned the rear of the Cyrano to white heat was also what cooled the plane down. Oh to be a man such as that, cooled by blood that caught on fire.

Booth staring at Clegg was Booth hoping that Clegg staring at him was really Recon staring at Trocar, as Booth was sometimes known *(nom de guerre)*. What Booth saw was the pre-African Clegg, face much the same but in a different setting, both heraldic and grand. What remained of the lank light brown hair looked wetted or greased flat, the somewhat scumbled parting on the right side of the head, the bulk of his hair combed sharply left, culminating in an almost Hitlerian forelock or droop. An incipient bald patch at the rear shone almost ginger in the harsh overhead sun that also picked out white in the sideburns and the one-day beard. Clegg's face had the angry pink of someone who never used sunscreen, and his entire face held a squinting scowl against the glare. Behind him, but not in the least shielding him, the cockpit cover of the Cyrano stood vertical, a huge hexagonal gauntlet, roughly rather than elegantly made, fixed in the Up position by a thick cylinder the color of champagne. Against this backdrop, Clegg's head looked threatened, as if some robot were gaining on him from behind even as, with one hand, his left, he clutched the apex of the windshield, his other hand positioned not to rest on the lettering that said KEEP HANDS OFF (or OUT). The veins in his forearm seemed swollen with recent exertion. All of him below the collarbone was engulfed by the enormous blue fuselage that sloped sharply away from him on either side. On the point of being engulfed by his machine he looked oppressed, awkward, stern, good-natured enough if pushed, but a man with too much else on his mind to bear photographers (Eric Schulzinger and Michael O'Leary), who had given up trying to coax a smile out of him. He was aching to draw that vast leatherette-lined lid down over him, even if he baked in the process; it would at least get him out of the direct sun and the gaze of the camera's eye. He, like a few others, knew what it was like to look forward in much the same stance and see the air coming at him at Mach 3, hammering the paint and the quasi-glass.

When Clegg saw Booth he saw much less, marveling at the youthful face flanking the bushy mustache: a face serious and pensive, almost studious, the close-cropped hair just about an announcement of tenacity. You would not argue with this youthful-looking tyrant; he would not argue with you. He had no expression to be evaluated, but features in gentle, abstruse combination that might have been those of someone kneeling at a grave, awaiting the soup, or signing a death warrant (with none of Nero's bleat "Why did I ever learn to write?"). Booth was sprayed with youthfulness, as everyone said; and it appealed to many to be bossed about by someone who only recently had been a teenager, or so it seemed. Orders came exotically from someone who looked like that; his face gave him a spurious compassionate quality and softened his sway.

Small wonder that those who spent much time around the two men began to look to Clegg to evince Booth's emotions. He did not always scowl or frown; indeed, he had a lavish grin that only the sun banished, and it often had a gratuitous quality as Clegg grinned for the sake of grinning, no doubt to egg the deity on. He was not above a bit of climatic voodoo, smiling to make the rain stop or the temperature rise. When Booth should have smiled or scowled, Clegg did sometimes do it for him, believing in expression both facial and verbal. In this way he became almost a translator or a transferrer, aching to snatch Booth from his taciturn slough and set him loose among men and women, a spinning top of charm. Booth's mask, handsome as it was, had pieced itself together over many years; it had not come all at once, and he saw it as armor, presuming that to be easily readable, especially by men under his command, was to become an easy mark. So his demeanor, one might say, was neuter, static, chilled, whereas Clegg's by contrast seemed expansive—he was too much of a show-off to be an officer, and all his gyrations in order to achieve the perfect sit of head, the right bulge of the lips, failed to upset his impulsiveness. He would talk to you, even at Mach 3, whereas Booth would be holding converse with the gods of the headwinds. If, as Bossidy said, Lowells spoke only to Cabots, and Cabots spoke only to God, then pilots spoke only to Clegg and Clegg spoke only to Booth.

A shallow person might have said they were addicted to each other and it would be true that, after becoming inured to each other, and then habituated, something narcotic began to take over. Flying, until someone gets killed, makes odd bedfellows, and it is said of wartime aircrew that they were able to stand one another only because anyone's chances of surviving a full tour of missions was slight. Death was the leavener, or being missing, wounded; Booth and Clegg had had their share of such vicissitudes, of course, but their symbiosis was a peacetime one likely to endure, although they'd thought it would last longer than it did, perhaps even in their mind's eye envisioning themselves on crutches being winched up to the canopy (not that high off the ground anyway) and buckled into a cockpit that doubled as a wheelchair for both. It was certainly one way to get extra oxygen.

There were other Cyrano pilots, of course, but none who, with the Cleggian or Boothian sense of fatality, accepted his copilot as a gift from the gods: just irritating enough, not insufferably brilliant, neither a gabber nor an introvert. Each had discovered just about all he needed to of the other's humanity and pilot skills. The rest was learned caution backed by that unknowable thing, the love of flying they shared on an almost inarticulate level, as though, Adolf Galland said, an angel were pushing. That said it for them all and helped them concentrate on the job at hand.

Flying next to each other had its appeal, far more than flying together in separate planes. The other could always, in theory at least, corroborate a certain sensation, if asked about it in good time—what Clegg called the Swansong Ache in his testicles when pulling too much g (why Swansong, he never knew; it sounded like the feeling felt); what Booth said he would fucking well measure one day as an old cracked bone in his forehead cut like a hot cheesewire when they swooped back to Earth. These in different aircraft would have been expendable, blown away in the commotion of each landing. Two pearls in an oyster is what they really were, of demonstrated high caliber but unknown as far as genius (or genie) went, still capable of being pushed beyond previous limits if only the occasion arrived. It did. They were. And now they were reaping the wholly unpredicted aftermath in the shadow of a defunct Cold War, hoping the world would soon dream up another squabble that demanded high snooping, an art easily lost in a mere month of inactivity. Clegg and Booth were sure that hordes of younger men, already breathing down their necks, would not be trained to succeed them. Where was the need? They, Booth and Clegg, should have been objects of study long ago, during obsolescence. No, Clegg thought, that's not right: we never had one of those, we just whooshed from full-blast activity to obsoleteness. There was nothing in between. We were overtaken by events, as people like to say, as if events were runners and humans assholes in aspic.

For Clegg, flying was heaven, ecstasy, the thing that dislocated him from his usual self. It was like the country house he daydreamed of, all corridors and porches along which drifted the music of a string trio, casual and pastoral, prompting him to stroll and notice how the wind altered the way the music sounded. He would never have such a home, he was sure, not even in Turkey where he had seen some with flower-strewn balconies. He was saving this idyll for later, for after later. For Booth, on the other hand, flying was a way of completing an incomplete self: no bliss, no rapture, only the sense of consummation as a piece of him reached out and found what it wanted. And now, of course, Clegg, though not while flying but while being interrogated, had found his angel: skimpy and volatile, but an amiable apparition worth waiting for, on whom he was glad to dance attendance. Aqua Regia; now, *there* was an acid worth getting fired up about. He longed to see her again, but had no magic word, no sign. An angel in the offing was no part of Booth's cosmology, of course, though he would tolerate it in Clegg's; Clegg was always a bit wacky, flaky, even gullible. To imagine something was to have it: that was Clegg's way, not empirical or manly. All Booth needed was a clear roster of his duties, although also a guarantee they would never defeat him or fail to fulfill. That was the weakness, plus one other, which we will come to later, that often left him wondering [who he really was.]

There were people in the service who could indeed do that: identify him and label him with no hint of fakery. If only they had done so and equipped him with the requisite tag. Being a colonel was no help. Nor was pilot status. Some wit should have come along from his retinue of clevers and dubbed him pious, like Aeneas, or greathearted, like Odysseus. Booth still had a little diary in which, written down when he was an officer cadet, his few Latin and Greek words sat in useless echelon, useful way back then, but never since. Actually his wordhoard made him better read than Clegg. Booth had studied his authors' obsessions, their catch phrases, whereas Clegg knew the reputations of all his books. Neither man had broken through the erudition barrier, but each had trafficked with the idea of being well read, envying the additional command it gave you, but unable to plant the idea in their lives. Besides, they had both had too much technical reading to catch up on, and constant updates to commit to memory. Somehow the mind that has constantly to remember a revised stalling speed cannot recall what Odysseus looked like, say, when he scared the girls on the beach. [Nausicaa's] name told everything about her, though, meaning one well suited by ships, and by their sea, by which she lived, in which like any washergirl she did her laundry (princesses such as she were expected to be useful), and from which she was not too put out by the arrival of a naked man (with whom she knew at once what to do). Such tales of awestruck recommendation would suit Booth and Clegg in another, later life.

A man going to the final redoubt of honor cannot, all by himself, develop the right heroic stance; he needs help from myth and literature, both anodynes as he sinks into the vast deposit of the dead, dying even if unable to swallow his fate, swallowing it better (so those ancients claim) if he can hitch it to the mighty universal turnover, the universal feast of death all are destined for. Better that a medal cork his mouth before it is too late. Better that some strident ovation, all brass no strings, crackle over his corpse; he will have heard it coming. A healthy irrelevant youth, his head bowed to accept the weight of his helmet, dies a warrior's death, as he knew he might have to. Into this context, a Clegg, a Booth, comes garlanded with honor and pride, able if anyone can to fudge up his own glamour, part of which consists in disbelief that he has survived this far, each time not expecting to return, yet never expecting in his heart of hearts *this* one would be the comeuppance, the last one, doom's dry thunderbolt. It is the only glory they have geared themselves for, but they are not ready for the humiliation that ensues. Not even after burrowing into dusty classics would they ready themselves for that, for nobody "writes up" the anticlimax: the court of inquiry, the interrogation, the demotion, the cashiering, the first pension check and all the red tape that goes with it. It is as well they never read Virgil and Homer. Bookworms they never would be, only derivative fusions of Tarzan, the Red Baron, Prester John, and Paul Revere, but virtuoso monks of the system all the same, plying the skies unseen, always too close to the sun, forever in fits of cramps, trained to exquisite finitudes that only a machine could mind.

"All over," Clegg said, fidgeting.

"Well, *that* part of it."

"The part that matters."

"Unless they have something else for us."

"Considerably slower," Booth told him, his voice full of tender melancholy. "You'll see." He meant unexciting.

"Rather not," Clegg said, absentmindedly landing an airplane on his thigh, the thumb again outstretched to serve as a wing.

"Then, Rupe, you needn't. It's open."

"You sure?" Clegg felt his entire lifetime's expertise being flushed away. No more cold fuel, white-hot ass, space suit, slight tremble of airframe as he squinted at Earth's curvature up in what he called the violet transits.

"Once a pilot, always." Booth used his heroic voice for this, determined to appear in the know. "Our problem is open-ended. Honest, Recon." For once Clegg felt this nickname did not fit. He was more of a Rupe now and knew he would soon begin to insist on it. Downed pilots, he knew, developed kinky syndromes; the lyricism of deprivation was not for them.

Men who have languished in the back of beyond may well, when they get it, be unnerved by their accumulated mail. Perhaps there should be a special service to supply them with mail that will not disconcert, with mediocre heart-not-in-it letters and faxes that have Expendable written all over them. Letters full of clichés might serve and reminders saying Account Forgiven. The shock of being reconnected with loved and loathed ones can be lethal. Not only is there the coarse encounter with communication at all, but also the impulse to reply after, so to speak, your language has altered, and the soft code of amenities has died an unnatural death at the hands of barbarians, among whom grunt and bark are Rilke and Ruskin.

What is Clegg going to do with an obsolete folder telling him he has a choice between *Ariadne auf Naxos* and *L'incoronazione di Poppea*? Belonging to an opera club based in a posh watering place, he has always tried to initiate himself to an art form he has never understood or had much feeling for: an uncommon problem, to be sure, and especially so for a man accustomed to flying three times the speed of sound. His grown-up sister, whom he rarely sees, is a soprano, resident in San Francisco, and their agreement is this: she will pester him little if he will try to cultivate a taste for opera—not for her singing in particular. Report and she will abstain from writing him. He has been marooned in Africa, so she has written him, her faith in the military postal system immense. Wherever he is, wrapped in barbed wire, he will get his post, or so she dreams, convinced that all societies are basically humane. Even on missions Clegg has carried with him a little book, just a few inches square, easily smaller than a sandwich, that compresses the plots of operas into one page each. When he has actually boned up before attending a performance, he has not recognized the opera, so vestigial and cheap the summary has been. So he expects nothing, reads the book afterward, if at all, and awaits the day his sister, Babe (formal version Babette), will confront him with a three-hour examination. He learns snippets and hopes to get by, destined never to be a cultivated man; but a cultured one, as if he were a pearl, yes. Hence his retrograde singing, less a performance than an outburst, less words sung than meaning avoided. It tunes him in to her, he thinks, or so he thought before Africa; now it puts him in touch with his [Aqua Regia,] brings her down and home from her own exquisite paranormal flights. Babe once introduced him to a beau of hers, explaining what he did, and before the other could respond Clegg had shushed her so loudly that everyone turned around to look.

"She's just boasting," he said. "Actually, I am a middle-of-the-road flying instructor. My big-time days are behind me." She almost believed it, so bedraggled he seemed in the act of self-identification. To her he was Prometheus Unbound, and the little gold eagle he wore in his lapel was not the one that ate men's livers but the emblem of high fliers.

Every now and then he would run through his list of musical trivia. He had tried to restrict it to opera, but wandered off the reservation. To begin with, he knew of three operas performed only once: *La Dame Blanche* by Boieldieu, *Lucrezia Borgia* by Donizetti, and *The Merry Wives of Windsor* by Nicolai. How anyone could work that out, he had no idea. Were all performances of everything logged somewhere? With nothing omitted? It was like counting the number of times a Mooney Mite had flown. More to his taste was what composers had died of, Scriabin of a facial carbuncle, Rossini of cancer of the rectum, Ravel of a brain tumor. He had heard that Ravel never had a single orgasm, but would even Ravel know that, he wondered. Chausson died in a bicycle accident, Granados was torpedoed, and Lully stabbed his foot with his own pointed cane. This was his raw material, ideal for pleasing Babe, though the spray of his data irritated her. At least her brother was, for once, functioning in the sphere of music; how could she talk of planes when he shushed her all the time? She had to admire his almost photographic memory, but it was crammed with latitudes and longitudes, rituals and procedures. There was hardly room in there for culture, though she could tell he needed it, living the barren life he did (she dubbed it Turkish Delight), deprived even of his favorite TV shows and condemned to spend most of his time with Booth, whom she loved for having once made a pass at her during a dinner. Whenever the two went back to the Skunk Works for some technical revision of the Cyrano, she roped them in for a concert, preferably an opera, and Booth said it was like being in a metal factory, he had never heard such screeching, while Clegg reminded him of the eminent deaths: Wagner, angina; Gershwin, brain tumor; Puccini, cancer of the throat. Booth cheered up at news such as this and began to smile.

Yes, she told herself, both born killers, not that you'd ever guess. They fly so high that thousands are only specks (in this she was wrong, thanks to supercameras). How come they do not need the counterpoint? I mean the other side of life? How come they're content with only one thing, as if all you lived for were coffee, foxtrots, or crosswords? She could never figure these two monomaniacs out, though she was an opera monomaniac, could she but discern the fact. Rupert and his friend went to the Skunk Works as little as possible, dreading the obligatory dose of culture, but Clegg never quite got tired of amassing trivia, certain that one day he would need all these particulars, when he was no longer Faustian Superman, or whatever name he went by in the dungeon of his loyal mind. That he had a sister struck him as bizarre; [he had never wanted sibling,] or wife, or relatives of any sort, just a plane that enclosed him and shot him forward, upward, like a sperm. His entire life had consisted of getting into pickles, messes, fixes, so that he had no clear trajectory (goals, ambitions, plaques on the wall) but only a ragged spoor left involuntarily behind him. Clegg and his detritus were a long-established company by now; he truly was that ancient dream of the fighter pilot, as envisioned by umpteen commanding officers, the bachelor with no ties—and by implication no worthwhile interior life, no love of peace, a more than lascivious desire to kill.

Well, he had had his career, but he wanted it again, brasher and wilder than ever, except he no longer dished out death, which point he would have pounded into Babe if he had only been able to tell her things. When he was finally released, honorably of course, she would be the most pleased soprano in America and they would perhaps sing something coy together, he and Booth for her, with her then joining in to make a tempestuous troika. He sometimes wished he could get close to her, but better not as she seemed bisexual, and she had dozens of acquaintance-friends who all asked him the same impossible question: What do you *do?* Once he had said "I hang around to fuck my sister," but this had only made him the life of the party. They would love him even more once his mind was gone and he sat in his wheelchair watching Robert Stack hosting [*Unsolved Mysteries.*]

Yes, he murmured. You don't have to be nice, or clever, or honorable. You have to be a husk, that's all, with your medals on your chest and an old marque of the plane you flew—to live in, see, the most streamlined of cabooses. You would be allowed to go bonkers in three moves and live in there, tight-strapped into the cockpit, with the ghosts of Chabrier, Wolf, and Donizetti, who went bonkers too. It is unlikely I would end up on a TV quiz show, answering tough questions about opera. What I'd like is to get through into the new century with something of the old excitement from the twentieth. A hangover from the old days for the new orgies. Come see the men who saved the world just by photographing the Soviets (and some others). How would that read on a billboard? COME SEE THE MEN WHO SAVED THE WORLD. . . . Not bad. They would play the *Flying Dutchman* overture all the time they were looking at us. This is Master Clegg, I'll be bound. Yonder's Master Booth, the meistersinger. By the time we were allowed to write our autobiographies we'd be too dead to write them. Folks could guess, though. How'd they survive all that radiation year after year? Well, look at us. We didn't. We're fried, folks. It sank through the lead and made us look like those old Japanese, the Ainu.

Once again Clegg was battling the contraries of life, the good that promised only good, the bad that promised only that. Only too ready to think well of the world, he was the last man to become a cynic, so he had found himself over the years bending over backward to minimize the horrors. God, in whom he irritably believed, would surely not have created a bad universe, even if He were into video games only. Still, the Booth-generated idea that the universe was one of the deity's doodles had given Clegg many a poor night's sleep and numerous uneasy days, when war, earthquake, murder, came to the fore and challenged benign thinking. He knew only too well that being hopeful wasn't being optimistic; they were different. You could be hopeful for a minute or two, even a week or a month; but an optimist held to a doctrine that covered everything for all time. So, to his credit, Clegg never said he was an optimist unless he meant in the round, *in toto*, as regards everything; but he heard people misuse the word and he rebuked them. He often read it too, as in "He said optimistically," whatever that meant. Clegg made a clear distinction between impulsive, impromptu hope, otherwise known as the spasm of hush, and the good cheer of the incessant holist. How, he wondered, could he fuse the two, saving the former for scattered moments, the latter for the continuum that included all moments? Was it possible, he asked himself, if optimism swallowed up hope anyway, as a lion might engulf a thorn? In that case there was no need to hope. Hope did not count. And optimism was not a thing you had to ponder: once you (he chuckled) opted for it, it was yours forever, even if dozens of things went wrong. Somewhere at the back of his mathematical brain hovered an equation saying: If you count up all the goods you otherwise wouldn't bother adding up, you find many more of those than of bad things. Life may not feel that way, but quantitatively the optimist was closer to the facts.

He also had another theory, having to do with speed. The faster you went, he thought, the more cheerful you became. Transsonicists, as he liked to call them, doted on euphoria, back-feeding their cells with the message that, if you expected the world to treat you well, it would. The very thought paralyzed him with joy: you could somehow talk the uni-

verse into it. Perhaps this was what he had been doing while being interrogated. Believe in yourself and the surrounding universe one hundred
percent, and out would flash Aqua Regia, the personification of your
goodwill, and all that acrid cross-questioning would turn out to have been
a charade—although one intended, he guessed, to appraise him for some
other role. Pray what? Out of the fire into the frying pan. Wasn't that the
general direction of civilized behavior anyway? So, perhaps he was not
going to be cashiered for bad luck but newly motivated, groomed, for
something else, less dramatic, more mental. The brass had its reasons.
But it would not be demotion to flying instructor, would it, though they
did need Cyrano instructors. Somehow Clegg knew there was more at
stake than usefulness or, at the other end of the career spectrum, a military lullaby. When he realized such things, bobbing up toward him like
the homuncule called a Cartesian diver, Clegg felt something lift in his
own head, a piece of him doing duty for the whole, a silver synecdoche
blazing like car chrome, reassuring him that his days included still
imponderable grails not to be hunted or collected but to be obeyed until,
in death, a huge set of matted loins trundled from the sky and sat on his
face, smothering him into awe. You cannot do this in reverse, Clegg
thought with his last engram when the divine monody began:

"Yew had a good time, Jewboy?"

"I ain't a Jewboy, Father."

"Well, yew are now." That was death, every bit as absurd as life, and
quite without grammar. Clegg went on thinking, certain not to be dead,
and wondered why, on his deathbed, or in the deathbed fuselage, he
should not sing, gibberish if need be. They want me for something. It isn't
over yet. I am still a pilgrim colonel. Makes sense. They wouldn't train me
for nothing, not at today's prices. I am the golden postscript. They told
him nothing, however, and he divined he was supposed to detect whatever was to come (role, mission, punishment) as something reflected off
Booth. They would shine it off Booth, and Clegg would catch, exultant at
being singled out yet again, his wordhoard undepleted, his hands fit still
to hold what ancients called the joystick or the control column. He
steered with his heart, maneuvering toward a genetic splendor he had
never hankered for, his honor given a retread. Whatever they told him to
do was his way of not rusting. What was that line about rusting in action?
He couldn't recall, but he didn't want to waste the remainder or rump of
his life. There was nothing worse than a rusty rump.

See, that was why he thought himself an optimist. Just when he'd
decided he was done for, he wasn't. Instead of being slit open from gill to
tail, he had been thrown back to grow full-sized. No wonder he had such

success with women, those nourishers of life; he was on the side of life himself, almost as if he had created the planet without help. Primogeniture of a trusting heart, he told himself, regaling his mind with such a phrase. He was the man who, of all people, loved people the most, warming to them with conspiratorial ardor. He knew now he would sing with greater aplomb. Babe would tape him, no longer holding back on the compliments, and opera would surge toward him, a clogged ovation. All this because his mind had turned a minor corner, growing its own uplift as if self-help were the major act of genius in the twentieth century. Glad as he was to have sneaked it in before the closure, before the nineties fizzled out, he hoped he wouldn't have to do it afresh every morning. If only self-help had staying power, rooting itself in the soul like celery, whose stalks—well, he abandoned that metaphor, knowing how metaphor thinned things out, sapping them of their blessed *is*ness. He knew now that Booth, eyeing him in the ready room or in the showers after a mission (a poor place to eye anyone if you are showering right), was losing him in metaphors, setting him aside, mailing him away like a parcel, deClegging him with punitive relish. He was a mindless amoeba. Or a slime-spooring slug.

"What you staring at?" Booth always asked.

Clegg said he was staring at his stare. "You sure as hell will know me again, Colonel."

"Don't you Colonel me in the shower with our swingin' dicks dangling."

"You know what, Colonel? You stare at me because I sit behind you all the time in flight. I've worn a little patch away, staring through the back of your helmet, so you glare at me in the shower. You always did. You always will."

The scapegrace earthiness of their banter had always astounded Clegg, who set some store by formality, whereas Booth regarded profanity, colloquialism, obscenity as privileges due someone of high rank. Booth never neglected a privilege, but looked askance at the privileges of others, whoever they were. Clegg had once, in his TV-viewing days, tuned in a local station whose freedom of access attracted an anonymous teenager who phoned in and regaled the host with four-letter words, hour after hour. Nobody stopped him. The host bumbled through. Freedom of speech kept the kid going while hundreds phoned in, only to find the kid never hung up. Not prudish, Clegg felt exploited and never watched the channel again. Booth had once confided to him that, had he not been a pilot, he would have been a radio announcer or a TV anchorperson. Clegg could see why. Booth had the right demeanor, hearty and imperious, and, unlike most anchorpersons anyway, had been to an Ivy League college. What he also had was that extra degree of homemade sheen essential to the media climber: ingratiation peppered with pride, bustle mixed with confected gentility. Booth could turn this stuff on; after all, it was an officer quality, prized by the brass, who were proud possessors of it themselves. Clegg was willing to be passive, to watch or listen, but also to disbelieve what the newscaster said, to imagine facts that never got into broadcasts.

Besides, Clegg had a touch in him of the naked seer striding heedless through the blast. What the news media denied him he imagined, knowing that a keen imaginer beats an onlooker hands down any day. Something restrictive in Booth put him off, but he pitied him for it, wondering how many things a man had to be good at to go blameless. It was not important to be an all-rounder, but you had to know where a civilization's mines had been laid, and Booth knew, showing a quite studied knowledge of recent technology, sometimes letting slip a technical note that surprised Clegg, who saw Booth as a role man rather than an information one, poseur rather than savant. No doubt of it, Booth kept up, devouring aviation magazines and (though Clegg had no idea) keeping several scrapbooks for different subjects. He knew the finest details of the plane he flew, and, aloft, would listen or look for malfunctions Clegg had never heard of. In fact, on return, Booth would sometimes get into arguments with ground crew about how to fix something, and he would always say, his final line, his sign-off "Look, you guys, I know how to make it not work, so I know what makes it go. Gotcha." None of this endeared Booth to anyone but Clegg, who rather enjoyed his bumptious know-it-all attitude, putting people in their places who didn't know there were places for them to go: sergeants especially. Booth was a full colonel full of himself. After all, he was on the brink of becoming a general, or he had been until Africa. The mannerisms of a general-soon-to-be had fallen away from him, and his high-handedness was once again that of his substantive rank. His political savvy and his engineering know-how never deserted him, however; he remained a man of parts whereas Clegg was a man of appetizing fragments, genial for himself to contemplate, whereas Booth allowed others to size him up and did no more introspecting than a chameleon.

"Tell me," Clegg asked him one day as they shared a chocolate bar in the palatial PX, "where is the disgrace in having a flameout?"

"A double flameout," Booth said pedantically.

"Well?"

"You never heard, Recon, about the messenger who brought bad news? Ancient Greek guy. They killed him because the news was bad."

"Myth," Clegg snorted. "Examples from real life, if you please. That was an ancient Greek joke, though I can see the Ivans doing it, oh yes."

"Then why not us?" Booth had a hectoring air, as if, having just finished lecturing, he retained the pundit mode for everyday chat. "Just think about it, gentlemen."

"Who's that? Who are *they?*" Clegg had heard enough and began to wander away, tossing the remains of the candy bar for Booth to catch.

"The correct terminology for it," Booth called after him, "is prejudice irrelevance. Otherwise known as guilt by association. Your poppa forged the guillotine blade. Is he therefore responsible for all beheadings? Of course he is. No matter how long the chain of causation. Sooner or later we are guilty of everything. Get it?" Clegg had gone, happy to think Booth a self-befouled unicorn who might have been more palatable without fingers. Sometimes he yearned for something to happen to Booth, just to bring him down a peg or two. There was decorum and there was lip service. The latter he would not engage in, the former he revered, but when Booth started in on his own twisted notion of decorum Clegg retired from the scene, knowing that Booth had in him something of the gunrunner, the pirate, the roustabout, and trumped up rules for whatever he wanted to do. Yet the whole idea worried him: perhaps everyone was indeed, if thoroughly connected through and through, guilty of something. There was always a link to disaster, which his gentle probing of the dictionary told him meant something wrong in the stars. Was it true, then, that he and Clegg were in some measure responsible for their flameout? What had they done? Was it that they just didn't know? Or was the whole idea a chunk of masochistic self-slander?

Now they were back home, among familiar words and supportive routines, it was as if time had slowed; nothing happened anymore, and habit gradually arrested everything. Whenever they recalled Africa or Turkey, though, their lives took off at full pelt, becoming vulnerable all over again. With him, like a talisman, Booth carried the details of Turkish Airlines Flight 981, its crash near Orly, the DC-10 hitting the ground at 490 miles per hour, killing all 346 on board. Takeoff and climb-out were perfect, but at twelve and a half thousand feet the latches on a faulty door gave way and the plane decompressed at speed, the cabin floor collapsed, and the last two rows of seats on the left-hand aisle fell into the hole in the caved-in floor and were blown out of the fuselage. Having no controls, the crew were powerless to control the aircraft. The inside pressure against the cargo door that failed had been nearly five tons. Booth brooded on this, taking a specialized interest in Turkey and its planes, and most of all adopted as his own call sign the catch line from a Turkish radio commercial popular in 1974: "*Acaba, nedir, nedir?*" or "Wonder what it is, what it is. . . ." This is what the DC-10's captain had begun to murmur only forty seconds before the jet collided with the ground. Something gallant there. One of Booth's few theories about life had to do with last utterances made by pilots, captured by so-called black boxes (Day-Glo orange, actually). "Mother" or "Shit" were the most common final words: hardly original, he thought, but look how little time most of the pilots had. Clegg told him it would be more interesting to study the famous last words of literary persons, such as the Russian Gogol, who cried for a ladder, a ladder. But Booth persisted, wishing the Turkish captain of 981 had said *acaba, nedir, nedir* at the very end instead of "It looks like we are going to hit the ground." How much cool and presence of mind, not to mention sensitivity to language, did it take to produce a real winner? The best he had found, or could remember, was one from an aircraft that actually landed safely. "I'll kiss you later," said the pilot to the first officer, a line that Booth rather envied, spurning "I can see the water. I got straight down" and "Hey, what's happening here?"

"What you call it?" Clegg asked him out of courtesy. "Ultimology?" Booth shook his head.

"I don't call it anything, not strictly, but famous last words won't do. Don't see why I should have to call it anything. Just passes the time."

"Does more than that," Clegg joshed. "It makes you feel there but for the grace of God go I. Well, don't it?"

Booth knew that, when Clegg spoke slovenly, omitting syllables or dropping his aitches, he was up to no good, so to be on the safe side he answered "*acaba, nedir, nedir,*" to which Clegg responded with one of his own Turkish phrases, got up by heart just to create an impression: "*tatli su ferengi,*" or *sweetwater foreigner,* as Istanbul-born Europeans were called. Clegg was joshing him for putting on foreign airs, not for collecting ultimisms or whatever he called them. Perhaps they were air epitaphs. Now, what would that be in Turkish? he wondered. It was amazing. They no sooner arrived home than the language they disdained to use became the one to flaunt, even if only at each other.

"Sweetwater foreigner," Clegg said with a punitive laugh.

"Oh yeah."

"You," said Clegg. "You all over, Colonel, sir."

Booth knew he would have to admit to his canon some statements from earlier in so-called black-box tapes. The best was rarely at the end, though the context then was more dramatic by far. Trouble was, the Cockpit Voice Recorder was a self-erasing, thirty-minute loop because, well, nearly all accidents in the air occupy no more than half an hour. Never, he thought, was he going to hear something as good as King Lear's famous line "Never, never, never, never, never," but he did recall a woman pilot lost over the Turks and Caicos Islands with all her fuel gone trying to get a fix from Grand Turk Tower. "I am on a heading of zero-nine-zero," she said. "I have left the island. Please keep talking to me—I need it." Ten minutes later she was gone, despite a Pan American Clipper in the area trying to find her. Damn, Booth thought, rapt again by the accident and the waste; she should have landed on whatever land she was over, or in the water near shore, while she still had power and didn't have to go down in the darkness into the ocean dead-stick. Some savior had burst up from deep within him, a Booth lost to most, but now and then resurgent from his younger days, when he could remember first solo and first cross-country, when he recognized he was yet another variant of mere sublunar man, destined to envy the hawk and the albatross and, by perusal of flimsy dials, to cut a calm track through seeming vacancy, his mind on the hubris while his hands managed the big sough of wind, easing and shoving, until, if fortunate, the same patch of the planet showed up beneath him again from which he'd burrowed upward. So he felt for all lost pilots, circling or going down, wishing he could with some compassionate extensor arm reach them and field them homeward, murmuring to himself in Spanish, like Ernie Kovacs, within his thick mustache, a few choice lines either of romantic airmen or hidalgo lovers. The panic button met the piropo. Or he was the newest Walter Winchell, crimping the airwaves with messages to all planes in flight, from wherever to wherever.

"Please keep talking to me—I need it." In his mind he was always talking to them, as if they had never left on their last flight, as if they had never launched. He was Mister Air Central, reeling them all in to safety, he after all the supremo of anoxic altitudes where no one else dared go, nearer to whatever lay outside the planet, whether the deity or just some immense refrigerator in the sky. Booth was never in a hurry to come down because, when he did, he made contact again with all the misery that men and their flying machines had gotten into.

No, he was not his brother's keeper, but he sometimes fancied himself Supreme Air Traffic Controller, marshalling them all into proper patterns, maintaining spacing and separation, every now and then transmitting fine words upward, and supplying deft exit lines in case of trouble. He was never one to trust to luck, though; until *acaba, nedir, nedir,* he had never had an exit line planned for himself. One he'd always fancied, however, was "I'm up to here in alligators," which got across the savagery of the turbulence as well as the visionary state of the pilot. In truth, Booth saw himself as a bossyboots and was pleased with that image. He loved words, not too fancy ones, and how they provided the ultimate grid through which planes flew, and all those five-letter words that marked the intersections of the invisible airways along which instrument-flight-rules aircraft nibbled their way, intercepting each aerial crossroads electronically like blind mice charmed with an alphabet. Yes, as in the old movie about the Lafayette Escadrille, when they rehearsed the successive legs of cross-country flight, away from the aerodrome, then Querqueville to Plumetôt (he thought the names were right), then Crépon to Carquebut, Carquebut to home. There was magic in even those ancient watering places, sites of innocent rituals preceding the most perfunctory bloodbath of all: one week at the front and life was over for the rookie pilot.

Standing at the squash court, preparatory to playing at least a warm-up game, Clegg began to tell Booth about Aqua Regia and found him much more sympathetic than expected. Booth envied him, he said. "Every man needs a Red Riding Hood, a Lady of the Lake." She wasn't quite like that, Clegg told him, she was fragmentary and elusive, not given to long stays or elaborate explanations; but formidable and timely, as much from outside circumstances as from within his skull.

"Plausible phantom," Booth said. "Next thing she'll show up in a topless bar and bite your nipples off."

Clegg shook his head, a gesture that had had no meaning in Turkey where the head jutted far back for No, and wrote Booth off as that pain in the neck the envious parasite.

"Maybe one day, Colonel, you will see," Clegg told him. "There's nothing I can say or do that'll prove my point. When I see her next, maybe you will too."

"Freemasonry among the deluded," Booth quipped. "I'll buy that, I really will."

Clegg knew that she was lustrous, sensitive, eternal, perhaps a ricochet from his mother, whom he had adored and whom he thought he heard calling him Rupert as he was falling off to sleep, not to recommend any course of action or to counsel, but merely to caress her lips with a beloved name. It was one of the things that kept Clegg straight, even in the turmoil of his nights. His mother addressed him direct, inspiring him with intonation. Her touch had been symphonic, her voice choral. Now, though, he needed an Aqua Regia too, less giving, less generous, more attuned to the dedicated soldier in him, offering not so much tenderness as gusto. Clearly, Booth thought he was partly cracked, but Clegg knew the place and role in this erratic world of supernatural creatures even if they figured only as sketches, hints, blueprints; they were there to mobilize his initiative, maybe to prepare him for his next assignment. A man could live, Clegg thought, half in this world and half out of it; inspired both from beyond the grave and by a force immune to categories such as the living and the dead, the real and the fantastic. Clegg's holism was as natural as clearing his throat, and Aqua Regia was as familiar, as domesticated, to him as a statue he had seen in some museum of Cybele bedecked with fruit that looked like scores of huge fever blisters defacing her stomach and waist. He was a good home for incongruous images, no doubt because his recent life had been absurd. The only image that left him cold was the normative one celebrating the everyday, the predictable, all of which had passed him by in the high desert. That was when he began to muster within his head the paradoxes and contradictions of life, the moments when God could not make up his mind.

Now they were playing, stiff and awkward, but making a gesture toward fitness. Scoring points mattered little, but loosening the muscles soon gave them the airy scamper of boys. Booth and Clegg skidded, slipped, collided, gasping and perspiring, even trying out shots with the racket held slantwise to impart spin. Once upon a time they were skillful players, able to judge within an inch or two where the soggy little black ball would land, and adept at occupying a dominant position in center court. Today they just slugged the ball about, forgetting to keep score, wondering what it was they had lost in Turkey and the desert.

"Hey," Booth gasped, "about the ball! The paradox of the fortunate fall."

Clegg had no idea what he was talking about, but no breath either to ask him with. Sometimes Booth mouthed saws from other cultures, like his incessant *acaba, nedir, nedir,* trying not to impress but to insulate himself from the vicissitudes of daily life, easily repelled (he thought) by runes, maxims, and dainty mottoes, almost as if he consulted at will one of those Turkish *niyetçi,* fortune-sellers, whose pigeon pecked out for you from a tray loaded with slips of folded paper an ineffable promise effed: *You shall receive a letter from your heart's desire.* No more than that, but it was torpedo fuel, abyssal splendor, there just for Booth and likely to send him slithering upward through the lattices of creation until he had achieved an eminence—height or rank—that rendered all further effort unnecessary. "Peck again, pigeon," he would say, "give me a better one." Or he would slouch away to a vendor whose tray used a rabbit as its deus ex machina. Above all, Booth wanted a cosmic guarantee that said full colonel was not the sticking place; he had done favors, and performed services, that entitled him. Yes, he told himself, I sure am entitled. No one knows how much I've done for them. I should get at least a tray full of pigeons.

Clegg had never responded to these fortune-tellers, having already decided a delirious but beneficent fate oversaw him, requiring only an attentive bow or two, or, faced inexorable battery by the material world, a whimper of sublime humility. The deity or the furies always backed off when the victim saluted or bent the knee, as much at home as an angora cat in Ankara. There was nothing lost, he claimed, in telling the universe how omnipotent it was, at least within the arena of his regimented little life. If you told, you went on with your life; you won a reprieve. If you refused, you felt nothing immediate happen to you, but not far away the destroyer of delight began to twist your noose of wire. It would not be long. Therefore, Clegg told himself, speak charitably to the world that bore you.

Living a satisfactory life entailed behaving as you would with Turkish hotels, on principle avoiding those that called themselves *Lüks* (luxury), *Kösk* (Pavilion), *Saray* (Palace), and *Belediye* (Municipal). Other warning words were Silk, Brigade, and Grand. It was better, Clegg supposed, to head for quarters in any establishment that scrubbed its fainting couches and armchairs, bluntly offered rooms the shape of a half moon, and attached its keys to taxidermied hooves of goats and other animals. Aim low, aim humble, he told himself, and all will be well. Seven hells may be in wait for me, but there are a hundred thousand bazaars on the way. Openness to delusion, he thought, was the overture to what he needed, and a certain reluctance to tell anyone what was going on in his most private being.

"Penny for your thoughts, Recon."

"No thoughts today, Colonel. Today is a nonthinking day."

"Well, then," Booth would chant, "penny for that. Now I know what was in your thoughts."

The repartee, sackcloth variety, calmed them and steered them away from serious military matters, which Clegg was only too ready to ask about when Booth seemed his drabbest, least extroverted, wrapped glumly around some stinking pain. But he never said to Booth "Penny for them." He just fixed him with his obsidian stare and waited for the blink to answer.

Next came the first of Clegg's *mellow* interviews, staged around a shiny oval table with coffee, tea, and soft drinks. Conducted by a few of the brilliant young savants who had seemed to favor Booth, this was more like what Clegg had had in mind all along: tinged with congratulation, envy even, and conducted with jocular finesse as if gentlemen had at last seized power and were using it for noble ends. The thing that bothered Clegg was the gentlest insinuation that Booth was somehow forfeit; or, if not that, then to be rebuked, blamed, cashiered. Gradually the questions became direct, couched in peachy amenity but bang on target.

"Colonel Clegg," one of the juniors began, "how would you rate Colonel Booth's actions in the desert? Was his conduct that of a senior officer, a leader?"

Clegg stalled, pleading ignorance; after all, they had landed far apart and had hardly had chance to compare notes when reunited. No, *since* then, one of the questioners said. "What did he tell you? How did it stack up?"

"Oh," Clegg said. "You mean stateside."

"Yes, Colonel. Thank you for being so attentive."

Sarcastic slimeball, Clegg thought, and then made his routine defense of Booth, both loyal and evasive.

They were after something else, though.

"Is Colonel Booth an ideal officer? Would you be surprised to see him promoted to general?"

Two questions, Clegg noted. "Yes. No," he said. He was playing it pretty close to his shirt.

"A patriotic officer?"

"Without doubt. A perfect specimen."

"What would you say if we told you Colonel Booth had—well, that there had been rumors about his loyalty?"

"Oh, you must mean mine," Clegg blurted.

"No, his."

"I would be shocked, and I wouldn't believe any of it. You guys—"

"No, Colonel," one of them interrupted, "*your* opinion of *us* can come later. As can any suggestions you wish to make. Please concentrate on the matter in hand. You would be shocked, as you said."

"I certainly would. Beyond a certain point, you don't listen to scuttlebutt about senior officers. There is always a certain amount of resentment floating about. Spite. The usual poisoned cremola."

"The—" This time Clegg interrupted. "Slander, if you like," he said, and involuntarily patted where he thought his heart was. He was also going to add *semper fi*, but thought better of it. Perhaps this was when they would crush his fingers or shove toothpicks down his nails, though the room, all flags and urns, decanters and silver cups, seemed hardly the place for torture; rather, one of the holy holies of sport, lacrosse maybe, or rowing. Automatically he scanned the walls for crossed oars, a coxswain's cap on a golden peg.

"Colonel, how would you behave with Colonel Booth if you heard something to his discredit, that he was a turncoat?"

On it went, with Clegg resourcefully twisting this way and that, at one point offering his theory of identity and how experience enabled you to define yourself in wider and wider ways, constantly enlarging latitude and longitude until the man within felt magnified, on the way to greatness of heart. All through this presentation, however, Clegg had the feeling that he was teaching ancients to suck eggs. These juniors or preppies had done this kind of thing in their sleep many times. It was how they had risen to power; yet he and they were in the Pentagon, not sequestered down at the CIA. So, he told himself, there are home-grown sophists. They give you the eye when you play their games yourself. Try something else, Clegg. They're on to you, though you were enjoying your little jaunt through self-defining.

So he said, "Booth, Colonel Booth is exemplary."

"You would defend him to the death?"

"Why the death?"

"Colonel, just because you feel under the gun, which you are not, don't feel obliged to ask too many questions."

"If not," he protested, "if I don't, how am I going to know what you're getting at? Something's behind all this. Colonel Booth's dandy." He knew he was offering a Booth who was a hundred percent whereas his true estimate varied between eighty and ninety, yet still pretty good. Booth was the man. It was no great sacrifice to rate him as faultless. If there were things wrong with Booth, these twits were going to have to figure it out for themselves.

On it went, tinctured with hints of insubordination, conduct unbecoming, disloyalty, even a hypothetical taint of treason, but Clegg held fast to his Platonic idea of Booth, just about the only friend he had left, at any rate the only one who could understand how Clegg now felt after all that had happened. In a sense, they were brothers in bad luck, and that was enough to inspire him to maintain a solid front. All the same, he caught himself, in the intervals of talk, during nourishment (he took coffee, tea, and Coke, in that order), beginning to want to change his answers in accordance with how Booth would answer about him, as he would no doubt have to sooner or later—perhaps was doing so this very afternoon of a warm July. Clegg was trying to resist second-guessing himself, and this set him daydreaming about Turkey, Africa, and the old days of training in the Cyrano.

"Colonel Booth," he said jubilantly, above a tide of minuscule quibble, "is a wild weasel."

"Just so," one of the group said. "What other animals is he? Which animal would he like to be?"

"Weasel's just fine for Booth," Clegg said, wishing it didn't sound so lame. Damn these yuppie-assed questioners.

"No ferrets, lynxes, wolverines, foxes in his private menagerie."

"None of those, sir. He doesn't mess around. He goes in and gets right to it."

"Flying," said another, going on a different tack, "does it give you feelings of superiority? When you land, do you feel better than your fellow man? Colonel Clegg."

"Humbled, sir," he said, "and almost irretrievably shrunken." That shook them.

An exaggeration, surely? Would that not hint at a degree of instability in the colonel? Was he proud to make such an admission? How would a desk suit him?

"I imagine," he said tersely, "you have plenty of them and few eager applicants, gentlemen."

It was almost over. His interrogators began to mill around the room, seeming to nod at the portraits of illustrious brass, speaking swiftly behind cupped hands, looking up or back at Clegg with barely disciplined agitation. If Booth had been there, Clegg thought, he would have been enraged. Clegg suddenly had the feeling he had been awarded some decoration; the ceremony was over, and he was being subjected to the usual kind of reverential joshing, obsequious envy, good-hearted resentment. He had known these feelings all his life, either as his own or visible in the conduct of his contemporaries like bright nuggets in a drab backdrop. It was familiar conduct, even if boring to watch. He parried and lip-served as best he could, not even demurring when a couple of well-spoken eggheads (as he construed them) gently pulled off his blazer and laid it aside neatly folded so as to show the squadron crest on the upper left pocket. If this was bonhomie, then he was the good guy, not forever, but for as long as the shindig lasted.

Off went his striped tie. The front of his shirt opened and bellied with the wind of their sudden movements. He was being ragged, that was it: a backhanded compliment reserved for heroes. Now they all turned their attention to him, tugging and sliding, heaving and laughing. Even his pants went away, his shoes, his socks. They had him on the rug now, yet with parasitic carefulness, urging him and cajoling, calling him Recon, until he stood there, helped to his feet in striped boxers and nothing else: a hero revealed, stormed at and exposed for what he physically was. This was as nothing to Clegg, who, having lived the military life as long as he had, was no stranger to bathhouses, barracks, communal heads, and the like; he did not flinch, he did not even think he was being looked at. He said nothing at all.

As they fussed him and refurbished him, each having stored in his mind what he wanted to know about Clegg stripped, Clegg recognized a familiar thought coming back to him, as it did just about monthly, haunting him without informing him much. It was better, he thought, to pour your best energy into your most demanding chore of the day, saving it up like air or fire until the crucial hour struck, and then using overkill to settle the thing. The trouble was, he told himself, your energy got dissipated, frittered away on this or that, so that when the crisis came you dealt with it feebly, just wanting it over, and never mind the outcome. How could a man achieve apportioned energy? If you never knew what was coming, how could you apportion anything? Save up a lot of it just for something trivial? That's what always happened. He decided living was not a systematic process, could not be planned, which meant you were always in a state of overtrained, underfueled readiness, like some boxers who went into the ring knowing nothing of their opponent, whether he was a first-round knockout specialist or one who warmed up over half a dozen rounds and, just when you thought you had him scuppered, became a raving monster who'd been resting, feinting. Clegg had a dismal sense he had not been up to today's affray, whatever else it was; he had come through, but blinking, dazed, puzzled by men whose main skill was hypocrisy. That was it: they played pretend.

At last, in a tone both disdainful and genteel, he spoke, moving his head this way and that so as not to exclude a single face. "Gentlemen, your touch is gentler than that of the Danakili who mine salt in the desert. In my time I have been roughed up in Bangkok, Singapore, Kuala Lumpur, Hamburg, Marseilles, you name it. You know where the Cleggs and the Booths have been sent by an enlightened brass. If this was your intent and your pleasure, roughhousing me after gentling me, after interrogating me as a total stranger, then well and good. I don't mind. In fact I welcome it, knowing the spirit of enlightened horseplay still thrives in the land I am willing to give my life for. Now, if that sounds a little corny to you, that must be because, among those of us willing to lay our lives on the line, it pays not to get too sophisticated or complex about it. If you have to go, you have to go. I am not one to bicker about my future. Do with me what you will. Maybe I have used up the best of me. Here I stand, you can see the old wounds and fuel many a wet dream with them. You have got me down to my fruits of the loom, but you have not gotten me to slander Colonel Booth. Maybe one day, when I am sitting in a wheelchair, ninety years old, I will allow as how he brushed his teeth crosswise instead of with the grain, but until then, naked or clad, I am loyal. Would you gentlemen please give me a hand with my duds now? After Africa, you feel the cold more than you used to. Thank you much."

Young effusive dodderers, they escorted him out into the midafternoon sunshine, patting him on the back and congratulating him. *Congradjulations* was how they said it, making him wonder if they had all come from the same prep school, military academy, university department, or indeed zone of warfare. Maybe they had, to a man, already won the Congressional Medal of Honor for astounding feats you would never associate with blazers and gray flannel pants. They had redressed him with the same elaborate, finicky care as they had stripped him bare. Presumably they now knew about him what they needed: an odd combination of mental temper and physical aplomb. The quality they hunted had blazed through from their naked colonel, and he had not been found wanting. Nothing lacking: that's what *that* meant. The skin he had bronzed in Turkey somehow evinced the savvy he had acquired in the Cyrano. It would not have been his own way of assessing a man, plumbing him, but it could conceivably work. He was surprised not to find Booth outside in squash outfit, lounging and grinning at him as if he knew all about the scragging that had gone on in that seminar room or holy of holies. But no Booth appeared. Here I go, Clegg thought, being conducted somewhere again. They keep marching me around and subjecting me to indignities. What am I missing in all this? What's the key? Am I more important than I thought, or just a whipping boy?

The conversation around him was not addressed to him, although he seemed to have provoked it. Almost all of the interrogation team wore horn-rimmed glasses, which made it hard to see into their eyes, even for the keen-sighted Clegg. The afternoon light was a caustic, uncontained liquid swill, devoid of tints often associated with it: salmon, beige, apricot. Instead, it seemed indeed a mass jamboree of hyperagitated photons, each capable of blinding a Newton, each none the worse for its journey from the furnace of the local star. Half blinded, Clegg wondered for a crazy moment if this were yet another test, with the local sun harnessed in a unique way to punish the malefactor from Africa. Clegg knew this was an insane idea, but today he was receptive to such thinking. Nothing had gone according to expectation, nothing had panned out as he would have liked. Perhaps he was at long last surrendering to migraine, something in the family on the female side, but he had no headache, not yet, and he doubted if the searing dazzle had anything to do with him.

Or with them. Suns were not for hire.

Or with Booth. Even his power did not extend that far.

The deity might have intervened, Clegg thought; after all, where did Aqua Regia come from? Was she not an emanation from the far reaches of space? Or a phantom from the well-known part of the visible spectrum?

One thing he knew. The constant piling up of unanswered and unanswerable questions created a kind of gas in the head, clogging and blurring, convincing him that all he knew was wasteful and all he asked was beside the point. If they were seeking to demoralize him, they were succeeding; but it was upset with a hint of prank, no doubt the way the young arbiters around him thought. They were in charge, and with abominable whimsy impossible to counter as it had no rationale, no tradition, no protocol. It could not be learned by rote, but only by jamming two personalities together, the one taking the impression of the other like a jagged wound in the heart. Clegg almost prayed to himself, knowing he would grant just about anything; the trouble was, he told himself in a fit of nausea, he wasn't a god anyway. They were conducting him to another, larger building, perhaps for execution. Who could tell? They would secure him with ropes to a vaulting horse, blindfold him with coconut matting, and then shoot him in the head after some wild card, say Captain Ernst Jünger formerly of the *Wehrmacht*, had inspected the scene and the arrangements; Captain Jünger had once been in charge of execution protocol for the German army, specializing in deserters, some of whom he had to coax to behave well. Clegg would be no more surprised to encounter the hundred-year-old Jünger than he would his ageless Aqua Regia. For reasons unknown, fugitives from other realms—the real, the imagined, the undreamed-of—were making their way into his mental landscape, dawning on him as it were, and bolstering his retinue of standbys. They were hardly old faithfuls or reckless converts to the code of Clegg, but they came unbidden and, joined together with tact, might make up a useful squad of—he wondered. Well, how about revenants and newcomers? Or, if not that, how about covenanters and cohorts? Who would be next? Surely there would soon be another Clegg, not Clegg the younger but Clegg the baritone, Clegg the peripatetic lecturer?

Blindfold on, blindfold off. A strong bouquet of winey mustard. Rotting chrysanthemums. But from where? Seated, he had to adjust his eyes to the screen; the dark had to rival the sunshine before he could see. They waited while he told them about it. Then the movie began, all about Booth, whom he saw making a chalk mark on a lamppost, sticking a wad of gum on a men's room door, ostentatiously polishing a pair of sunglasses in front of a pet shop. It was Booth all right, but without those three things: his severe demeanor; his almost Turkish fling backward of the head; and his peculiar glare, aimed at the periphery but mellowing as his eyes focussed nearer to him until, as he looked at someone or something only an arm's length away, his gaze converted to doodling-sentimental, all of a sudden chastened by worldly wisdom into that of the Tartar with a honeyed heart.

What on earth were they trying to prove?

Booth a spy? No more than Machiavelli was an astronaut, Clegg muttered, or George Washington a chess champion. No, not spy: agent. No, not agent: undercover man. No, not that, but traitor. Then which? Clegg asked. No, they said. "What would you do if Booth turned out to be a traitor? Would you denounce him?"

Irritated, yet undermined, Clegg said "How can you denounce when you do not know?"

They did not let him get away with that. "We are telling you. He has done extraordinary things. Would you care to know?" No, he answered; he would, however, very much like to talk with Booth, not necessarily about espionage, but about elitist rancor. He did not say this, but he thought it with right pungent fervor, beginning to know now why he had been treated so bizarrely since rescue.

"Forgive him, then," he said. "He's A-one. You should clone him instead. Ask Captain Jünger over there. He knows all about executions and traitors. It will all go off well if you get him to organize it. He's the cat's whisker at that kind of thing. If you're looking for a seemly finis, call it what you will, ask him how to bring it off, in a clearing, with trumpets, stethoscopes, cognac, and sunglasses for the honored victim."

His allusion to Captain Jünger did not faze them at all. They were learning how to cope with Clegg, whose mind did a kind of sideways levitation and vomited green gruel when asked awkward questions. "Yes," said the thinnest of the questioners, in the seat behind Clegg, "Captain Jünger never misses the annual reunions of those Germans who hold the Blue Max, their most prestigious decoration. Doesn't that tell you something about him?"

Awed by knowledge or superlative lying, Clegg said, "It tells me that hundred-year-old men get lonely. How many more reunions has he left to go?"

He enjoyed this company, though, even if they libeled Booth. It was rare to find an assembly of men who, when you made a conversational allusion, followed you with it and gave you full reign, even shooting their own hobbyhorses to let you do so. But highly suspicious as well—too ingratiating, Clegg thought. They have already charmed the pants off me this afternoon. Booth a spy in Turkey? They must have been reading my mind. Booth even had a flag in his bedroom, with his medals pinned on it, citations and certificates and all, a Kipling American jingoist if ever there had been one. Now they were going to ask him to shoot Booth in the head or keep an eye on him for the next ten years. Oh, it could never be anything as crass, as misinformed as that. Then what? Clegg felt an urge to weep.

It was not as if he had taken a special vow to Booth. Loyalty between them took care of itself through military routine: an order was an order; and, although Clegg liked to joke about the marine, *semper fi*, quality of their bond, it was more like a conventional relationship, with mingled devotion and complaint. Clegg was beginning to discover the onset of another view of Booth, one both poignant and grave. He had done some feckless things and it seemed he would have to pay. That was a gross view of things, Clegg thought. A complex man such as Booth was bound to attempt erratic, tactless maneuvers merely to prove, if one accepted an aerial version of life, his virtuosity. There were aerobatics, weren't there, of the moral sense? Of etiquette certainly, as Clegg was the first to confess about himself. Flying the Cyrano earned them various penalties: loneliness, discomfort, envy, an overdeveloped sense of their own importance. Both he and Booth had become accustomed to these accompaniments of their paramount role, and both had argued that, along with the technical and hands-on examinations they had undergone, they should have received some schooling in what they had agreed to name Cyranism. What they did wasn't like flying just any old plane, and their missions were far from standard. If there were penalties, there should be guidance and redress. Their minds should have been looked after better.

All this occurred to Clegg at speed, and he vaguely wondered how often he would have to roll-call subjects he and Booth had worn to death, knowing it was too late for the brass to do anything about either. He and Booth were on the verge of superannuation, but they had not thought about it, they were too busy flying, surviving. Time had sidled up to them, each thinking it was the other's shadow, and now, like certain athletes and newscasters, they had to count themselves "past it" while still relatively young. So what if Booth had been eccentric, letting off steam, dressing oddly, doing antic things, talking weird? Wasn't that the privilege of the prematurely used up? Clegg had an uncanny sense of doubleness: he and Booth had thought about these things often, but had never discussed them. Or had they discussed them without ever thinking about them? How could a man be bored by such painful novelty?

Am I zeroed in on the target? Clegg had an awful sense of looking past it so as to spare Booth. If Booth had indeed indulged in monkey business with the Ivans or the slopes, he would no doubt have to pay for it over and above the payment due for being what the military thought was old. Thinking of Booth thus, Clegg saw him dwindle in rank, all the way from colonel to light colonel, major, captain, and two kinds of lieutenant. Now he was an air cadet, bristly and eager, older looking than he was because of the mustache, but somehow innocent, eager to believe, indeed an aeronautical postulant. This was the Booth he most admired, when the man's (or youth's) sheer openness of mind seemed a form of mental initiative. Nowhere else had Clegg seen a passive thing such as receptivity seem so active a gift. Perhaps, he thought, that's what it is like to be a young clergyman, taking it all on trust, building faith on it without really knowing much about anything, until, slam, you get cancer and have to decide in a hurry if you've lost the faith or are going to stick with it to the end, obtuse as an old tiger. Clegg sometimes felt he knew the preambles to other careers than his own, but never gave himself credit for the knowledge, arguing with himself that certain careers overlapped more than anyone knew: the mystic and the high-altitude reconnaissance pilot, the monk in his cell and the lighthouse keeper, the author at his word processor or yellow tablet and the explorer, like Admiral Byrd, alone and jittery at the pole.

Then he noticed he'd fixed on solitary men who felt the repercussions of other beings without getting to know them from within. I am a sort of privateer, Clegg decided, wishing nonetheless he knew more about a word that, having occurred to him from God knew where, did not necessarily fit the occasion. He was drifting, meandering, half worrying if his kit was all right, left in the elegant suite they'd given him. He had so little to lose. Somewhere, was it in Borneo or Germany, there was the locked trunk with the rest of his kit in it, unopened for twenty years, his name painted big in white (*Captain* Clegg then) on the outside of the lid. What was in that? Books, a tie press, a trousers press, a flashlight, maybe a revolver, some flags and helmets, a pack of rainbow condoms, a gross of foam earplugs, some saved-up newspapers. Such was the clutter of an unresumable life. Surely the perfect ritual was to bury *your old trunk* for alien prospectors of the planet to find eons later, a time capsule to give them a news headline. He laughed, his mind having served up to him the ultrapatriotic image of Booth, pressing his pants by sleeping on them, smoothed out between a blanket and a carefully folded American flag. Clegg had always joked that he could see the imprint of the stars and stripes when Booth stood erect in good sunlight. Now the man was being rumored to be an informer, a spy, and he asked himself, How many spies, informers, were rumored to be high-altitude reconnaissance pilots? There was no reciprocity between slanders these days.

Should he tackle Booth and get the truth out of him, so as to know better how to protect him? Or should he keep quiet, as a friend should? All he knew was that he would sooner betray his country than his colonel, he could not quite say why, but it had something to do with a country's miscellaneous unknowability, the number of other people available for the chore, and the astounding degree to which a separate human (separate from the mob) exerted a spell on others without even trying. To the proposition that a country was full of millions of comparable individuals, Clegg had no reply beyond his not knowing them. What use had they been to him when he flew all those recon missions on their behalf, to keep them safe? They had not even known where he had been time and again, and to them he was merely a cousin several times removed of Captain Gary Francis Powers, the bad-luck boy of an earlier era. Clegg and Booth were like two old renegades, ex-Communists, former bandits, once upon a time prized for eccentric deviation, and now brought to book. It was up to them to save themselves and find careers the names for which were so obscure their bearers might never be found. Docent, say, at the Kandinsky Museum. A sizarship or a postmastership at an Oxford college, the latter especially advantageous because it suggested a bogus, misleading career in the post office, where a subsidiary career in passports would throw pursuit off the scent in yet another way. His mind kept churning, but clearly he needed to catch up with Booth, unless he was already manacled in another part of the building. Was there, he wondered, a pentagram behind the Pentagon, cachet of a military magic known only to Pershings, Lindberghs, and MacArthurs? Without help, he too was going to fade away, like that old soldier in the barracks poem.

By now, in this well-upholstered limbo of the investigation phalange, Clegg had begun to query Booth, not so much outright as through metaphors. Getting nowhere, not even with such evasive invasions as the story of a man who had the mannerisms of a spy, and that of the pilot who invented a self-incriminating story of himself, Clegg began to quiz him directly over the broccoli-and-cheese soufflé.

"What on earth did you do, Colonel? They seem all riled up."

"I did my duty."

"But did your duty entail something extra?"

Booth was nodding, unlikely to stop.

"How so?"

"You know how mosses are a kind of pioneer plant," Booth began. "Well, it was like that. I was a pioneer."

Clegg could fathom none of this. Was Booth deliberately obfuscating things, or was this the only way to do it? Was this the one way he could bear to do it? If so, what *was* it?

"I was asked," he resumed, "and I said yes. You've heard of the spy who came in from the cold, and ice station zebra, well, it was nothing like that. I myself have read a fair amount of spy thrillers, and it was more like taking a registered packet to the post office. I was to pretend I was bogus. Skunk Works we called Spunk Works. It was as easy as that. The information I passed on, with all the pomp and circumstance of spying, was fraudulent, but carefully devised. So far as we could tell, they never found me out. Now, of course, they have no use for me, neither *them* nor our own people. For years I fetched and carried, and I do believe it was no flameout we had, but something planted on board, but by whom? You see my predicament."

"A double life," Clegg whispered.

"Hardly a life at all," Booth told him forlornly. "What can you do when they ask? You amass a good name, a fine aroma, only to be asked to do something such as that. It doesn't bear thinking about."

"Jesus H. Christ," Clegg said quietly, as if remembering a long-forgotten quotation. "We were blown up."

Booth had stopped nodding, but now he began again, his face haggard in its tan, his hands washing themselves with dry tenderness. "Maybe both sides had a hand in it. Have you thought of that?"

"To be quite candid," Clegg told him wearily, "I hadn't thought of it at all. You astound me, Colonel."

"Well, get used to it, Recon. The history of our missions isn't going to change. I imagine we'll get a medal now, for surviving, and then be lowered into twelve foot of wet, fast-drying concrete."

"Only if it's *written*," Clegg was murmuring. "We might still make a living dipping toothpicks in mint. You know how it is in hospitals. They have Intensive Care, which suggests more attention than you'll ever need or be able to tolerate. Intensive Care has a complementary opposite called Extensive Indifference. The two things go together. So: they'll both overattend to us and ignore us as well."

"Blather, Recon," Booth said. "Believe me, buddy boy, they have more than enough facilities for turning us both into metal polish. Don't you worry. If we get away with our lives, it will only be because they want us to—so they can go on observing us and filling their blasted notebooks. I may not have learned much in or from the military, but I have come away with the distinct impression that they do what they damned well please, especially when they have help from the civilian contingent. Why, man, they can make sabotage look like a quotation from the sermons of John Donne. No man is his own prophylactic. They can get up murder as an extended inter-library loan. Anything can happen, so much so that, as you look around you at ordinary things, dogs being run over, children buying ice cream, old people pausing on their walkers, it all means something else you don't know about. Innocent fascia, I call it. I feel safer if I have a phrase for things. You'll never know what got you. Somebody taps you from behind, says 'You dropped your paper, sir,' and he's gone while the cyanide wafts up from between the pages, and down you go. We have arrived at exactly the moment at which we no longer dare do anything commonplace, or, for that matter, anything special, such as flying the Cyrano. I'm sorry. You are hardly an accomplice, Recon, but you are part of the team. Would they get me and spare you? I doubt it. We may have only a few days to go. I don't have to tell you, as von Moltke told his friends in Tegel Prison, it takes twenty minutes to strangle at the end of a rope. 'Brace yourselves, gentlemen,' he said. Think of yourself as Gandhi or Trotsky: a target. Maybe that will help." He hunched forward as if confessing.

Clegg said nothing, sensing a lion had ripped a huge hunk of him away, sentimentally known as the rest of his life. Was Booth lying? Who was telling the truth? If it was no use questioning Booth, it was no use asking anybody anything. The answer, duplicitous as ever, would come in classical Greek, wrapped in a bottle that exploded when opened. The senior-junior yuppies in gray serge trews had scuppered him quite, even someone as innocent as he, a onetime lover of astronomy. How could anyone with such vast interests be considered guilty of anything? Clegg moaned inwardly, convinced that he could lie low for a year or two in a remote slum in Liverpool, England, in a place with a name like Toxteth, talking with a fake Beatles accent, hair dyed orange, a safety pin through each earlobe. No? Surely Booth was looking on the black side. The ample coruscade of knightly behavior fell away—was there even such a word as *coruscade?* The ample palladium of knightly behavior sagged. If only he could remember what a palladium was. It was as if all the words he needed with which to characterize his predicament had slipped away from him, and he was left with words vaguely appropriate because resonant, but words whose meaning he didn't know and had never known. It was just like his singing; he mouthed something unctuous or grandiose and left it at that. His songs were very sung.

"How could that be?" Booth had asked him something, but Clegg only drawled.

"Disguises," Booth was saying in an almost hysterical rant. "If only we had time."

"Yeah, by shit, Colonel," Clegg shouted, "and a plane to get out in. Preferably jet."

"Piss-obvious, Recon. The slower the better. An old crop duster. *Two* old crop dusters going in different directions to spray different fields. You never know. They do have a landing strip nobody knows about."

"Or we could bluff it out." Clegg seemed cheerful, grateful perhaps to know something definite. He hummed. He broke into gibberish song, aiming at itinerant angels who crowded the room like feathers settling. *There* was the dimension that would save him, the source from which Aqua Regia came, all glowing wholesomeness and sensuous polyvalence. What on earth was he dreaming up now, in the teeth of catastrophe? Booth seemed to have run out of ideas, seemed almost inclined to wait things out, resigned to his lot, whereas Clegg—optimist rather than grace-hoper—believed in other ways out. Had they done their worst, felling the Cyrano over the Danakili desert? Or was there worse, with poisoned umbrellas and electrical spaghetti?

"Let's make a run for it, Colonel. Now."

"Where to? We'd never get out."

"You want us to kill ourselves."

"Not yet. We should take some of the bastards with us."

"All this time," Clegg told him, "I thought these jolly little bumboys were on your side. Were *yours*, Colonel. They had it in for me, and after a while I didn't give diddly-squat."

"Brave Clegg. Keep calm, man. We have to give the impression of coming back to normal. Essentially, they have us in two ways. One: as condemned men. Two: as playthings. Maybe the two come to the same end. Playthings to experiment with for the good of the Corps. How do you like them apples?"

Clegg almost choked, swiftly abandoning heroic notions for a common or garden yen to go on living: *Unsolved Mysteries*; the glass of water set before you in American eateries before you even speak; fifty or sixty channels; the little red flag that tells the mailman the box contains a letter for pickup; ironing boards that fold down from the wall in motels; drugstores, drugstores, drugstores; automats; the gratuitous politeness of Texans; the demotic courtesy of calling men "sir" without the least military connotation. A wave of homesickness raced through him and spilled away; he was already home, dammit. It certainly didn't feel like it. In Turkey you always touched gold while making a wish in full view of the crescent moon. What should he do here? Lick a hundred-dollar bill while saluting the sun? Suddenly Clegg saw that the country you yearn for while away is never the one you return to; its refrigeration during your absence attenuates and blurs it, converting it into a fallible icon you should abandon at the Customs counter on return. What are you trying to smuggle in, Colonel? Oh, a scale model of the United States, sir? Sorry, we do not permit contraband. In the wrong hands, at home, this could be disastrous. No, we do not give receipts. Where did you buy such a bauble?

Now Clegg knew how energized his mind could become by vignettes, cameos, of the beloved place. Or by images of startling scenarios, such as the one that first lit the fires of aeronautical yearning: someone had told him of a flight up to the Arctic Circle, there and back before lunch, memory heaving with delight at having such a view during lunch. To have just, only just, been feasting one's eyes on the Circle, a few hours before curried lasagna — that was a rapture worth signing on for. He had never investigated the concept, though, leaving it in the realm of aubade, serenade, symphony, tone-music, ignoring such prosaic matters as the aircraft's range, speed, and ability to refuel. He never quite believed in it, especially as the plane had been an English Electric Lightning, a marvel in its day. So it flew and reflew unchecked, a make-believe exotic renegade hopelessly inferior to the Cyrano. It had been a beginning, though, a kick-start guaranteed to change his life and turn him into an air-farer. Was there such a word? There was such a man. There were thousands, all of them heroes whose philosophy was that they were expendable, as if they were sugar, flour, molasses. It was amazing: they would leave mementoes behind them (nothing went with them on missions), but they themselves would evaporate into the smoke, the flames, the ocean, noble for having allowed themselves to be used. Where he found this notion of expendability, he was not sure: it both terrified and exalted him, reminded him that anyone in uniform had forfeited his life to begin with. The idea was not unique to the Japanese. Whenever he looked at the chest of a fellow pilot and saw the abbreviated braids of medal ribbons and decorations, he knew he was looking at carnages that now and then had surrounded them. So they were all givers, donors, even he and Booth who prowled the world like long-sighted paparazzi, meaning no harm but doing some, and they were certainly taking risks. To live one's life safely was way below this: a life of quiet, lucrative vegetation uninvigilated by death. In a way he was glad of war, mistrust, the mindless bickering of big-stick-touting nations. He was grateful for nations, languages, flags, the differences that festered and stymied diplomats. Had he been flying combat missions, as of old, he might not have felt so sanguine. Such theories as he had about self-sacrifice had come to him in a phase, the most recent one, of flying peacefully, belated because earlier he'd never had chance to think. Now he was Clegg the ponderer, calm and lofty, a warrior no longer, but Recon the looker and examiner.

Booth's view of all this was classical, which is to say public and unemotional, whereas Clegg's was private and romantic. Asked to be a double agent, or whatever the term was for what he did, Booth had readily agreed; duty was duty. Clegg would have made a mess of it, he was sure. But there was this: if you added a role to your role, then a day might come when your second role proved unnecessary; but your first role might by then have become undetachable, a permanent lamentable weld, whereas a Clegg, homogeneously simple in his role, would have no such problems. How, Booth wondered, to drop the habits of a lifetime? Was there not another niche for him, for them? Would NASA take over all the Cyranos much as the military had taken over the space shuttle? First the jet pilots yielded to the astronauts, he thought, then the astronauts yielded to non-man-rated missions — or soon would. Sometimes his mind, his overtaxed and bullied mind, had the disheveled crispness of paperwhites, gone dry and now unresponsive to water. Had he doubled his role for double money? Not quite. He had done it out of honor and the desire for excitement, because the chances of being shot down were so slim. Smarter men than he had polished their *summas,* kept their noses out of combat, and joined step together to become a durable elite, not merely civil servants but civil honchos operating the world by numbers and curves. It must be fun to be one of them, he decided, watching the virile fraternity of the Booths and Cleggs flying off to bloodshed. Oh, now and then one of them blew his brains out or died of AIDS, but the majority went on to huge pensions and neat villas across the Potomac, some even becoming endowed professors of geopolitics at an age when hard-slog professors retired with a sigh and half salary.

When Booth allowed himself to hate, he did so with officious relish, knowing he was a rare specimen. It had never occurred to him that the bogus data he passed to the other side might have sent a test pilot to his death. Surely they checked it all out in a wind tunnel first? He was not sure, did not care. It was not his fault that the reported angle of incidence of a certain wing was half a degree too much, or that the smuggled-out aerofoil from the Skunk/Spunk Works was imperfect and likely to cause a spin. Such worries were for the brass, or for their bouncy, bright juniors, cream of Harvard, Yale, and Dartmouth. If the Soviets had not been such aeronautical plagiarists in the first place, they would never have needed to worry; they loved nothing better than capturing a plane and then making slight changes to it so as to have an ostensible new design. Booth's knowledge of other nations' aeronautics was woolly and vengeful, but he did not honor savants linked to demonologies. That he seemed to offer the spectacle of a distinguished officer gone to rot bothered him not in the least; his pride in himself was sacrosanct, so much so that he had forgotten where he had hidden it. If there were anywhere a polity, a *magna carta*, for the double agent officer, it came not from the military but from drafters of international law whose edicts appeared garbled and magnified in the movies, as when Doolittle's Tokyo raiders appeared in a Japanese court and were condemned to death. He remembered that movie as if it had been real life for him, and Doolittle his military daddy. Lined up, the captured American fliers had an almost jaunty air, confident that as military personnel they had no place in a civilian court and would swiftly be marched away once the point was made.

Bless them, Booth always murmured at this point. One of those Nips, maybe the sallow narrow gent with the pointed beard, set things going, Booth reminded himself, and then it was Greenbaum, a captain, who made the statement that rocked them on their ears for its fervor, its weight, its marshalling of an ancient language to vindicate a team of brave men in the twentieth century, and in the lion's mouth. Greenbaum referred the court to the Geneva Treaty, not entirely sure they were familiar with it, and began to quote, lungs pumping hard although clearly he had never had to make this speech at any other time: not a plea but the trumpet of honest indignation tinged with wry contempt for anyone who could not grasp a point as simple as this. Captured combatants, he told them at the curbed shout, are entitled to the protection their own state is unable to afford them. The judges on the bench scowled at this bit of evasion, or so Booth recalled, having sat through the movie a dozen times, too engrossed in the proffered charter to remember its exact wording. He remembered its emotional lunge, its uncompromising direction, bringing the good news from Aix to Tokyo. On thundered Captain Greenbaum, a lawyer from Queens as Booth remembered it, a burly, correct figure to whom the God of the Old Testament was more real than any puffing samurai. There was a hiatus at this point, perhaps mere agitation while Greenbaum took a deeper breath and returned to his onslaught with the broadsword of common sense. "Their lives," Greenbaum told the court, "ceasing to be *jura publica*, under the dominion of belligerency"—and now the Japanese officials realized he was not going to translate his Latin—"have become *jura universalia* when seen from one point of view and *jura probata* when seen from another." It was magnificent. He might have made it up on the spur of the moment, smacking them also with some such trumped-up thing as *jura cosmica* and *jura apo-*

dictalis. Facially, the *sangfroid* Japanese were on the run, backing down from what they could not fathom because they could not track it from one logical turn to the next, which he Booth snapped up with the ease of a barracuda. This had been one of the great days for two languages, its orator a made-over attorney from Queens of all places, a man newly crashed into the sea after being steam-catapulted off a carrier in a B-25. What an event. Booth knew he would like this speech engraved on whatever tomb he got.

Glorious, intransigent, Promethean, metal-hearted Greenbaum stove on with a "thus," hectoring them now, having already brought them to their knees with his triple cross of public, universal, and proven. "Thus," he boomed, "by a double portal they reenter—" Booth glowed, thrilled, began to shake with commemorative joy. *By a double portal,* he whispered. Greenbaum was inspired. What a phrase, worthy of Tennyson or Whitman. Had he spent much time rehearsing the speech in his infested, dank cell, or had he, geniuslike, come up with the phrase on the spot, under the white heat of all that murderous civilian scrutiny? "By a double portal," Greenbaum was going on, "they reenter the sphere of normal relations. Though separated for the time being from any political community, they once more belong to humanity and themselves." Behold the double portal, Booth instructed himself. Don't let it ever get away from you. This was enough, surely, but Greenbaum had more; he would never shut up, he was right about everything. One minute his practice was restricted to the minor lots and privet hedges of suburban Queens, but next was opened wide to the *gesta* of comprehensive epic.

Some logic from on high was propelling Greenbaum, who no longer read from paper but did impromptu law with his clients loosely grouped beside him, a charmed, vindicated clique, knowing he had gotten them off. On he drove, adding sanity to logic, still flushed from the delivery of his double portal. "And, as of their lives, so of their liberties," he resumed, settling into a rhythm culled from the Declaration of Independence, affirming the independence of American airmen from Japanese fanaticism, with the disunited press of the whole world watching in that courtroom. "It is of their combatant liberty alone that belligerency can dispose." Booth had never been able to figure out when Greenbaum was quoting or when he was being a pasticheur from Queens. Where did the quotes go? "So you see," he said crisply, being Greenbaum again, "Your Honor, you can't try us in a civil court." Had the chief judge answered him in querulous Latin, smearing challenge with trumped-up *homo belligerens* and *res extensa*, the whole ball of juridical wax, Roman-Dutch and hinged on a pin, something might have been achieved. But, the applause quelled on pain of death, the judge, affecting to have understood, answered in crackling Japanese, ignored the entire point about the double portal, and proclaimed the civil court's validity. After all, these American airmen had bombed a city of civilians; it seemed beside the point that it was the capital city of a warring power. Booth seethed while the fliers were condemned to be beheaded, honorably, the Japanese maintained. He of all men understood the double portal, the innocent ambivalence the military role required. To him, because the airmen were no longer combatant, they became civilians. It was clear. There they stood at attention, mute witnesses to their redundancy; they were no more warriors now than they were tennis players, chessmen, or bean counters. The movie incensed him, but he always watched it when he could because it provided him with a polity, he who had gone one better than most other pilots, acceding to request, not obeying an order. He never clicked his heels. He was never a *jawohl*-er. But when he said his crisp, emphatic "Sir" in response to a question, it was as if he had clicked the heels of his mouth. "Yes, sir" uttered with ravenous profanity was his *cri de coeur*. And Captain Greenbaum, beheaded in spite of his courtroom pains, remained a hero in Booth's head, not so much imaginary as dreamed, then lauded, saluted, loved.

Only poetic justice, taking a Roman holiday, would thus have equipped classic Booth with an avatar of justice and romantic Clegg with a phantom lady. It was what both needed, therefore perhaps what they needed to embellish. Clegg no more needed Greenbaum than Booth needed Aqua Regia. Yet Booth was dealing with someone almost real, whereas Clegg had a ghost to domesticate. Two men living in the penumbra of velleity sucked the rusk of self-solace. One found an angelic nurse (so far), the other the personification of an alibi. Would Aqua Regia vanish, then, and Greenbaum lose eidetic standing? Clegg would end fawning on personable shimmer, a Red Cross lady, and Booth would go settle in Queens, bon bourgeois after all, a fake Greenbaum forgiven.

Booth was well aware that much of the information he had passed to the Soviets had been identical with what appeared in specialized aviation magazines: not the popular ones slanted to owners of single-engine monoplanes (Pipers, Cessnas, Beechcraft), but the mostly tedious-to-read organs of technological probing. What puzzled him was that the Soviets, who scoured these advanced magazines for top-secret leaks, had not twigged his data were out of date, or public knowledge, or just plain wrong. How could so paranoid an industrial-military autocracy have missed the obvious? Had they been asleep at the switch all that time? Or did no one care? Or,

more imposing, were the Soviet invigilators so sloppy, so careless, they failed
to pick up even the most obvious clues? He rather enjoyed the duo of two
fanatically inimical societies bored with their own safeguards. Theoretically,
if all the top-secret stuff got into the magazines anyway, there was no need
for a Booth to supply it in secret. If Booth was handing it over wholesale,
there was no need for the magazines to do so. But then, he realized, there
would always be magazines of that kind; so his role appeared utterly
redundant, not worth the extra funding. The truth must have been that those
who pored over American aviation magazines of the highbrow sort didn't
understand English too well. So the whole enterprise went on in a fog,
adding to his incomprehension of the Soviet system.

Then he thought again. If what he had passed on had been bogus, it
would have figured in the Soviet mind as baroque addendum, not
patently muddled but puzzling, worth a few years' testing in a wind tunnel. Maybe they never quite knew the difference between magazine data,
ostensibly trustworthy, and the nonsense he passed on—it was so technical that even he, with his copious grasp of aeronautical principles, could
not appraise it. So he had not been redundant after all, but had provided
enigmatic red herrings designed not so much to fly as to throw up on serious blueprints, a kind of virus really, designed to complicate the reception
abroad of facts retailed in magazines. He was paid, so he must have been
of use. Now he saw it. He had been like the tinsel dropped in World War
Two to muddle Nazi radar, and he wondered if the whole operation—
Booth plus magazines plus others nameless then and nameless now—had
not been a gigantic scam: one hoax alongside another, calculated to make
comparers think one was genuine, but which? That must have been the
truth. Booth must have been as his idol Captain Greenbaum might have
said, echoing the phrase *amicus curiae*, friend of the court, *amicus confu-
sionis*, friend of confusion.

How difficult it was to try to evaluate your role and performance by foreign criteria. He would never know his true impact, his chronic standing,
as a double agent; what he had been ordered to do had opened up, even
in a mind as dedicated as his, a host of hypothetical readings that, codi-
fied, expanded to infinity, losing him like a rocket's stick. How did it go,
that survey of his possible nature?

He was ordered to provide bogus data.

Ordered to do so, he nonetheless secretly did not do it.

Ordered to do it, he sometimes did and sometimes didn't.

Not ordered to do it, he sometimes did it anyway, culling information
from top-flight aviation magazines.

Doing it, he also provided the Soviets with genuine top-secret data, which they either recognized or tossed out.

He then provided his own bosses with bogus information from the Soviets.

And soon he was riding a circuit of misinformation, invisibly crippling both sides in the interests of peace. It wasn't a bad idea: the double agent tripled. Was this what was meant by the phrase playing both ends against the middle? Peering toward the horizon, where ideas died a spurious death, he saw sublimity in the role of the man who wins by feinting.

Then Booth became bored with self-analysis, telling himself the whole thing was over, the Cold War was kaput, the shadowboxing was frozen in its final stance. All he knew was that he had been different, a man more evolved than many, a kind of military Marx Brother who played the code machine, and who, having fallen for what was fake, had never recovered, preferring it to both axioms and empirical observations. He came out a man transformed, and the magic that changed him was his own.

Who knew what the Russians thought anyway? What could you make of a nation that assembled its discarded airplanes in a huge field forty minutes' drive from Moscow, letting them rot and shrivel in that appalling climate as if they really believed they were close by Tucson, Arizona? Fancy leaving those formerly top-secret machines out there for tourists to gawp at, almost as if at long last revealing some variant of the truth. Booth winced, wondering if he himself belonged in that dismal meadow of tussocky turf, put out to grass like even the Fulcrum and the Bear, as if the mighty muck-a-mucks were saying, always, here is where we went wrong, again and again. He who wants his wound healed must first reveal it.

Was that what the Soviets meant? The field was a museum, but hardly one that cherished and celebrated; a thousand decrepit phone booths might have stood there instead, or tractors, or snowplows. Clearly, a top secret was tops for only so long, as in the West, as in the U.S.A., which was mighty careful what it put out to heat up in the desert sun outside Tucson. The Soviet version implied aversion, disgust: Let the Russian winter hammer these obsolete martial toys. Oh for rust, dilapidation, field mouse droppings. Booth thought he had seen a Luddite's auto-da-fé, in which metallic robots breathed their last, unfortunate not to have been cows or sheep, pigs or fowl. Metal was the key, he told himself. In the old days, when foreign governments sent smart emissaries among the Soviets, the Soviets always bestowed on them at the last, in a kind of politicist coup de grâce, a titanium samovar. Why? The Soviets had too much titanium, so they spread it about a bit, taunting other countries that had little. *That* was why one or two models of every discarded plane sat al fresco not far from

Moscow, scarecrows for the Star Wars era, raw material for uncountable samovars. It was their Stonehenge, he said, there to warn commissars about the perishability of all things, ideas especially. Booth, no commissar, had been a useful double agent, but his mind had never been in it, nor his heart. Both now came to life even as his day in the sunlight waned and turned foul.

It was so much simpler when he began training on a Northrop T 38, which handled similarly to the Cyrano. To be sure, the training was severe, but life back in the Sacramento Valley of California wasn't that harsh; he was a major among captains, majors, and colonels, all with three and a half thousand hours' total time. Not that the T 38 stretched by eleven inches, making it the Pavarotti puppet that unfurled from a certain comedian's fly during an especially raunchy act. The Cyrano just happened to be a plane that heated up at Mach 3. Tactile, Booth called it, doting on the thought that, for flight, he wore a silver tuxedo and, during the van ride out to the flight line, plugged in his portable air-conditioning unit. These were the divine physicalities of his calling. Once, supposed to land at Farnborough for the air show, he had reached Amsterdam before the Cyrano had slowed down enough for him to turn around, and that after flying from California to London. Trying to reconstruct what genuine things he had handed over to the Soviets was quite different; if he had done so, and, being Booth, he surely had, they would never have noticed. He did it to see what happened, and nothing did. Had he even reported that, when the Cyrano reached maximum speed, its wing skins crinkled from the heat, making chordwise corrugations parallel to the pell-mell flow of air? Anyone examining a Cyrano's wing would have been able to establish that. It made sense too: spanwise corrugations would have made no sense at all because the airflow ran from nose to tail. Did you become a traitor, then, if you blabbed something that logic could deduce? Booth thought not, but he needed to think that way, wanting pardon or vindication, having substituted casualness for duty. Nothing made more sense to him now than a night refuelling of the Cyrano, during which his fishbowl visor flashed chromatic with a thousand disco lights fired by Verey pistols aimed at the same target. The light show almost gave him vertigo, but what lulled him was the thought of all that JP-7 slushing aboard, some sixty or seventy thousand pounds of it. This had been not life in the fast lane but the life stratospheric with the machine leaping out ahead of the sounds of his presence: half a mile per second, almost six miles higher than commercial jets, with only a weather balloon for company, giving the whole mission a flavor of World War Two.

Yes, he remembered, watch out for those damned balloons. Flameout happens during high-speed maneuvers in yaw. Every motion has to be ultrasmooth, or there will be an inlet upstart and the Cyrano will flame out, expel its shock wave, and suddenly begin swapping end for end, a balletic disaster at supersonic speed, mashing the pilot's head and bruising his eyeballs. I know all that. It is written in acid in my brain, which is why we are still alive. Booth remembered, despite all his vices; I, Booth, testify that we hardly ever left a contrail, unlike our Soviet brothers, who liked flying smoky planes, perhaps as the plume of bravado, whereas we, humbler and niftier, got in and out without a sign. In laxer moods, Booth had yearned never to be a pilot again, but a member of the ground crew, wearing foot muffs when walking on the aircraft and, after the landing, waiting half an hour for the Cyrano's surfaces to cool down, unless, taken by a fit of zeal, he wanted to plant both hands on the hottest part of the fuselage and give himself a cicatrix, just to show nephews and drinking cronies, raising his palms with hieratic grandiosity to reveal the pink, corrected fish scales his skin had become. That was one way to become a man without fingerprints, and the newly landed pilot could do it as well as anyone else; he only had to take a deep breath and apply his hands to the titanium.

Thought came of T. E. Lawrence holding his hand above a lighted match, burbling on about the trick of not minding, but Booth dismissed T. E. L. as a grandstander, preferring the icon of exhausted pilot, still in knightly chain mail, incinerating his sensitive hands with self-effacing aplomb. The trick, Booth told himself, was not to show off.

Leave the Cyrano out for long in the Marysville sunshine and its porous tanks leak fuel because they're unheated and not pressurized. Booth sighed, then gloated. There was always a trade-off. For a long time, he had been amazed this lethal-looking dark blue dart had anything so prosaic as an undercarriage—just tires and struts—that dangled like a drunk's suspenders (his image). In theory, such a plane should never land, should have been born in fire and put a girdle round the Earth nonstop. In the days of its design, the man who dreamed it up offered fifty dollars to any employee who could find anything simple, buyable-off-the-shelf, about it. His fifty dollars were safe, Booth knew; the Cyrano was an amalgam of singularities, some of which he might have passed along to the wrong party, only doubling up the tales the aviation mags told. The Soviets had never come up with any such plane, and they had never won the fifty dollars.

On the whole, that distant raid on Tokyo had been simpler than his life was now. Ejecting became a metaphor that told him Russian pilots were better at ejecting than at anything else; they were always pitching themselves out of their aircraft at air shows, at low speed and low altitude, landing without harm. They went up only to pitch themselves out, betraying (he thought) a culpable hankering for circus. He would always go down with his plane from now on, he decided, but what plane? Why were those Russians so good at ejecting? Was it that they knew both sides plagiarized each other and, during the shuffle, some bad ideas got canonized, with tragic results? He could not tell, but he suspected. Planes based on rumors made torrid footage on the evening news. He yearned to go back and have a different life, preferably in some less illustrious aircraft that chugged along low above canals, factories, and golf clubs and had to be refueled in the normal way, by landing, every couple of hundred miles. Puddle jumping, they called it. Visual Flight Rules (Very Faulty Routing) rather than flying by instruments: Instrument Flight Rules (ironically remembered as I Follow Roads, whereas of course the roads followed by the IFR pilot were blue lines on a chart). These spells of Ludditism had begun years ago, but he had fought them off, ascribing them to the latest malaise, weariness with technology, akin to the disease that medieval monks used to suffer from—*accidie,* or spiritual debility, which was perhaps what happened to men when they realized daily they were not gods, though leaking hubris from every pore. He wanted—what did he want? He wanted not to want. He wanted to be air, gravity, anoxia, the weirdest mix of flight, music, and nostalgia. Oh to be an *aramski,* he said, the best Russian rocket, needing nothing and never needing that lack of need to be regarded.

How many times had he wished for something impossible, echoing an old fanatical philosopher who said he believed something because it was impossible, which was to say that such a thing as he envisioned just could not *be.* What was ridiculous, to him, was not that all was possible because God was dead, but that once you believed in God although everything seemed absurd you were lost. You had reached the stage at which everything that ever was was a reason for believing in God. Booth's head began to whirl. The mess he was in was metaphysical, nothing to do with aviation. Man was not on the planet as the guinea pig in some exercise to do with belief; man was an earthling by accident, neither with nor without purpose: just not thought about, not considered. Booth began to shiver in the presence of something so vast, so awful, he wanted to kill himself because the prospect of death amidst such travesty was so unthinkable. Here was something different from the kind of thing that upset Clegg, such as (one of Clegg's mottoes) "Loyalty above all else, except honor," which struck Booth as almost a logical maxim. Here was the end of the mind's power to control anything. Stand fast and be gobbled up, he thought; take a stand on senselessness.

Yes, he whispered, grapple with the lack of intention.

Be neuter.

Don't cry.

Don't pray.

Don't understand.

Be as passive as lettuce, teak, potassium permanganate.

Remember the formula for explosive hypergolic.

Take redundant *explosive* from preceding.

To test anything, fly it to Arctic Circle, expose it to the light there, then bring it back.

Don't confess.

He remembered taking his aged [parents] for their weekly drive, through graveyard after graveyard on request, so they could test the waters of design, the inroads of time, the graveyard wind. Maybe, in fifty years' time, he would be doing the same thing, but for death, which cut down the preamble. You could usually count on it to do that.

"Penny for them," Clegg was saying in a jolly rhythm.

"Sick of this place?" Booth expected no answer.

Clegg just gestured, a shrug melded with a slight lift of the head.

"Let's join up again," Booth said. "Let's enlist."

"As in the old days."

"Depends on what you mean by old."

"Senescence repelled," said Clegg. "Boy, do we work at it."

"Shit shaping," Booth told him. "We gotta shape."

"We ain't shapin'," Clegg answered in his broken-down plebeian drawl, "we dead, brother."

"You can say that again."

"We—"

"Don't," Booth said, on the offensive. "That's more than enough for one day. They will ship us out real soon. You can see it in the *summas'* eyes."

"As in the movies."

"As in no movie you ever saw, Recon." Booth poured the remains of his sun-weakened drink into his cowboy boot and winced. "I knew a man, an aviation mechanic, who became so essential to all the private pilots he could shut down a whole airport just by going on vacation. Then he came back. Once he went off to Florida and never came back. One by one the local pilots flew their planes away and *they* never came back. That was called the denuding of Wimpole Ferry. Knew a guy too who kept hearing some Ravel on the radio, went to the stereo shop and always bought something else because they never had in stock the CD he wanted. In no time he had a stack of the same CD, the only Ravel they ever had. Thus do seekers after the holy grail surfeit themselves with sameness."

"You're talking funny again," Clegg said. "You need to get some sleep. Pronto."

"Tell you what, Recon. I'm a killer," Booth said. "A dumbass out-of-the-night killer."

"Well, Colonel," Clegg said, irritable, "why don't you croak off *back* into the flaming night. Where they want you."

"There's always your sister."

"She's coming to town."

"She'll go back married, then."

"Dumbass trip if you ask me."

"Diplomats are great ladykillers," Booth told him. "You better lock her up from the colonels with their meatgrinder phalluses."

Clegg had heard most of this rigmarole before, especially when Booth was both horny and mystified. Eager to know what was going to happen to him for having betrayed a national trust, he became verbally belligerent, half adulating death because it, so the rumor went, closed down all wondering.

Around the internal pentagram they marched, heads erect, thumbs in line with the seam of their pants, eyes fixed on a point a hundred yards away, Booth both giving and acknowledging salutes (more the former than the latter). They were in dress uniform, like two accelerated pigeons: two of the possessed, allowed to prance like popinjays until the coup de grâce, a smart examination done on computers, requiring them to compose a three-hour essay in English on one of the following topics:

1. Banality in power politics.
2. Terrorist style.
3. The Ploesti Raids.

At a disadvantage, Clegg wrote on a theme dear to his heart, Turkish obscenity, while Booth, understanding none of them, did the impossible and wrote on restarting the Cyrano's two 30,000-pound-thrust J58's. They thought exams had long gone, but this was part of the new novelty, concocted by the high-strung yuppies in suits. As they did so, plans unfolded for their eventual rebestowal in civilian life, the whole idea being to conceal two albino mites in something like the score of a Schubert sonata, infinitely minifying them into the texture of the paper. Never would they visit that open-air museum outside Moscow, or receive a titanium samovar, see yet another Russian eject, or ever mine coal. They would be subjected to what was called compatible ablation, which provided a job and a hobby, both taken seriously until further assignment, and the final quietus. Clegg would have to share in Booth's restriction, for having done nothing but be along and sing.

"I'm sure somebody's looking out for us." Booth sighed. "There can't be nobody."

Booth failed to answer, lost in his daydream about the Cyrano's engines, trying to wangle into his thoughts a sentence he had read in a Spanish magazine: masculine society, repressive, now and then just has to allow the existence of some woman both extravagant and rare.

They had still not been allowed off base, and the more they felt land-locked the more they dreamed back to flying or to life in Turkey. Clegg, having read the daily newspaper aloud for half an hour, much to Booth's annoyance (he put in the earplugs he always carried with him), then began talking what he fondly hoped was sociology, haranguing Booth with the idiocy of modern shopping. "Everything used to be so heavy," he said, "until we discovered how to freeze-dry, which was when we began bringing everything home as a powder. The groceries weighed nothing in those days. Then, would you believe it, they decided the water we added to the powders wasn't safe, so we had to start bringing our water home in huge jars. The groceries weighed twice what they ever did. Now, tell me: is that progress or not?"

Nibbling at the corner of his *Washington Post*, Booth mumbled something Clegg could not fathom. He assumed Booth had agreed and so launched into his next topic: how to dehydrate water, so to speak, in order to bring it home as a powder.

"The laughter of Chinese women," Booth pronounced from within his cocoon of semisilence, "is like the wind curling around a corner door-post. Honestly." Clegg gaped midsentence, reluctant to change subject, yet wondering what had sent Booth to China. Clegg had not noticed the earplugs; when he talked to Booth he looked away from him, offering his voluntary to the sky, the furniture, the floor. In retaliation he launched into a memory of the Topkapi Palace, for three centuries the residence of the sultans. Each year, he told Booth, who knew, there was that performance of Mozart's *Abduction from the Seraglio*, at the so-called Gate of Felicity.

"I know," Booth retorted in spite of his earplugs, "right next to the actual seraglio in fact." He, Clegg, and Babe [Babette] had attended a July showing, little mindful of the fact that the Gate of Felicity, *Bab-i Saadet*, sometimes known as the Gate of the White Eunuchs, led into the sultan's private quarters. The opera happened between the harem and the emerald-full Treasury, against spray-painted panels that belonged in a motel. The trick, as Clegg learned, was to look beyond these ephemeral vulgarities and focus on the minarets and towers.

"There was a huge *çinar* tree," Clegg said, "with the orchestra grouped around it. Bells and cymbals as well."

"Don't forget the fire engine," Booth said, removing one earplug as if it were a concentrated and solidified infection. "For safety's sake, but to show off too. Remember the folding tin chairs, the Gate of the Bird Cage, the Gate of Salutations, the Mantle of the Prophet. So many bloody gates. I suppose by now they have a Gate of the Gulf War."

"And a Watergate," Clegg said. "Do you remember, there was no program of any kind, and if there had it would have been done in that weird little Arabic script, real tiny, called *ghabarah*."

"Meaning dust," Booth said, removing his second earplug.

"Learned today, aren't we, Colonel? It was invented for sending messages by carrier pigeon, so as not to overload the bird."

"More brains than you find at the Pentagram," Booth said, sighing and flying his open palm around him.

"And more consideration too. Anyway, the Mozart. In German, as I recall, which seemed okay to me, though Babe fussed about it."

"The power comes and goes," Booth yawned. "Electric."

"And the glory too."

"It went out three times," Booth said, "and they finished with flashlights, the headlamps of the fire engine having failed to light up the stage."

"I liked it best," Clegg said, "when they were singing in total darkness, almost as much as the way they released those doves to a final chorus sung in Turkish."

"Well," Booth told him, "if you hate opera, that's the place to go. It would have been better if they'd had a real seraglio."

"How do you know they didn't? Did you go and see?"

"You can be sure they didn't."

"In Turkey you can't be sure of anything."

"Here we sit," Booth answered, "like two Lawrences of Arabia seconded home to the War Office, to talk with Mr. Dryden who happens to be home on leave."

"In Tunbridge Wells."

"No," Booth said, "it's more like the officers' bar in the Mess in Cairo, and flunkeys keep bringing us drinks. We are soon going to go upstairs to see Allenby and be cross-questioned by him."

"Criss-cross-questioned."

"However you like. We have turned the desert upside down."

Devastated men, they had come home and then summoned up all skeins of imagery that would make sense of what they had gone through, just so as to feel no longer alone. Not enough airmen had been through such experience as Booth and Clegg had. There was no constituency of press-ganged salt miners. Hence their aberrational liking for T. E. Lawrence. Hungry for *Doppelgängers*, they remembered carelessly and, for succor, clung mentally to the slight Valhalla of cap badges (eagles volant and three-masted barkentines) or even crudely delineated blondes painted on the noses of aircraft, there to seduce death and tweak a last erection from the doomed. Yet all this felt outside of them, requiring a stride and a jump. They would have preferred icons that slid out of them, reared up as idols for adoration, and evaporated into a cloud of gunsmoke. Aqua Regia came from no war zone, and Booth had only Captain Greenbaum at his disposal: a wraith and a wrath. Aqua Regia could not be counted on, and Captain Greenbaum had been beheaded alongside those he defended. These were skimpy talismans. They needed burlier effigies, culled from some august rigmarole in this or that theology or beefed up from a mere quotation. Accurate forebodings were what they wanted, enabling them to lodge and settle without needing to wonder what it was that they had been through, how it had begun and how ended. They needed it, for symmetry's sake, to have a beginning and an end; the middle they knew about, but not much else, and it was no use consulting the senior-juniors, those already balding rookies with eleven degrees each, for they knew books only. They talked the talk, but that was all, and their nature was shot through with technocratic fuse wire that always gave the lie to impromptu generosity.

"What do we need," Booth asked, "that we don't have?"

"The key to the back door," Clegg told him. "Somehow to get off the reservation before we become really old, man. Off the reservation and into the seraglio."

Booth gestured vaguely at the red, white, and blue umbrellas around them as they fluttered in the afternoon breeze. It was a resort, really, all the prettier for being within a military encampment, like jollity's riposte to Armageddon.

Right in the middle of appraising his predicament with some geniality, Clegg would have an entirely different thought, all of a sudden anticipating his corpse, loathing it, yearning never to have one, wondering how to pass from being in extremis to crystalline algebra. No rotting in between. No smells, no greenness, no corruption. Fire would help, he thought, and a plunge into the briny. It was not so much himself he worried about (the defunct one peering at himself) as those who outlived him, having to look at a Clegg who did not look back at them, as if he had become the universe itself: tree, cloud, wave. He wanted no lid creaking over him, no prayer venting its mildewed phonemes in his unhearing ear, no office or unction done with oil or myrrh. He thought there were ways of evading these procedures, if you planned far enough ahead. The trouble was, when he began to plan, to review the miscellaneous circumstances of life lived, he found things so amiable his resolve broke down, and he had to confess to himself that, in spite of his morbid leanings, he loved life, like a tiny child in a huge vat of custard with a wooden spoon. It was not the subtle things he doted on, but fly-in pancake breakfasts, advertisements for which he remembered in detail although he did not have, as Booth had, a photographic memory. Pancakes, eggs, sausage, coffee, doughnuts, homemade cookies, the poster might say: "All You Can Eat. Adults $3.50. Under 12—$1.75. Under Five Free." You would get there, flying, if you aimed for the intersection of coordinates 43°5' and 76°32'. There was a turf runway 2,850 feet long, a communications hut with wavelength given for radio, and two kinds of fuel. It began at seven-thirty and lasted until noon, sponsored by the Adult Fellowship of Port Byron First United Methodist Church. Who cared about the shell, he thought, if the nut was ripe? These meets could wring his heart, far as they were from the solitary prowl of the Cyrano, almost linked to harvest fêtes and strawberry festivals. Other posters boasted a more studious intent, or had more of the witch-doctor touch, offering to astound with the Triple Cities skyline, New York's rivers, hills, lakes, and valleys. "Bring your camera and plenty of film," the posters exhorted takers; "Be prepared for that one thing in life you will remember always." A straight line led from that unique sensation to the Cyrano; the sense of wonder could be amplified and projected, even if the vehicles involved were not "new clean and well maintained aircraft."

So he spent time testing death against commonplace delights, asking himself if there was a given ratio, neither too many delights nor too few. You had to be prepared to go when called for, by children (as he had previously recognized). Fly-in pancake breakfasts were a kind of family life, he thought, especially for those who had no other family life. You could save up all your heartiness over a year and then splash it about as if you had invented it. Noon was a harsh time to end such affairs, but the carrot for that was a quiet snooze in the hay somewhere, easing eyelids that wouldn't lift. Who, one Sunday, after all the pancakes had gone, and the

World War Two bombers had emptied of children, had urged him into a huge empty hangar in which there were squadron-drilling birds, pointing at a solitary plane in the far corner, prized property of Aeneas Greatbatch, now eighty-four, some kind of Cessna, a tail dragger, white and yellow, then whispering in homage, "The wings are one big fuel tank. It has enormous range. You could fly to Florida without refueling. He had the wing specially adapted." Greatbatch of the epic, antique name, New Zealand if anything, would not sell, of course, though all were selling around him. So far as he was concerned, the wing that was a fuel tank could remain adored in the hangar corner, an unplayed symphony that had seen great days and preposterous distances.

These were the moments that haunted Clegg, that both worried and heartened him during his military career. Hardly anyone had qualified for such a sterling life as his, but everyone had gone to the limit in trying to emulate him and Booth, flying three-quarter-scale Mustangs, for example, spending their time and their children's university money on resuscitated Spitfires and Messerschmitt 109's. The invitation to the waltz was always open (or to disastrous peripety). Six shots of mixed whiskey to the good, he could tell dozens of stories about a man who sold his plane to another man who, that same day, crashed it while buzzing his home to announce his return. These were a kind of just-so stories, explaining how so-and-so got a wooden leg, or a burned-off face. There was an oral literature of aerial disaster, and it went beyond mere hangar flying and came out over campfires in the creaking frost of the Adirondacks, in the pilots' lounge at sunny Santa Barbara where the terminal looked like an adobe castle. Clegg knew. This man who sought bits of myth to live by, even patching them together to make an escutcheon (what did that damned word mean, why was it right?), saw how flying led to thousands of irresistible stories all predicated on a yearning of ancient aboriginal man who flew far away in the whirling sparks of his fire, doing the impossible. Icarus came to pancake breakfasts, he was convinced of that, and the sage, supreme pilot on the airfield looked enviously at the Citation jets lined up, little refrigerators ready inside to cool the drinks, big plastic red disks choking the round mouths of their engines, then surveyed his rather worn Shrike Commander, 1948 vintage, and said as how it had better lines than the jets, more character, more grain.

Clegg knew what he meant, urging him not to polish the spinners, or correct the craze in the windshield, or refit the armrest in the front cockpit right. "It's a work of art," Clegg had said, "those are just machines. It's a *creature* with durable personality." Even the Cyrano, slim, fast-as-light pencil, was only a machine, though its lines were Gothic as shit city and when you came in to land those watching said, Here he comes again, balls to the wall, as if he had taken afternoon tea with God Almighty. That pilot was usually Booth, the austere and lanky one, but they joined Clegg in the compliment, the envious infatuation. Clegg had seen too much and now was trying to unsee it, or go backward, minifying the huge events of military flying, inching back to grass strips and Piper Cubs and the airstrips with classic burgers and the rinky-dink motels perched on the brink of the airfields, with dank beds and black toilets from the mineral deposit in the water in those parts; unflushed for months, those toilets fostered a charcoal glaze that many came to see and left undisturbed, thus infusing the black with picric yellow of a surreptitious hue. Somehow, he thought, this idyll was still available, if only you paid the right price, only it could not be death, could it, only, say, pain, humiliation, aging, loss of face, burns, fractures, the shakes.

As a young man, Clegg had exulted in long summer nights, wondering if they had been brought into being to persuade humans that life went on forever; the sun worshipper survived all. Then he began to wonder why non–sun worshippers, for a time, survived too. That distinction without a difference gave way to a piece of rumored knowledge: if you saw daylilies blooming out in the middle of nowhere, or along a deserted highway, it meant that a human habitation had once been there, maybe a garden. The same was true for certain kinds of hawthorn trees. Clegg had always believed there was a knowledge beyond knowledge; you had only to tune in to benefit.

Not that he was a mystic or believed in the occult. He trusted in the magnification of the known, never happy to draw a boundary, to make an enclosure. In the long run, daylilies gave him more pleasure than summer suns because the allusion they made was more human. Thus trained to welcome an unusual point of view, he was an ideal student of Booth, especially of the new Booth, supposed double agent who got into the business without thinking about it, and became a real spy only on a self-imposed dare. Yes, Clegg decided, Booth had a keen sense of curiosity, wanted to find out what it felt like to be doing the authentic thing. In that sense, he was more an experimenter than anything, eager to put himself through certain hoops and bend himself into unfamiliar roles: an actor, a poseur, a mimic. There was little political skullduggery in his behavior. Dream as Booth did about a stalemate between two identically equipped powers, he didn't really care, not as much as Clegg, the peace lover, the infatuate of harmless aviation, did on his most honest days. Booth enjoyed human variety, most of all within himself, and could be tempted into just about any zombie's waltz if you guaranteed him novelty. In this sense he

resembled the man who suffered from chronic boredom, the antisophisti-
cate who insisted on being surprised by everything. Seen genially, Booth
wanted to celebrate the full measure of the world, finding, as the old classical tag put it, nothing alien to him.

On the surface he was your full-blown humanist, unwilling to discuss
humanity on too narrow a basis; underneath, though, he was always asking for something that was never there, fanning a grandiose appetite
doomed to trough on vacancy. Martinet, radical, and freethinker, he was
an attractive man, but only until he was baulked, when he would become
something of a tyrant, a law to himself, a devourer. That he could lead was
indisputable; whether he could get men to follow him was doubtful. In
small combinations of men, he was superb, whereas when dealing with
large numbers he tended to bluff his way, speaking from within a standard
persona. Never would he, like Rupert Clegg, linger with delight on a certain medal's highly polished background or the design thereon of a full
and lush laurel wreath laden with berries—traditional tribute to someone
who has excelled. Nor was he sympathetic to figurative lions, tridents, helmets and shields, bugles, hunting horns and attitudinizing pumas. Or
popes. Booth lacked the modeling instinct sometimes dominant in
Clegg, which included reverence for a miniature world known as the
microcosm. You could not believe in this last, Clegg had always felt,
unless you believed in the macrocosm: trusted it to go on being itself in
spite of you. And by *believe* he meant look up to, take energy from being
included in, feel ennobled by being implicated with stars and planets,
moons and asteroids. Clegg's only trouble, the point at which he gave up
pondering the universe and his place in it, came when he told himself the
macrocosm included all [microcosms.] It had to, there was nowhere else
for them to be. Therefore any microcosm must necessarily reflect all
other microcosms, and how could anyone find out about *them?* It was a
devilish problem for Clegg, almost tempting him to think the macrocosm
was nothing but a heap of spurious [microcosms] and, all in all, hardly
worth a rotten peach. He nonetheless went on with the gross, tedious job
of aligning himself with natural forces, stationing himself in relation to
classified astronomical and biological phenomena. This was why high-
altitude photography appealed to him, setting him far from the things he
snapped yet allowing him the whoopee at the blowups that came later. It
mattered to him that he had been born not to be a cipher but one of the
elect, exploiting uncanny power in the interests of a polity presumed
kind. He was unsure about the polity, but not about its benefits. He liked
having something to ponder, to augment. Booth was more hard-boiled.

Brooding on these matters, Clegg began to doubt his insight into

Booth; his elaborate findings were nothing but stagy guesses. You could never know a human being that well, and you should never want to. If only he could decide why Booth had sold out, or if he had done anything of the kind and wasn't just boasting. Sometimes, when Booth went too far, there was Clegg behind him, pulling him back with catatonic tact, not interfering but making of himself a block, a petrified pedestrian, personifying stillness or a polar point. An invisible cord linked them, or so Clegg thought, perhaps overrating his tutelary power. *Yup*, Clegg said, talking antic, *the phrase for him is he screwed the pooch*, for which there is no forgiveness. Why, then, was it not *him* they interrogated so fiercely?

There was a slowcoach quality to life, Clegg instructed himself to remember; it always trapped you. Either you were thinking too slowly or you were not thinking in the right categories, which were one jump ahead of you. Therefore, he theorized, Booth was condemned and he himself accused. Probably true. Or Booth in some way was already executed while he Clegg was condemned. Did it pay to leap ahead in this fashion, merely so as not to be surprised by the edicts of the powerful? He gave up on any such burrowings. The only thing to do was deal with Booth as before: friend-cum-ally-cum-chastener, hoping for clarification once the pair of them were away from Washington the white.

I am stuck, he thought.

There is no one to come and get me.

I am the only one of my kind; Booth is legion.

What is lacking in me is the gift of fury.

Can I be made new soon enough?

Some called it the anteroom, a place where officers of all ranks could slump into an armchair, nibble toast, sip bourbon, and worm their way through the newspapers, now and then dozing. What were the rules? No politics, sex, or religion, although few heeded them. There was little conversation, this being the scene for taking stock and repining. On the day in question, in fact their fifteenth here, Booth and Clegg worked their way through the games available: chess, checkers, darts, and pool, spending less than ten minutes on any, haunted perhaps by a supergame that combined all four, a game to remember, in which chess pieces at attention on green baize could be felled by rolling balls and checkers might be nailed to the field of play by darts hurled with unthinkable force. Surely, Clegg thought, someone could concoct a new game, omitting perhaps the darts and checkers. He vowed to find something to kill the time with, whose score would remain in memory as something sublime and unique. Here they were in uniform, newly fitted out, with nothing to do. The tailor had cuffed him sharply in the groin with the side of his hand, asking him which side he dressed; Clegg could not remember, and today his penis lolled central. How come he couldn't remember? Why did it matter? Did they leave a little extra space on the side in question? Couldn't you change your mind, from left to right or vice versa? He liked the implicit coziness of the notion: a little *cul de cock*, but he disliked having to remember where it lay in wait. He disliked being reminded of it at all, since it had always got him into trouble, at home and abroad. He recognized in himself a certain innocence about hygiene, but his innocence extended to other matters. P & C supermarkets, he'd thought, meant Polar and Commercial, or at least Pennsylvania and Connecticut, but it was Price Cutter, quite without the dignity of the A & P's Atlantic and Pacific. Now, Polar and Columbian would have been imposing, he thought. Booth told him these things and disillusioned him over the four games.

Only an hour later, Booth, making a gesture, pinned his medals and decorations to his skin, hiding them within shirt and jacket, but nonetheless making a beginning on some outrageous form of immolation. Right there by the tennis courts, Booth stripped off his jacket and then, as Clegg noticed the bloodstains, whipped off his shirt with a paramilitary flourish. Perhaps he had applied Bactine first, to his skin, or aftershave lotion; but no, he had done the deed raw, with exhibitionistic flash. Clegg tried to puzzle out where Booth had stolen the idea, but he couldn't recall any of the famous self-mutilators from Lawrence to Schwarzkogler. Surely this was the feat of the day; he wouldn't do it again tomorrow, and that made tomorrow slightly more interesting than anticipated. No doubt, Clegg decided, this was the way to annihilate time, with a punk cicatrix. A more ambitious method was to misuse military impedimenta, ditching a Cyrano to make an impromptu reef somewhere off the Bahamas, or Cyprus, or having honorific flags cut into shirts, swagger sticks given to orchestral conductors, and spin chairs that created vertigo given to dentists to create something else. Properly organized, such scandalous misuse would demoralize an army in no time, sending at least the senior-juniors back to college in search of yet another degree. At the back of his memory skulked those Royal Air Force pilots who, in 1956, had retracted their wheels on the runway rather than go bomb Israelis as ordered during the Suez crisis. Now that amounted to military disobedience, much like Booth's passing over of top-secret data. It lay within the scope of every officer, but most never attempted it; Clegg fancied the idea, nothing outrageous or flagrant, but similar to what one German called the domestic form of immigration. This is to say Clegg was not as ingeniously inquisitive as Booth, but unruly all the same, not your by-the-book light colonel. He wanted life to ripple, to shine, suddenly to excel itself as if challenged into poetry.

Why, he never really knew, but was most willing to explain it in terms of legendary Babe, a premature baby put at once into an incubator unswitched on. So she had fought for breath for two hours and had come out of the experience weakened in both heart and lungs, with reduced resistance to infection and recurrent sinus trouble. That she had forged on to become a singer of opera astounded him, as if she were seeking out the very thing denied her. She was resolved to sing, voicing her lack or that of others, not only rising to the occasion but engulfing it in a wave of will and scorn. Pushing her slight physique, she went from distinction to distinction, a vocal Icarus whose buoyant rebukes to her brother about his ignorance of her art pleased him no end. Yet, surely, she was always straining, shoving, gulping, all of which she concealed, but only with preternatural vim. No one noticed the crescendoes of her slight form, the degree of magnification she subjected her delicate voice to; some perhaps wondered at an occasional instant of fatigue when she made an uncalled-for pause, deflecting time from its mindless trawl while she created for herself a window of absence, closed to all others, open for her, until she resumed like one of those Turkish birds in its too small wire cage next to the Egyptian bazaar. It was as if the hearer's heart had stopped in synchrony with hers. Clegg always knew, of course, having attuned himself over the years, yet always wishing he did not know so much about the Byzantine chemistry that made her sing. He had freed her long ago; she sang apart from him, and in an idiom he found antic and crass. Yet to the sound of her pampered voice raised in song he responded with near-suicidal empathy, as if he had wrung melody from rock, a trill from a heart of romaine lettuce, a warble from a dead bird. Indeed, Babe was his miracle, and his calling her that indicated his incredulity; she would always be the infant in the nonfunctioning incubator, so much so that the word *incubator* mutated in his mind between *suffocator* and *exterminator*. When he felt most keenly, he flailed, unable to pin things down with words, but desperately aware of the flood of feeling that harrowed his heart, as if he were to blame for her having to become a stoic Promethea.

Booth, however, less emotionally involved, took her in his stride, aware of her problems but willing to accept her as a hundred percent, at least until she was struck dumb. She was a woman, petite and Irish-looking, with generously sculpted thighs and arms. Indeed, Booth remarked to himself, the arms of Norma Shearer, actress of old. What more could a man want? So they had often been a threesome, Clegg delighted to see and hear her, yet quite mystified by the element in her that responded to debonair, correct Booth, who almost qualified as a clicker of heels and ever maintained that faintly automatic rhythm in her presence: he bowed, he scraped, he sprang alive erect with feet together as if spurred. She enjoyed his military façade, assuming nobody could be like that through and through, which he was. Thus far, however, she had not discovered this, and he was just about on the point of getting away with it.

It took Clegg only a few hours with Booth to become accustomed to the ragged jingle of his medals beneath his shirt and jacket, the sound of a child playing with a wind chime a hundred yards away. A faintly melodious Booth was a novelty, most of all when he started reminiscing not about himself but about other pilots he had known personally. "That Yeager," he mumbled, leveling the rim of his drink with the horizon from which obelisks poked up, "he says how he had no seat in the X-Fifteen, but had to lean back against the tank of liquid oxygen, mighty cool if you ask me. I mean cold. The same man, flying over a German who was running from a crash-landed aircraft, shot him in cold blood after thinking the matter over for a full minute. My own view of flying is more peaceful. Test-flying is more like it. I am not one of your shooter pilots."

Why was he telling Clegg this? They took their meals together, unescorted (but doubtless bugged), free to talk and trough, but almost as isolated as evildoers, officers who had not lived up to the military code. Clegg would have understood better if armed guards had frogmarched Booth away for betraying his country. He claimed to have talked about warp drive and distortions of space-time that could whisk a spaceship from one star to another in a trice. He had even prated of the [Alcubierre drive,] stressing that the entire space-time in a cylinder between takeoff and target is crushed into a thin sheet. On the other hand, a space vehicle might be set up with such a sheet behind it, which then expands to propel the spaceship across the distance in between. Once the trip has been made once, he explained (or so he claimed to Clegg), certainly by the first method, the segment of space-time remains crushed. Rockets would just ply the minor distance in between. This, he said, was Alcubierre's warp principle. The problem, he contended, was that if this kind of shrink-and-fly method became popular, the universe would soon start getting smaller. Planets in the way, which is to say embedded in the thin sheet, would be eradicated. When Clegg heard Booth propounding all this, he at once set aside the notion that Booth was off his rocker. Far from it, he had the math to prove his hypotheses.

"What would happen, for example," Clegg asked, "to the planet supposedly close to [Beta Pictoris?] Would we just abolish it, steamroll it into dust?" Booth never answered such questions in words; in this instance, he maneuvered his hands, pretending to be handcuffed, and shrugged, then made a sweeping motion. That, presumably, was the end of the planet. Now Clegg realized their Cyrano lives were a mere extrapolation point, for Booth anyway; he got his bearings in the most abstract way and then soared over Einstein-Rosen bridges into white holes. For some reason he found the simple similes of the constellations hard to accept. Leo a lion? No. Centaurus a centaur? Perhaps. This was cumbersome stuff worth a sigh of belief, but he had more faith in things less imitative, such as the vexed calculus of plasmas and gasses. Somebody knowing Booth well should have predicted this shift in him from traditional aircraft ballistics to abstruse universal holism. Booth had gone beyond and, in his dealings with the Soviets, had only reported the universe as he found it. Here was no case of a man betraying data from such a discovery as Yeager's about supersonic flight: how, when a plane went supersonic, its elevators no longer worked, whereas an all-flying tailplane did. This secret the United States had successfully kept from the British, the French, and others for years, at a distance regretfully watching their attempts to control supersonic craft with inadequate control surfaces. So there was a tradition of keeping mum, even among test pilots, and this was technically what Booth had breached; the truth, however, was that he'd told nothing that wasn't in the public domain. And, Clegg figured, the senior-juniors here had discovered this fact after elaborate investigations. Booth might have been reckless, but he was no blabbermouth. What he told was the rhetoric of a Universe enthusiast: nothing more. It was Clegg's nature to think the best of people, so he went on thinking it. Having arrived at his charitable scenario, he stuck to it, wishing he too had Booth's grasp of quantum gravity, warp drive, and the rest of the spatial conundrum with which the twenty-first century was going to drive itself mad.

"Would you go?" Booth was urgent, playing with his custard.

"Would I go?"

"To [another star,] if asked or invited. If there were a way." Or, he might have said, an out-of-town narrator.

Clegg had an answer ready, one he had been waiting to slap on Booth for ages. "I would rather stay home and watch the different way American women chew gum." On he went, describing the front chew, the side one, the ways women had of caching the wad. What men did interested him little, he said; but masticating women, working the nervousness out of their systems with symphonic jaw movements that both exercised and made fragrant, that got his attention all the time. Only American women chewed gum, an act both potentially lascivious and wryly surreptitious. This meant that an American woman's features were never in repose but always gearing up, so to speak, perhaps in the same school of thought that said conversation made a ready man; well, mastication made a ready woman.

This was bigoted, Booth scoffed.

But entertaining, Clegg said. "I'm trying to get you out of yourself, Colonel. Einstein-Rosen bridges? I'll be damned."

"Recon, don't ridicule what you don't understand."

Clegg shut down, abandoning conversation, and plunged into his apple pie, devouring symbolism first, pastry second.

They were fliers, not thinkers, but lack of practice had made of them avocational wonderers, each in his own way. Booth was far away, transcendentally obtuse; Clegg was the man with the electron microscope fixed upon a wad of gum. They had been lucky to have still been flying: they were exceptionally good at it, of course, and a classic team in brimming good health. But they had been waiting for the ax to fall as their eyes began to falter, their prostates to swell, their reaction time to lengthen. Yet they had been heading in different directions for a long time now, and when an eminent entomologist pronounced that science was humanity's finest achievement, Booth said hear-hear, but Clegg let out the cry of a wounded wistiti. Art, he had said, was the greatest. "Oh well," Booth told him, "if you're going to be sentimental, Recon, the greatest human feat is the Resurrection, then: a god on earth like a man on the moon."

"Hog knackers to that," Clegg told him. "It isn't technology and it isn't science. Science was there to be found, to be summoned up, called upon to come out and show itself for what it was. Technology's brighter than science. It has more willpower in it. But art, that's not applied, Colonel, it's invented, it's concocted. It didn't have to be the way it is, none of it. There's even missing art that, if found, would change the face and history of art. Science's like water-divining. Art's divine to begin with."

As for flying, to which both of them looked back with fond ennui, Booth had always enjoyed landing, even after the bone-racking boredom of a long mission. There was something Platonic to it, not only landing at enormous speed, tucking the stick back in his belly so as to flare, then easing the nosewheel forward until it squeaked. To this maneuver, there was what Plato called virtue: efficiency in performing an assigned function. These were words Booth had retained from his undergraduate days, wondering if he would ever find a use for them, and in what sphere. To land was to resubmit to Earth's laws and, during the flare, when the Cyrano hovered between slow flight and renewed contact with terra firma, to become wholly passive, which had to be done with sprightly finesse. It was always something of a triumph for Booth to come back to the runway after an aeronautical experience so fantastic, during which he became a robotic superman. What pleased him most of all during landing was the way the aircraft, perched at a high angle of attack, seemed to be praying, with a lurch this way and a yaw that, exposing its private parts and under-belly to the grand magister of loins. Praying with its penis: that was what the Cyrano penultimately did, and it always worked; air relinquished the underpowered glider the Cyrano had become and tarmac accepted it home once more, as if it had been nowhere away and that at an altitude of only ten or fifteen feet.

Predictably, Clegg enjoyed takeoffs most, not that he despised the Pla-tonic or the passive. What was clinical in Booth was dynamic in him. He loved the thrumming trundle of escape velocity, the streamlined shudder that afflicted the plane during takeoff run and stopped suddenly as soon as the Cyrano was airborne. He doted on the lunge and roar, even though it was far behind them, and the abrupt, rampant shove almost vertically into the heavens. He could not get over the thrill of this, the leaving something for evident nothing. He wished it could be even faster, louder, more per-pendicular. He regretted it when the plane settled down to its admittedly astonishing cruise speed; the fireworks were over then, at least until return. Clegg sometimes felt during takeoff he was melded to the fuselage itself, irremediably, and his own energy was shoving the wings forward. Supersonic was good, he felt, but he wished it had been hypersonic, which was over five times the speed of sound: New York to London in less than an hour. And, of course, once he achieved that, he wanted half an hour, his desire culminating in travel by transporter beam: one nanosec-ond, a feat he thought might be accomplished by mental resolve. Here at home, or even along the disheveled highways of Turkey, drivers careened along at sixty or fifty-five, impatient with the vastness of their country, with the sheer concept of distance. To walk was to fail, Clegg knew. A success-ful man wanted things flashing past him on both sides at something like the speed shown in a holographic movie he had seen about general and special relativity. A tram in Bern, Switzerland, had flashed along at the speed of light through a commonplace street, and everything had shrunk. Or so Clegg recalled, as usual sucking the emotion from an experience whose facts blurred the instant he tried to recover them. The feeling of going fast matched the other one of being unobliged, of being linked to nobody and nothing. It irked him that he would never live to see [travel between stars:] the kind of thing that Booth, in a more scientific way, dra-matized in his mind. Certainly the brass, in choosing these two for high-altitude reconnaissance, had chosen well, tuning in to the far-seeking hunger they had felt since boyhood. Each man, in his own peculiar way, assessed himself as hugely appropriate, dreaming he gave off even at the movies or while playing pool the metallurgical radiance of space flight: not astronaut, alas, but aeronaut, once a distinguished term.

Now, of course, they had been handed an almost philosophical problem: denied the Cyrano, did you knuckle under to something as primitive as a Piper Cub—dashboard instrumentation scarce, speed low, range negligible—or as sophisticated as a business jet with two engines, speed brakes, autopilot—the lot? To give up flying would be a heartbreak, but to continue it in mediocre terms would be even worse, even in the bizjet. Perhaps skydiving, the pilot's abomination, would be better, or seaplanes, or sailplanes.

"You got that ole yearning?" Booth had not spoken to Clegg at all during tea, which they took on the military lawn, under stars and stripes umbrellas, partaking of scones, fruitcake, salmon sandwiches, muffins, cottage cheese, and various kinds of toast kept hot by electricity in silver stands that might also have held envelopes.

"I got it in the barls," Clegg answered in similar brogue, "but it hurt in de heart."

"Wanna get up there and spin?"

"Wanna get, git, up there and parachute down."

"Naw, shee-it, Recon, that's for weekend amatoors."

"Wayl, fuck them amatoors, Colonel. I sure would love to get me some ole flyin' pay."

"There's that."

"Not to mention the old thrillum stuff," Clegg said, warmed by coffee (no tea for him). "Got to get mah jism flowin', Colonel."

"We'll ask." Booth eventually did but was waved away, told he was too valuable. Was he, then, going back to the Cyrano? Was Clegg? Skunk Works and all? The senior officer among the civilian-suited senior-junior officers said nothing, but put his hands together in an Indian greeting, bowed, and walked away.

"Well, what in the Billy-Bob-Jackson fistfuck bollockfest did that mean?" Clegg was trying to muster obscenity and hitch it to down-home vulgarity, but too upset to make an intellectual or baroque triumph of it.

"Telling us to piss off, Recon. They haven't done with us yet, comrade. I wish to God we'd a stayed in Turkey. Leastwise they had entertainment."

"You mean among those nignog miners." Clegg above all did not want another dose of the desert.

"Not them. Where they carry cats on their heads in the markets and sell them to the highest bidder. In cages."

"Yeah," Clegg said thickly, as if transfixed.

"We could kidnap a plane somehow," Booth said lamely, not expecting Clegg to respond.

"We could bomb the White House."

"Leastwise film it," Booth said with a dismal laugh. "They sure wouldn't be expecting us. Napalm too. Let's do it."

Clegg poured more coffee and chomped into an éclair, forcing white cream sideways against his mouth.

"Look," Booth said, pointing at a jet gleaming sardine in the sun, "*they* fly over *us*. Screw 'em, whata they know?"

"Apprentices," Clegg mumbled through cake and chocolate.

"You said it." Curving on that military meniscus, their lives had only slither power, as if they were being left alone in order to run down and let the second law of thermodynamics have its way with them at last.

The more squash outfits they asked for, the more they got. Sweaters, shirts, underwear, shorts, socks, all those hideous ribbed and gusseted shoes in which America coddles its athletic feet. It was clear that, if they wished to hit the soggy little black ball, they must do it with sartorial flair. So they soon looked dapper, never improving their game, but able to cut an elegant figure on and off the court. A surplus of towels and facecloths, robes and natty little silk scarves, came their way as well, bolstering the idea that officers got the best. Usually they played midmorning and midafternoon, actually getting their bodies into good trim, and becoming more or less familiar faces among the ball-hitting fraternity. Booth played with geometrical cunning, Clegg with abundant follow-throughs; but they did begin to feel the burden of an underflexed body fall away. The more tired they became, the more spring their steps had. And they stopped cursing every mishap of the ball, instead taking a deep breath and swallowing the cussword. They enjoyed the game, but they enjoyed more the prospect of its being over, when they could swig lemonade and adjust their dress.

"It wouldn't be difficult," Booth said to him. "It's all a matter of a familiar piece of landscape on the move. I mean, if we dressed up as French soldiers, or a couple of German civilians, it wouldn't work."

Clegg could not remember what either looked like.

"Oh, something nagging at me," Booth said. "I don't know what. All we have to do, bully-boy, is walk out carrying rackets and, preferably, a big Coke with a straw deep into it. You see that door over there? It isn't locked. All these guys care about is who gets in. We could walk through, buy two sodas, walk past the Rockflat Building where the decoders live, then circle the little branch bank, skip the toiletries kiosk, and walk out to the parking lot. Who's going to stop a couple of patriots who haven't bothered to change and are going to drive home in their sweats?" He sighed, having discharged an enormous obligation.

"Drive away in what?" Clegg was not feeling energetic. He yearned for air-conditioning, fans, a cold bath, a cold towel, ice cubes on his belly. Anything but another of Booth's energetic dreamed-up escapades. Cooled off, he would lie back on pristine sheets and clip all the moles off his body, working from one armpit to the other. He wanted to be smooth and cold. He hated the sticky condition in which light objects clung to your hand as you tried to set them down. It hardly occurred to him that Booth was planning an escape from this, the suavest, most considerate of retreats, into which you almost had to beg to be admitted. He could see no point in getting out and then being unable to leave. But Booth, more thoroughly trained in escape and evasion, had thought matters through.

"Doable?" he said jauntily. "It's fucking feasible."

So, after a pause that quieted their racing hearts, they did it, fetching nothing from their quarters, but striding ahead with the right combination of fatigue and euphoria, two huge sodas blatantly on show, and around their necks towels, scarves, sweaters with the arms tied together. A summer scene, they hoped. As they walked, Booth, miming intense post-mortem play, swept his racket this way and that in imaginary shots. Past the Rockflat Building they traipsed, then the bank (closed), the toiletries (also closed), and the bamboo door to the parking lot, a key carelessly left in the lock, and, oddly, a dead chipmunk on the grass verge.

They were out, no sooner out than inside a Ford Escort that Booth hot-wired. "Half a tank," he sighed. "That should do." With curt, neat military waves at the guardhouse staff, who didn't even bother to stop them, they moved off into the semicivilized world, breathing jerkily now, on the best reconnaissance mission of their lives, aimed north, but what did that mean in a world of beltways? With them they had money and a cream for hand blisters, so they cursed impromptu decisions at the same time as deciding that, if they'd discussed the matter, they would never have gone. Quick now, Clegg told himself, Turkey or Africa?

In a long northwestern veer they burst out into Pennsylvania, wondering if it would soon be cooler as the sun sank. Booth cursed his route as the sunset hit him in the eyes, but squinted hard until Clegg, fumbling in the glove compartment, found some horn-rimmed shades. They had stolen the car of two janitors, Schall and Seinfelt, who would even now be damning them, little knowing their lineage and rank. Not too fast, Clegg told Booth. "In Pennsylvania they fine you a dollar for every mile per hour over the limit."

"It isn't fines I'm worried about," Booth said. They totalled their money (just over two hundred dollars) and studied a map. At their first gas station a young girl with stark blue eyes asked them for a ride up the road, only a mile, and they turned her down, knowing what sort of trouble they could get into. Off they rattled into the dusk, talking about the Pittsburgh airport and the chance of helping themselves to something that flew at over five hundred miles an hour.

Then Clegg said, "I wonder who owned this piece of crap, it must have set him back at least a hundred bucks. Geez, it sounds just like a Nazi bomber. Let's dump it soon. Look how people get out of our way, like we had car leprosy or something. Did you ever hear such a clatter, such a seething noise? Maybe it'll explode in a few miles."

"Nah," Booth drawled, "it makes us invisible in a funny sort of way. Magic Lamp stuff, with the battery shot. These old slant sixes, they got old-fashioned character, Rupe, they make a kind of metal mincemeat of themselves. Hide in plain sight."

Dining at a McDonald's they felt they had partaken of a neglected American sacrament (they had been too much east of the Bosphorus) and Clegg phoned his sister, leaving on her machine the enigmatic cry from the heart "The goose is loose." He would have to call again and tell her all about it. Now he drove while Booth snoozed. They were heading for Pittsburgh airport, at whose FBO (private terminal) you could always steal a Cessna or even better provided you walked through the foyer with the right moneybags swagger. Told to remove their keys, pilots did as they pleased; people might well want to hijack a commercial jet with a range of several thousand miles, but who wanted a puddle jumper fit only to get them into an even worse place halfway across the county? Both Booth and Clegg were a little out of touch with civil aviation, as indeed with the types of aircraft parked on the Pittsburgh private ramp (some of them with considerable range). It was going to be easy, Booth told him. "I been there before."

"I suppose we could always go to the Russian Embassy in Pittsburgh," Clegg said tactlessly. "They'd fork out for an old fellow traveler, wouldn't they?" Booth grunted and waved a hand at the sky. "Choose your plane. What would you like? You ever fly that stuff at night?"

"*I'm* flying?" Clegg said. "That's good. Now we'll be sure to be buried in Pennsylvania. Under deep green grass." Haughty Booth sighed.

"Now, you tell me, Colonel," Clegg said as if he wanted to know or did not know, "how did we ever tell from their faces which of our fellow pilots were going to be killed? Is there some sign in the face? Is it the guy who looks nervy, or morbid, or just plain unhappy? Is it the ones who look as if they're going to get cancer anyway, or crash their cars? I've never been able to figure it out."

"Who you been looking at, Recon? You been staring at Booth? I'm not the one, buddy." They changed places again.

"No, I mean if a certain guy looks a bit cross-eyed. Does that predispose him for being killed?"

Booth gave an elaborate cough, usually his preamble to a long authoritative statement uttered at sardonic speed. "Maybe the guy who looks too sensitive. Easily wounded, you know. Hell, there's a joke! Or the one whose skin looks too thin. Or those with small ears, small hands. The ones with curly lips like their momma just kissed them and wouldn't let them go. That kinda stuff. Or those with neat little curls pressed damp and oiled. Guys with small noses, which meant they had tiny dicks. Sure, you could pick them out. Then what do you do? Hey, son, you got the look of death, don't you fly that little old mission today. Hell," he broke off. "These civilian drivers sure never took no driver's course. All over the road. You gotta drive defensively or your ass is grass." He hit the horn, fisting it until he had a clear space in front of him, vacated by people trying to avoid the maniac behind them.

"You slow down," Clegg told him. "Mind what I told you, Coinel, about the fines in Pee Ay."

"Yeah," Booth said, "some poor little fucker trying to find the bottom of the scud in the mountains. You can pick him out in no time. Got that flush to his face, weepy look in his eyes, lips trembling. They go right in 'cause they never *believe in their luck*. You gotta believe in your good fortune. Like us today."

"Here we go," Clegg moaned.

"You asked." Booth muttered something under his breath ending in "take you for all you got."

"Colonel?"

"Nah, I was just thinking about all the false exculps."

"The—"

"The stuff they hand you when the going gets tough. Hey, they say, you just say what's in this envelope, about what you were doing with secret information, and it'll go all right for you."

"They did?"

"A script, see, which you think will clear you, but craftily worded to convict you. Not quite like those Jap courts in the war, but similar. Mind you, there they was dealing with Japanese-speaking lawyers and was never told the truth in English. Then they lynched them. They are not going to lynch me, son. I'll set Pittsburgh afire before they get to do that to me."

Clegg agreed voluminously, eager to please the hot-rod driver, anxious not to get caught watching *Unsolved Mysteries* in some luxury hotel, yet eager to step sideways now into permanent civilian life: no Cyrano, no interrogation, no narcotic injections. "Colonel," he said in breezy invitation, "when we get there let's circle the city."

"What's that mean, Recon?"

"Look around downtown."

"For a hotel."

"Not necessarily, just to get the feel of a—a *place*. It's all been in between, there's been no destination."

"They'll take us sure as fire."

"Now who's got no faith in his luck?"

Booth lapsed into silence, for once driving with stern meticulousness, eyes on the dim road, lips mouthing an indistinct prayer to his ancestors. "Fuck driving," he said.

No answer. Booth wanted afterburners. His impatience had begun to kindle. Crawling along the rind of the planet had never been for him. He thought of Pittsburgh as a friendly city whose residents were never too sure of themselves and yielded readily when challenged. All he needed was a plane.

So they circled, as Clegg suggested, cursing the signs that misled, cheering the ones that at first seemed not to mislead at all, in the end getting lost in a small enclave that contained a huge skyscraper of a hotel and various entrances to it. They both had credit cards, but no idea if they'd been canceled; nor did they wish to leave a plastic trail. So far as they knew, no one yet knew where they were, squirting in and around not far from the Cathedral of Learning. They decided to cross the river, hoping for some place— some dungeon, some kennel—more modest, eyeing all the parked cars they saw. Now they swung past a derelict-looking redbrick building, a warehouse or a foundry, and saw a parked Chevy next to a slipway on which sat several foundered ferryboats, noses deep in the river but half the hull in the slops on the slipway. Clearly they had been abandoned, but neither Clegg nor Booth had any idea why they had not been dragged away to clear the riverbank. Back they went a couple of hundred yards, then walked back and tentatively explored the flooded riverboats, finding one with a dry floor, actually a dry room, on which they jumped up and down, testing. Away went the rats. Out came a couple of battered folding chairs. The blaze of neon from the hotels across the river was enough. Booth reversed his chair and leaned forward against its back while Clegg peered into the distance, wishing they had stayed in Washington.

"What a shitty finale," he said.

"I'll tell you something you don't know," Booth answered. "I heard it a long time ago from a young lad going down in flames, lazy spiral. 'Where you're not wanted,' he said, 'you shouldn't want anything.' Imagine getting up the heartspew to think of that while going down!"

"Salute," Clegg said. "I salute the poor bastard."

"Just so long as you don't milk your tits on my pants."

Clegg snorted. "You're getting maudlin again, Colonel. It must have been all that driving." But Booth was fast asleep, a runner breasting the tape that was the chair's back, having arrived at speed.

Unsure of his footing, Clegg advanced to the stairway, mounted it, pushed open the little door, and stood on the minor bridge, facing the same view as before. It could have been downtown Tucson or Boston: an unidentifiable cityscape mirrored in the water, rippling and shimmering. Now, he thought, with a supercilious smirk, he was truly a modern man, perched on the brink of tomorrow without the slightest idea of what to do next, here in a city where he was not known and, really, as distant from it as from the cities he had overflown at unthinkable altitude for years. His horizontal gaze became vertical, and he longed to cross the river, confront the megalopolis that lay beneath him.

What happened next would have happened better had Booth been awake to witness it, or so Clegg thought, watching the buildings opposite shuffle and merge on the water surface, changing color and perimeter. Aqua Regia rose from the river and reared up to extraordinary height, no doubt to daunt him, still incomplete as before: no hands, no legs, but crimson in hue and with a face of nebulous completeness. Without pause she began to harangue him for being, as she put it, pointlessly late; she blotted out entire skyscrapers. Not that her tone was mordant, or even scolding; she just recited the facts without emotion, stressing most of all that she had his good interests at heart. He was not, she said, Booth's deputy or number two. Nor his lackey nor his subordinate. He was a distinguished pilot who should behave as such, she whispered. "RSO," Clegg informed her. "I was his Reconnaissance Systems Officer, which I guess is just a peg below the actual pilot. Never mind. *I* never did. Why should *you*, Mam. Are you a dream? Am I dreaming you or are you dreaming me?" It was almost as if he should address her in a different language, maybe an ancient one, so as to give all he said a gloss of eminence that reinforced the formality of their exchanges. He felt at such a loss, vouchsafed her radiant, chromatic, giant presence but unable to stand up to her verbally. She was there, in Pittsburgh, and he was here, also in Pittsburgh, but he was missing the import of her appearance. Surely a mistake had been made; she should have aimed for someone else, Booth even, say Jim Sullivan, Bill Flanagan, or Tom Alison, Cyranists all, and men more worth conferring with. If she were here to goad him on to something, or to deter him, she should get on with it instead of just floating at him now and then, all style and mannerism but no gist, no bottom line. That she was company impressed him not at all. It occurred to him that, [if she were an angel,] then angels were not there to jolly you along, make you feel good about yourself, but to nag you into doing your best. Angels were kindergarten teachers with wings, already sexless because that was how kindergarten teachers were.

"You could go away, Mam," he said ungallantly.

She did not move but intensified her scarlet glow, seeming to consume herself red-hot near the midriff: part of her blazed anew, then sank, leaving a blazing scar, which then faded. Such was one of her languages. He had heard that mermaids and other such creatures came into being based on characteristics of the person they haunted, so there was from the outset a common bond; the beholder was viewing some aspect of himself, and therefore not critical. He would be inclined to be receptive, even gullible. Yet she had told him nothing, had no doubt not even noticed his escape and his departure for Pittsburgh. It was clear, however, that she did not visit only during interrogations; she was a random caller, as likely to turn up in his bed (if bed he had) or while he roosted on the john, at his most alone.

"Give me a break, Mam," he said hoarsely. "I am Recon, the RSO, that's all. Tell me."

"You misunderstand," she told him in a voice both mellow and raging, the sort of voice he'd last heard in the movie of *Hamlet*, with Hamlet's father's ghost sounding muffled by armor, distance, and death. "I sometimes appear as stars," she went on, "or comets. [I can be anything.] I just choose to be this way. I could be a salivating giant. This happens to be one of my manifestations to airmen. I am arbitrary, yet lethal. My silence halts your mind. If I will it, you will never speak again. I am the source as well as the fount. Do not irritate me or I will be obliged to promote you into being some other life-form. A dog. A snake. A bamboo tree."

He bowed his head, certain she was only an apparition and could be banished, should he wish it. He wished it and she stayed put, if anything rippling more hugely, developing a definite pair of eyes and nostrils. He had heard of serious pilots' being mesmerized during long missions, such as he and Booth flew in the Cyrano, by movie stars, who then with mouths as big as bomb craters kissed them (enveloping the head), gave them blow jobs (losing the glans between two teeth), and generally took them over for a while, making them feel trivial and negligible. Was that what was going on? Who was she, then? On whose Hollywood pillow had he dreamed too much? Nobody recent, he was sure, because he remembered none of them, but perhaps somebody between Myrna Loy and Sharon Stone. Oh, Jennifer Rubin, then, of the bulbous lips and sea-blue eyes, or Barbara Hershey, of the voluptuous strong jaw. He gave up. The face in question was too vague for him to recognize, the body too symbolic. He was trying to unwrap a cipher from within an enigma and assign it to a studio. Still the huge apparition, neither shot at by river police nor flown through by patrol plane, hung on, imposing and ghastly, neither his nor anyone else's, able only to talk in riddles. She was a clipper, an albatross, a sun dog, hotfoot from the seventeenth century, where she had been waiting far too long, until mankind invented Cyranos, just the kind of technical little quirk to tempt them out of hiding. Titanium Goose. Maybe she came out of hiding, in an oak tree at the time of Charles II of England, in order to attend the 1974 Farnborough Air Show. Or (and he half fancied this explanation) she came to him out of sheer competitive anger, irate at such a performer as the Cyrano, able to do an angel's job and carry two men at the same time. That must have been it. She was Madama Angelic Flight, put on her mettle by a plane originally intended to be an interceptor. So he either knew it was a zombie of his own invention or he dreaded its massive powers, confronting him as it did with no brochure, no program, no pilot's operating handbook. If Clegg indeed saw something, then he did so with spleen and contributive grandeur. If you dealt with something so awesome, you should surely deal yourself a card from the bottom of the deck. Didn't old Steve Wittmann, air racer par excellence, whose first pilot's license was signed by Orville Wright himself, con his pursuers by banking a little away from the course while barreling straight ahead? This made those behind him lose ground and increase their distance. That kind of maneuver surely didn't include broken glass, but Booth never had found out all that happened to Clegg when they were repatriated and questioned. Nobody, least of all Rupert Clegg, would tell him. So the answer was nothing at all: nothing to tell meant nothing happened. Booth knew well that pilots, addicted to calm behavior, believed in talking calm so as to stay calm, the drawback to this being that nobody believed you when you said you were in real trouble. If there was no panic in the voice, there was no help in the controller. Vaguely Booth recalled something about a guy who, thick with ice and descending fast as an almost nonaeronautical vehicle, achieved supercalm and did that famous line concerning being a little old snowman up here. Down he went, unworried about. The better the image you came up with, the safer ground thought you were. So, if like the girl in the

Bahamas you panicked and let it all hang out, you at least stood a chance of being taken seriously, even if you had none of surviving. It was better, he reasoned (the colonel dominating the private pilot), to go down being taken seriously than just to crash. Honor with him was far from frivolous, and he wondered if Clegg's broken-glass caper, indeed his broken-glass philosophy, had dignity to it or not. He thought not, quickly assembling all the graveyard spirals he'd known about and what the crashing pilots said the closer they came to impact. No great lines, he thought, and, sadly, the best one he recalled came from a movie, as from one of the reflected fires in Plato's cave. He couldn't recall it exactly, but it was a message, something like "Tell Cag he was right. I was thinking of Connie." That was all. Most exclamations were maternal or fecal, which was not surprising since final, basic things were afoot.

Clegg, however, hardly noticed the shredded glass, culled from an old lightbulb floated toward him on the slop coating the floor down below. What a privileged being he was, being made privy to the world of the interstices, in which what mattered mingled with stuff from the world of absolute zero, where nothing moved, where no energy was. That was one way to look at the ravishing domain of what was active, where he had recently been. What assailed him now was the static, in which color figured as motion, almost, and you had to come to terms in your own fashion with what loomed up in front of you, shocking, numbing, enthralling. He liked the notion of her being a fifinella, the genius of a locus that was everywhere: the muse of machinery, fixing on him because, well, he had been so badly treated by the bald-headed Phi Beta Kappa boys. She was not Nurse Cavell or Florence Nightingale, but she had something of them in her, along with specks of Mata Hari, Mae West, and Amelia Earhart (that spotty pilot). So she was—Clegg pondered hard, involuntarily squeezing the shards in his palms as he thought: nourishing spy-slut idol, or something simpler such as the angel of flight. He preferred the word *fifinella*, though, evocative as it was of whimsy and dolls, Italian pastries and peroxided poodles.

"You're deep tonight." Booth sounded hoarse and somewhat unfriendly, no doubt unwinding from the day's events.

"Just working out which religion I belong to. Along to." Clegg sniffled with that cold coming on.

"Thank God for rivers," Booth exclaimed. "Just look at all that god-damned light. Kind of a midway, ain't it?"

On an impulse, Clegg moved sideways and drywashed the glass off his hands into the rocking slop.

"You scratched a mite?" Booth didn't really want to know, but he sensed Clegg wanted him to ask, so he did, with debonair brevity.

No, it wasn't worth talking about. There was nothing like freshening up the front of your hands, airing the red meat that underlay caressing. Clegg grew from bold to reckless, permitting his female gremlin to emit from the red place she inhabited a grotesque klaxon sound, ear-rending and paralyzing, incomprehensible but lethally loud. Or so he told himself, marveling at his ability to withstand her onslaught. He told Booth, but Booth shrugged, said Clegg was under the influence and had better be seeing a doctor soon. Fingers in ears, Clegg asked him to listen, pointing to ground zero, but Booth scowled and said something about jet engines. What? It's jet engines over at the airport, Recon.

"That airport is thirty miles away."

"Then you got superduper hearing, buddy-boy. Don't you go messing about with me. I hear what I hear."

Clegg gave up, doomed to be alone in his ecstasy or his tribulation. She would not come for them all. "Look," Booth said, and Clegg saw riverboats, sirens screaming, coming toward them, louder and louder as the Doppler effect took hold, and then fainter, what a surprise, as the streamlined vessels swept past in search of a better malefactor. A huge, ammonia-smelling wash poured over the unsubmerged part of the ferry they stood in, making it wallow and almost capsize. Had they been below, they might have been swamped.

"How'd you like one of those babies on your night off?" Booth was teasing, but he sounded genial.

"No riverboat for me," Clegg said. "I can live on air. And some booze. How come we don't have a bottle on this night of nights? Too tired to pick one up?"

"You don't understand, Clegg. We are on the run, man, not cooling out on the way to Bermuda to meet a coupla dames. Here we are, like wet rats on a leaky something in the Pittsburgh River, and you complain about the amenities."

"More like the Monongahela," Clegg said, airing his geography. This was a sore point for Booth, who once upon a famous time had almost failed an examination by calling Madagascar (as it was then) Ceylon (as it was then too). Some quick tutoring had put things right, and in any case no one took seriously the report that a distinguished pilot had his geography that wrong. Inclined to inculpate the examiners, the general population of pilots said what they always said: The brass were out to get you 'cause all they flew were desks. This was just another ploy and Booth was a demonstrably honorable man.

Clegg was still hearing sirens, Aqua Regia's or the patrol boats', longing for a smooth, quiet night on the river. From here to where? Right now he didn't care, but he knew his mind was in just the mood to hear a helicopter's roar in the tiny exquisite filigree toiling spider in a boot cupboard or a roar of afterburners coming from the blurred mouth of a fifinella, the face about one hundred feet square, slap bang across the glittery Pittsburgh night. Not a prestigious backdrop, though thousands huzzahed it these days, Golden Triangle and all. Clegg had kept up his *National Geographic* subscription all through his career and not that long ago had closed a door forever on a cupboard of unopened issues. He could never take them with him, he knew, so now they were proud Turkey's own, and he had left a whole world behind him, including an issue (perhaps) about revivified Pittsburgh, that Slavic Sheffield. It was clear to him he heard things Booth could not. They were sometimes in different dimensions.

Yet not now. Booth was getting cussèd, stripping himself naked of his squash whites and teasing Clegg to do the same. "Ain't seen you nekkid for ages, Recon. Git your ass loose." Why bother? Booth was already naked in the river moongleam and the shed light from the skyscrapers across the water. He looked like tall alabaster, with silver scar marks catching the light as he fidgeted and urged Clegg on. "Git them off, Rupe, old son." For reasons unknown, but maybe wishing not to be intimidated, Clegg stripped off with his painful hands and shuddered at the night air, wondering what Booth intended. Surely not a swim in rat-infested water full of torn metal and nailed-up two-by-fours. There, he was naked, about five feet from Booth, who looked undernourished, having lost some weight at squash. They turned, scoffed, and began to rib each other, having a vague sense of doing something un-American. It would be better if they were asleep, should they be caught naked. Or dead: that would solve everything. Or suffering from typhus. There were scores of ways out. Instead, they stood almost at attention, each as if making forlorn admission to the other that their bodies had wasted in their stratospheric role. They had withered in sedentary ballistics. It was hard to conceive of it, going so fast so high as if sitting in a library, poring over Lord Baden-Powell's *Scouting for Boys*.

They shared a secret, a fleshly one, but it had no interior, was no multifoliate infolded rose. Having seen each other naked, each knew the other was a separate man, unknowable and unreachable, apart in his pain and his joy, and they would no more dream of shaking hands naked, or mutually embracing, or slapping each other football-style on unshielded rump, than they would of not returning the other's salute—in this case, Clegg initiating the compliment, Booth returning it, then Clegg (a touch pedantic) acknowledging that, and Booth saluting all over again while muttering why the fuck doesn't he move on, move along, we could be here all day fanning our faces. They could get caught up in such minutiae of etiquette, not because it meant that much to them, but because it eased tension, or it would have done had it not started a new tension of its own, as if two marionettes had been given free will but could not shake the preliminary tremors of old habits. Something like that made them uneasy with each other, but not when naked. It skinned them, so to speak, to be without uniform and underclothes, gave them back to the ragamuffin human race. Perhaps too it made them feel younger, less fixed in formal entity, closer to baby pulp or teenaged malleability. The pain of needing now and then not to be anyone hit them both, especially after long missions, among which this hegira to Pittsburgh was one, less sleek than the others, but a salient departure with court-martial written all over it. A bow ended this nude duet, with Booth re-dressing first. In no time they looked ready for tennis again, except that this would be tennis in the dark, and they had the look of dapper yuppies, aloof and stranded in their tugboat dark.

Booth told Clegg a bedtime story, fudged up from severe and coldsteel memory, evicted from the head and banished; if only, Booth thought, memory *were* biddable. He reminded Clegg of the old F-100, the so-called Super-Saber, popular name Hun, with whose tail the engineers tinkered, shortening it to make the Hun deadly, then lengthening it again. "Remember roll-coupling, Rupe?" He most certainly did, and all the adverse yaw. "To land at all," Booth whispered, "you had to haul back like a sucker on that fucker. Pull back for all you was worth. Or she wouldn't set down, she wouldn't settle, and you would always have to be ready for the go-around, as if the smart guys designing her had not thought about landing her. It had not occurred to them boys we would have to land it. Big sink all the time. And then that poor bastard whose Hun staggered around at the vertical, flame pouring from his tail like a Roman candle gone crazy. All over the runway he hovered, trying to get that nose down, but the nose went up and stayed up, just like one of them vertical takeoff jobs. Leastwise until he did something else wrong and ploughed it in, making a million little old pieces of it and his darling self. He was not the only one by far. Hell, we started calling that stutter-dance of death the Saber dance. Blame the goddamn compressor and about a dozen other components. Yet, yknow, it wasn't that bad a plane once you knew you was messing with a rattlesnake that stalled at one-fifty knots. Imagine that. One-fifty. Jeez. Then they come up with the One-Zero-Five Thunderbird, and the Navy sent 'em back, wanted the old bastard-bird the Hun again after all. Hellfire, metal fatigue, slats, North American forever sending out the bad news, they was a long-suffering firm in those days. And the Eff-One-hundred two-seat was deadly too. But, you know, they is all deadly. The only way is you master them and show them like a dog who's boss. What you think all that Super-Saber shit cost in old dollars, Rupe?"

Rupe was asleep, sprawled on the deck of the bridge, elegant in his squash attire but very much in Booth's way. Shaking his head in superior-officerly disapproval, Booth strode over him and went below, wondering if Clegg had ever noticed changes in his colonel's demeanor. Booth was hunting an analogy. What was it? The data he let slip had always been on the conservative side, yes, always well within the performance envelope: none of the astonishing stuff. The Soviets would understand that, he had thought back then. Ah, here came the reciprocal half of the analogy. At air shows in foreign countries, the Soviets had always put on restrained displays, well within the aircraft's capability. That was it. So here was he, understating or litoting everything, and there were they doing the same in action. It made him one of them, surely. It was their way. Of course, he long ago had realized that, with litotes (or what he in his technocratic fantasies called LITOTE MODUS ADEEN) you always applied an expansion factor. In no time, those who dealt with you always read, say, 2.1 as 3.7; you had only to get them started, on the right inferential road. It was one way of blabbing without opening the mouth wide. *Hamlet,* to put it coarsely, would be only a few soliloquies and the play within the play. A part stood for the whole. Now there was a name for that. Synecdoche.

Thank heaven for memory. Clegg had been snoring, and soon Booth was too, his feet not far from the wash along the warped-down end of the submerged lower deck. It was almost as a survivor of submarine warfare that he lay down, said his nightly prayer to himself (urging, cajoling, exhorting) and wished never to be recovered. Yes, he thought in quasi-lullaby appended to his long F-100 speech to Clegg, it was the Turks who took on a lot of Super-Sabers, a whole bunch. Now, was that just to prove their manhood? How would I have looked in one of those badly cut Russian uniforms, with a bandmaster hat and all that cheap-looking commissionaire braid? Sartorially they always looked a third-world country. The too big caps had always bothered him, the peaks bad enough but the big old-fashioned gramophone records of the top appalled him, prey to wind and proportionate only on a seven-foot man.

In the amphitheater of his dreams, Clegg was presiding at a court-martial of the senior-juniors, who all stood before him with their pants around their ankles, waiting to see if they were to be jailed or shot. Some delicious caressing sensation that always moved on had him in subsidiary rapture even as he debated their fate. He wriggled and twitched with delight, making the accused follow his movements with agonized care. How could he concentrate with all these epidermal squiggles going on? Which woman would caress him thus? Up he leaped in real life, still half asleep, rummaging in his shorts for whatever ailed him, little knowing a carpenter ant was on the brink of his rear end. Down flailed one hand, then up the other, but too late; the ant bit home into his fundament's tender glacis before he twisted off its tiny head between finger and thumb, some miniature globe of coal that would not be crushed. An ant had awakened him from a delectable court-martial — the dryest of dreams — with a savage chomp, and he took it as an emblem of bad luck. Could an ant poison you? It was summer. He was dressed for sport. How could an ant eventually *not* find its way upstairs? How far might it crawl into his insides against peristalsis obdurate as an army led by Patton? It was bound to have bogged down in the tide of advancing clag. No risk, just a big heap of ignominy. Even the ants were against him, egged on no doubt by the fifinella. He noticed Booth had gone, no doubt for an evening swim, or to hunt a bottle of liquor.

Perhaps they would end their days here, near the home-from-home of Pierre Boulez, about whom Babe had told him more than he needed to know. It would not be so bad, would it, the two of them never found because Pittsburgh failed to tidy up its rivers. During the sea war in the Pacific, Booth had told him, new professions developed, including that of onboard salvage as kamikaze planes piled up on deck: a new wartime carrier skill that got the carrier shipshape again as soon as possible. Now, if Pittsburgh were any kind of a copycat, these waterlogged ferries would not have been here to begin with. And. He wearied, wanted so much to sleep again, heedless of the amputated thorax in his shorts.

Where was Booth? He wanted another lullaby. Talk to me again, brother, of the Eff-One-hundred and its turrible vices, sir. I can stand to hear about them as I drift to sleep, drowning in the postindustrial slop. No. He had to do it for himself, bleakly envisioning the big chubby noses of the Kittyhawk and the Hawker Typhoon, the spindly shuttle shapes of the Westland Whirlwind's nacelles, the sharp-cut corners on a Lysander's wing, the broken-kneed low-slung stance of the Chance-Vought Corsair created thus to accommodate an enormous propeller. Clegg knew his aircraft when he allowed himself to. He had installed within his memory salient features that his addiction to the Cyrano had virtually blotted out:

knowledge befogged, but still accessible when he relaxed and drifted down among the oozy weeds of sleep or drunkenness. As patly drilled as Gurkhas, fierce Burmese troops recruited by the British for their empire, these tenderly remembered planes scooted through the graphite grays of his trances, ferrying him back to earlier airfields and other air forces, barking their pistons for him on other war fronts, even diving to rescue him from the vitriol briny as he, the most recent Clegg, bit the bubbles in a vain attempt to be a Cartesian diver. There was no need of Booth and the Super-Saber this time. Clegg baled out, a stunned ox, determined to resume his court-martial of the boy-interrogators who flashed their keys.

REM sleep entered him into the dark violet of the stratosphere, making him a pilot again, but denying him the dream of before, now presumably someone else's property or obligation; Clegg now found himself in a mosque with six minarets and replacement stained-glass windows, by his ankles exquisite tiles of lilies, tulips, roses, cypresses, and vines. For a while he thought he was in some sumptuously appointed aircraft hangar. The minarets outside were missiles in their silos. And then he was strolling through traffic in Taksim Square, past flower vendors and telephone poles painted white at the bottom. As he passed he slapped the white to see if any came off. He was looking for the tomb of a young woman, the Sword of the Prophet, and in the first court of Topkapi the left-hand tower, sometimes used as a prison for those among the eminent who had profaned the sultan. Between the two Norman-looking towers was the Gate of Greetings, which in a dream had a cheerful sound. His true destination was the harem, of course, where plashing fountains kept conversation from being overheard, grilles protected the Sultan's life while he took his bath, and one dark corridor, the Golden Way, saw gold coins scattered on festival days. Clegg mingled with the Black and the White Eunuchs, urgently looking this way and that for a flash of hair and thigh, like someone regaining a language he had lost, wandering from room to room with or without the crowd of tourists, wanting to live in style, to be recognized as a man with a magic carpet.

During the night, their thoughts conjoined on Turkey, but they were not men linked by dreams. They rarely shared dreams, so each assumed the other had restorative sleeps minus the impetuous enamels of ordinary slumber. Each thought the other an efficient rester whose mental machine needed no mumbo-jumbo pick-me-up. They not only dreamed, however, but reminisced heavily together, dislocating entire chunks of experience in order to inspect them from all angles, almost as if to prove to each other they had lived. The day would come when their time among the Danakili would haunt their dreams and their daylight hours, but it had not surfaced yet. [Mersa Fatma had vanished] into the abyss of unfathomable time, neither creature nor cipher, but when back among them would set them fretting and guiltying, initiating the constant revision of what they had done: two men paralyzed by recrudescent conscience, probably at the moment at which they could least revise and renew themselves. So long as they two stuck together, they formed a barricade against the past. Separate, though, they would find the past making easy inroads, challenging them to come clean, to bring suppressed details out into the daylight, just to see if they remembered correctly. As for now, they neither remembered nor forgot; some of what had happened was not there, not on their screens, embedded in their logs. The trick, Napoleon had taught, was to put each experience into a separate drawer, then close it, so that the chest of drawers, in other words the resident mental censor, might not make comparisons. Clegg and Booth had slammed shut all they could, but there was no way of sequestering the emotions, the fear and the worry, that came to the surface as incessant ripples, responses to events now gone, but also responses to events yet to come. They were worrying about the future, but nothing specific; the main commotion came from behind them, perhaps because they had suppressed it at the time. Now, an imperious sandstorm, it pummeled their backs and actually blew them into position for the next endurance test.

When Clegg awoke, all he could say was "Bloody river."

Booth said nothing, but privately cursed his spine.

Across the water, the hotels stood silent and unlit, dun obelisks awaiting an earthquake. There were trains, though, snaking along the nearest bridge, grinding and screeching, then turning away rejected. Without moving, Clegg watched a dozen go by, wondering if that might be their next form of transport and if he might become yet another Gray Ghost, like a character he recalled Richard Farnsworth playing in a movie. Would he like to be a hobo? Ride the rails all the way to San Pedro? Best of all would be this ferryboat pumped out and refloated. They could resume their escape, this time by river.

Booth was grumbling at him from below; then the sound stopped, and he heard Booth walking up the sloping asphalt on his way to the parked car, an odd figure in his squash whites, an albino waif adrift in the penumbra of industrial civilization, a far cry from the pilot of a Cyrano newly arrived from Turkey and Africa. To be here in the glad rags of plutocratic sport was a near-obscenity, but no one was about in the pallid dawn, only a few genuine river workers in haste to get their hands again into water that smelled of gas and gangrene, that felt like Vaselined pus. Booth's unbelievably competent mind was full of thoughts about food: bacon, ham, eggs, fried bread, cornflakes, muffins, bagels, even a steak or a slab of hamburger. He looked on foot, wondering why [July felt so cold,] then by car, shaking his head at the whitewash swastika that had appeared on the front left door. Someone was onto them or on their trail, he thought, trying to provoke them into something reckless. In the end, led by his nose, he found a small greasy spoon that accepted credit cards, and bought everything they had including home fries and stewed tomatoes. The menu, he convinced himself, was Bulgarian-Amish, but food was food. He drove back at speed, greeting Clegg with an incoherent song and a joke. "What would you call a pasta fetishist."

Clegg could not even muster a plea for repetition. He waited, wondering, his stomach a dead balloon, his eyes two proverbial pissholes in the snow. Booth woke euphoric, but Clegg came out of sleep only in a matter of hours.

"A fettuccinishist," Booth said, dropping a bag, such was his merriment at his first mental flight of the day. Were the next as bad, he would drown himself in the noxious river and leave Clegg to shout down the river police and the FBI. "Here's food," he said. "This'll set you free."

"It fucking better." Clegg coughed. "I been inhaling that river gas all night. It kills the rats, it kills me."

"This here breakfast, Rupe," Booth was saying with stately severity, "happens to be your best Bulgarian-Amish. Yew git some of this here swamp bread and fart your worst. We ain't in Turkey now, but your French gourmet cook is, like, not on the premises."

How could he be so sprightly so early? Clegg stayed up on the bridge, having reached halfway down the steps to take a parcel of food. Now he chewed as if hypnotized and washed down mouthfuls of a cola on whose can he saw a bottle. What a world, he thought, when your ghosts don't feed you and your comrades-in-arms drive you crazy with early-morning good cheer. I feel quite ornery, as ever at this time. Thank God for the click that tells me when my day has begun and I am fit to be left alone with my fellow humans. Somehow he had bumped his toe, no doubt when flailing around after the ant, and now he judged it, thinking he had perhaps bruised the nail and it would drop off: a clue to his pursuers, a souvenir from the bridge.

Then it was like spring's flowers coming out in a single hour: Clegg truly awakened, plying the already faltering Booth with talk of the squash court in which Enrico Fermi had begun his researches into nuclear fission. Booth grunted. And did all spies wear gray fedora hats? Didn't that give them away? Booth, scandalized, shook his head, murmuring something about men in baseball caps. It was a matter, Clegg at last recognized, of choosing a direction or of waiting there on the river for a posse of Washington bully-boys to come and arrest them, take them back to playing squash. It [was July,] so their athletic gear would not attract too much comment unless they headed too far north. The trick, Clegg said, was to head for any college town and bust into the home of some departed professor, reading his books and feeding his goldfish. A romantic notion, this antagonized Booth, who pointed out Pittsburgh too was a college town. City, anyway. "Just think of all the empty dorms," Clegg said, certain of his point. "We could have half a dozen rooms each." Booth wanted to head for the airport, then fly north, having "commandeered," he grinned, an Aero Commander. A wan joke, this, not to Clegg's taste. Did they want to stay put, replete with breakfast, until the river patrol's high-speed squadron came for them, with rifles clipped to the upper insides of the gunwales? It was a matter of energy, really. Were they up to a sustained flight, with all the planning it entailed, the masks, the deceptions, the meager food, the broken sleeps? Or should they make a final sprint to some prepossessing town where the local airport was not too conscious of security?

Off they went, two worthies off to play some summer sets, rackets under their arms, almost as if they had come from one of the hotels opposite. "Why doesn't your magic lady tell us what to do," Booth said, "and provide us with a magic carpet?" A close observer, however, would have noticed how rumpled their shorts were, how grimed their shirts; how their faces had taken on a wan, distraught look, as after staring around them in bright sunlight for too long. Was there also something disheveled about them, in their gait something seedy and fractionally shady? The gestapo would have nabbed them in seconds, but the Pittsburgh police had not even been alerted, and the one patrol car that saw them was not primed for squash players who looked like accountants from the nearby Conference Center, the only odd thing about them being that they were on the wrong side of the river. One river guard, high on his drab deck, saw them, exclaimed, then settled back to his morning paper, which later he would adapt into a model boat and float downriver just for the sake of creative contribution. He had thought of emigrating to Australia, a frontier where things happened, but dun and friendly Pittsburgh held him in its smoky thrall. He would never know what had passed him by: just a couple of exercise mavens out for a morning trot, maybe catching a couple of butterflies on the way, betting a sawbuck on the game, knowing they had a nifty breakfast awaiting them back at the Vista, where breakfast was a lordly buffet.

Of course: this was Sunday, slack day on his portion of the river. He had been promoted to the river, leaving Earth behind, and next would be flame or air. He hoped for air, meaning helicopter patrol, but saw he would first have to bring off several remarkable coups: killers, grand larcenists, dealers, and addicts. Little of this happened in Pittsburgh, though, where the main crimes were cultural. The city even had an Armenian poet laureate, to whom all the other poets paid court. Everything there was Three Rivers, except the police and the symphony concerts, and it would indeed soon be the Three Rivers Patrol and the Three Rivers Symphony Series, much as, farther east, where the diagonals of Pennsylvania crossed on the site of Pigskin U., a famous football university had had all its endowed chairs named for pigskin, never mind how jarring the collision in such titles as Pigskin Professor of Jewish Studies. Perhaps this bullhead monotony amounted to gentrification: was it cruder to pigskin a scholarly appointment than to have no endowed professors at all? Officer Ruckert Lieder knew little of this. Pittsburgh was as Pittsburgh did, and some Ariel unknown to him had cast a girdle around a city, shutting out all outside folkways. It was into this unceremonious burg that Booth and Clegg had come, picking out of the air the impulse to be soon gone, away from the smoke, the potholes, the Middle Eastern delis, the contempt for Philadelphia and Harrisburg (and all other Pa. towns). All they had to do was empty their bladders and drive, committing themselves to their credit cards, little knowing that no one was following them in the actual sense, but on a map, thanks to a transponder in the carefully planted Escort (the only car on the lot not locked).

Now Trooper Friend joined Ruckert Lieder, and they masticated their cheeseburgers together like two crows at the same raised fence. They would never have qualified to be Cyrano pilots.

Now Clegg offered a penny for Booth's thoughts and was told about the German woman pilot, Hanna Reitsch, who test-flew the V-1 flying bomb. It glided like a piano, she said.

Clegg was thinking of all the unused shower caps in the Pittsburgh hotels, passed on from guest to guest over the years. He would dearly have enjoyed the Vista and its ample views of the river.

"Here we go again," Booth said, "still at large."

"What a comedown," Clegg answered, "after Africa."

The grotesque sawmill vibrations of the Escort were too much for them, accustomed as they were to the Cyrano's pure lunge that left all propulsive commotion behind. They were spoiled, to be sure, pampered supermen relegated to a trot, a fumble, a dodgem-car type of motion. Even a Piper Cub would have suited them better, but neither man had felt up to hijacking something at the private part of the airport, and then of course inviting trackers. No, better the car than brief fun at seven thousand five hundred feet, heading for Elmira or Binghamton. In the red Escort they had scores of choices, heaving gently from Pittsburgh eastward or westward without having to change altitude, away from the airport to Etna and Fox Chapel, Verona and Indianola (Clegg's favorite), on back roads reconnoitered with philatelical precision, getting them to Milton and Punxsutawney, Weedville and Penfield (Booth's preferred because it reminded him of brain surgeon Wilder Penfield). They took a wobbly, indefinite route, as if blown by winds this way and that, mimicking flight, drift and yaw, not from Cyrano experience but from earlier flying when the plane was air's pawn and they crabbed their way forward, surrendering themselves to the sensations of off-course, voluptuous and lordly so long as someone kept an eye on the map and the roads below, the outdoor theaters, viaducts, lookout towers, racetracks, perennial and nonperennial lakes, dams and piers, oil wells and flashing lights, obstructions and group obstructions, obstructions with high-intensity lights, power lines and catenaries, water tanks and coast guard stations, the full variegated swell of structures that lurked in the planet's nap.

Flying, Clegg thought, was an odd medley of things, his final finding being that sometimes you went on flying as if the plane was not there; it had dropped or ducked, sideslipped or vaulted, and there you were, princeling of your own slack impetus, suddenly jarred back into your seat again, set back on course after what could only with irony be called an excursion. That was the charm of it: you needed the machine in order to get going, to get the airspeed high enough to create low pressure on top of the wings, and then you were made, part in charge, part passive, drilling your uneven way through an invisible liquid that brewed legends and took lives. It was impossible not to want it, but anyone who got it got something else: a satanic view of fallibility. It was not that the ground was unforgiving; it was that speed and gravity cornered the ego and made it wince. Up there you paid for all the impatience of drivers on the ground; going as fast as they wanted to, you consummated their dream and the dreams, as Pentecostals say, of all signs following. In his early days as a pilot Clegg had yearned for the ground unrolling beneath him to be painted white and pink and green, just like a map, with clearly identifiable roads and railroads marked, name places on towns, rivers of palest azure, mountains of cordovan brown. It would have been so much better than the haze-ridden blur, so hard to figure out, so unlike what it seemed when you were aground. He wanted vertical constancy and all those gracefully explicit symbols plastered on, solid blue for perennial lake, dotted blue for nonperennial, an actual sign reading Misty 3 Moa for military operations area number three.

After a while he became accustomed to flying over undifferentiated elephant hide and took pleasure in instrument flight as he watched himself slither along the strict narrow airways printed over the merest facsimile of what lay beneath. He learned to avigate, as airmen sometimes say. None of what bothered Clegg bothered Booth, whose mind had developed a curious receptiveness to the hindrances and conventions of flying; he didn't so much put up with them as calm his mind to the right level of alert behavior. He did it by numbers and incessant bookwork, not only learning all he should so as to ace his examinations but acquiring all kinds of miscellaneous extras, never mind when he might need them. The holes cut in the wings of Messerschmitt 109's were crude and jagged, but who cared so long as fuel poured in? The same plane had a steel plate behind the pilot, to protect him from fire behind. And, in the years between the world wars, when the Versailles Treaty limited Germany to a hundred thousand soldiers, the German High Command construed this edict as referring to a hundred thousand officers.

All this was Boothiana, almost as if, instead of going on to become a Cyrano pilot, he were going to be an antiquarian aeronautics expert, an associate professor of sky somewhere, creaming all and sundry with recondite knowledge. Knowing such things, being so gratuitously well informed, gave him an extraordinary mental (and speech) rhythm that bothered people. He sounded as if talking down, forever implying that, if you learned to fly without recognizing the historical context of the act, you were an industrial yahoo, fit to twist screws but not to fly. In Booth the legendary three-dimensional giftedness of men came to the fore, as was appropriate in a profession that sometimes required celestial navigation and the pilot was inside a transparent sphere on whose walls reposed the huge ciphers known as constellations. Clegg had a feeling for the stars all right, but Booth knew what they were for and used them even when he did not have to; it made him feel part of the universe's radiant sphericality and put him in a position that revealed some small galaxy merging with the Milky Way ever so slowly by human standards, but slinking inward like a lover or an infatuate, sucked in and broken up by the cosmic football game.

While Clegg drove, Booth scrutinized the map, exclaiming at the little towns that huddled south of the New York–Pennsylvania line, at all costs not wanting to be found in New York State: Elkland, Lawrenceville, Fassett, Sayre, Brookdale. To the north of them there was little but Waverly, close to the line, anyway, and he wondered why. Clegg said the line meant nothing in any case; what you couldn't find from the air was no-count stuff, but he allowed as how he'd like, someday, to fly along the line from Genesee to Susquehanna, even as far as Hancock in the very northeastern corner of Pennsylvania—or was it New York? These confounded road maps misled you all the time. Prompted by a different, though related thought, Booth said he'd like all the towns to be like Athens and Troy, both in this area; as you went north you ran into Ovid, Cicero, Homer, Ceres, but no Tacitus, no Sallust, no Quintilian (he was airing his knowledge today, inert since God knew when), and just perhaps no Euclid. Classical revival appealed to him because it made a region homogeneous, sending the tourist back to the guidebook, even the classical dictionary. His mind was like that: precise and scholarly, as adept with words as with math, but preferably words written down, math done quietly. Indeed, words dealt with like math. He took the wheel again after they had stood furtively in a thicket emptying their bladders. "It's okay," Booth said. "We both got one. Yours stubby and fat, mine long and thin. Long and thin goes too far in and's always making babies."

"Not so's I've noticed," Clegg said, clearing his throat. "You've been too busy for that, Colonel."

Booth spat on his hands and rubbed them on his squash sweater. "This is great country for an open-air pee."

"Anywhere's to pee in," Clegg answered. "You gotta notice the difference between peeing and flying, boss. If you wanna pee, any field will do. If you wanna make a crash landing, then you gotta find a suitable field, long enough, not ploughed, no wires, no trees. Why the hell am I telling *you* this?"

"Nervous with your piddler in your hand in the open air, Rupe. You'd never go off at the mouth like that if it was all zipped up like a million dollars."

"Well, fuck my fanny," Clegg said.

"Fuck it yourself, Rupe. Remember, the faster you fuck in Pennsylvania, the bigger the fine gets."

They sailed through open-feeling Elmira without a thought of Mark Twain, neither of them able to stand his so-called humor, and picked up

Route 13 at Horseheads, aiming at Ithaca (of course: what more classical?). On the sectional that Booth was now using instead of a highway map, he saw what he remembered. The runway was more or less parallel to Lake Nausicaa and there was a private strip, Skyhook, south of town, and then another called Tom 'n Jerry. Yes, he mentally doodled, the runway there might be made of ice cream.

"Ben and Jerry," snapped Clegg, "sir."

On they cruised, at last sighting Ithaca far ahead of them, looking down on it. Perhaps there still, Booth said, was the madman Haiz, who ran the FBO (private terminal) and spent all day talking on the radio, executing hypothetical flights to Vladivostok and Lake Chad. Haiz was a cosmic mind.

"Yeah," Booth said, "look." Clegg saw Virgil, Seneca, Hector, and Scipo (which surely should be Scipio), and burst into irreverent laughter at Booth's odd preference for classical names, as if—what was it? As if their presence made the surrounding terrain more august, more renowned, much as some folk thought Paris was all the more literary for the writers' names affixed to its streets, even the names of those you couldn't bear to read, or hadn't bothered to. Booth had this Greco-Roman thing, part of the military complex that included heel clicking, correct saluting, proud bearing, medals pinned to the skin of his chest. When they had retired to the thicket to relieve themselves, Clegg had half expected to see a medal pinned to Booth's foreskin, or even lower down, with the ribbon and gong acting as a kind of penis sheath. But not this time: that, Clegg told himself, would come later. He was sure the medals no longer decorated Booth's chest; he could not hear them.

"You going to call the tower, for old times' sake?"

Booth snarled something about the sun's having gotten to Clegg and increased speed, slicing through downtown like a demon, as if he knew where he was going. He was heading for the airport on the 237-degree radial from Elmira, aimed at the Holiday Inn, perhaps, in the days when the Holiday Inn was uptown in Lansing and the Ramada was downtown next to Woolworth's whereas in later days the one replaced the other for reasons unknown and the new Ramada got an extortionate, lavish facelift. Here came those comely two tennis-playing lads, eager to wash the stains of travel from them, but not yet their memories of Turkey and Africa. "Look," Booth said, pointing at a couple of Cessna 152's getting into the pattern for landing, their pilots little realizing how their genitals overflew the old Holiday Inn nonstop at about twelve hundred feet, a juxtaposition no one cared about.

Booth parked, checked in, used the key, and was in the pool in the interior courtyard before Clegg had a chance to figure him out. What a relief to be out of their squash gear. In the mall next door, they bought jeans and Cornell T-shirts, bright red baseball caps and pointy Brazilian shoes, slip-ons, reduced from twenty dollars to ten because no one, there, ever bought those kinds of spivvy shoes. They were only a couple of miles from the airport now and its revolving green light, the holy grail of upper Volta, awaited their impetuous convenience.

When Clegg tugged off his brogue and began to massage his toe, complaining and wincing, Booth strolled across the room like a venerated prizefighter who had just lost several pounds by starving himself and made a distant inspection. "Ingrown toenail," he said, and at once began the treatment. "We could rush you off to a podiatrist, but unlikely we'd find one today. The thing to do is soak it. First thing. Then I will show you a miracle with a small ball of fluff." Clegg soaked the offending toe for half an hour, not wholly in the bath but perched thereon, using the folded-up nonskid mat as a cushion, wondering why he never kept his toenails perfectly trimmed. Then Booth squatted beside him, tucked behind the nail a Popsicle stick ungathered by the maid, and, in slow increments, worked it sideways. With a neat, sighing twist, he forced the nail's edge from its anchorage and bent the corner forward, installing between it and the quick a little ball of fluff tugged from the coverlet on one of the beds. Then he let the nail spring back, which it did slowly. Clegg saw blood and pus, but he felt no more pain. "When it's long enough," Booth told him, "we'll snip it off." He found a Band-Aid in the little supply cabinet (unusual in a midprice hotel) and dressed Clegg for war. "You're invincible again, Rupe. You just think about the rocket pioneer in prewar Germany whose rocket exploded. He died of a chunk of the engine in his heart. Or the line boy new to the Messerschmitt One-Six-Three, who dipped his finger in some *C* or *T stoff*, the propellants, out of bravado or in some mood of genuine scientific curiosity, and out came only the bone. The pilot sat between the two tanks, a human sandwich! What's a sore toe to that? You'll be fine in a day or two. It'll be sore to begin with, but you'll recover. My mother taught me such things. And there's always the tube of paste you put on ever so gently. We don't want a cripple as we begin our new life, so-called."

Astounded by his competence and solicitude, Clegg wondered at the other parts of the man, usually so boisterous and leaderly. Now and then he behaved like a male nurse, suddenly having had a vision of human ailment. Or (and Clegg surprised himself thinking this) he was so intolerant of the least malfunction he made every effort to preclude it or to fix it. He would go to self-abasing lengths to keep the show on the road. Then he would say, with resounding panache, "Let's get the disaster on the road again." Very much the disabused colonel. Clegg tried to find *Unsolved Mysteries* but could not, little knowing it came on at eleven, on the cable, severed siblings, battered children, kidnapped innocents and all. Another night, he would be appeased and life would begin to regain some of its lost symmetry, pattern and reliability. Clegg had argued that they should use a motel, claiming they had so much back pay they might buy a boat and sail on Lake Nausicaa.

Some minor financial rearrangements, such as verifying their back pay in a California bank, and they would be authentic citizens again. Just maybe, Booth thought, they want us to sink out of sight into the knitted wool of society, complete with ID, driver's license, Social Security, the lot. They want to smooth us away. They want us to smooth ourselves away. At least we no longer look like tennis players, though in a trice we could reassume the part. His innards yearned for the nearby airport, where now and then something landed or took off; he could hear the lawnmower sound of the weak-engined Piper Warriors, the huge aural froth of turbo-props, and rarely the bottled-up thunder of jets or the raging commotion of reverse thrust. He wanted to be there, running things, or taking the active: no more dithering, no more earthbound to-ing and fro-ing. He wanted a straight line.

Next day, Monday, was a kind of metaphysical Christmas. A package awaited them at the desk from Federal Express, containing all their documents, bank statements, ID, credit cards, and a thousand dollars in cash. If anyone had been intent on carting them back to Washington, he must have changed his mind. This was the invitation to the waltz, to a spendthrift aftermath, the senior-juniors no doubt having recognized the futility of interrogation. "Rupe, boy," Booth said jubilantly, "we've been let off the goddamned hook."

"They know where we are."

"But they don't want us."

"Then there's no need to run."

"No," Booth said. "When they need us, they can always grab us. No problem. They could always locate us. I do declare we've nothing left to offer them. We're running on empty."

"Then it's like paradise."

"It's more like the Heavenly Sextant," Booth said. "You know, that part of the sky in which there seems very little, a grouping made from unclaimed stars. There's whole bunches but we haven't managed to see it so far. That's where we are, Recon. Up to us to make our mark."

Clegg dry-washed his face with his hands, wishing his toe did not still hurt. He was quite prepared to play the role of invalid, foot propped up on a pillow, tucking into eggs and home fries, croissants and marmalade. This was going to be the time of replenishment, the long period of forgetting, the lull in the bombardment. Life was shelving them at last and all that Brassoed rhetoric about surging up in the world and defining yourself could go and perform upon itself the anatomical impossibility. Booth, however, was not through yet, ready to go and bluster Alan Haiz into taking them on as pilots, line boys, test pilots, radio communicators, paid friends: anything. Then they would find lodgings both spartan and ample, close to the airport (maybe a trailer), and borrow flying magazines from the local aero club, thus reacquiring the litter of an obsession.

THREE

A One-Way Ticket to Palookaville

een once but hardly taken in, the green metal hangar shook to the sough of a lambent August breeze wandered north from the Gulf of Mexico. Its rusted metal, hot to their touch, would have to be ground away before paint came near, but neither of them felt equal to the chore and made a mental note to have someone else see to it, which meant it would never get done, not with the anticipated press of passengers and the constant shifting in and out of one or two planes. The future was a great rectifier, and, besides, both Booth and Clegg had still not recovered from the shock of being still on the run, as it were, and actually involved in the rental of property, even a run-down aircraft hangar whose huge door, unmoored at the bottom, swung outward when they tried to budge it, having long since pushed its rollers from their clogged-up grooves. When it was truly windy, the two doors floated away from the structure as much as fifteen degrees, tugging at the top runners with almost enough force to pull clear. Something deciduous about the hangar appealed to Booth and Clegg, echoing whatever it was in themselves that unnerved them now they had survived Africa and capricious questioning by the senior-juniors of the Pentagon Star Chamber. A pair of has-beens, latterday flops, canceled retreads—whatever the right phrase for them was—they saw their newly acquired hangar as the manger of great things, the way out of obsolescence into mother-of-pearl rebirth, faintly startled to be thinking in images so lyrical, so tender, though not so much when Booth, his hand clamped on one end of a swaying door, said without warning, "You saved me," with almost a tear, and Clegg had to work his jaw muscles hard to regain his composure.

Had he really said that? If so, what was he alluding to? The desert? Or the interrogation? He had no idea, but he was sure Booth would amplify his statement once engines were oiled and trim tabs set. Intellects vast, cool, and unsympathetic had squinnied at them, like overlords of the galaxies, and found them wanting, yet far from culpable, perhaps too passive in the face or the rear end of disaster. All that was over, however, although Booth kept mentioning Trotsky, a Porsche Booth had once owned, Boethius (whom Clegg knew about), the Ivy League (which piqued Clegg), *The Financial Times* of London, and the constellation Centaurus (which they had in common). It was as if his past were moving in on him to reclaim him and, indeed, set him back more than a mite, reversing his time line in the interests of habits almost forgotten but now stoked up again. All in between had been found wanting, and Booth seemed headed back to his origin, at least in the easy recollections of casual speech.

Clegg wondered if he too, in everyday chat, had started harking back to—oh, the Battle of Britain, his tie rack, his beloved pool, his wounded feet, but could never catch himself in the act. Fabulous hairsplitting, Clegg decided, wishing he'd gone to a campus where they worried about such matters and gave you a degree for doing so. He had always longed to meet the Oxford professor who, having lectured on good and evil for thirty years, had said in the end he could always tell the one from the other: one tasted like butter, the other like margarine. When a towering mind said something like that, Clegg knew he had wasted his life; he could have said it too, at a much earlier age than the Oxford professor had. He wondered what someone such as he, newly mortgaged for an air-craft hangar, a twin-engined plane, and Satan knew what else, was doing thinking about such men, whose lives had played no part in his, but fizzed through it like neutrinos on their way to Australia, lighting up the slum in which his imagery rotted and the windmill in which his mind ground ideas to acorn dust. Why, he was becoming quite Boothly or Boothish, wasn't he.

Now he remembered Shumaker and Young, flying the Cyrano for NASA (until *their* engines flamed out over somewhere unpalatable). So did Booth, but Booth had no time for memories of such men: mere deputies. He preferred to remember Alan Haiz, paralyzed after a stroke and eager (if such a word were not too vigorous for his mortal languor) to be rid of his properties, such were the costs of his long-term care. It was as if Icarus had fallen prematurely and auctioned off his wings. Haiz the polymath had broken down and Booth, for all his misadventures and their aftermath, felt obliged to keep the Haiz tradition warm, copying that encyclopedic rigmarole of his to the letter, changing nothing, not even scouring off the rust, indulging in no paint and no whitewash, letting mice and sparrows have their way with the hangar, continuing to let rain and wind and snow in, even peeing in the same old corner as Haiz (a cor-ner of wall audacious chromatic yellow like a permanent lamp flashing). It was all right, he told Clegg. Continuity was all.

And, Clegg thought, proto*cool*. A smidgen of insubordination.

"Did you say proto*cool?*" Booth looked needly and irate.

"Now, would I say anything so daft, sir?"

"You better not proto*cool* me, Rupe."

He said he would not; he promised, scout's honor, swore by the Pitts-burgh river police, by Aqua Regia.

"Only good shit in here," Booth said with a near-lisp.

"Count on me, Colonel." Clegg looked away. The man had begun to crack at last. *You saved me.* Little did Booth know: Clegg had almost sold him down the river a couple of times. Each instance stood out boldly like a crucifixion against an open furnace: once in Africa, once during interrogation. Clegg would never forget and had recently been wondering about the bond between two men, one the other's senior in rank (Clegg only an *acting* full colonel), and, as before, about the words *subordinate* and *lieutenant* (in lieutenant-colonel). A soldier had to know his place, Clegg thought, especially in the ambit of death and torture. Pain cleared the head, did it not, especially under frightful circumstances? Pain in comfort was one thing, with morphine or one of its derivatives enclosing you in soft lawn; but pain admixed with horror was a wholly different thing.

"I never saved you," he told Booth.

"You don't remember," Booth told him. "You're getting fuzzy, Rupe. Here we are. You're going to fly the plane and I'm going to man the phones. How's that for a suitable return? Anyway, you got the look of a man who saved somebody. The savior of the moment, Rupe, no holds barred."

Clegg demurred, but it was no good: Booth had made his mind up and was awash with fellow feeling, gratitude, awe. He had (Clegg thought) invented something to rejoice about and nothing human or divine was going to take it away from him. They were going to be so busy soon, back to puddle-jumping aviation, a dollar here, a dollar there, here in the Finger Lakes that all had names like Owego, Oswego, Otsego, as if the local Indians had suffered from etymological lockjaw, unable to devise more than a few patterns for their words.

Their plane, a twin-engined Piper Apache, 1962 vintage, had a solid, reliable look. Bought cheap from Haiz, it had belonged to a country doctor who loved it and always kept it hangared dry. All its contours had a rounded, folded-over-itself look suggesting (to Clegg anyway) an old rose defensive and hunched. Nothing spiky about this plane. Nothing snarky. It was a trundler, a lumberer, a beast of the field. It didn't yaw much, float in its own ground effect, or dip a wing when stalled. It was not a plane in which to kill yourself or intimidate a native population when you roared over them at zero feet; rather, the natives would look up and laugh at a rocking horse broken loose. It chugged. It reminded Booth of a faithful old dog, always waiting to be told what to do, and then more or less doing it. Buying it had been an act of faith in the future rather than in the future of the plane itself. Booth and Clegg would be around to see it sent to the knacker's yard or installed, cheap, in the playground of a suburban school interested in aerodynamics. It seemed to demand a name, but Booth and Clegg resisted the temptation to give it one, preferring its national number's last digits: Six-Seven Poppa (for *P*). It was bad enough to call a female gremlin Fifinella, but to call a battered Apache Trudy or Egbert was anthropomorphism gone berserk. It remained a vehicle, a conveyance, whose sharply splayed retractable gear made it seem more modern than it was, though half of each wheel stayed out in the slipstream to cushion the Apache during a crash landing.

Well-attuned Booth observed, during the first test flight, that this bulging half wheel reminded him of a Bellanca Viking, and that ushered it into the fold, gave it a speedy relative in the family tree of cushy agile airplanes. At 191 miles per hour, its carlike profile seemed to desert it, but only perhaps because the people within leaned farther back under the pressure of a wind restricted to the tumult outside. Sensing how fast they were going, they leaned back to be of good cheer, weighed down by two hundred pounds of baggage behind them. With the door not an exact seal, the Apache made a fearsome clatter, but Booth and Clegg intended to equip passengers with earplugs, three all told with two pilots, the copilot helping passengers with carefully prepared displays, maps, postcards, pop-up models, and model planes. Their original idea, not so bad really, had been to acquaint passengers with the landscape beneath them, the topography of the Finger Lakes, making a journey into a seminar, a novelty flight into an act of communion. To descend afterward, respecting air and flight, that was the raison d'être of what they came to call Perigee Airways.

"Got it, Rupe," Booth had exclaimed. "Apogee Airlines."

"Away from the Earth," Clegg said, murmuring. "More suited to a NASA rocket isn't it? They won't be getting *that* far away from good old terra firma."

"What then?"

"How about Perigee? Along the Earth. That which hugs the earth, quizzing it, peering into its pores. Airways suggests different ways of doing things whereas Airlines brings up the whole business of flying straight-line vectors. We'll be doodling around more than flying as the crow."

Booth backed down, as he could do with surpassing graciousness; he sometimes, to Clegg, looked like a somewhat past-it Luftwaffe ace especially with sunbleached hair, the severely rinsed blue eyes, the frown lines from squinting into the sun too much. You looked at him and thought, he seems too noble to go to waste. He has not delivered his all yet. The mustache is far from German, but his name might be Erich Sommer, old pilot of the Arado 234, proud that his flights in the greenhouse cockpit gave him no armaments to defend himself with during camera missions.

Indeed, once, he had encountered a photographic de Havilland Mosquito over the English Channel and each had recognized in the other an unfanged sibling and proffered a lazy, curt wave of grudging acknowledgment. There goes he. Here go I. Like beach photographers asking folk to say cheese or *Sieg* and to keep still for at least an inhalation.

In profile the Apache was an image of four hundred and seventy horses (imagine!) pulling almost five thousand pounds. Imagine that on the ground, Clegg thought. I have never seen seventy horses, have I, but I have often been in the presence of five thousand pounds. The first version, Booth reminded him in a scholastic tone, had only three hundred horsepower; they were not so generous with horses in those days. Booth wondered why. At first Clegg fumbled for some notion of its being humbler to fly with fewer horsepower, as if it were more decorous to take up fewer horses (horses didn't belong in the sky anyway), but he then decided it was all a matter of improvements in manufacturing technique, so the horsepower inched up from 150 to 160 to 235, what a big jump at last. Later models came with swept fin and rudder, an all-moving tailplane, and extra cabin windows, but not 67 Poppa, along with which came a rigger and engineer called Chaff, himself the owner of an Ercoupe, a plane guaranteed not to stall or spin. He ministered to several planes in and around the FBO, checking them periodically and when they got bumped a little. Chaff was subject to sudden departures to destinations unknown, but he usually came back with a copious tan, having delayed the entire airport (the general aviation part anyway) for weeks. It was rumored he was a spy for the Philippine government, but Booth pooh-poohed this slander and suggested he had to go away to have a heart bypass. Poor bastard, he merited sympathy, Booth said.

Yes, Clegg decided, it was fair to call the wing a Hershey bar: the outboard panel was certainly that, though the inboard one had a slight taper to the leading edge. Even the engines had parallel lines when seen from above, and the fuselage seen from the front was of boxy cross-section. None of this troubled Clegg, who had seen too much streamlining in his day, too much ignoring of the simple fact that almost any uncouth shape could batter its way through the air, given enough power. He was in favor of the clumsy and the outrageous, such as the first airplanes flown by the Lafayette Escadrille and the big lumbering flying boats of the Germans, more boat than plane. If, on accident-prone Aeroflot, he was supposed to go from Moscow to Vladivostok, he would take Austrian Airlines to Tokyo, a Japanese bullet train north to Niigata, then board a flight back to Russia to Vladivostok. It would be safer to do it the long way round, he thought, and he didn't mind the extra time at all.

So let the Apache be a Chevrolet.

If only the world were more humdrum.

Had less chic.

Then he would be more at ease, totting up the first year's take: fifty passengers all told, one a week, at one hundred dollars per trip. Not bad. Yet not enough to cover repairs, check by Chaff, and hangar rental. He tried to think of something new, different, that would make the sun of their Airways come up. Why was he worrying? Booth was supposed to be the accountant, the one who decided when Perigee Airways would have to mount a fly-in to save itself, touting hot air balloon rides, chicken dinners (half a chicken, coleslaw, roll, and macaroni salad for five dollars), skydivers, gliders, State Police helicopter on display as if it were a coelacanth, Pitts rides, Elk Flyers, and of course breakfast (pancakes, sausage, home fries, eggs, coffee, orange juice, all you can eat: $4), not to mention hamburgers, hot dogs, drinks, etc., all day, evoking an orgy during which life and airplane rides would never end, food and drink would never run out, and the dark would never swallow the daylight. All this would be his responsibility, along with invitations to warbirds, war heroes, home-builts, pilots of replicas, and minijets. All of a sudden Clegg realized what loyalty was: you gave yourself to the other because you liked him. You might have liked him for years without actually thinking him worth your livelihood or your life. You just went forward and put yourself on the line because duty required it, and then liking, followed by whim-of-the-moment servitude. Was that it? What was this huge affiliation he was trying to think about? When had orders begun to shade into fondness and that into caprice? There had to be a worthwhile basis, or the gesture was fatuous.

In olden Germany, Germany before there was a Germany (unless the Germania of Tacitus, a Joseph's coat of tribes), the holiest bond between men was between an uncle and his *swestersunu*, his sister's son, lord in heaven knew why. It was so, quite arbitrary, not worth brooding about. It might easily have been brother and brother, but it was not. In this case it was colonel and lieutenant-colonel, bound to each other by braid and shoulder insignia: an impersonal deal, but not between Clegg and Booth, who had cemented between them something to do with danger. Clegg smiled, willing once again to settle the matter with a metaphor; in England, he recalled, the least damaged German aircraft from World War Two found a final resting place at RAF Cosford, also the site of the RAF Hospital. It was as if lovingly restored and polished Arados and Messerschmitts did duty for medical cases the hospital couldn't solve, and superlative omnicompetent alien aircraft were there to egg the doctors on to ever finer triumphs, Pyrrhic or not. Indeed, the wounded that some of those German planes had created lay on cots in the Cosford hospital, never to be moved, perhaps assigned a bed that looked out on the silken flesh of Nazi warbirds, almost as if there were some bond of honor between the victim and his destroyer's tool. It bore thinking about, Clegg thought, but only at bedtime; an entire day devoted to the fiery bond between enemies would be a day more than wasted.

Clegg would be happier doing a practice run up Lake Nausicaa, pointing the bulbous insect-spattered nose of the Apache into the press of sea-gulls, with the setting sun on his left almost cupric with fatigue, and over on his right as he approached the electricity-generating station some thousand gulls milling about over the coal heap. It was hardly a romantic scene, but, low over the water, he exulted in it, in its very mundanity, glad to be photographing nothing, unobliged to a passenger, sensing the first cold of evening wafting through the slot at his feet, watching the engines match each other on the dials, fantasizing which lakeside mansion he would eventually buy, which seaplane he would acquire to grace it. When a solitary fisherman waved to him, he waved back, knowing they could see the smile on his face, wishing the Apache were a seaplane and he could land to have a beer. Up to the lock at the head of the lake, big enough to hold a battleship but used mainly by small boats that portage might have dealt with. He flew back along the lake's other shore, tapping the storm scope as it revealed bad weather over near Binghamton, then switching it off. Told by the tower to execute a short approach, he swung a tight turn, 45 degrees at least, and then prepared to land, but, because of some quirk in the light, found himself unable to see if the three under-carriage lights were on: three in the green. Up he went in a go-around to an altitude spelled out by the silky-voiced female in the tower and started the whole thing over again, now number three behind a Cessna and a USAir de Havilland Dash-8. This time he saw the greens, set down the mains with a slithering pop sound, and eased the nose downward, aware of having executed what was known in the trade as a greaser. It was no different from a thousand other landings he had made, but it was domesti-cated. This airstrip was more home than any other had been, and he had already formed an impetuous affection for the red and white approach lights, the fluid white lunging electric pulse of the so-called rabbit that showed him what line to follow, and the Christmas tree display of runway lights proper, lit for him in all their pomp. The Apache was much more his toy than the Cyrano had been, yet it was a serious instrument too: benign, seasoned, cozy.

Having parked at the ramp after waiting for permission to do so from the tower, even though not a single other airplane was in motion, he thought again and headed for the broken-down hangar, starting the engines up again like one who had lost his memory while aloft. With the buckling, billowing doors open, he attached the cordless battery-powered towbar to the nosewheel and backed the Apache into its hangar, thinking it was not like any number of horses. How could you move horses with a machine driven by a friction drum? He had the hang of it now and would not shove the tail too far inside, as he had done at first with Booth yelling at him from the back wall. It was something to be doing this instead of leaving the job to sergeants and corporals whose livelihood it was. More of his life seemed to him under his own control. He did more. He touched more surfaces. As if to prove his point, he leaned into the nacelle, into the full aroma of gas and oil that floated slowly away from it: a smell of burned paint and singed damsons evoking for him a cabin in the woods with a predatory grizzly hovering at the window. He would never have sniffed at the Cyrano; its hot afterbreath was too hot by far and its skin scorched. Another emotion he felt on shutting down for the night was guilt, guilt at leaving the plane all by itself in this derelict one-plane hangar, almost as if abandoning a dog to an inferior kennel. So he contented himself with patting the Apache on the nose, site of a hundred dead insects, but an inevitable result of flying low in the evening. Using his last strength he lugged the hangar doors shut and secured them with a length of chain that went through two rust-holes and clipped together: poor burglar deterrent, but the hangar was hard to find, and what was inside it could hardly be absconded with. Unsatisfied with this whole line of thinking, Clegg cursed all vandals and Vandalia their home. He concluded with another metaphor, this time wishing he had for his life the equivalent of the little round mirror on the side of the nacelle; it told him if the wheels were down, though not if they were locked. Just now, they felt down, looked down, but the greens were not explicit.

Next day, as they waited by the silent telephone, each sprawled in a deck chair whose fabric had seen better days and deserved a thorough wash anyway, Booth began talking about the Junkers 87 dive-bomber and how its unretractable metal legs had canvas leggings around them, for all the world as if they were human ankles. "Eyelets," he said jocularly, "and little straps that buckled."

"Those Germans," Clegg said. "You'd kind of expect it of them. The other side of the atrocities was the fondness for cute forest creatures. Maybe they thought of the Stuka as one of those."

"The other side of the leggings," Booth resumed, "was the explosive charge in each. If you lost one leg of the undercarriage, then you blew off the other one so as to make a better, more symmetrical forced landing. It made sense, really."

"It raises the question," Clegg said, "of those pilots who couldn't tell if they'd lost a leg or not. If they thought they had, and were wrong, then they would bring into being the very situation the explosive charge was intended to prevent. One-leggedness. Hey, Doctor Booth, my toe is healed."

Booth dipped his hands, then made them climb abruptly. "I am full of stories today. I never told you about the lousy Russian oil, did I? Has to be thinned with gasoline when the weather's cold. It causes cylinders to last not very long. Space shuttle astronauts use their Tee Thirty-eight Talon trainers to make weekend trips to resorts and ski slopes. Now, that sure is one way of building up your monthly fifteen hours. When the Pond racer crashed in 1993, at Reno, there had been a fire in the cockpit."

"You're a fount of information today," Clegg said.

"I'm a fount anyway."

"You tell it like nobody knows it is, Colonel."

"Well, if that phone will never ring. Full flap for landing causes a high angle of descent, but not a high angle of attack. Full flap *reduces* the angle of attack." There he was, reciting the recondite algebra of his calling, someone babbling in his sleep by searchlight, switching now and then to information with more bite in it. "Hey, Rupe, did you know? There's a female flying as flight engineer on a Cyrano. How do you like that apple now? Flight test engineer, and her husband, also a flight test engineer, they got it covered, they got it nailed down, Rupe. Talk goes they are now using Cyranos to help develop an American SST."

"Like I said, sir. There is so much I just don't want to know anymore. Brain economy, I call it. Now, that cute little Velvet Uncontroller in the tower, with the sexiest voice in New York State, she's more interesting, at least to this soldier of fortune. She flies a stool, I guess."

"Who?"

"Velvet Uncontroller, I call her. The bedside manner with the bedside voice. I wonder who *she* belongs to."

What was happening to Booth had happened to professors of literature, who, on retirement, had been known to quote *in toto* all the works they'd taught over the past thirty years or so, not to make a point, but to keep the stuff alive within arm's reach. What they had exploited for so long had now become a reef to fasten themselves to, and life without it was a massif of vacancy where no one belonged and nobody had any future. Indeed, the phone *had* rung, three times, but to no consequence. Someone had asked what kind of plane they flew, and was it a biplane. Another person had hung up saying wrong number. A third had asked about their ad in the local paper, advertising Perigee Airways: scenic tours, postcards, chromatic visual exhibits, recorded commentary played over the speaker. This caller asked if he could bring his Boy Scout group for a reduced rate. None of this helped Booth out of his fierce, steaming doldrum, or Clegg from his lethargy. To be pensioned off, that was bad, but to sit at an airport all day waiting to go, praying for customers, that was worse. Maybe the ad was wrong, rhetorically speaking. They should have taken a different tack, touting instead sunset flights up and down the lake, with salmon pizza and Conestoga sparkling water. What did people want? Not just to fly a carrier from one place to another, or a plane to parachute from, or a plane that delivered newspaper to remote country areas.

"Hell," Booth droned, "maybe we should invite them to come fornicate in the backseats, Mile High pin provided. Or make an appeal to potential suicides. There's gotta be a more officerly type way to do it. We're not businessmen, Rupe, we're high fliers, we are men who used to have a golden mission with our assholes lifted high. Now this, all our dough mortgaged."

"At least," Clegg answered with a forlorn, patient headshake, "the brass are leaving us alone. Or whoever they were. Babe's coming to see us, see how we're getting on."

"She'll see in five minutes how low we've sunk, Rupe. Tell her not to come."

"No, she has to go to New York City."

"Then she should overfly *us*."

Every airplane at the airport seemed to have a mission: a BP Warrior went away on oil business; a big yellow floatplane from some Canadian wildlife company sat on wheels that merged into floats, then thundered away to investigate creatures of the wild. The huge Gulfstream jet that Clegg coveted (only thirteen million) was outbound for Pisa, Italy, on a trip for the owners: six people with four seats apiece. Cessnas, 152's and 172's, came and went, landed and took off again, always cleared for the option, creating at pattern altitude a perpetual aeronautical ronde, a circular buzz, that was almost a treat to listen to, splendid for its periodicity and steady mutation. Watching, Clegg marveled how, at certain angles to him, a speeding plane taking off made no sound at all, then made a grinding noise as it slowly climbed, and he wished he'd read more about Doppler effect and Doppler himself. He and Booth sat in a vale of ignorance, able to busy themselves with an evening flight up the lake when the air was calm and solid, but not to interest the populace in aviational diversions. If they'd had a Cyrano to tempt them with, what a story that would have been, or even one merely on the ground, condemned like those planes that sat in the Tucson sunshine dry-moldering, their teleology defunct. He could see that Booth was going to crack before he did, sliding into the past, into the roll call of crashes and mishaps in which men as good as he, better even, got into messes that ruined them and many others, when pilot error marred everything, even the thousands of technical marvels that functioned flawlessly all the way down to the crackup. Stalls, spins, ground loops, loss of engine, breakup of the airframe, flight into bad weather, all helped savage the wonder of the thing that flew, defying the bird and the insect, surpassing zeppelin and airship and balloon, squeezing distance as if it were Play-Doh. All this compressed into mute pastiche of a planing seagull. Clegg almost wept at the tawdry glory of them now. Booth's bones were softening; you could see them in his face, sagging and turning to glue. The pair of them would not go someplace else, not yet, but they aspired to a rainbow at whose end a provident angel sat with a silver chalice full of myrrh and ambrosia.

They waited several more days for the phone to ring and might even have welcomed from Washington a call to return now for final judgment: Make your way back to base by whatever means you think fit. Booth recalled an incident from World War Two in which Nazi paratroopers descended on a Dutch town, then took streetcars ticketless to their next destination. It was a wonder they had not stopped off to watch a football game on the way. There was no limit to human originality, whether others regarded it as uncouth behavior or not. The airport here was a new one, but relics of the smaller, previous one remained: a little restaurant, the Happy Landings, that always belched vile smoke and still functioned, and the former terminal, now occupied by the art department of the local university. After a hot dog each in Happy Landings, Booth and Clegg took the Apache up for a run around the pattern, just to keep it honest and move the oil around. They flew as far as the electricity-generating station, then turned back. Booth flew with almost capricious abandon, but his mind was on the job; suddenly, he cut the right-hand engine (word he said as *injun*), and the Apache lurched sideways with a wounded moan, nosing down and away until he switched the engine back on again, recovered heading and altitude and laughed at Clegg's dismay. "What do they allow for that maneuver?" He was proud of his ability to do an engine-out. "Eight seconds?" It was not long for, to begin with, realizing what had happened if indeed it happened without warning; then heaving controls into the still working engine, turning the plane left (as today) while it roared to go right and down. It was imperative to rehearse this disastrous eventuality, but Booth's nature required its most dramatic format, doing the thing at five hundred feet instead of two thousand. Clegg complained, then fell silent as Booth spoke crisply into the immaculate sound chamber of the David Clark Noise Attenuating headset—gel ear seals and supersoft pillow head pad—"Rupe, *you* test on your own time. Today's my test. Not so bad, eh? She no sooner gave up the ghost than Booth got her flying straight again."

"You're a genius."

"No, Recon, the guy who first thought of twin engines is the genius. If you have a plane with one engine behind the other, you never have that kind of trouble. There's something to it, isn't there?" Booth made the Apache do some elaborate little wiggles as he bored in on the Ithaca VOR and runway 14. The honest truth was that, should there ever be a fare-paying passenger, that person would be in good hands; two such perfect pilots were almost too good to be true, even in a plane so different from their military one. It was, as they so often said, a piece of cake, a doddle; Icarus was driving Ben Hur's chariot, for whatever purpose, and, in Booth's case certainly, superlative airmanship figured against a background of aviation trivia remembered with felicitous hunger, cramming Clegg's ears with the stuff of many books, even more hangar-flying talkathons. This time Booth explained to Clegg about the Junkers 188, whose nose was all glass, which betokened the bomber version, whereas the fighter version had a solid nose. At some point it occurred to Luftwaffe pilots of the Ju188 that, if the fighter version were given a glasshouse nose, Allied fighters would get a nasty surprise, getting the fighter when they thought they had easy prey in the bomber. So several solid-nosed Ju188's showed up with glasshouses painted on the nose, to disastrous effect. Booth loved these little tactical maneuvers, lore from a war he never fought in, and passed them around like good advice from the Ancient of Days, insisting on the technical ingenuity of the Germans, who rarely cared how something looked so long as it was efficient.

Clegg always agreed; he loved airplanes every bit as much as Booth did. Booth had once told him a story about espionage or information gathering (not flying technique this time around). He had found out something about Russian aircraft design and felt the information should be handed over to the key man at the Enrico Fermi Institute. He had gleaned his data from a Russian aviation magazine. After a long journey he arrived and presented his find to the appropriate scientist at the Enrico Fermi Institute, who it turned out had already read the magazine in Russian. Such an event, Booth proclaimed, demonstrated the unreliability of the accidental method also known as Autolycus Retrieval; the scientist might have yawned and gone to sleep, losing his place in the magazine and missing the Russian article entirely. Clegg laughed and agreed, or agreed and laughed. Booth was obsessed with his undercover past, none of which, Clegg thought, had amounted to much, though he certainly took risks with his eyes wide open. Things were different now: they rejoiced in reprieved mundanity, asking little, getting nothing in return. Booth was fighting his way through World War Two much as Clegg had participated, mentally, in the Battle of Britain; but "all that," as Clegg summed it up, was salvatory daydream, used up and blown away. Clegg needed less drama in his margins than Booth did, contenting himself with distraught memories of something vaster and less understood: the laws of thermodynamics all the way from One (the conservation of energy) to Two (the tendency to run down into chaos) and Three (the unavailability of energy below absolute zero). Clegg had spent much of his life clinging to these laws, never quite fathoming them or needing them professionally, but seeing them as a challenge, a dare, just like a little torero charging out of the schoolroom for a bullfight in full cosmic view. What effect the laws had on his military career, he wasn't certain; but he could see glimmerings of thermodynamic changes in his career seen as a whole: energy kept from one job only to be infused into another; getting more and more run down, more tired; and knowing that what he had left, by way of gusto or vim, lay out of reach, like a pin entombed in an iceberg. The mishaps of his life made a little more sense than usual when he installed them in this Draconian context. Indeed, he felt they were more God's fault than they were before and actually marked him as one who'd had special attention from the deity.

"You land it," Booth suggested.

"Got her."

Down they went in a swooning rectilinear lunge, gracious as a thin dowager fainting into a vat of cream. Oh, they were so good at this, even with no one aboard to feel the lack of thud. Booth had already figured the cost of this little jaunt and was wondering when their ledger would show something in black apart from doodles and amusing asides. Babe wasn't coming after all, Clegg told him as they resumed their deck chairs for the afternoon vigil. Good, Booth thought. I wanted her to stay away. Clegg and he craned their necks to look at every car that passed the gate to the hangar. Why shouldn't someone out for a summer drive decide to have a summer flight as well? The Apache was not in sight, however, and their ad in the local paper was going unread. Clegg decided a different technique was needed, so he came up with a scenario involving a certain Segundo Cielo, famous Italian travel agent famed for discriminating choices of venue in the Finger Lakes; after all, was he not an expert on the Italian Lakes? Clegg drafted the text of his new ad on the back of a fly-in breakfast leaflet, peppering his prose with interrogatives and such ill-recollected phrases as *dolce fare nente* (sic) and *lago azzuro* (sic). The idea, more or less, was that this Italian travel maven had seen the Finger Lakes and had gone out of his mind at their beauty; now ensconced in a palatial suite in the local Ramada, he was allowed on public access TV to talk about his experiences, and in a thick, confected Italian accent. The prose text would go out on postcards on the flip side of a picture in which the Apache gleamed white with black and ocher trim, its door figuring hugely at an advantageous angle. As Segundo Cielo said, "door big enough for a giant."

"You know," Booth announced, "there is no money for color postcards. Back in the old days, when the Germans put an air force together disguised as a commercial airline, they actually rejected one plane because its door was too small. An early Heinkel. Imagine the gall, the chutzpah. No, they said, for a commercial airliner, this door is too small. Imagine."

"Segundo Cielo," Clegg said, contorted with spurious humility, "he say: Apache door accept truck. You bring truck. Segundo Cielo fix. Hee feeex."

Booth grunted and told Clegg to fuck off in Italian.

"We have credit, Colonel."

"We have debts, Recon. Day will come we'll have to pay them or sell the plane. I'm the accountant, damn it."

Nonetheless they went ahead, commissioning printing and having Clegg (the town's newest celebrity, Segundo Cielo) boast on Channel 13 about the lure of the Apache tracking up the Lake and back. There would even be a reading of the famous poem by Lamartine, he said, garbling every language as he said so: "*una poema francesca appelé loch, Die Loch, di Lam Lamartine.*" Just to get them in the mood. Prices low. Cabin spacious. For twice the price they would do it three times, like hard-up trollops. All the same, Clegg's Italian persona began to grow apace and his Italian, fermented by enthusiasm, began to smooth out, no more correct than before, but more confident, more blasé.

Some malign deity had been watching. Their first clients, repulsed by Booth, were two colostomy sufferers who had been nowhere for years, but wanted to see the lake from the air, heedless of the effect excitement could have on their prostheses.

"There's always the potty," Clegg said. "Trust Segundo."

"Then you can clean it up," Booth told him with combative disdain. "I don't want them letting a simultaneous big one go in a freshly cleaned cabin. No, no, no."

"Don't be so retentive. We want customers."

"But not a shitstorm."

In the end, the two passengers climbed aboard, enjoyed the trip and had no accidents. Booth, writhing in the right-hand seat, yearned to yank one of the engines and shake the two passengers to bits, but contented himself with showing them postcards and photographs while playing the Nausicaa Waters song loud enough to drown out the radio that sprinkled the air with transmissions from other aircraft, all answered by the Ithaca Tower, this time not the controller with the sexy voice. The two passengers, the Fitz-O'Briens, had even paid and left a tip for the pilot. Finally Booth and Clegg were in business, but only, it seemed, with the maimed: the deaf, the blind, the crippled, the spastic. In no time Clegg and Booth had acquired and developed special skills that amounted to therapy. Most of their clients (one nurse, two patients big or little) just looked out, even the blind ones, transfixed by the noise and reassured by the similarity of the Apache's cabin to the interior of a car. There were no crises, no throwings up, no screaming, no tears, in the main a series of awed reticences in the presence of two howling engines and the lakescape gliding on beneath them.

Segundo Cielo, now out of his hotel home and plugging an audiocassette commentary ("No need to fly; just buy!"), had prevailed. "Hell, Colonel," he said, "we could have gone all the way to December and ended up with not a single passenger."

"So now we're rich?"

Clegg gave up. Booth wanted a fortune to come pouring in; instead they were beginning to be paid in word of mouth, and Clegg wanted the airline to be called Cielo Perigee or Segundo Perigee, both of which Booth called mouthfuls. The name remained the same, the prices did likewise, and the handbill became more imposing, more expensive, folded up into the monthly TV cable bill. They even evolved a bombing run and a simulated accident (one engine cutting out) for the braver of their clients, but stopped short of aerial copulation's Mile High pin. Finally Booth had something to write in his ledger, and his logbook as well, installing facts numerical and verbal in copper-colored ink, his handwriting a feat of stunning calligraphy that made Clegg envious and got him wondering what he could do to rival his colonel. The man had unsuspected rift valleys of estheticism running through him. One day he might paint the plane lavender and call it Beauregard Airlines: Come aboard and practice elocution. Then he might regale dinner-jacketed guests with tales of the Second World War and pass out flowers, pepper-mints, and rose-hued glasses.

What Clegg did, after sifting through the debris in the upstairs offices of the nearby art history department, was to open out a huge drawing of an unskinned Cyrano, once part of an ambitious promotional display in the lobby, and paste it to a gigantic square of plywood, carefully smoothing out air bubbles with a damp cloth. The wood warped a little, but he was prepared to put up with that. When the paste had dried, Clegg propped the backed drawing on a table and decided what to do. When he had a chair, he began, his tongue curled excruciatingly out the corner of his mouth like some elongated bait. With almost fanatic care he inked in cer-tain portions, the nosewheel and its struts, then wrote some words in a tri-angular shape near the cockpit. As he warmed to his work, it became clear he was both coloring in the Cyrano as if by numbers in some elementary coloring kit, and sketching his autobiography with rudimentary cameos: in a word, illuminating the drawing that lolled before him, showing a small boy eating the corner off a loaf or playing the piano. It would take months, he thought, as he slid extra support under the plywood's corners and drew up closer to him various ancillary tables for inks and dyes, brushes and rags. He was a monk of old, allowed to decorate in personal terms the text he was illuminating. Surely this was better than being tat-tooed all over his body. Slowly, various little glimpses of the Apache began to appear on the flanks of the jet, all numbered 3367P, and white trimmed black and ocher.

Lounging outside the hangar, Clegg fancied himself once more far back in time, on an RAF airfield in the south of England, keen for the sig-nal to scramble, his warmed-up Spitfire waiting for him. It was the aroma of cut grass that brought this on, the unalterable blue on high, the faintly ammoniac smell of gasoline approximating salmonella of the brain. If it was summer (and in Clegg's mind the preferable season was summer), then it was time to down the Luftwaffe; an old pipe dream kept bursting through and making of him a war hero, the kind of dandy man he had never been, far from bravery, cowardice, honor, glory. Up he flew and downed two Messerschmitts, then returned with only enough fuel to land, part of his memory reminding him, however, that the German pilots had only ten minutes or so over the target. He cursed them all, van-quished them to the mingled symphony of summer wasps and bees, drag-onflies and red admirals, swifts and swallows and seagulls, the constant studder of grass mowers, the swirl of torn-looking stratocirrus. This was a good season to die in, he thought, though the problem with dying in pretty circumstances was that you didn't want to leave them; better to quit in February, when all was black ice and severing winds: you were glad to go to the realm of ultimate numbness. He had heard of the afternoon of a faun, had heard Debussy's music, and the afternoon of a pilot was even more delightful because his dreams were not only of the mown greensward that flanked runways all over the world, but of flights never undertaken until now, in cushy flying boats and austere rocket planes. He was in them simultaneously, apportioned according to his interest, least of all in reconnaissance planes. If Booth lay and dreamed, he said little about it, and Booth was the more political of the two, so his dreams, Clegg supposed, were drenched in *Machpolitik*, dominated by the worry that had followed a career of dutiful ambivalence. Clegg dreamed an idyll, Booth a corrida.

Out of dreamland, Clegg supposed he could tell the time by what planes left when, if only they were on time. Since there were so few jets leaving, all to Pittsburgh, he knew these by heart, especially the afternoon one at 3:40 P.M. whose departure he usually greeted with a mumbled "There he goes, almost on time." He and Booth could take this flight, be in Pittsburgh after fifty minutes, have dinner, patrol the shops in the terminal, and take the nine o'clock plane back. Home by ten. What a glorious waste of money. He preferred jets, although he had developed a soft spot for the Apache, as for some medieval life-form. Since he had begun working on his big drawing of the Cyrano, both tinting it and sketching little scenes from his childhood, Clegg had come to think of himself as an anchorite, man of the bare cell, the harsh-fibered habit, and was even thinking of transferring himself from the trailer he shared with Booth, only walking distance from the airport, to the hangar itself: a condign hovel, bedless and unheated, windowless and without running water, all to—what would it be? To flog the spirit, to tame the heart, to kill expectation and purify desire. Perhaps the hangar would not do all this for him, but he was up to giving it a try, at least so long as he bedeviled his head with such obvious-seeming problems as why they had been allowed to steal a Ford Escort, why they had been allowed their pensions and an honorable discharge, why there had been interrogation at all. There was more, but he could not always summon it to mind, instead recognizing a blur in which guilt met indignation. This was not how he had expected the finale of his career to be, and certainly not Booth's—surely the man had been tapped for promotion to general.

"No," had been Booth's savage comment, "only to particular."

He was like that, able to render the emotion of the moment without explaining it. You knew how he felt, but rarely why. It made him a dramatic companion, but an enigmatic one too. Clegg rather liked not knowing certain things about Booth: his core and the tassels at his perimeter. He felt about the Apache as a broken discredited ringmaster might feel about an old, broken tiger with no teeth and myopia. Not for him the accurate perusal of a day's takeoffs, checking them against the clock; the rippling red tongue of a Baskerville hound dog on the nose of a Nazi warplane was booty enough, whatever squadron the dog had stood for back in the dreadful days when, unless you were very lucky, you had only a couple of weeks in which to earn your Blue Max. Both men had accepted the low profile of Perigee Air (as they now called it—air's nearness to the ground is what mattered most). It did a moderate trade, usually with the unmoneyed, sometimes with those whose vision of earthly existence had broadened to include the ecstasy of flight poorly financed. Up Booth and Clegg went with their rag, tag, and bobtail few, eager to prove something to them while the Apache held together.

"Name a quicker way to shave," Booth said, quaking.

"Decapitation," Clegg answered, trying hard.

"Calcium permanganate and hydrogen peroxide! Whoosh. Or hydrozine instead of the permanganate."

"I see," Clegg said. "We are launching rockets today."

What was this Wernher von Braun tincture in Booth, the blend of superman and ace, dynamic technocrat and latterday Prometheus? Had it always been there, or only since Africa? It was hardly a qualification for civilian life, only if the bearer turned to skydiving, say, or stunt flying. Booth had lapsed, but his imagination roared on at red heat as if he were waiting for the next conflict, the next plateau of agony to erect itself above everyday phenomena. Booth had been overjoyed when news came that Winston Churchill had been cleared of a scandal having to do with Pearl Harbor. Had he known of Japanese plans but failed to warn the United States? No, Booth had always said, and now it seemed he was right. Clegg had never cared about this supposed ruse to draw America into World War Two, but he could see that someone with Booth's politicist leanings could make a steak and kidney dinner of it. He was more concerned with the relative flop of Segundo Cielo, travel agent, to his mind a brilliant piece of copywriting flummery. Why had it gone nowhere? Why, on a scale of 1 to 10, did Perigee Air achieve only 2 or 3? Not that he and Booth were competing with major airlines; their only competitor was Brent Swoonpasture, an architect who, now and then, ferried people to and fro in his Piper Aztec, but hated to fly on instruments and therefore went up only in the benignest weather. His tiny operation, formally Cayuga Sky, became known locally as Fairweather Hansa, a joke with a spiteful Nazi tinge in it perhaps because Swoonpasture, locals said, used to be

Schweinpastete, or pig-pastry, euphemism for excrement. Clegg had never been able to figure out the convolutions of all this; he knew only that Perigee Air was steadily beating Fairweather Hansa to the punch, which was like saying a paralytic danced more jigs than a corpse did. Something like that. Here they were, mired in grassland, overflown by yellow finches of extraordinary delicacy, just about getting by, better at goofing off than at anything worthwhile, but having behind them a baronial hinterland of golden feats, two conspicuous careers and many thousands of hours. What was wrong? Was this the latest version of the witness protection program? Could it be that, whatever they did, the senior-juniors intended it, so long as it aimed downward into despond?

With some help from line boys and a few art students, Clegg managed to shift his plywood Cyrano from the upstairs of the university's art department to the hangar that held the Apache. The safest wall by far was the rear one, against which they managed to rear up the plywood rectangle, bending it a little. Now the rock-still Apache loomed at the outside world against the ghost or skeleton of a much more advanced airplane, but the bits of color Clegg had added shone dully from the interior, fool's gold or chinks in the wall, admitting ingots of sun. He liked the effect, but also the presence of the Apache while he daubed and inscribed, honoring the spectrum and digging into his childhood for scapegrace escapades. He wanted, now, to name the hangar. If the plane within could have a name, then so could its sheath, its resting chamber. In the end, having dismissed Gibraltar, Cape of Good Hope, Madagascar, Civil Evening Twilight, Glory, Chubasco, Consolan, Greenwich, Lux, and Mean Sea Level—his mind had been not only in a fine frenzy rolling but also doing loops and dithering spirals of affectionate recollection—he settled on Valparaiso because he remembered it as meaning Valley of Paradise, twin town to Niceville in the Florida Panhandle: an ideal city by the sea envisioned and executed by a certain John B. Perrine, only fifty miles from Pensacola, scene of some early escapades and definitive Cleggiana. Besides, the name evoked Chile, and the almost universal human yearning for a place of gold, a vale of innocent sublimity. Whether a run-down hangar with loose-dangling doors would fit the bill, he cared little, knowing any shed that enclosed the stodgy, reliable, timeless *Apache* had to have something good going for it. If, as Booth said, a Messerschmitt 109 was a coffin whose low canopy was for corpse viewing, then their rented hangar had all the lilting grandeur of a fully erected tent in the desert with lavish rugs unfurled beneath it for desert-callused feet to tread. It all depended on the mind observing; one eyeful of the dormant Apache and you were fit to embellish the hangar. Had not Sir Walter Raleigh once upon a time spread his elegant cloak over a puddle to save a lady's feet?

He forgot the exact analogy, but knew he had been intending something to do with tactful grandiosity, gracious descension, if that was a word at all (today it was). When he had finished an ornamental replica of the DC-9, he might donate it to some aviation museum, to the local airport, or just leave it in the hangar. He might restore it to the art department premises, with the authoritative wave of an unmistakable altruist. It would be something to do during the interstices of life, in between braces of colostomy passengers or of good-natured mongols. He was ready for the future, and busily anthologizing the past, from Pensacola to Africa, from California to Biggin Hill. Should he have invited Booth to join him? His mood was that of young RAF mechanics who, at places such as Cosford and Biggin Hill, cleaned and reoiled the aircraft of distant wars, bringing each machine back to airworthiness as if a distant, opaque rule had come into being: so long as only one deadly sample of a warplane survived, it was honorable to fly it again, in the colors of the victor. How rarely such planes crashed after loving reassembly: better work than was ever done on them during the flame and crackle of war. Five Spitfires in line abreast on the ground would break Clegg's heart, he had not known so many of the few had lasted that long. In the old days, those with instinctively Christian souls had been called *animae naturaliter Christianae* (he adored a word that could end in *-iter* without putting anyone's teeth on edge). Well, Clegg was a natural apostle of flight, guardian maven of the flying machine, actually sentimental about flight, which Booth was not. Clegg caressed the tumblehome of canopies, the outswell of the glass, like someone making free with a Michelangelo statue. He was that kind of man, as capable of a cliffhanger's high as of a pedestrian's toddle. Was there somewhere, he wondered, a sharp rim that cut the living off from the dead?

Or, after a sufficiency of years devoted to suffering, did your corpus of irreducible myth begin to pile up to such an extent that nothing stayed clear, as to the Swan of Tuonela (Sibelius's) that undulated along the life-death line out of sheer diffidence? Feeling belatedly improvised after so long a career in the Cyrano, he decided that gestures made late in life had prophetic force. There was an acute, symbolic relationship between the number of years left you and the emblems you made for yourself; the later the emblem, the more potent, almost to the point—if you got it right—of saving yourself, winning a reprieve by relentless exercise of mind. Behind his emblems (the hangar, the Apache, the nude Cyrano, were emblems) lay something else: a pursuit of sweetness such as he dared not admit to, not among hearty men, anyway, though Babe had heard him out on the subject, deftly steering him toward Richard Strauss's "Im Abendrot" for the sweetest duskscape of all. He had listened to a cassette and swore the music was the most meaningful, the most moving, he had ever heard. It was beside the point that Strauss, the henpecked Nazi, had not been an honorable or a courageous man. He had sucked in plenty from the oversoul, and that was that. Why, he had even found the gall to say that his *Metamorphosen*, supposedly an elegy for bomb-ravaged Germany, was actually a dirge for sundered opera houses. War, he was supposed to have said, could not be all that bad if it put paid to thirty-odd opera houses. Babe fed him such comments, along with Strauss's reputation for vanity, meanness, jealousy, and pique. Adept at the card game *skat*, he bilked his colleagues, and in Bayreuth in 1933 he won so much from the members of the orchestra that Winifred Wagner had to reimburse them before they would agree to play.

"Beside the point," Clegg told Babe. "There spoke through him, there *streamed* through him, an agonizing succulence you find in almost nobody else. Bastard he may have been, he caught the honeyed mucus from God's unwiped nose and made it into music."

"He also," Babe had said, "in 'Of Science' in *Thus Spoke Zarathustra* cooked up a canonic imitation in fifths to demonstrate how to solve life's riddle with science. He's really your boy, I think. In *Don Quixote* he has a knight and a squire flying astride a wooden horse, or at least thinking they are. There's a wind machine in the opera to add realism. Most of all, though, there's *A Hero's Life*. What more do you want than that? He may have been a twit, but he was a lively minded twit. You'd better listen to his music." An enigmatic woman with doors in her that never opened to knockers, Babe had told him all this years ago, and her attempt to convert him to opera had nearly worked. Clegg had felt the sweetness in the music, had assigned it back to God, who was using Richard Strauss as his go-between, and almost considered the matter closed. To listen to "Im Abendrot," as he often had, was to obliterate Strauss the meek hunk of shrew-bait and fan to life Strauss the visionary slave. Not so bad, Clegg had decided. He did quarrel with the Nazis after all, about collaborating with Stefan Zweig, and went off to Switzerland. Was that any worse than Thomas Mann's departure to America and a cozy life on Pacific Palisades? Listening to more of Strauss, Clegg decided, might attune him to something in life not available to others, to that preternatural fecund sweetness he dreamed abstractly of except when, as fairly often, he reclaimed a childhood image from the can of molasses that showed a dead lion with a beehive in its belly and admonished consumers that out of the strong came forth sweetness. Babe might never educate him to opera, but he might under her distant guidance conduct himself to the never-never land of beauty that pooled on the tongue and sent it into pineal rapture.

"Those Brits, they sure had it," Booth was saying in one of his universal apropos, uttered mainly to indicate attentiveness in general rather than to make a specific point. "Dja ever hear about the Royal Observer Corps's badges for excellence, Rupe? They took tests, can you imagine that in the middle of a war? Mainly in aircraft recognition. These were the guys who stayed up nights and spotted German planes. Daytime too. All they had was binoculars. There was a cash prize and a whole series of cloth badges. Light blue Spitfires on a black background. After another test you got a red Spitfire. Then a series of five-pointed stars, one, two, three, after which you swapped your red Spit for a gold one, and then all you had to look forward to was another gold star under your gold Spit. Imagine working all that out while the bombs were falling and the Heinkels were droning. Just think of all the work their wives and girlfriends had with scissors and needle, taking the badges off and sewing the new ones on. That is phlegm, Rupe, that's why they won the war. The Nazis came over in droves and the God-loving Brits regarded the whole mess as some kind of Boy Scout competition. I tell you, we joined up with the wrong guys."

Clegg allowed as how the RAF and he were not total strangers. Not mentioning his daydreams about the Battle of Britain—that sky full of knives, smoke, and diminishing contrails—he said he understood the rigors of the test piece during bombardment, and recalled something by a literary gent, a Brit, about the imminence of death being able to concentrate the powers of the mind abominably. "Yes," he said. "The Royal Observer Corps. They also sat on roofs to identify flying bombs. But the the V-two, they never saw *them* coming, or heard them much."

Clegg's receiving apparatus had switched to chimney swifts, such as besieged the airfield and the hangars, giving their chitter calls an hour before sunset, starting with a long drawn-out formation, line astern, then switching to form a ring, which then broke, every morning, every evening, into a line, each giving a superb display of V-gliding in which a bird snapped its wings into a V over its back and glided fast for five to ten seconds. The more he watched them, the dizzier he felt; they flew all day, near to but remote from earthbound living, habitués of sublime monotony: bladelike, curved, scimitaring sky as so many human pilots managed to do at prohibitive expense. How different that was from what he had once heard an outstanding doctor, after examining him, describe (as if after spartan rehearsal) as large, sessile, soft, velvety, villous adenomas.

That was the magic, truth told: to have the intestines in flight, thrown around the sky at several times the speed of sound, yet maintaining their gradual munch and squeeze, their push and lunge. To be in two conditions at the same time, that was paradise, so that those who looked for you in the one failed while you swaggered away in the other. Clegg was nothing if not sensuously attuned, believing that if you clapped eyeballs on the physical pageant of things you would never feel like an isolato, an outrider, a fringe-freak; the core would keep you straight until you decided to let it have you and aimed yourself in or to turn your back on it forever and headed out for the cosmic wastes eager to turn to dust.

Clegg had no idea that Booth, having seen the transfer of his embellished Cyrano from art studio to Valparaiso, had begun to fidget, sensing that he cut too insignificant a figure in this parochial circus. He began to plan Booth's Answer, nothing in the manner of Clegg, but something more human, less work-intensive. Proportions, they were what mattered, and the weather on the day, the schedule of planes up and down the runway; so it would have to be a Saturday, when traffic was least. He would probably have no audience but Clegg and whoever was in the tower, babying or chiding them up and down. Carrier passengers could not see the runway now, as if the new airport had been designed to keep the vulgar side of things out of sight; people boarding through a metal tunnel might think they were entering a spacecraft, not an airplane, and would be flung to their destination untraditionally. Perhaps this blind the passengers sat in was a means of increasing the mystique of flight, so no doubt they should have been blindfolded and equipped with earplugs if only to loft them into the right ecstatic state. People intending to fly Perigee had no such problems, actually having their noses rubbed in the murky imperfection of low-cost air travel to make them appreciate it all the more, especially when, at last, the Apache pulled away from the rotting hangar and fizz-buzzed into the open, heading for the grand territory of a ramp only just purged of deer and gulls. To be in the Apache, taxiing between a DC-9 and a de Havilland Dash-8, was a unique experience readily classified as loss of face or gain of shame, except that it had a flagrant, antiquarian side reminiscent, at least to Clegg, of how the aforesaid Brits drove their ancient cars from London to Brighton, shedding parts and sometimes blowing up. Then nostalgia reverted to its old meaning of road pain and a motor car, as the Brits (and maybe the Turks and the Danakili) called the thing, became a pretty sacrifice to a brutish god, so blatantly a contraption it was more related to a mousetrap than to anything by Peugeot, Mercedes, Maserati, or Duesenberg. Clegg doted on such atavistic maneuvers, on the persistence in the twentieth century of a structure's forebears, on the cranks and couplings that Luddites still looked back to unless they peered backward beyond the wheel into the mists of trudge. He was both Luddite and superman, he thought, unwilling to surrender either, as happy to watch the armrest inside the Apache's right-hand door begin to peel away from its mount as to hear the dissonance of metal fatigue in a 707, that swan of speed.

Just now, with an assist from the USAir magazine, he was drafting a new card for Perigee's passengers: a grandiose, mock-humble plea that began *We welcome your comments concerning your travel experience on Perigee Air because your impressions of our service are important to us. Write to:*

He hesitated. Should he put Segundo Cielo or Rupert Clegg (Col.)? *Deborah Thompson, Director of Consumer Affairs, USAir P.O. Box 1501, Winston-Salem, NC 27102-1501. Thank you for flying USAir* sounded better than anything *he* would write. He wondered why, then forged ahead with Rupert Clegg, doffing Col. for Esq. in the vain hope that class would minify rank.

Next thing, Booth had various lengths of wood delivered to the hangar, to Valparaiso as Clegg would put it, and Clegg marveled at the sturdiness of some, the flimsiness of others. Clearly, some of this wood was sturdy balsa, but balsa all the same.

"You're going to be busy," Clegg said, gesturing at the wood, the cans of spray paint, the cord and nails. "You planning some kind of crucifixion, sir?"

Booth was nodding, but with no great conviction. What he chose not to tell Clegg was that, since Clegg had taken over the back of the hangar with his mock-up, he Booth would be doing something of his own so as not to seem helpless, inert, out of fresh ideas. Booth knew what he had to do, but it was not a crucifixion or an improvised scaffold outside the hangar. Two things were going on in Booth's mind: he wanted to make some kind of show commensurate with Clegg's, and he wanted to get back on friendly terms with Clegg's sister, which might not be too difficult to do (he already had some snapshots of her, and Clegg had others); Booth remembered her as an elegant, forceful blonde, a bit zoftig, but what the hell, she was a woman with whom he had some kind of standing start. It was as if he suddenly remembered the race he was born to, the heterosexual side of himself, long closeted away. Neither operation would be difficult, and he quite candidly admitted to himself that he wanted to show Clegg up, cut him down to below lieutenant-colonel size. Then he might move on, perhaps to something else aviational, putting behind him all notion that he had let Clegg down, especially when they arrived back stateside. He could have saved him all that interrogation, couldn't he? They had wanted to know how much backbone Clegg had left, and Booth needed to know why. Was it that Clegg was still of some use to them whereas he himself was not?

Clegg had been reviewing himself again, forlornly coming to the conclusion that he was a man on the brink, chronically hurt by the presence of vacancy. All those miraculous buffers that people doted on—magazines, clubs, friendships, teams, letters, books, phone calls, newspapers—had no appeal to him at all and did not serve to insulate him from thoughts of death and dissolution. He knew of nothing, save flying, that could blot things out, neither the cordial exchange of formulas with equally needy friends, nor the smiles of neighbors, the hugs of dear ones. He knew that he, who had had so close a brush with death it might be called a blind date, was on death's waiting list and would soon be processed as if, instead of having already paid some of his mortal dues, he were starting from scratch, obliged to muddle through the entire rigmarole all over again, uncomforted by the comforts of the average sensual man. In Africa, Turkey, Pittsburgh, he had been teetering on the rim; he had no roots, he did not belong, and his lifelong conviction that a lively mind needed no roots, but could thrive anywhere, had taken a beating. Some could float, but not he. Some could walk on water, snow or jet fuel, but not Clegg, the born savorer of surfaces; a badge on your epaulet meant nothing, and you might just as well have parked a wad of chewed gum there instead. It was important to keep busy, but that was only a stopgap; it didn't change the basic predicament, it only deflected the mind that chose not to know better. If anything, he was like that image in a Miró painting called 48: a rudimentary black spider made up of four shaky lines crossing one another against a snowball. That would do, even as a badge of identity: Clegg the radar spider waiting to be apprehended.

Working fast with saw and smoothing plane, Booth made himself what he wanted, but took the work outside on the grass, some of which he blackened with spray paint that failed to hit wood. Bang-bang he went with his little hammer. Then the sickly pear-drops smell of balsa cement floated into the air as he glued his pieces together, telling himself he needed a calm dry day for this, not one of those squally ones that kept even the Apache at home. Drawings he made, after looking into the distance where the runway lay baking beneath its mirages. Winter would close down all Perigee business, even though the air by then would be solid and heavy, ideal to fly through with a trio of greenhorns. By winter they would have to find other employment or saunter off into the witness protection swindle. Perhaps he and Clegg would head for the lecture circuit, giving improvisatory talks about their flying days, shooting a line as the British called it, then moving on; after a year of that, he thought, the two of them would believe their own lies, so they would somehow acquire a call-in talk show, radio only, predicated on the big bands and therefore highly specialized at best.

Now Booth tested, steadying himself against the rusty wall of the hangar. He did not fall. So he checked a couple of components for weight and trudged to the runway end with his burden of lumber. There he fitted his feet into the slots, then took them out again. Clegg, watching in breath-held relish, walked over to join him, amazed at what he saw Booth trying to do. The wind dropped altogether. Lucky. No airplane attempted to land or to take off. It was the hour of the custard pie, the toasted bagel, the swig of hot tea. Perhaps no one was looking, save a couple of art students over by the fence usually frequented by yellow finches. Now Booth began, kneeling so that Clegg could arrange on his head the huge hat made from balsa wood and painted black, easily fifteen feet in diameter but light because Booth had made a framework and covered it with tissue paper. Gradually he stood, keeping the vast hat balanced, undisturbed by wind. Clegg would draw this apparition later to reassure his memory. Now he helped Booth mount into the stilts, also painted black. He reeled once, then got the hang of things and slowly began his perambulation along the runway, swaying and reeling but somehow keeping straight while two vertical balsa rods kept the extremities of the hat from drooping. What the control tower thought a gruesome, fatuous apparition began to make its way from somewhere near the Vasi lights to the first taxiway, would never be recorded; but Booth, ever a Euclidean Proteus, was able to imagine, and of course he had Clegg's crude sketch to fall back upon. Slow as peristalsis, he advanced, chanting something obscure and lugubrious, looking ahead only, a distorted priest on the march, tall as a gantry, wide as a windmill laid flat.

"How you feel, Colonel?" Clegg had no idea what else to say. Booth was parading, that was it, and in a dimension of his own making. The Danakili had done this to him. He was annunciating something, to be sure, but what?

No answer came from Booth, but he stopped singing. His floppy balance on the stilts weakened, then he regained it with an urgent laugh, actually increasing his stride as he got better at the walk. He had heard the expression "You talk the talk, but can you walk the walk?" Now he was walking the walk, wordless as a wheelbarrow, and making something of an impression as several line boys came out to see and secretaries from their competition at Nausicair appeared with cups and saucers. Barney alias Beauregard Booth marched on for president and company, heedless of the hidebound world around him. He was again at eighty thousand feet.

Just imagine, Clegg was thinking, he can do that to himself, he can make himself do that to us. In his TV viewing, Clegg had come to marvel at well-groomed men with expert demeanor and solid standing in the community, bankers, accountants, or pharmacists, who suddenly vanished under mysterious circumstances and then, perhaps months later, were seen again, seedy, shifty, unshaven, seemingly prey to amnesia, making nervous phone calls on an outdoor phone close to the door of a tavern. It was as if these men, absconding or abducted, had set into motion some foul gravitational rhythm that felled them, took them, and then served them up to themselves in parlous condition, a condition they had yearned for, as if the whole procedure of being respectable had become too much for them and they wanted to experience the ephemeral joys of living at a lower level, eyes down half-shamed, jowls chumbling with unexplained tics, hands always on the go with a pound of frozen fish for sale in a pinkish plastic bag. This voluntary or involuntary relegation of the self had haunted Clegg as soon as he began watching *Unsolved Mysteries*, sometimes only a half-hour show, sometimes an hour, other times an hour and a half, so much so that in no time he became a dab hand at disappearance, noting patterns that recurred (the faked suicide postcard written left-handed by an orangutan, or so it looked; the lifetime friend who waved at the missing person as he went by in a captured-looking car but got no reply, no sign of recognition). Clegg soon reached the point of assuming half the people in the world were missing, some of the time, and he had noticed that those missing as children turned up, just so long as they had been led away by Arctic-faced adoption officials, always into stern boxy cars, whereas those children who just vanished never turned up again except as corpses by some riverbank or in a Dumpster.

The adults interested him most, and he half wondered [if indeed UFOs were taking samples at random, as some returned abductees claimed,] or whether the kidnapping instinct in the country was running riot. Those who were criminals were usually caught, thanks to the police-blotter nature of the program; those who just walked away or were led vanished into Dante's nether-never land, the object of much well-dressed lamentation on the show, and well-rehearsed summaries by the detectives involved. Clegg had long ago concluded that many adults in his beloved country, that liked its rifles more than its freedoms, wanted to be in another place than the one they were in. They moseyed away, leaving their wallet and checkbook under the driver's seat of an abandoned car, the sprinkler going full blast for days all through toad-strangling thunderstorms, and communicated with their loved ones again only through the most fallible means, and with imperfect, stilted, stunted, uncharacteristic messages that did not add up. From all this you would conclude that their loved ones were not loved ones after all but only stand-ins for angels, Liliths, demons appalling of aspect but otherwise honey-pretty. It was almost as if Clegg, downed in Africa after sleepwalking through Turkey, had been an unsolved mystery himself: one of the lost, an Atlantis man in the end, for whom various sadists sent postcards home for him, to his sister or his commanding officer. He had not been through it, but he knew the emotions that fitted the design and he sometimes wished he too had been abducted by UFO, CIA, or gangsters in a scarlet car. That fate had surely befallen Booth. You had only to watch him, balancing and swaying out there, something dreamed up by Mary Shelley, after his sudden departure from the race, his entry into—what was that new role of his? Bergamasque-Dracula-Gilgamesh–Man of a Thousand Faces? Clegg could not pin it down, but he saw his superior officer suddenly turned into the scarecrow of his own plight, trundling down the runway like something out of no-man's-land, not lyrical, not elegant, not moving or frightening, but enigmatically outrageous. What on earth, literally, would a DC-9 do when its captain saw Booth ambling from one end of the runway to the other, slow as a *mutilé de guerre?*

Pull up or fly right through him, crushing bone, balsa, birch, the lot? Certainly Booth was wide enough to be seen, but not substantial enough to cause a go-around. What then should the $100,000 pilot do? Somehow land over him, beyond him, reminding Clegg of how St.-Exupéry had once deliberately bounced his landing plane over an object on the runway: one of the great, definitive, uncopyable landings, and in semidarkness too. The answer was altogether more awesome. Booth would withstand the arriving jet, allow it to fly through him, and *survive*, converted into Toledo steel by the encounter. You had to believe in him if you wanted him to prevail. He had gone out there to declare himself as an unwieldy, incommoded being worthy of respect, perhaps even an equal of the ever-decorating Clegg, late of the Cyrano.

Reluctant to waste his breath, Booth whispered to the tarmacadam, telling it to save him, hold him firm. It did. By the time he finished he would have blisters in unusual places. How did he look? Would Clegg photograph him in his latest incarnation? He was determined to go the full length, 14 to 32, swaying northwestward, unable to slow up in spite of the tower's entreaties.

Now he was abreast of Clegg, or rather *it* was, this mesmeric apparition like a huge inflated crow parading past in silent pathology, his mind in the Cyrano, his feet in the stilts. Thank heaven, Clegg thought, for a quiet day at the airport, but the tower had already sent everybody packing, told them to fly time-wasting rectangles at a distance with the terse explanation: Something on the runway. They all assumed it would be deer, having heard it before. After all, how could the velvet-voiced siren, Uncontroller, plausibly tell any pilot about a specter on the runway in stilts and massive hat, inching forward dead center at seven inches a year? It would never do. It would never gibe with the manly code that said obstacles were fauna, only rarely flora, otherwise planes less fortunate that had crashed or crash-landed and were burning away according to all three laws of energy. Then Clegg saw part of Booth's act for what it really was: a throwback to old barn-storming days when wingwalkers turned saliva to salt. Booth was a wing-walker on the ground, an aerial pole-vaulter, as well as a filch from a Mardi Gras, and might continue as such until arrested, brought low from his stilts and uncapped of the vast disk he had appropriated to himself, stealing from Saturn or the saints in books of hours.

He had become a walking saucer.

Defeating Clegg's illuminated plywood.

That was enough, then. His pass was executed.

Clegg yelled to him, but had no answer, no acknowledgment of any kind.

He began walking after him, then sprinted to catch him, and walked beside him, feeling *dwarfed*. That was it, wasn't it? Booth had made his point, still captain of the Cyrano long gone, as unaware of demotion as Stonehenge of lightning. He did not have to die to make his case, nor, as the wind now rising proved he could, take flight beneath the gigantic sombrero.

Booth began to take flight, lofting himself with infinitesimal poise. Or rather he was elongating himself in the neck, almost an Indian rope trick. Now that hat was lifting free of him, untethered as it was, and actually beginning to waft backward in a faint emulation of wind shear. Back went the hat, outrigger struts dangling, then forward, to and fro according to some oddity of runway breeze. Next, as was proper, the hat resettled on Booth's crown, and he moved gently ahead, hugely tentative, unaware of Clegg or anything else, just inching forward as if in the presence of unthinkable galactic wastes, in one way traveling faster than any space-craft, in another hardly moving. It all had to do with parallax, Clegg said. We understand these matters, we air force bums. Where is he going? Won't he get tired? Has he eaten beforehand?

Someone must have known where Booth was headed, back, forward, slightly sideways, an inch or two up, because as the wind lapsed and Booth's hat took root upon him again, perhaps urging him onward with kinetic energy gleaned from ground effect, a loud crack sounded across the vacancy of grass and asphalt, just the noise made when someone went out to frighten birds off the runway and its approaches, rarely killing any but making the gulls and crows head for the lake. Someone had shot at Booth and, presumably, missed, sending a bullet into far-distant trees or a genuinely unlucky driver on 13 North. Clegg waited for shot number two, but nothing happened and nobody showed, nothing moved. Who could have attempted such a thing? Booth was odd, but did he have enemies, political foes who wanted to put paid to him without the presumed satis-faction of hands around his throat? Could he perhaps have rigged a photo-electric cell somewhere that fired a gun at some weird angle when he arrived at a certain point, as now, at the Vasi lights on the runway's other end? Clegg doubted it and took cover behind a gasoline truck: not so prudent, really, but he had not recognized the truck as a bomb. Booth had not budged, an obliging stationary target for whomever. Even an amateur marksman could have picked him off where he was. Did the hat spin? Or cant? For Booth it did, spun just a little by the bullet's mere con-tact, but only from, say, 300 degrees to 304.

Now Clegg saw Booth be vulnerable, having initially succumbed to the apparition as something lordly, potent, stark, only to revise it in a flash as something helpless, fuzzy, limp. He could race up to it, to Booth, and fell him, wrestle him to the ground, saving him from the next shot. He knew about trajectories and how bullets often rose too high even when aimed low, along an exact parallel with the ground. Booth should be pressed so low he made an instant foxhole, each shot missing him by half an inch as in those carefully designed military exercises in which greenhorns scuf-fled prone beneath strands of barbed wire while machine guns, set at a millimetrically perfect traverse, scissored the air above them. Had any man had a Kirlian aura to him, it would at once have been shot away. Clegg regained his equanimity, deciding to stand where he was, waiting to see what Booth would do. If he had not heard the shot, he would be moving ahead, and he was, well past the thick white stripes that marked the runway's end. He had passed the huge numbers (wrong way round for him):

32

and was in the position of a plane that had, as the trade idiom has it, run out of runway and had to leap into the air or hit the trees, the remedy being to add power. He did nothing of the kind, of course, treading humbly as far as the puddles and clay furrows left behind by backhoes and other machines devoted to runway extension. In theory he could have walked right into Lake Nausicaa had he kept going and so become the first man to enter the water on stilts, descending as they sank into the mud.

Again Clegg shouted, but Booth heard nothing, now come to a halt again as if waiting for someone (more zealous than Clegg) to catch up with him. Indicting himself as the poorer part of this partnership, for not daring to leap the intervening space where only one bullet had passed, Clegg found long-forgotten Japanese words invading his mind: words he had never used but had become familiar with in his travels, musing on syllables that became the flotsam of his life. First came *sempai*, meaning the dominant member of a duo, in this case clearly Booth, who had the right princely undeferring qualities, and then *kohai*, meaning the secondary person, who had the right qualities of, say, an ensign ever ready to defer. Was this a correct account of their relationship, or a sentimental travesty? Indeed, anyone who thought in such terms as these was deforming all partnerships, all bonds. Life, Clegg thought, was never that clear-cut; he and Booth swapped roles all the time and needed no rubric to satisfy their sense of self-esteem. He was aware, all the same, that he still called Booth "Sir" and "Colonel," which was all right even in civilian life, he supposed, but in the long run parasitic or fawning. By the same token, Booth called him "Rupe" and "Recon," and was casual in doing it. Clegg would never have swelled orotundity so far as to call Booth Beauregard or Barney, not even if they had known each other a hundred years. Alas for fealty, he thought; it makes obeyers of us all when, really, in every sense, our minds are revolting.

Booth had turned around and was facing the other runway, which had a bump in its middle; you couldn't see one end from the other. This meant that taking off was a matter of trust: you always assumed the other end would be there, and the intervening five hundred feet between bump and end. Nobody removed half runways in the night, of course, so pilots who expected it to be there weren't taking much of a chance. All Booth could see was the bump, and, not having heard or felt the shot, which had nicked his vast hat, he began to walk the other way, quietly humming a marching song jumped as readily to his lips as *sempai/kohai* to Clegg's mind. It was a lewd, simple song about Eskimo pussy being mighty cold: "I don't know, but I've been told." It shortened the runway for him even as he began to wonder how many marches to and fro he would have to make before Clegg took down that plane on plywood and changed the hangar back from a studio to a place of worship. Again the hat wobbled and hovered, then floated backward, requiring him to halt until it came forward again into exact place. He had never done this kind of thing before, so, he reckoned, he was at least with Leonardo now.

It had just occurred to Clegg that, in spite of Booth's being his superior officer and therefore inferably his superior in pilot skills, it would not have been Booth who would have been called to the colors first for a kamikaze operation. For such a terminal flight, all that was needed was someone expendable who could fly a plane reasonably straight for not too long, and then aim it downward at an enemy ship. Nobody in his right mind would waste Booth on such a mission, which the Cleggs of this world had been flying for years. The sea bottom was littered with their skeletons woven crudely into the smashed superstructures of the planes they had sunk. Clegg caught himself transposing; *if he had been Japanese,* of course, this might have been true. Being junior to Booth, he would always be expendable. Yet what Booth was doing now might tilt the scales a little. He was going too far Booth was; he was going to cancel his illustrious bond with air supremacy and come tumbling down. If only, Clegg thought, I had the paraded sedateness of certain speakers, who could put things just right, managing to insinuate the truth without the least degree of rancor or animosity. You could fell a mighty being only with genial arrows. Where had he seen it, in whose driveway? To keep illicit parkers out, someone had stationed a legless lifesize nymphet in a bathing suit, across her middle a plea: Please don't block my driveway. She got the nosy parker's attention and the driveway stayed clear. But it wasn't a matter of addressing Booth politely and saying, Give it up, old man, you have lost control. Just look at the image you recently cut. It was a matter of staring him down until he condemned himself. In a local eatery, Clegg had noticed what looked to him like a replica of the English queen erected on a plinth of scrolled ironwork above the taps for soft drinks, the holders for extra-large, large, and medium Dixie cups. Asking, he was astounded to be told no one knew what the three-foot-high statue stood for. When they found out, he was even more put out: this creature, with the face of a cherubic doll, wearing a bulbous crown padded with crimson silk and red velvet robes, was the Baby Jesus. In front of him he held, like a skittle, a smaller Baby Jesus identical to himself, almost like a baby removed from the womb in standing position.

"Not the Virgin Mary?"

"No," the Italian owner told him. "It is the Infant Jesus in Majesty holding the Baby Jesus."

"All the way to infinity," Clegg had joshed. "Smaller and smaller. Why isn't the littler Jesus holding an even smaller Jesus?" End of discussion. That was to know far too much about something ineffably holy where it stood, caked with ten years' grease. Its function was to behold those coming into the restaurant and warn them to behave themselves; the Baby Jesus had his eye on them; so did Baby Jesus minor.

Clegg envied the unintroverted citizens of the world, able to go about their business in the presence of inscrutable symbols that brought him up short. Compared to the Baby Jesus, Booth was Satan peering into the abyss and finding not a friend in sight. On the one hand, driven into responsive activity of an artistic kind, Clegg had purloined plywood and a drawing of the Cyrano as well as the role of a medieval monk: not exactly garish, as he saw it, and dignified, harmless, appealing. On the other hand, Booth parading up and down the runway in massive hat and standing on stilts was asking for trouble and that was why he had been shot at. It was clear that whatever power was supervising their fates, Clegg had found a quiet modus, Booth a modus leading to quietus. Soon, Clegg would have to replace Booth.

The prospect did not displease him either; he had been a maid in waiting long enough, always a bridesmaid, et cetera. He never doubted for a moment he had the requisite qualities, but for what? Perigee Air? A cadet could run it. Well, then, the living effigy of Cyrano pilots? The personification of the aerial hero and to hell with Richard Strauss? Clegg felt the great day coming, but began asking himself how much he would care if those in power cashiered Booth altogether and turned him into a passenger, a drone. Distant thunder suddenly not so distant cut his meditation short as a huge shape lumbered into view from the runway's end and settled into a nose-up position right over where Booth had been. The tower had given the okay, unable to see Booth anymore. The jet floated toward the white lines, caught in the exquisite miracle of slow flight, neither landing nor flying but seeming to pray to the ground, feeling for it, first one way then another, touching only to flinch back because not level, but then settling, wide, fat, and farting until it eased over forward onto the nosewheel as reverse thrust deafened everyone there. What Clegg could not see was Booth lying prone in the mud, having in effect launched himself forward at his first sight of the DC-9 approaching, barely more than a disk with fins, silent as tarmacadam, yet gaining on him at over a hundred miles an hour. Not even time to fling himself aside, not encumbered as he was; all he was able to do was pretend to be one of those creatures whose carapace matched the meniscus of the ground. Fortunately he had been so central that the twin jets passed on either side of him, heating him and ruffling him some, but doing no lasting damage. Deafened, he bit his tongue, held his breath, stabbed his nails into his palms, and prayed to the freemasonry of discarded pilots for one last chance.

Little did he know that, soon after the DC-9 reached its ramp, a small green car chugged its way from the tower toward where he had been, where he no longer was, having decamped into the bushes beyond the runway's end. It was from this direction that he had been shot at by the unknown assailant; but Booth found nothing and lay there quivering, aghast at his loss of the gigantic hat and the stilts. A performer needed his props.

Then he heard Clegg blundering toward him, calling, whistling, uttering a fastidious cry never before addressed to man or beast: an undernourished yodel that failed to bring Booth out of hiding. "They want to speak to you at the tower, Colonel." That was usually the coup de grâce for a pilot in Booth's predicament. Not even a retired colonel was going to get away with runway parade, runway invasion, runway blockage. That he might have been mashed to a pulp was beside the point. Clegg yelled again, this time with conventional coarseness in the theory that, the more impatient you sound, the sooner your quarry will show. Booth stayed put, willing to hide out in the barrens for months rather than face the inevitable inquiry. He still had no idea he had been shot at. Well, Clegg wondered, has he or has he not? I must be imagining things? If only we could find the bullet. If only, at this point, they could arrange for two rocking chairs on the verandah of a sumptuous hotel facing the lake, any lake, with tea and cookies on a small table between them, a putting green and a croquet lawn in front of them, and, not far away, a robust launch departing ahead of a gunmetal swirl for a trip around the waters, past golf courses, agricultural museums, fancy villas with eight TVs, tiny country churches like birdboxes in between the mansions, and a pall of expensive cigar smoke wreathing the entire vista with nasal demisemiquavers as the fully formed sun drove lower and lower.

From now on it became hard for Booth to get to sleep; he managed to drift off only if Clegg read to him from a volume of accident reports, or read to him such items from a magazine, somehow banishing the ghost of what might have been by insisting on the worst. Or, sometimes, Booth read to Clegg until the book or magazine fell from his hands. Their mode of reading was casual, requiring many paraphrases of the boring parts, omissions, and occasional elongations of matters too juicy to be read in their own sweet size. Now and then either of them found dramatic oral exchanges between tower and pilot that required histrionic emphasis and, after that, a short pause. There was one history, of a young Mooney pilot who left San Antonio in weather conditions clearly beyond his skills. Yes, he had told the Flight Service Station, he could go to instruments if he had to (and he would *have* to, they told him). He spoke as if he did not understand instrument flying, insisting on a route he called "Zero Eight Zero to destination Clover Field," which was not the way to say or do it. It was suggested he accept another routing, of Vector-198 to the Eagle Lake VOR and then direct. A note of derision and chagrin crept into Clegg's voice as he went on with the reading while Booth lay back and tried to envision tragedy in the making.

"He loaded his wife, mother-in-law, and infant child into the Mooney and requested clearance at three-eight in the afternoon. *Uh*, he said, *we've filed our plan and, uh, uh, uh, need a course of Zero Eight Two to Eagle Lake and then Zero Niner One to, uh, Clover Field south of Hobby.* While he kept asking for what he wanted, the clearance-delivery controller kept trying to give him the course he needed: *Vee One Niner Eight to Gland intersection, direct Hobby, direct*, as well as the usual altitude, frequency and transponder code information. Oddly enough, the frustrated controller did not insist on a readback but let him tootle off with the word *Copy*."

Booth, who had heard this one before, but responded to its retelling like an aficionado to part of a certain operatic aria, doting on the outrageous finesse of it, broke in and said from within his narrowing tunnel of sleep: "Don't tell me. He took off in appalling conditions from San Antonio, with a ceiling and visibility so poor the tower controllers couldn't see runway or taxiway. Then he said *rolling*, and took off into the murk. Rupe, tell me the bit about the controllers, when they talked about him like the bad boy in school."

"The tower controller asked his colleague in the radar room *Departure, did you turn Eight One Kilo?* And he answered, 'I'm not talking to him.' So the tower controller called the Mooney pilot and requested his heading only to hear *Eight One Kilo, uh, needs a course of Zero Eight Two to Houston.* This pissed the controller off, so he issued an order instead, saying, *Mooney Eight One Kilo, you fly a heading of One Two Zero*, using the good old imperative and don't you jackhoss me anymore. There was no answer, and Mister Uh-Uh-Uh, he flew off closely followed by a Piper Cherokee."

Booth half woke and said with jubilation, "Now it gets interesting. They know he's on One Two Zero but they don't know if he's there by accident and they turn the Cherokee to One Eight Zero to avert a collision from behind. In the confusion—" He yawned hugely.

"In the confusion," Clegg resumed, "the tower controller mixes up the numbers of the two planes and the Mooney guy answers something intended for the Cherokee. Imagine! The Mooney pilot never responds again, no doubt in an all-befouled-up sulk. Back in the tower, conversation rages, with the departure controller saying, *What's Eight One Kilo going to do?* Then he asks the tower this pathetic old question: *Are you sure he's even airborne, Bobby? Yeah,* comes the answer, *There's not a target or anything out there now—there's not an airplane, there's nothing out there.* Truth told, that Mooney was all over the place until the right wing tip hit the ground. The fuselage went between two big mesquite trees, losing both wings. And the cabin with its passengers flew another hundred yards until it hit a substantial tree trunk. No fire. All dead."

"Recrucify the Infant Jesus," Booth droned, "you wouldn't get me taking off into conditions like that: Two Zero Zero ceiling, visibility half mile. No way. What puzzles me is, he knew he knew nothing about instrument flying, but he was determined to go. Maybe to show off. But why should he think he could get away with it, less than a novice, when experienced pilots wouldn't even attempt it?"

"He was all balls, Colonel. They often are. They spend a quarter million bucks on a deadly toy and then they prove just how deadly. I guess somewhere in the mental procession from purchase to death there happens a moment of sublime heroism, at least as the guy sees it, in which he is giving himself a chance of doing something almost impossible, and then he finds he has the balls to keep his lunch down and his bladder tight and his anus puckered while doing it, after which he knows he is still alive but for not much longer, maybe a minute or so, long enough to mull the matter over before he hits. I don't know, Colonel, but there's more balls and bucks than there is brains." Clegg saw himself back in Turkey, holding forth in the officers' club, opining about flight at eighty thousand feet, about which he knew too much. They listened to him there, at least until Booth entered the room.

"Let's assume," Booth said dreamily, "this guy wasn't trying to wipe out the family in one fell swoop. So he must have thought he'd figured it out for himself. Look how he insisted on his own route, like somebody downtown asking a policeman. *Telling* him. The autopilot would have done it for him, but what did this fuck know about autopilots anyway? His VCR must have plagued the jism out of him, not to mention the can opener. He became disoriented almost at once. He was an amateur trying to do a professional's job. I'm glad he isn't in the sky anymore, ready to kill us all." That was enough. The drug had worked, the enemy had been routed. Death, on whose side Booth so often found himself, had won again, and for good reasons. It pleased Booth to think there was a logical justice in the sky, keeping the good guys alive and the dunderheads in the ground. Clegg felt some sadness, a streak only, but wished he did not have to recite these accidents to the somnolent Booth, to whom violent death was a specialized pornography; it made him come in his mind and gave him a good night's sleep, and perhaps he would have enjoyed photographs too, a smell at the ripped clothing, the sundered fuselage. Pilots could become so good they felt callous and, when some poor inexpert slob bought the farm, forgot the reverence for magic in his woeful performance, the tender openness with which he started out to get his ticket. Booth joined forces with the headsman. Had he not, after all, survived his own catastrophe, for none of which he had been responsible? He must have felt invulnerable, even in sleep, Clegg thought. Look how the DC-9 missed him only the other day. Look how the bullet skimmed his hat, leaving him ignorant. Who am I to tell Booth someone shot at him? Where would the evidence be? Why does he like me to read that other one in a high voice, the bit by the woman in the crashing Bonanza when she says *going into the mountains*. Her last words. What's the charge for him in that? Why did she bother saying it? Perhaps to adjust her own mind to the unavoidable possibility that it was all over for her and the mountains were her last, last thing.

Yeah, death, Clegg told himself, death in comparison with which everything is interesting. Imagine being as close as she was to that stultifying comparison. It was as if his thought awakened Booth, who had seemed in a deep slumber, half snoring. There were his eyes, negating the sleep already had, and he was asking for the Falcon in Lake Michigan. Clegg was glad; he could do this one in short order and nod Booth off again with a précis. There was no need to read it out loud; after all, eleven o'clock was coming up and with it *Unsolved Mysteries* on the tiny Bohei TV, made in Korea.

"Okay, the Falcon," he began, Booth eyeing him in a manner close to hostile. Get on with it, Booth's glance meant. "The cause of this one was the parking brake in the Falcon Ten. With three detents, it had to be dealt with carefully. Off. Park. And Emergency. If it's not Off, a light low down on the between-seats quadrant shines to warn you. The pilot claimed he had released the brake on departing the parking area and had not used it subsequently while he was taxiing or while waiting to take off. However, investigators found, and this is what sickens you, the Falcon Ten taxis quite well with the brake set in Park, and detailed studies of the brake handle found in wreckage proved it had been in Park on impact. Then they looked at the brake pad material, which had been overheated to something extreme, and then suddenly chilled, as would be consonant with the Falcon's plunge into Lake Michigan. So it took off, but not airworthily, *with its brakes on.*"

"Can you believe it?" Booth asked. "Talk about a five-million-dollar toy. I have heard of guys taking off with the towbar attached, or with the elevators locked, but this—now tell me the part about the crew."

"The Falcon," Clegg said without referring to the ripped-out article, "floated for a while before going down in twenty-five feet of water. Not too bad, I reckon. Depends on who you are, what you're made of. Scratch the copilot, who died of injuries. The pilot swam out through a gash in the fuselage bottom made by the entire nosewheel assembly being torn out. Lucky guy. As for the four passengers, they went through the overwing escape hatch and trod water, held on to floating seat cushions and actually got onto floating hunks of ice. A fire department helicopter was able to fish them out before they got too cold. It's obvious, Colonel. The Falcon should have aborted, even if it still hit the lake; it wouldn't have hit it so fast or gone out so far. Instead, they elected to take off, impeded, and went nose-first in."

Booth had drifted off again, partner to those five in the water, dreaming his down-in-the-drink dream, mourning the costly jet. When they die, he knew, they all die together, the expensive like the cheap. It grieved him to have a complex airplane bite the dust or the water; he thought of all the welding and circuitry, the formers and electronics, devoted to making it behave as required. Then some yahoo came along and made a pig's ear out of technological poetry. In his dreams he sided with the Germans who, although often wrong about air strategy (too much emphasis on versatility; the cult of the two-engined bomber), were technical aces, always making the engine accessible, and the guns, and forever packing the wings with automatic slats that kept the plane from stalling. Air pressure kept them within the wing's contour, but out they popped as soon as the airspeed fell toward stalling. In another life he would have been with them, shivering on the Russian front outside his Arado reconnaissance plane, knowing all was lost. Perhaps he felt for the Russians because the Germans were so good.

Against his better nature, Clegg had fallen to reading yet another of their bedtime stories, the one with the woman saying (in an earlier transmission), "Bonanza Seven Two Five, we're in trouble, we're losing airspeed fast, going into the mountains." That was at two five and two three seconds. Only three and a half minutes earlier, all had been going quite

well, and the exchanges with Oakland Center had been mellow, composed, patient:

"Bonanza Seven Two Five, ah, how's the ice on the wings now, sir?"

"Seven Two Five, ah, ah, a little more icing."

"Okay, is it still building up or does it appear that it slacked off now?"

"Seems to be staying on the wings, Seven Two Five."

"Okay, sir, are you getting any more?"

Clegg shuddered, noting the minimal passage of time between "on the
wings, Seven Two Five" and "getting any more?" Only seconds, and the
amount could increase, even as you watched it dust you down.

"Seven Two Five, negative." Clegg sighed relief and went on reading,
holding the magazine far from his eyes as if to avoid contamination.

Soon after this the woman took over the mike and loggers working
northwest of Redding, California, saw the Bonanza appear from the
clouds and, with a revving up and down noise, seem to spin, blast into the
ground at 3,300 feet, to be followed only seconds later by a ruddervator
that pinwheeled down from the bottom of the overcast. That was the left
ruddervator falling; the right-hand one had been dragged down after the
rest of the airplane, still being connected by control cables. Clegg tried to
imagine the pilot's wife and her state of mind, knowing she had taken
over the mike in the final seconds of their lives, as if she, the nourisher of
life, might call on some prevailing force to save them at last. In fact, Center's last question, to the pilot, had gone unanswered. "How are you doing
now, sir?" brought no one into action aboard the Bonanza, so Center
made a longish suggestion: "Suggest you, ah, descend now and maintain
niner thousand and if you can, reverse course and proceed back south-
bound." Then just the woman and nothing, the pilot having lost control
of the airplane. Clegg was mighty glad they called you "sir," suggesting a
courtliness or knightliness of the airwaves, an exaggerated courtesy that as
often as not fortified a nervous pilot and, merely because he was being
addressed in a respectful manner, made him find courage he never knew
he had. He became a hero because he was being addressed as a gentleman by a gentleman who probably had no such elegant motives but said
"sir" out of mechanical good nature. Clegg liked the "uh"s and "ah"s as
well, surmising they were indices to honesty. People were thinking under
pressure, not always able to produce the perfect answer at heartbeat
speed, and indeed sometimes pausing before the most ordinary word or
number. Chivalry, he decided, calms the heart and stills the churning
bowels. We have all been there, our mouths too dry to talk with, our
hearts doing a jackhammer in our chests, and then some total stranger out
of the uncaring invisible ether calls you sir, and you feel knighted. Surely

that was the way, even with student pilots: strength through civility was the proper motto. No wonder he still called Booth "sir," not that Booth needed buttressing; he had too much courage as it was. No, Clegg enjoyed the sense of collegiality the finesse brought, the sense that they were among the elect and used little pomps that other men could not rise to without seeming effete. Envy not the controller, duty bound to turn novices into master pilots with a little touch of patrician calm. In such a world, Clegg thought, it was a wonder anyone crashed. He had missed nearly fifteen minutes of his TV show.

Yet tonight was one of those nights on which Clegg was unable to concentrate on the haggard, whispering narrator who always seemed to know more than he confided, or on the simulated faces of the lorn, the bereft, the permanently upset, pictured on the show in party frocks, baseball suits, PFC uniforms, wedding dresses and tuxedos, all of them with lives gone palpably wrong for long or short spells. This was the texture of life lived next door to death, sometimes put right by a phone call; but even the life's presence on the show did not guarantee it irresistible allure. It could be dull, tedious, something durably generic. All the same, even the dullest life seemed an object of ceaseless fascination contrasted with death, about which, Clegg reminded himself, we knew nothing at all, even less than the Higgs boson about which there had been so much debate in scientific circles—what was it, and why? Clegg had no idea, but he knew when things had no qualities, and death was one of those things. He understood why Booth doted on these gruesome bedtime stories, reassuring him and making him feel he had done a great many things right amid the mayhem of his calling. There, Booth would keep thinking (or so Clegg thought in his Euclidean way), but for the grace of God go I. He died in every fatal crash, emerged smoldering and bloody from every nonfatal, and actually seized the controls in some, saving all souls aboard like Gulliver leaning out of a windmill and lifting Alice from the bottom of the well.

What kept Booth from sleeping well or attending to the admittedly tiny requirements of his daily round was his command appointment over in Clemensville, facing an inquiry of the Federal Aviation Agency, which had taken a dim view of his saunter up and down the runway. What little flying he did would soon be greater by far than the flying allowed him. He had broken laws of all kinds, but at least not in an airplane, so his crimes amounted only to self-abuse and self-endangerment. He was not even sure if suicide was a crime anymore, or the attempted version; surely you were entitled to *off* yourself whenever you wanted. In any event, all he had tried to do was fulfill himself on the plane of imagery; he had tried to cut a figure, like somebody dancing in a public place. No, he might have distracted the pilot of a DC-9 during the landing process, and that was bad enough. An aviator, Clegg had told him, ought to know better, and they would ram that point into him. So he would drive over during the evening, pitch his tent (as he liked to say after Africa) in a motel, and meet the feds bright and early, full of ingenuous mature excuses and a complete recital of his aerial career. In the end, surely, they would apologize, create him an instant astronaut, and forgive him on the spot. He had not even been to retrieve his costume, hat and stilts, leaving them there for posterity to ogle or to mount like oars high on a wall, a brass plate attached outlining his prowess and saying exactly when. Booth had immortal longings, not necessarily to be accomplished in the Apache. He could have flown over for his interview, but he had been grounded, so that would have amounted to yet another crime. Yet, to him, grounding a Booth for an escapade on the runway was like jailing an acrobat for picking his nose. To hell with authority, he thought, that has no savvy, never knowing when to leave a man to the invasive suasions of his own conscience: the agenbite of inwit the ancients used to prate about.

So Clegg had been obliged to keep his imagination fed, not merely with violent misadventures but with the almost Jane Austen quality of controllers' exchanges as they discussed the day's entrants for disaster. "Read me the Squirrel, Rupe. How did they begin, those guys?"

"*Go ahead, green.*"

"*Watch that guy, he's a squirrel.*"

"*Nine Eight Two. Jacksonville.*"

"*Green light.*"

"*That Navajo don't have a transponder.*"

"*I ain't seen him yet, where is he?*"

Thus departure control and the tower local controller, identifying someone who was bound to give them trouble before the day or the hour was out.

On went the tower, Clegg said, "like they had nothing else to occupy them, the pisscutters. Tower, he says *That's him just to the east, heading, uh, he looks like he's turning Zero Seven Zero, I'm going to turn Eastern.* Departure chimes in with *Yeah, turn Eastern northbound, that's easier.* Now, that was Zero Seven Four Zero Zero Eight. We next hear something lively from these boys at Four Six minutes Four Five seconds, when Departure says *You're right about that, I turn him One Seven Zero so he decided to fly Five Zero.*"

Booth exploded with immoderate guffaws although he had heard this before; a permanent risibility had infected his being, the world being full of savage lunacy and moribund obtuseness.

"Fly Five Zero," he echoed, chortling and hiccupping.

"Then the tower," Clegg resumed, "says *Yeah, that's what I'm telling you. The guy is, the guy is a squirrel.* And Departure answers him with more cynicism than you might have expected: *I don't think he's any more instrument rated than I am.*" Clegg nodded and stood to stretch while Booth continued repeating the one word "squirrel," helpless with laughter.

"Then, oh not many seconds later," Clegg said a bit louder so as to prevail over the laughter, "Departure takes a deep breath and tells him, *I really do hate to do this to you this early in the morning, but watch that guy, I don't think he's any more instrument rated than I am. He's, uh, I've given him about twelve turns in the last twelve miles.* All Center does is say *All right, thank you.*" The parrotlike quality of some of these utterances awoke Clegg to the mundane monotony of human thought, even among controllers. Once they got an idea, he decided, they pounded it into the ground; and why not if it went on amusing the Booths? That squirrel stuff sure got them going at breakfast time while a pilot was getting into deep trouble. When the right engine went out, the same controllers began calling him *sir.* It was like Lewis Carroll saying one Alice was worth ten Janets. The guy in the Navajo was the same guy under different distress. But Booth didn't want to hear the onset of trouble, even though, to Clegg, talk about *he just lost an engine, coming back to me* was enough to tickle his spine. Booth wanted him to get to the severe stuff, like the soliloquies in *Hamlet* or Ariadne's elegiac arias on Naxos, when Departure said *November Seven Four Nine Eight Two, say souls on board and fuel remaining in time, please.* That sure lost you a heartbeat, didn't it, with its overtones of *Captains Courageous* and the ripe old days of the *Titanic,* unable to count souls on board or anywhere else. Then came the answer as the Navajo did who knew what under terminally imperfect control: "*Nine Eight Two—three souls.*" Clegg coughed awkwardly though he too knew the text by heart and was subject to no surprises. "*I have about six and a half hours of fuel, uh, I seem to have gotten part of the engine back. I'm working on the fuel thing now, so I'm heading back anyway for the moment.*" A little skein of fool's gold, of optimism, running through the bedrock of fatality; Clegg was savoring it, but Booth had raced ahead, asking for the end, the declension into idiocy when faced with a recalcitrant machine. Clegg again omitted stuff, went for the pitiful saliences, pilot to pilot:

"Niner Eight Two says *Roger, Three Zero Zero right* only to be corrected with Approach's *No, sir, that's a left turn heading Three Zero Zero.* He can't hold the heading," Clegg announced in his dreary bureaucratic way. "I guess he wants Booth and Clegg to help him out."

Booth was more sympathetic. "Show him almost getting it right," he said. "Give me the countdown, Rupe."

"Niner Eight Two says *Roger, Niner Eight Two, having a lot of trouble with this engine, it* (here he becomes unintelligible, no surprise to me) *goes in and out on us, uh, I don't know.*"

Booth nodded with fierce, juvenile energy.

"And then Approach puts it all together, he too unintelligible to begin with, which must have encouraged the guy in the Navajo no end and his accompanying souls. *Niner Eight Two is four miles from DINNS, turn right heading Zero Five Zero, maintain two thousand until established on the localizer, cleared for ILS Runway Seven Approach.*"

Both Booth and Clegg allowed a long silence as they preheard and honored what came next, the pilot of Niner Eight Two again beginning with unintelligible babble, then letting it all hang out: "*got problems, oh my God* (unintelligible) *Mayday! Mayday! . . . lost control . . . God . . . in a spin . . . oh my God.*"

The two passengers survived, badly hurt, after the Navajo hit tall trees in a marshy area, hit more trees, and then went four hundred feet farther.

"Look, I gotta read you this," Clegg said. "There was oil pouring from the oil access door on the right nacelle, see. The dipstick was gone. The number five piston had a hole burned in it. And there was burn damage on two connecting rods, and the rod bolts on six had failed. This guy had eight hundred hours total time. He was good enough to close down the malfunctioning engine and make the ILS approach single-engine. He just panicked out when he could have made the decision to shut that engine down and work with that situation."

"You wise, invincible prick-fucker," Booth snapped at him, "leave him alone. The guy is dead. He ruined his family. I want to hear what one of them said. Was it a woman?"

Clegg read, slowly and earnestly after the rebuke. "*I was just so scared I put my head down and I was holding on for dear life and they were screaming and saying we got big trouble, big problems, big problems, and Larry was screaming something and Steve said oh my God I can't believe it, oh my God. . . . All of a sudden we hit some really heavy turbulence or something and our altitude dropped and we were going down and all of a sudden the plane just went crazy. We just lost control and started diving. First we went straight up and then we started going down. I was looking out the window and I saw that we were going down straight at the trees and then we leveled off right before the trees. And that's it, that's all I remember."*

"Yes," Booth said gently. "That's our stock-in-trade, Rupe. You and I are two guys who dominated that emotion and live to tell."

"How come, then," Clegg answered, aware of deviating from some norm even as he said it, "it don't feel like survival? It feels like we went down with some goddamn ship. Honest."

"Surface feelings, Recon. Deep down we are survivors."

Clegg could not quite muster the sense of triumph; he felt mesmerized and lethargic, no doubt a result of reading accident reports aloud to a man who appreciated them too much. Would they have fared better if he'd read to Booth from *Hiawatha, Dracula,* or *Treasure Island?* He groped for favorites, but concluded he hadn't read many books, or couldn't remember those he had. He had read his share of Eric Ambler, Leslie Charteris, and John Buchan, but the only titles he could recall were not by them at all but by more demanding authors, or so he guessed: *Gulliver's Travels, Crime and Punishment, Erewhon.* And there was one flying novel that had held him, *Pylon,* and one about a German U-boat called *Das Boat.* He wondered why there had to be German in the American title, but supposed it was a matter of flavor, something lost if you said *The Boat,* which could have been about Noah's Ark. Clegg's relationship to literature resembled a free-falling parachutist's relationship to given points on the Earth's surface: the Empire State Building, Dutchess County Airport, Lake Nausicaa right under him: uncertain and tumbling, prey to extraordinary shifts of attitude and trajectory. Usually he liked reading to Booth, but there always came a point at which he, Clegg, wanted to throw up. No one would realize it, he thought, but there were planes tumbling out of the sky all the time. Never a shortage of disasters to fit the accident columns in the magazines. Not commercial carriers, not military, and not business, but private or what was known as general aviation: amateurs, really, who could never get the flying bug out of their systems. They flew into lousy weather, stalled and spun, ran out of fuel, did crazy stunts to impress their relatives or women friends, and that was that: an elaborate toy totalled in minutes. He sympathized with the aerial yearning, but deplored the feckless rodomontade of the pilots.

Look at the guys in the Navajo, the subject of his most recent elocution in that graveyard voice of his. A shot magneto had kept them on the ground for hours. They were three guys heading for the Bahamas. They left Long Island after midnight, reached Florida in time to meet a tropical storm. When they took on oil, the left injun took seven or eight quarts, the right one three. Talk about indices to bad fortune. When at last they began to taxi, the Navajo went off the taxiway onto the grass. Then followed the scenario he had read to Booth, graced (as he, Clegg, saw it) with such mellow formalities as saying "with you" to the tower, Departure saying "all right, sir, say intentions," as if nothing bad was going to come of all this bungling and bad luck. They all called the pilot a squirrel anyway, so they had an attitude from the outset, which must surely have worsened their attitude to him as the day wore on. They called him sir all right, but underneath the amenities there was this tone of pawnbroked respect. Tower complained to Departure *It took us thirty minutes to get him on the runway. Uh, uh,* as Tower would say. Then, at a later point, Departure seems to whisper gossipy fashion *Hey, how do you think I felt?* And Tower answers *Okay.* Around this faltering guy has grown a cocoon of incipient slander that maybe did not affect him, though it easily could through timbre and intonation, whispering behind his twitchy back. Then Approach tries to say something, but it comes out *He's gonna be, gonna be, he's gonna be . . . after Osprey One Five Two.* They were wondering where he would fit into the conga line of planes coming in to land at Jacksonville (JAX), their only duty really being spacing and separation, although they did many other voluntary things as well. *I'm gonna call Alert Two,* Tower says. Approach, almost chidingly, tells the pilot *Try to fly the best Two Nine Zero you can, sir.* The pilot answers, a bit crestfallen, *Roger, I appreciate any help I can get,* little knowing he has only a couple of minutes to live: coupla, as they say in the trade, and they did not go to the Bahamas at all. "Roger, sir," Clegg whispers, appalled by something so simple as a fatal accident, selective in that two survived. He would much rather they chartered the Apache and allowed him and Booth to fly them, real slow, to where they wanted to go, affable banter all the way and not a whitened knuckle between them.

In his mail next day, arriving just before noon, Clegg found an envelope plastered with such words as URGENT and CONTAINS TIME-ZERO MATERIAL, which already got him grumbling, inside a message imprinted on a pseudo-certificate: *Rupert Clegg, Pack Your Bags You Have Been Chosen for a World Class Florida/Caribbean Vacation Package including—* He stopped reading, knowing that at last he was a civilian, a citizen. Lower down, the certificate suppliers addressed him as Rupert: "Rupert, your Exotic Cruise Holiday includes" and he stopped reading again, instead flipping the certificate over, only to find an uppercase exhortation: "RUPERT DO NOT DELAY." Nonetheless he set the thing behind the candle on the mantelpiece, behind the typed nonschedule of what was now Perigee Air. Maybe this, he worried, was how Segundo

Cielo should have handled Perigee, with a little pizzazz and much use of first names, ransacking the phone book for victims. It looked trustworthy, but it was too full of hard sell and behind it, somewhere in a Miami lawyer's office, there was the usual afterbirth of boilerplate. Booth had been sent one too: just the thing to poison even further the bad mood the FAA had stirred up in him; this very night he would drive to Clemensville, a motel, and ready himself for his hearing, a colonel on the mat.

Booth was still sleeping when Clegg set out for Perigee Air, cycling past two trivial streets—Bosmun Lane leading to Bosmun Products and Sylvan Avenue leading to Better Dairy Herds—then turning left across traffic to the ill-repaired airport road on which sat Langmuir Lab like an obsolete train station, yet no more so than the defunct airport only fifty yards from the elegant new one in which the afternoon sun, aimed right at the check-in counters and the agents' eyes, had made the airline buy sun blinds and supply protective glasses. Sometimes, knowing a whole day's uninterrupted vigil awaited him, he would enter the polished lobby of the commercial carriers just to greet Feffie, Judy, Michelle, Sherry, Nikki, Marsha, Tina, Buzz, Ken, Frank, and Mark, who ran a tight and sociable ship, composing without trying to a light militia of the lower air. Today, however, with a touch of cold making the air breathable, he headed straight for the hangar and got to work on his illuminated drawing, now and then tapping on the plywood to still ghosts and invite lady gremlins. He had not witnessed his fifinella since Pittsburgh and now doubted she would ever reappear. He was becoming quite the dodo, the hangar potato, he thought, though the cycling kept him fit and eager. By the end of the year, they would have spent their savings, but would still have their pensions, and of course the Apache. A local museum might fancy it. The new airport might like to hang it in the lobby, slowly twirling like the mobile that used to dangle in the old Pittsburgh terminal (he had heard the mobile now stood outside, paneled with canvas, a toilet for airport workmen). Nothing endured, he knew, not even the National Transportation Safety Board that sat in judgment on all accidents and pronounced who or what was to blame.

After Booth had left, saying he would have eggs and ham halfway as if for breakfast at dusk, Clegg began to fret about him; not that Clegg wanted to testify, or had been obliged to (he saw nothing, he said). It was just that he had some foreboding, a metallic pluck in his heart, on top of a sense that he should be with Booth on his big day, even if only for moral support. It did not take him long to have the Apache gassed, tugged out, and revved up. There was little traffic at this time of evening and he was soon on his way IFR to Clemensville, only a twenty-minute flight. Surely he passed directly over Booth at some point, but he lost time getting a cab and then riding to the motel.

Carefully calculating his tip, he scanned the motel's parking lots for Booth's car, found it, and was just going to launch himself toward the door, 112, when he saw a man of medium height approaching it with a plastic bag: maybe a pizza delivery done in civilian clothes. Balding, a little tubby, the man had a high forehead and a babyish face. Clegg stalked him and waited as he knocked. It was no doubt one of the FAA officials, or so he thought until Booth opened and the stranger raised his arm. Clegg saw the silencer, heard the click, and fast as a Cyrano clamped his hands around the other's windpipe while Booth, recovering, seized the pistol, allowing Clegg to twist and finish him off, throwing him aside for Booth to drag toward the Escort. Into the trunk he went, floppy as a bag of onions. Booth and Clegg had worked together before in the alleyways of Istanbul and needed minimum conversation to get things moving.

"Who the hell?" Booth was shaken.

"Those pretty-boys in Washington," Clegg answered, "are on your case again."

"Two seconds more," Booth told him, "and I'd have been a goner. Your timing sure is great, Recon."

"Let's get this sucker into the lake. The tower closes at ten, so that's the time to do it." The rest of the evening they devoted to clean-up work. They drove to the airport, loaded the unknown assassin, flew to Nausicaa, dumped him off the right-hand wing into the lake, Clegg maneuvering him from behind, and then flew back to Clemensville, where Booth was determined to meet his questioners. Clegg took another room in the same motel since he wanted Booth to sleep and he kept late hours anyway, staying up until at least 12:30, when the last *Unsolved Mysteries* ended. If life had ever been dull, it had certainly changed its nature now. They had finished him off so fast, and there he was at the bottom of Lake Nausicaa with his dinner hardly digested, his life having flashed before him in black and white, his victim full of eggs and ham. Clegg wondered why, if Booth had stopped to eat, he had not been the second to arrive; but he had seen Booth eat before and knew how he subjugated food, as if he had a flight to take up in five minutes' time.

"Hey, we should do this every night." Clegg was allowing some levity into his sense of anticlimax.

"Then let's make a list," Booth said. "I would hate to die before having settled with everybody. Boy, that was sure a bone splitter of an evening. Quite like the old days."

"Nothing like," he heard.

"No? Was it gentler?"

"No," Clegg told him, it was not gentler. "We weren't as good at disposing of somebody. We've improved."

"We'd better not make a habit of it."

"Depends who comes along. What about those bully-boys in Washington? Was this guy one of *them?*"

"Nice having your own plane," Booth said. "Stick them in the right seat and slither them out, just so long as you bank the airplane right. I mean correctly. To the right. Gravity does the rest. I had never thought about it. No ID, hardly any money, but lots of ammo. I wonder what they were going to pay him for whacking me."

"Whatever." Clegg sighed. "Your price will be going up. At least we've had the satisfaction of meeting the enemy and doing him in. I hope he doesn't float to the surface."

"Cinder blocks are best," Clegg told him. "By the time the ropes rot, he'll be nothing but skeleton. Don't forget the lampreys. People won't swim anymore, there are so many lampreys in the lake. Lake Nausicaa's become Lake Nausea."

"Tomorrow won't take long," Booth said. "I'll tell them I was practicing fancy dress for a party. For an art students' ball!" His exhilaration had a malign edge, and now he was betting against himself that no one would be there to confront him at nine o'clock tomorrow morning. Thank God for the motel, he thought, as an institution: the privatest place in America where most of its intimate rituals get transacted, where nobody cares what you do, and anybody who does is like the Nightman in that movie *Touch of Evil*. Dennis Weaver the Nightman who knows nothing and is responsible for nothing. Next to crawl spaces and cellars, the motel is where the dark side of us lives. Or in the bomb bay of a derelict bomber. He wondered just how many hit men got as neatly taken out by two colonels trained by the Danakili. It had been quite a feat considering the coincidences — Clegg might well have stayed in Ithaca, or arrived late, or Booth might have skipped dinner and therefore arrived early for the waiting gunman. Clearly, someone was living right. Now the silenced gun puzzled fish in the gloom of the lake bottom, doomed to rust and clog while he and Clegg flew the Apache to some haven safer than the Tower of London. It was a matter of choice. Nothing held them back. Then why wait for tomorrow's interview? Why not get out now? He was a colonel and he wanted to see their faces. In a way, he wanted to be approved of by his enemies and given the signal to depart. He wasn't sure of this. He and Clegg had their own guns, military issue (but not the ones they signed for years ago; these were filched, like so much else).

The hardest thing to decide, Clegg concluded, was how logical they were being, under such pressure, in such a weird situation, never knowing where the next onslaught would come from. The Apache was more conspicuous, he thought, than the car, but less so than a Viking jet. It always had to be parked, but maybe they could always find a grass strip with nobody there to see what went on. Could they live from grass strip to grass strip, then, sleeping in the plane if they had to? It might be more logical to buy seats on a commercial carrier, get wherever they were going, and lie low. Suddenly logic was something locked in the phonemes of an obscure language. His head felt squeezed, neutralized, out of shape. If his brain was what he was thinking with, it was letting him down. He had heard of what some shrink called the misprisions of panic, but he had never felt them so keenly, not even in Africa. It was really difficult to hide without the help of the authorities, and even then only when you weren't being looked for. The smart thing would be to get their hands on another Cyrano: nothing could catch them, not even a missile, and they would be out of reach forever, yet obliged to dump the airplane. No Cyrano was going to be theirs, he knew. Ideally, one should land an Apache in a war party of Apaches, preferably at one of those repair depots devoted to Piper aircraft, but Apaches were becoming rare, indeed sought after, so perhaps the thing to do was leave it behind. A car was much more anonymous. Or so he thought. Why was his mind faltering? Well, he didn't polish off a thug every day, did he now?

According to Booth, the best thing was to feint: that was, to pretend to fly away and then come back, *sneak* back. Fly east to Tacitus, hang around there for a day, then scoot back to Ithaca and hangar the Apache pronto. As Clegg saw it, that wasn't much different from staying put and going to the movies a few full days in succession. There was no need to feint, he said. Nor, he claimed, did it make much sense to slink off to Tacitus, then head for somewhere else. What had Tacitus got to do with it? Booth said something about one flight's being on a flight plan, and the other not, but that wasn't quite the point. "Oh," Clegg said, "one would be IFR, and the other unannounced. What are we getting at here? We don't seem to be very good at escapes unless someone helps us. For example: we drive the car into a Galaxy transport and have it skylift us to Seattle. That kind of trickery. Then we live the remainder of our lives in a boxcar, never exposing ourselves to the light of day."

"I just feel a need to get out of this town," Booth said. He meant Ithaca, not Clemensville, where, when he presented himself at 9 A.M. at the designated office, a bubblegum-chewing secretary told him the meeting had been called off and he was to stand by for rescheduling. He might have known; indeed he did, but he wanted to witness it in the raw, like someone who had never seen a disemboweled yak. Now he was in the clear, his duty done; or, rather, his duty exterminated. The question remained, however, at least to his sometimes Jesuitical mind. Had they not shown because they knew he would be dead? Or had they heard that their "operative" had failed? Surely, he thought, he was one up on them by having put in an appearance. He was not as habituated to the mores of the planet as he thought he was, at least to the ways of its bureaucracy.

In the end, they did stage a flight to Tacitus (pop. 3,467, elevation 1,282 feet), where they found no one attending the Unicom; so they landed with maximum care, looking all around them for unannounced aircraft, and found the place deserted, four jets parked with big stoppers in their nacelles, and some Cessna 172's. Not a soul in sight, but the office was open, the coffee was brewed, the water cooler functioned, and there were current magazines in the toilet. Not a bad, though dusty place, Clegg thought. What do we do here? They used an old shirt of his to polish the Apache, then squatted in the long grass beside the ramp with a six-pack and a cold pizza. After finishing their snack, they made paper airplanes from sheets of paper filched from the notice board inside and reinvented aerodynamics, Booth doing especially well with a little glider under each of whose wings he fitted with paper clips a cone-shaped tube as long as the wing was wide, small end facing back. This made the air squeeze itself up in order to get through the narrow hole and made the glider speed up, developing extra energy from being almost jet-propelled.

Clegg smiled, impressed, convinced, distracted. The Booth of old was still alive; the spy of yesteryear was still at work. Where, Clegg wondered, had Booth found *that* idea? Had it been burgeoning in his skull for years, or had he stolen it? He *had* stolen it, as Clegg should have known had he not forgotten his aviation history. It was, to them, a pretty scene with white and multicolored gliders wafting about in the faint breeze, with two grown (self-regarding) men strolling about after them, plucking them from midflight like someone trapping butterflies, with not a soul to watch, no plane landing or taking off. It was limbo, comprehensible if you only put the right questions. There was no refrigerator inside cooling the drinks because the drinks were all aboard the Falcons and Lears, tepid now but cooled in only minutes when the jets spooled up. None of this satisfied Clegg, who argued that a general aviation facility should always have cold drinks on hand, never mind what the jets contained. Then a cream pimpmobile drove up, disgorged four men in natty suits, and drove away. In ten minutes the jet was gone, cleared to its airway, and Booth and Clegg resumed their gliding game, trying to make their gliders fly in formation, but failing.

Already they had forgotten why they came here, and Clegg thought he saw ghosts of pilots entering and leaving the hut that enclosed Tacitair, that uneasily confected trade name nailed above the door, in white letters on brown paint, done by a mentally deficient lemur. In order to agree with one another, they restaged an old debate of theirs: style at the expense of everything else versus saving the planet at all costs. What intrigued them both was the invention, the unique turn of phrase, the thing that was never there before, to measure or to utter, versus what they called wholesome-mindedness. They cared little for conservation and knew they were not popular for this; but their lives had gone to injuns and performance, to heights and speeds, to record breaking and the platinum albemarle of technocratic prowess, often mistaken, as Booth and Clegg knew, for an angel. In a perfect world, some flying saucer would swoop down now and capture them, restore them to their magazine subscriptions and families on a distant planet whose only approach to Earth had been theirs. It was not a perfect world, though, none of it, nor even a quite good one. In a way, nothing was worth doing; nothing further, anyway. If they were in a poem, the last stanza had ceased, the poem's momentum exhausted with the end of its last syllable. It had been a painfully long stay, an endurance test, in an exacting dimension under the sway of aberrant tyrants. Had they volunteered? Yes they had, on the understanding that, where they hailed from, their lives on return would be doubled in length (where they came from, since no one died naturally, lives were terminated on schedule according to education and feats).

Or so they dreamed, if indeed they had come from somewhere else, the contract being that they would be retrieved when their time was up, as in Keats, but without their being able to anticipate the event. So they were passive short-timers, aware of exhaustion or completeness but unable to think into the matter further. Hence their pretty picnic on Tacitus airfield, a *fête champêtre* for two, executed out of innocent improvisation. They did not know they were waiting, or why those who had served them (Aqua Regia, Babe) had not reappeared even when they were supposed to, or were vehemently hoped for, like figures breaking free from a custard and wielding arms and legs for the first time. Theirs was an untidy tour of duty, both marred and embellished. The only clue as to who or what they were consisted in their ages, exposing them as just a little too old to be flying the Cyrano if indeed they had really had their previous experiences in the service. In the center of their career(s) floated a time reversal that gave the game away, or would have if anyone had looked closely, asking how did they manage to pull it off? Hadn't they done too much already? They had come because of this planet's basic adoration of flight.

In fact they did not return to Ithaca (an act much celebrated in Homer), but dawdled on, now and then going for coffee to the main building, sometimes snoozing, at other times arranging their paper gliders on the short grass (a disciplined, on-parade look to things) or the long (strange levitation on a green hairbrush). Something was prompting them from within, an impulse they had not felt before, but it was suasive and final. Easy picking is what they were, but nobody came after them; nobody ever would. They droned on in immaculate serenity past noon, into midafternoon, exchanging memories of Turkey and Africa, Washington and Clemensville. It seemed to them they were passing through some lattice of time that enforced upon them lighthearted dormancy. Clegg thought about a midge he had swatted against a page of a book he was reading; he had then slammed the book shut, embedding the midge in the texture of the paper, its entire being and cardiovascular system ending in a pink smudge, generalized so fast. Yes, he thought, its life would have been better than a secret. Booth looked on, nodded approval of Clegg's dream, and launched each of the gliders in turn with a strong fling, as if making a seriatim declaration.

Now, simultaneously, as if switched on, they began murmuring lines they could never forget, but which had reached their home planet somewhat skewed: written in the seventeenth century, but not transmitted at the speed of light until three centuries later, garbled bits from the epic *Parade Los* (and its sequel *Paradi Reggae*) with, for archdiviners, certain significant saliences evident even to the general reader. One went:

> beyond this deep whatever draws me on
> or sympathie or som connatural force
> opens at greater distance to unite
> things of like kind with secret amity
> having secretest conveyance

with no punctuation, lost en route. The other, uttered simultaneously by Clegg, was as follows:

> copartner in these regions of the world
> leastways disposer lend them oft my aid

> even my advice by presages and signs
> graced answers oracles portents and dreams
> grant they may direct our future life

also unpunctuated. Their names came from these haphazard, unique quotings, as did their mission, their careers, their terrestrial idiosyncrasies, all this thought unworth pursuing only by those who never yearned for a hint of other life, no matter how flimsy, how poor. The Miltonic style, messed up as it was, had spoken to someone an unthinkable though very Miltonic distance away, and it had proved sufficient. The same thing might have happened on Earth when a ten-line fragment of some *Galaxy Lost* blew in on the cosmic wind or wafted in as part of some undirected panspermia. Zeal had brought Booth and Clegg to their earthly destiny, and love of flight had seen them through. Now a paralyzing nostalgia brought them low, settled them into waiting status, equal to no other form of activity. Booth yawned, Clegg slept. The airscape of Tacitus remained silent. Nothing stirred, not even the bees and dragonflies of an auburn autumn afternoon.

When, at last, Babe arrived in something that resembled a Citation jet, old model, urging them to board without so much as a word or deplaning, the pair of them got up and walked unsteadily aboard as if reunited for the first time. The jet taxied, took off, climbed steeply, then achieved a metamorphosis of its molecules that would have awed Ovid. Where they all three went after that could never be known, least of all by the police cars and armored cars that encircled the airfield, sure of finding Booth and Clegg along with the Apache in the ring. Whether or not, with their local life spans doubled, they would engage in yet another mission might depend on something as subjective and random as the quality of writing that got through to their superiors. Or as myth. The night lights of Ithaca, seen from high up on South Hill near Ithaca College, resemble a swan. Nabokov's Lolita, nubile and playful, was really a girl who attended Belle Sherman Elementary School, not far from where he lived. All else is mere refrigeration.

FOUR

Rosebud

The man slouched at the gravy-brown desk is flying it. Its slave. It extends the whole length of one wall. Were it smaller, he could resist flying it, though his will is a slight thing nowadays. Even if he could resist its length, though, he could not resist the massed screens of the monitors piled one on top of the other all along the desk. Computer screen. Storm scope. Tremors of the graphite-gray memory. White digits on a background of varying colors. Or, on the radar scopes which bring home to him storms near and far, flares of yellow, green, and red, the last being the most fearsome weather of all. In these colorful displays, as he lolls and dreams, he thinks he sees Latin America burning, a scarlet wedge at the bottom right hand, matched by a green Africa in the opposite corner, but that is only rain. Africa is wet.

Only a screen, he says. Only screens. Stacked up on a desk. Amazing it holds the weight. Seven or eight of them. He seems unable to count beyond five or six. All he knows is that he sits here, sits out the days and the nights, tuning in the colors, the numbers, garnering news of the world. He loves that wood of the desk, the fake grain of the consoles, the warm dun-green steel of the cabinets. Once upon a time he never sat at desks, but now desks are his all, and what he heaps upon them. All that red weather. Sensed. Sounded. Touched with an electric wand that fans across the glass, dies, then sweeps in again from the other side, ceaseless and constant. Then he feeds the data, the givens, into his computer, sometimes called his transmuter. His hands tremble for joy. He force-feeds it, but there is no overloading it. It does not in the end yield a prize pâté from its liver. He could be staring into the end of the human world. He knows South America is not on fire. He knows Africa is not being drenched. He stares at the flares, the thimbles of molten light, until they dance and lose their veils. He sees how screens shut out.

Then he sees his clearest, sees thunder cells the denuded crimson of gaillardia pulchella, that gaudy dandelion of the Outer Banks. He sighs. The hell of his life is reaching others at last. In his transmuter he stores up the storms. On the screens the incoming planes move like moths, but not on the same screens as the storms, although they both tear the same air apart. Where, once, his heels were winged.

The man slouched at the gravy-brown desk is flying it. Nothing moves. No keening of wires. No blurt of squashed air needing somewhere to go. A modicum of darkness in his face hints at pain. He flies his pain and it flies him. Into each of the rounded screens in front of him, a looking glass into which he heaves heart, mind, limbs, and breath. Whatever else he has. He taps the keys of an aerial abacus. There, at his desk, in the shabby low room in a two-story cement blockhouse that might double as a bunker, void of dead as yet. But he has hopes and he flies them too.

Just walkably far away loom the huge granaries, the hangars, that enclose the planes he is no longer allowed to coax through space. If this burns him, he is cool. If he knows he is being observed, he does not flinch. The tanned small hands ripple away, making the silent sonata of enormous lift. To where no human ever was, so gross a journey. He will die at the desk, he knows, at something less than minimum sinking speed. All the big noisy tin birds locked up behind him in their asylum. Rust. Creak. Inert as rain spouts. He only half eats. He lives not locally, but on Greenwich Mean Time, almost always five hours ahead. So he will die before his time. He will have been gone five hours before they lift him from his chair and load him into the last surviving yellow biplane in the world and float him with it afire into the lake. For now, though, with each minute he goes ahead he falls a jiffy behind, or more than that. The twinkling of an eye. The drop of a hat. Two shakes certainly. Think of him as a dwindling Methuselah whose agate eyes have stared into the sun too long. The sun has stared him down. As in Africa, where he lost his soul. Booth his name, would he but answer to it, instead of 502524. Just sometimes he answers. A tease.

To and fro. He tries to think of that. It will not come. It must be to or fro instead. He tries that. Miraculous, it comes. Fro today, then. No, he is in between. Denied a direction, he circles through the ruined choirs of his mind, backing, backing away, until, grinning his half-millimeter grin, he almost develops a red shift, but as soon develops an air force blue as he strays into view again, forward as forward can be. But not so fast. Fast in his day, he is now a stationary man, well on the way to qualifying as a beacon. One of the fuzzier ones beloved of moths and gnats. Or like some child in school sitting up straight, a tiny paragon of attentiveness. Arms folded. Eyes on the blackboard. Ears tuned in. What could anyone say worth all of that? A shy swot he is. The hat on his head should be blue, of softest cotton with mesh gussets to hold the shape. Instead it is orange or red, from that region of the spectrum, cut as only he knows from a wind sock of fluorescent dye-fast vinyl coated with nylon for long life, approved by the Port Authority. Three-and-one-half-inch bill. Twin fronds of oak leaves there. Scrambled egg from some last breakfast before taking off. No one has found the leftover wind sock, but surely the wind that blew up or down it can blow across it as well, wherever it flutters or fills to mislead.

Behind him, ignored, hangs a plaque informing the world at large that aviation in itself is not inherently dangerous. But to an even greater degree than the sea (he hates the sea) it is devilishly unforgiving of any carelessness. He laughs. Or incapacity. He snorts. Or neglect. He winces and almost begins to cry. Plague, he thinks. Not plaque. His mind roams away. His hands feel on his behalf. One screen is umber now, as if, outside, were only a stratosphere the hue of crushed violets. And he going faster than a nondawdling bullet. Happy days. They will not rise up from their graves. To hassle or to haunt.

In his mind's eye, while or because he holds his breath, old horrors come again. He is mining rock salt with bare hands that bleed. He is mining red salt. Cudgeled by black Danakils, those captors his raptors. Again he faints, choked on his babble. With slowcoach grace, hushed lepers prod his face. He mines red salt again, with exposed quick of finger. Things to come are already upon him, like next year's weather all at once and overwhelming.

To or fro. It hurts him now at the desk that he never cared enough. Did not in the desert give one jot about his friend. Out went the flame. Up and down went their capsules. And all he cared about was Barney Booth, who would have let the other one, his buddy, die. He did not even think the words: *I do not mind it if he dies today*. That would have been attention. He did not think of him at all, him unthinkable as if already dead, and an unremembered one at that.

Next, one man marooned in the mountains as trapped as any sentry in his box. Utterly alone with wind and hawks. This is the buddy, permanent in his fix as a saint in a stained-glass window.

Next but one, a man captured by salt miners. Working. Working. Shoved. Badgered. Starved. Of all phases in his life the dominant. All his cries, yells, all helter-skelter racings of his heart, start here.

Even now, looking away, they catch sight of themselves just then, peeping forward to the bliss of looking back on it all. The coming through the going through even before going through with it. The difference, though, makes havoc of one who finds nothing to fill that vacuum of the heart where his buddy used to lounge or tap-dance in the full spate of his early middle manhood. In prime condition, really, ripe as a cauliflower, ready to cut and sell. A goner. His image peeled away. All the good-byes unsaid.

Harsh, Booth says. A done thing dies. Done, it lingers, like a fox cub in the doorway. Lingering, it fades at the tally-ho. Faded, as with all things whose vocation is to fade without a murmur, a gasp, a sigh, a little cheep-cheep, it is here today but gone tomorrow. That is the universal scheme, the butter on our bread. You count on that until your dying day, although you know, in the core of your going, it's not without demur. Oh no, you resist, you clear your throat, you blink to signal anybody. This is what happens to everyone else. Whereas I will it away with a sniff. Inhalation that does not happen. Reflex that does not flower.

He resumes. You go on clean. Betray again if you are good at it. Wipe the slate and start over with an incurable newborn smile. It's okay. You'll never do it again, you tell them. It isn't me at all. I was temporarily out of me. Out of things. Hit the wrong key, folks. Barney Booth, once you get to know him, isn't like that at all. He grows on people. He flowers in their gaze. Mister Reliable.

He wanted ever after to be good to that cast-off Sancho Panza of a friend, wholesome likeness to himself. Rupert, he says. What a name. Rupe is better. Or even Rue. Two men the same. Muscle. Bone. Flesh. Juices. Beard to shave. From time to time, little white squirts from some self-engrossed bulb inside them. Two chips off the selfsame block. Only one of them damned.

Little word, damned, but he believes it. The two of them live on. Even an inferior living is living according to cosmic record books as big as mesas. Barney, for one, desks. To desk has now become his private verb. While Rupe, aloft as often as not, flies charter flights, a chauffeur glorified. Their future wears a hood. Their past bears acid stains, old underwear turned into dust rags. They smile at artificial flowers. They befriend what is left of each other. And only Barney knows. Ever ready for the so-called loss of life, as if life were gas escaping from a communal balloon, he had schooled himself. Not too close. Never too intimate. Know their names but not know them. Keep them a victim's arm's length away.

It never worked with Clegg, whom he surnames when being strict, whom he first-names, oddly, when trying to be even stricter, winning a cheery smile he puts aside like a paperweight full of tiny crystal flowers. Old asphodel. Clegg has no idea of what happened in the desert, or of what is happening now, but continues in miraculous blithe mutuality. Two men, back from the dead, with hairs growing still in their nostrils. Most of the old bodily rigmaroles. Not so deft as before, nor so honed as if muscle had alchemized overnight into the springiest of steels. But alive. Ticking. Compos mentis. Warm-handed, hearty. To go on friends until doom-crack.

But this deskbound one, the desker, he can hardly bear the heart-full grins of one who never wished him dead. Or uncared so far as to have him die unthought-about. As if remorse shading into shame has failed to wipe out lovesick disappointment.

Now, to prove himself still capable of motion, he thrusts himself two-handed back from the desk and heads for what he calls the Can. The Head to Clegg. Bathes his face at the basin, humming a desolate tune. Sees his face in the mirror, wishing he could see past that apparition to the Big Dipper, or, more prosaic, Utica, in roughly that direction along the land. Ceiling and visibility unlimited, he murmurs. All down the sky from top to bottom. But, in the dead air of the men's room, he just washes his face all over again, spluttering. Madman, in the northern hemisphere, he wants to see the Southern Cross, and all he does, with hands undried, is walk outside to a dim spot behind the FBO, where dew and rain resist the sun, and, kneeling, plant the palms of his hands on the dredged-out, spongy grass, as if renewing contact with complete simplicity, and watched by that other, Clegg, who wordlessly notes in the man's movements something sly and random. He watches Booth straighten up, bunching his shoulders in toward his neck just like a wrestler before round one. Clegg slinks away before Booth turns, and so misses the shoulders coming down again. Booth walks as if waiting for the engine of his walking to kick on. It does not, and he feels as if he will never reach the dun green door of the FBO. His being is one red-hot thought. To be indifferent, not care if Clegg lived or died, is just the same as strangling him over and over again. He sees himself approaching, hands upraised, and saying, *It will not hurt, oh no, this is what I do to you nonstop.* Into the open with it, just like a murderer.

And Clegg, with his boylike smile, just says *Hands off, I'm delicate. Your hands are green with grass.*

Booth will go to the can again, even if only to savor the shock of his appearance in the glass. Can this be me? This wasted face? These used-up eyes? The faint tan like a darkening from within? This is a man in a men's room. A glutton for punishment. His crime is mental only. The punishment is too. He nods, goes in, plies his screens again to bring in the pageant of bad weather.

Oh, Barney Booth. Conscience a cinder. Heart a golf-ball hole. You deep-sixed him like an empty bottle, with no message aboard for posterity to marvel at. Yo ho. Hosanna. The legendary bell tolling for humankind does not toll for him. Or the one tolling for him for it. He lives on. Squanders what is left of him, in robot motions toward what loosely is known as night, more exactly as the time between the end of evening civil twilight and the beginning of morning civil twilight, as published in the *Air Almanac*, converted to local time, which he does not heed.

Shoves forward nonetheless. Thattaway to the sun. With his body on local time, but his mind on Greenwich, what he needs most of all is the beautifully pertinent navigational aid known in the trade as Consolan, for transoceanic travel, although it guides only. It has never been known to console. Whence and whither is beyond him. He needs a system that steers him, knows where he has to go without his knowing what makes it tick. No tune. No commands. Just once, he knows, as he flails and dithers, he snapped like week-old toast. He could have yawned instead, and that would have been harder to do.

Somewhere I'll find you, he hums to the glide slope. To something this final, he thinks, there should be a thunderous prelude, a whole array of Vasi lights, red and white, to tell him he is making his final approach too high or too low. Red over white is right. All red is too low. All white too high. At thirteen hundred feet from the threshold he finds the far bar of lights. At six hundred feet from the threshold the near bar. From the near bar to the far. How he yearns for that. It sounds like an indefinitely postponed promise of refreshment, as if he were crawling through Dublin or Munich. But it is only, all told, twelve boxes of light, arranged in four sets of three on either side of the runway. What symmetry. What helpfulness, even at night or in snow. If the pilot making a night approach desires to have the brightness of the lights reduced, he need only ask the controller in the tower.

Grease it down, then. But he is as exempt from honor as devoid of grace. Again he falls earthward from that hulk of ruined titanium, away from all human forms of bliss. Free to. He interrupts that train of thought. Free between the near and the far bar, between the end of evening civil twilight and the beginning of morning civil twilight, to ply his Consolan. Free to go callous for the rest of his days. Free to talk himself back into his own good graces. Knowing it needs, he tells himself four or five nautical miles away from the threshold, the mind provides. Pride grows a scab. That is natural. That is the law. Look. Adjust. Line up. Not too heavy-handed now. Two fingers will guide it.

All so seemly. As in the color filter assembly. The upper two thirds are red, the other third clear. The lens effect thus achieved makes white light when viewed from high up. Red when too low, as aforesaid. But pink when seen from the horizontal center of the slit. Forty thousand candle-power to bring home how many horses? He tries to divide the one by the other. Vice versa. But nothing goes into anything. He no longer knows how much horsepower he has. Maybe no more than the harnessed heft of four shrews. Not so bad. Just that little will get him down safe. He would love to land on the land.

He has been interrogated to death. Like Clegg. All modes of interrogation save inquisitor in leather mask, breathing pure oxygen. Has answered on a basis so selective as to entitle him to instant membership in Infernal Fibbers Incorporated. Saving face. Saving soul. Two men in the desert, lost for more than a month, then, through some mathematical sleight of hand, questioned about it for five months more. Odd ratio. Smacking of the cabala.

All wrong. He has lost touch with knowledge, has too often explained himself to those who, amazed at his survival, refuse to make sense of it. Or of Clegg's, high up in the mountains with Booth below sea level. Never give up, he always heard himself saying. Get through at all costs. A little coil of tungsten will, he told them. To bend but not to break. But what fueled his will to live had been the willingness to have Clegg die. And this can never figure among things tellable. Is only there as the thumbprint of a bleached abstraction's ghost. Missing believed killed.

For such leftovers he lives on. He foams inside. He churns. Tummy grumbles all the time as if some tiny animal has taken refuge there, spastic with fright. Officerly duty, Barney knows, says look after your people, whatever else. Like a Moses with epaulets. That is the law. In that, an F grade. Not for failure, but for friendlessness. Fraud. Fie.

Yet why ever after haunt himself? Belong to the order of perfect beings he might not, but he yearns at least to belong to that order's second or third class. If not as an eagle, then as gull. Crow. Cabbage white. Wasp. No matter so long as winged.

The so-cold universe, from which he delicately takes hints without ever wishing to, goes on enveloping him. Able to accommodate his every thought, his chronic pain, even the in-suck of his imploded heart. There is no other penalty. Remorse is no carcinogen. Guilt has not struck him dumb or blind. He stammers or stutters a fraction, though. No longer quite sees how to shape his mouth to talk or kiss.

On he goes, desking, tapping keys, sometimes using his heel as a high-speed hammer on the dead polish of the floor. Jittery. Athrob. Ready, if he can only find out how, to put his mind in place of the universe. On he goes, from rage to weakened gentleness, then to a more assertive gentleness, a louder prowess, with his fresh image like one newly shaved growing on him daily until he almost believes, shall we say credits, that he has come through unscathed. Mended at last. If ever hurt. He turns into a walking hopper of aviation lore. No end of it. He knows. He says.

He flies all the flights humanity has never flown. From Hell to never-never, from Coventry to Nod. Just for the record. A Leonardo-Daedalus, he imagines all the undesigned and unbuilt planes his maimed imagination can supply. So much so that, as he combines or twists his hands at subtle angles of attack and planes his palms above unthinkably distant hunks of it matters not which planet, he seems master of both archetype and prototype, feeding into his transmuter, as he calls it, the lowdown on the air. In the nights testing himself on far-fetched data while swigging his own brew of bouillon cubes dissolved in coffee black as soot. His cup of bollocks, he says.

Several times on slack days, when Clegg has no charter to fly, the two of them wander to the bench next to the parking lot and watch the traffic coming in. The distant buzz of an engine will do it, or a sudden flurry of talk from the tower. Squinting their eyes, they try to see the white or gray whateveritis sailing into view above the curvature of the earth, flying not level but along an arc that leads to them. Two whitenesses they see are wings. Like pilots on some poop, they stand and wave, hailing the new-come marvel, Booth with sallow envy, Clegg with friendly skepticism.

I'm a stranger to all this, Booth says wanly.

No way, Clegg tells him. Once a pilot, always one.

He's coming in too high.

Chop and drop, Clegg answers. Look how steep he's coming down now. I do a bit of that myself.

Booth stares at him: With passengers?

No, when I'm on my own. Never with passengers.

See how it changes, Booth sighs. It turns from a gray into a whiteness. Funny, how they all of a sudden become real. You never expect them to.

As far as passengers go, Clegg laughs, I carry a paddle with me, and if anybody acts up I tap them with it. Works wonders.

Now, Booth tells him, I know why business has fallen off. You paddle them?

On the contrary, I'm the soul of politeness.

Well, Booth says irrelevantly, I've no soul at all.

What he has instead, he feels, but never says, is something like diffused dawnlight trapped in his head. The mental equivalent of a death rattle. He loves to watch the planes, but his heart does not go out to them as they arrive, all waft and freight, slowing and tilting back, touching down and heaving slightly forward as they slow. He wants a new life, even if he has to crouch on a wing to get it, and clutch with all his might not to be blown away.

Clegg plants a palm on his shoulder, telling him to stay. Clegg has to go. Booth watches him limp away, wishing he too were as whole a man as Clegg, as able to josh and touch. He walks right at a group of birds, scattering them, and walking abruptly at them where they settle next. Today he is willing to be nothing grander than a pesterer of birds. He is as much at home as an Inuit on the bank of the Ganges.

Earlier mental standbys from Table Mountain to the constellation Centaurus, from Trotsky to the ruddy-faced role model General Cyrus W. Shumaker, give way to uplift images of great aces from the history of flight. Billy Bishop. Cobber Cain. Paddy Finucaine. Dean Hess. Richard Hillary. Biggles and the Baron. Senior partner of this little airline, this little line in air, with that nemesis his friend hugged tight against his heart, he sometimes thinks that what they share is too routine to be endured.

Eff Bee Oh, he murmurs, for FBO. Fixed Base Operator in the trade. The very name evokes immoveability, in the teeth of impermanence. But also something underhand and unworthy. The word *operator* hurts. Operators big time or like him small are bad. Except for wireless operators, quaint term from an early war. And when the term means driver of some vehicle, yes, as applied in certain states, not of the heart, by Jiminy, but of the Union, not, by Jehoshaphat, between man and woman, man and man, woman and woman, man and beast, woman and beast, beast and angel, angel and the implacable tender deity. His mind overshoots constantly and he does not correct.

Fixed base also stands for the pilot who no longer flies. Grounded after a series of escapades, he takes pride in being cussed. Or accursed. The words have fused. Has twice taken off and landed with towbar fast to nosewheel. Has once begun to taxi with one wing tied down. Repeatedly mistuned his radios when feeling bloody-minded. And, on too many occasions, taxied across runways in use, just to get a cup of bollocks on the airport's other side. Using airplane as rickshaw, airport as street. Has also deliberately landed on runways not in use, and in the deepest grass. Taxied from the nearby highway across a parking lot and buzzed his engine at a Snowi-Cone, demanding mint pistachio, sugar cone, jumbo, above scything roar of propeller. Thus Barney Booth Esquire, [hardly at home on his home planet,] but a genius of air otherwise bound to buy the farm. A menace known. But as a menace in agony, which blurts and pips like Morse through his garbled heart, the least known of men.

Quiet the eagle that nibbles him yonder.

Quiet the Rupert who watches him slink beyond the pale.

Quiet the khaki screen in which Booth sees his face.

As fixed as geology, he runs the the office as its officer while Clegg and some juniors, such as the brash Lammergeyer, cocksman and health fanatic, fly the charters. Odd sound of the word *charter*, to Booth at least. If not of Magna Carta a surly echo, then of early navigators heaving up on the mouth of the Hudson. In their vessels heaving. Heaving to. As in Hove. Yes, that was epic, indelibly so. Crowns. Garlands. Cheers. Titles. Ordinary men dubbed knights. Or was that in the Indies after all? He wonders who he has been in other lives. With so many leftover cravings for glory, cloaks, his name writ in fire while they bury him in floaty petals. Only he knows, he does not tell, what over the years has arrived in crates and been sequestered in locked hangars, or in the whitewashed-windowed rooms above the Eff Bee Oh. Or what has been flown in after the control tower shuts down at five in the evening, the hour of the lifting of the arm. And vanished from human ken. Heads from beheadings? Foreskins from ancient wars? Dynamite disguised as walking sticks? Working models of his conscience made in bronze or teak, oiled with blood of Christian lambs? Oh no. He buys up model trains.

Daily he redesigns the plane of planes against the day it will be perfect. Predatory. Sleek. Faster than the rotating Sun. Heavy as neutron starstuff. And murder to fly.

Whenever he changes position, or relaxes, at his transmuter, murmuring about subroutines and arrays, or mouths utopian runes about the first job to do after entering a character (turn the next character on the screen, he whispers, into an inverse video version of itself), he lifts right hand, tautens palm to convex, cants up thumb, and cruises or sails the streamline of his hand against the icefield of the wall, each millimeter of motion, as his pulse taps in his wrist, the equivalent of a thousand miles. Sighting above his knuckles at some invisible horizon knobbly with penguins, he lowers the tip of his middle finger only its nail's width and banks the hand slightly, half murmuring Ho Boy or Boyo, until the second and third fingers topple down, an undercarriage, and the airplane of his hand droops toward a landing nowhere on the stairs, coming nearer and nearer his face until, massive as a starship hotfoot from [Proxima Centauri,] one of his favorites, it blurs, closes the view, and drifts forward again.

Up flicks the finger gear. Then the middle finger drops only to rise at once, and the rest of the hand seals around it, an arrowhead if you permit that image forming while the thumb still cantilevers out, strained to the utmost.

He has no name for this bird in hand, but is always maneuvering it against acres of flabbergasting ivory light, planning angles of descent or bank, turn or tilt, and trying to accomplish ever faster that last downflick of the middle finger, after which the hand re-forms like a horizontal para-sol snapping shut.

Who'd not warm to that? To someone unused to watching him at work or rest, even rummaging through those hidden crates upstairs or in the locked hangars, he seems to be trying in vain to salute or to wave good-bye to someone direly far away. A tic, this, a mannerism, it wins him the repu-tation of playing blind man's buff all by himself, all the more so when he brings his thumb right up to his eye and traces the hand's gyration with his head touching it.

Grinding a small engine between his teeth, with a tiny crescendo com-ing down his nose, he zooms and wheels below the dewline of the win-dowsill, a chump of parallax, a slave of slow incessant motion. Then, land-ho, the world outside lumbers back into view like a moon's rump above the nacelles of his knuckles and the ordinary world goes giddy-up again.

Several times an hour he does this, and when they cry Barney, hey, Bar-ney, hey there, Barney Booth! he invites them aboard what he calls the spaceship of pain, fresh in from [the Rhesus Condor Rift,] via the Coal-sack Solomons, his only cargo something so bad that no phonetic system can hold it. So he says. The harsh quotient of everything. Frosty rather than toasty. We are the afterbirth of a cosmic abortion that almost took. Panspermed here by one more compassionate than us. His face dithers as always at that line. They watch entranced as the grown man plays imp, fool, clown, Judas among the nincompoops.

Then he is quite explicitly saying something else, about a cursor, in which word they think there is an *e*. He excuses himself, telling them it is time to store. They go away, regaled but snubbed, even Clegg, that most mystified of men, in whom the milk of human kindness has burned away to a crisp for reasons unknown. Just, Clegg broods, as if we were still out there in Africa. BB has never gotten over it.

Only sometimes Booth has. He knows they are already filing aboard, settling into horizontal seats behind his goggled eyes. Those who don't know where they are, he chants, are more than eager to go far. Riffling through magazines and sucking mints, they are his passengers in the strict sense of not earning their keep on his team. Before the short-field takeoff, in a cross old wind, he shuts the turbines down. Mere will will ferry them all the way to the Category Three System where tulip bulbs of light in rows fifteen parsecs long grow weary of being bright. His eyes feel full, so prickly that he has to cough to free the tear ducts. He shuts down his trans-muter for the day. Says I forget the address of the first byte. Knows what the one product of his transmuter is. Ends in um. Let them dub him dare-devil, barnstormer, flying fool, a menace to all mankind. He'll one day show them such a time that each of them will need to write a dozen auto-biographies, in mercury on slate, even to convey a glimmer of that sinusoidal ride. Look, folks, no hands. Things to come are upon him. Raw slipstream gnaws his face.

Why did memory boost itself so much? Why did something remembered loom ever bigger for having been brought back? Sweet in the gorgeous forenoon, were they two once upon a time together? Heart all balm, he answers: Were we ever! Him the pulp, I the rind. When last in evidence. In mind's eye an apple, in mind's apple a worm. I once was navy blue. He begins to quiver, a fraught aspen. Correct a hand if it outstretch o'er a poorly bird. Eye white. Face charred, Loins flayed. All the usual honors.

If time may be paged. No. If time may be read. And thus paged. This is more like it, Barney Booth. Book of life back and forth, as if to say I am not reading, nothing so ambitious. Just dipping, dipping. To and fro. Up to work and so to bed. Up at dusk and down at dawn. Now there's a program, felt in the heart as a power-on stall. Hip-hip. I'm waiting. Hip.

You won't. I wouldn't either. Not required except of dunderheads. Required only in the down and out. Aren't there any out and down?

Booth's eyes hurt from gazing at the storm screens. When he looks away, the colors of the indoor world look wrong. When he looks back, the colors are harsh, they have no glow. Worse, he seems to see through things, and knowing there is a technical explanation for this doesn't help. He raises his hand against the overhead light. It casts no shadow on the desk. He can see the tube full of white light beyond his arm. He feels ready to climb the wall, questing, thirsting, for something forever beyond reach. Here comes Clegg with a weather report, but Booth sees the door behind his trunk, and the slight gap in Clegg's left eyebrow extends right through his skull, behind it only a smidgen of door.

The light's all wrong, Booth says. I'm seeing round and through things.

Eye fatigue, says the practical Clegg. You need some sleep.

Or a green eyeshade?

What did you say? Clegg asks again. What?

I was just remembering, Booth whispers, what I said when we were in the desert: You people there can help us much. I said that into the microphone.

They could. They did. From such flukes are miracles made. All for this. It was the same in Africa as here. Your eyes got so fouled up, you couldn't see straight.

Clegg has gone, urgent about his business, thinking that Booth sometimes couldn't get to first base in a first-base factory. Humming an Italian song he's heard on TV, he heads for the hangars, bemusing them all with his workaday cheerfulness as he does his ditty: At Benevento by the bridge-head. A war song, he thinks, from the time of Mussolini. But, just perhaps, from World War One, when there was fighting in the Alps. Then he comes back, smacking his forehead for forgetfulness, and calls his mother, pins down the weather, the cramp in her leg, how long it has been since he visited her, and then resumes his airward walk. No longer humming.

Booth rubs his eyes, applies spit, which dries into a crust. Salt. Like his first glimpse of the salt flats, where he landed. Then as now less part of his fate than watching it happen to another usurping his own face, about whom he does not care.

One last time have that old minute. Even if only the shade of it like a fish-scale wanning thunder light. Have. Half have. Have not. Runner recoil-ing from go, get set, get ready, unlimbering into the past as the crack of the gun travels back down the barrel into the blank.

He tries again to get this interior thing said so as to close the frequency down for ever after. To remember it exactly right must be to make it go away for keeps.

Now it comes. Hi, Bald Eagle. Hi, Clipper. Come on in, we'll take care of you. Soppy switchback, hear this prang. No, that was another time.

He tries again to get it back, and glaze it like an apricot. Than which, he huffs and puffs, under the sun by tolerant moonlight nothing less than a pearl contains the oyster. Was that a prayer? Lordloveus for such an inside out. Here a touch. There. Touched all right. All Africa my domain. Our help in rages past.

Now, here it comes, thistledown amid the rumpus. He has to hold on tight.

I can see above us. Copy. The stars are shining. Out of ten for eleven. Cleared for base and final. Squawk ident. Say again. We are not quite sure, ah, who we are. Descend and maintain. Copy. Brah-voh Brah-voh is with you, Zulu Tower. Do you read? At this point we genuinely care. Please keep talking to me, I need it. Ah, affirmative. We're going in.

Comes a high-pitched whistle, just possibly one of exclamation.

Oh, that's wonderful. I'm in a kind of little pocket here. Just a bunch of spit and fluff. Thattaway. Gotta let down. Yes, sir. Hold on a second. It's. Remain this frequency, sir. Yeah. There's too much over. Negative on that. No further contact. Do you read? Bravo? It's. Negative on that. Buga-booth over. But not everything else. Only his voice ended.

Then he is not at the desk anymore. Find him in the john, taken short. Or, hunched in three or four black greatcoats, coast guard castoffs, lurking behind a hangar, eyeing the runway as if it leads upward to some crock of gold. Shivering, whatever the weather. Worrying about his bank of screens, already being tampered with, unplugged. It is his life-support system. Holds him up, a scaffold of visual clues. So he is often to be caught scurrying back, his tallness somehow folded over. Fly unzipped. All those greatcoats badly arrayed around him. Eight sleeves, but only one with an arm in it. Four fronts with buttons and eyeholes, but these mis-combined from coat to coat. He storms ahead within his bundle of felt. His hands grapnel forward to his chair. Wheel it away from the desk as if it weighs a ton. Then he slides it gradually toward the twinkling screens, whose greens, yellows, reds, flutter and shimmer as if falling loose from the pattern in a Persian rug rippled in the wind. *His* image, that. I am always a soft touch, he scoffs, for any palatable image.

Otherwise he soothes his mind with how life, a flight plan of sorts, amounts to a series of way-points. In the flight plan you select them, in life not. Unchosen, then. Result of flukes and greasy happenstance. He knows how he was in the instant of being saved, never again to mine red salt for his raptors.

What a way to go, he says, in that muddled ecstasy. The way untaken. I lost my way and it has found me again. From hell to hospital direct. No in-betweens. Gentlemen, he tells them again and again, even years later, through ragged lips, between one way-point and another there is an infinite number of. He weeps a gasp. Unknown halfway houses. How he looks he learns from their gazes. Eyes almost sealed with rime ice that is salt. Nose split and swollen from a punch, a dunt, from some stave. Teeth the color of walnut shell. Hair white with pain and sun's bleaching plus salt scurf. Gulping air rather than breathing. Heart in its cage bumping about like a baby rabbit. Scabby. Scraped. A stench of swamp coming off him. And they still have not found Clegg, his buddy, marooned in the hills.

Now he glows again, back at his desk. He cannot pick up this bed of roses and walk. The colors feed him. Tiny crackles of static discharge give him tiny thunder cells to soldier through. Now he coos, on the verge of merriment. Once again he has trundled to the john. Then back. Or viewed the forbidden runway, ill-buttoned-up in coastguard black. He hates the sea, but not its coastline's coats.

Into a microphone whose other end has no one in tow he cautions someone. Yeah, well, sir, the thing is, we don't want to go by generally. We want to be, ah, precise. Is he on the edge of your scope? Ah, he's oh-five-oh, headed for Chemung Forest. Yeah, the vortac there. Yeah, Alameda, wait a minute, here comes something. Just in sight. I wasn't painting a dad-gum thing out there. Here he is now. They have let him go. Can I hear cheering? Well, let's hear it for him, then. He was dropping fast, Alameda. Can he reach the hills and land on top? Generally, no. But this one time.

He wilts, trembling. It is where he has been, a zone of air with no place name. All air's the same. Not so. All air's different. Some of it's as different from some air as terra firma is. He begins a devout-sounding murmur.

His shoulders lower. Head poises as if to butt the lowest screen, which paints the slewed St. Andrew's cross of two intersecting runways. Now his hands fly, tapping buttons that say shrunken imperatives. To him or the machines? He wonders. Stby for stand by. Cyc for cycle. But stab for stab. Hitting Wx for weather, he gets weather, red at the core, leaf yellow and grass green strewn around it like tumbling crocuses. His image again. He jeers. He stabs. An almost vertical green line points to a faint diamond that might be a star, but only, says the screen, three thousand feet high. A small star, then. A baby sparkler. Not so. It is merely another way-point. Fed in. Spat out at the stab. Now he goes to target alert, shakes his head viciously, though a tear forms. Then hits Frz for freeze. Nothing stirs, least of all the yellow F button he's depressed.

Now what? He has gone to scan. Slowly the entire landscape of [some planet or other] crawls across the screen, sketchily presented, daubed with storms. He looks for somewhere with no weather. No such place has yet been born.

Then as ever he and Clegg are twin airplanes hurtling through the same storm. Ships passing by night, with voices oddly shrunken by distance and lightning.

BB: Bravo Bravo level at two zero. That you, Romeo Charlie?

RC: I have you good and sharp. Out of one niner for one five.

BB: Romeo Charlie, okay, I'll take lower too.

RC: Okay, sir, descend and maintain. Romeo Charlie.

BB: I can just barely hold it here. I got some kinda silver thaw out there, like small sharp animals popping holes in the metal, ah, I wouldn't recommend it. Each one has kind of lots of paws. Bravo Bravo.

RC: Say again, Bravo Bravo. Romeo Charlie is with you and, ah, he sees nothing of the kind. You okay? Bravo Bravo, did you copy?

BB: Bravo copy. We'll just keep on coming in.

RC: Romeo Charlie. Looking. Heavy what did you say? I did not get what it is that's heavy, sir.

No, they never flew that flight together, or apart. It is the flight from truth, fancy, and all other enchanters. Booth actually hopes not to collide with Clegg on the ground. Two men together, at one in their work. One innocent, one the fiend of his mind's eye, yearning to tell yet dreading the aftermath.

So time's points pile up. The one man cannot hear what the other does not say, but wonders at his scowls, his grunts, his spastic half salutes, then gets on with his work, leaving that other at his desk, who wonders why the sky does not fall. The burn in his heart is harsher than a sun.

If and when he gets right down to it, spells it out raw: *My friend, I gave your life away even though it was not in my gift,* it will come out sketchy, shortened, every bit as formally urgent as the lingua franca that streams above them in the waves of air, up where the vectors are called Victor.

You know who, he'll say. Romeo Charlie, I am with you. You-know-who is with you at last. Out of pain for truth. Just a bunch of fluff and spit. I can start you down any time. It is going to hurt us both more than either of us. Copy? Sorry, I need higher. Moderate icing. Real snowman here has, ah, missed approach again. We'll go right on to—

Where, he does not say. It is never there. In his mind, in spite of all the screens, he crashes repeatedly some 120 feet short of the threshold and continues up the embankment onto the sod-overrun area. He always has three eighths of an inch of ice on his leading edges, and lesser amounts clinging elsewhere, mostly to vowels and consonants he will not use again.

How the screens hide. He sees that at last. His face yet again in reflection grins that wry pout, as if heaving closemouthed. Can he be alive? A twitch blurs him, then he settles down. A blink wipes him out, but not for long. One lax lip is a little puffy, not from scrimmage but from being gnawed. Then he smiles, the insane replica of the field of the cloth of gold, but sucked dry by the snowberg of the rest of him. Only the hand, half halting and wholly crystalline by now, signs a benediction over the screens, pauses, weightless with light pouring through it, and braces itself, ready to hold.

Then has to be content with living in the present, able on days of severest blue to murmur his little call, *Cavu, cavu,* as if begging the screens for seed. Over his head white vultures are gathering, he knows it from how they interrupt the sun's light. He wafts them away with an idle wave, but they are willing to wait, touring around up there. Banking, canting, all lazy spirals. Not vultures, he knows, but chubby-bodied little white speedsters with long sharply upcanted wings. The fin seems to swoop forward as if to outstrip the body and the wings. Eager to be there, wherever there is. At his throat. Deep into his liver. Each one's nose is a probing dome, and there is nothing but air between them and him.

They are in his mind, it's obvious, but they will fly out of his mind when they attack. Ten or eleven four-seater monoplanes with slant sprig aerials perched on their backs. Gross exhaust pipe under the nose. Big lamp in the nose blinding him. His hand goes up to ward them off, to push back their buzz. *Cavu*, he cries, knowing his call is no call but flying slang. Ceiling And Visibility Unlimited. It might be more profound. Other calls are of mallards, eagles, loons. Never mind. He claps his hands, whether to rejoice or wake himself up he does not know. When will they descend, out of the mind, to break through the cushion of air about his body? Only under the desks will he feel safe, or shrunken and tucked in a drawer. His flesh crawls, to or fro. It gets nowhere. His eyes tear but do not spill. He hears his voice, again attempting the call as if he were stranded in a marsh, yes, or on a promontory scabbed with cactus. Walking a plank of thorns. Then he shrugs, does a tuneless whistle, cups the back of his neck with one hand and kneads the muscle, freeing his head to move forward again toward the screens.

A hippopotamus in winter, he murmurs. I am that ungainly. Those are vultures I have flown. I have steered those vultures with these hands, these feet. Landing, they can float all the way down the runway. They love the air. In flight, the panel in front of you buzzes nonstop, something between a fizz and a death rattle. In the older models, the fuel lever was on the left-hand floor, an awkward and almost lethal site. But now it's in between the pilots who can sometimes hold hands over it by friendly accident. Stiff ailerons. Map light mounted in the yoke, too close to the lap. Too much tweaking of the throttle needed. A vernier screw would have been better. He knew his way around these vultures, even in the dark. Their mediocre turning radius made him think of plows. Cost an arm and a leg, and then the other arm, the other leg, but if streamlining's what you want, they have that, massively smoothed out to oblige the two-hundred-knot wind they float in. Brisk. Impatient. Snouty. Bred from the fighter planes of old, but pretty-striped black, red, on bone-ash white. Their sound like that of the hammers of hell. Their smell shoe-leathery from the upholstered seats, but now and then, when up on high, tinged with the acid tang of ozone. Oh yes, it is one of his mothballed dreams, a dream of fair to middling Mooneys, Irish, he thinks. They come and go, but mostly they circle and hover, awaiting his summons.

Whose the fault, then? He could be there right now, cleaving the sky with the others as company. [A white flash among tin swallows.] Riding a moderate chop. Levelling the wings with an almost delirious flick left, then right. Left buttock, then the right. An overtone of sex from the long-lost planet of the flesh. High enough to need oxygen. Whisper and purr of that [like an alien] invading his nose and throat.

Now his right hand half forms the fuselage and wing, aiming beyond the weather. His eye sights from behind the canted thumb, cross-country from Van Nuys to San Francisco. Any imaginable journey will do, so long as it gets him out of here. And whatever he says like some of the planes is retractable. He means the wheels. Sleek shine. He prays to that. The streaming wind invisibly hugging the metal. He gloms on to that. Dusk-landing, with the graphite-blue mountains behind him as he turns at the first taxiway, nose light blazing as if someone were sitting reading a book in the gloom under the whirling spinner. Lunging waddle forward at almost no miles per hour. The runway already violet behind him within its cordon of Christmas lights. The broad polished snout nodding its way to the tie-down point, horse to its trough. Hiss and creak. The whole plane flexes in a parody of givingness, which is why it does not come apart aloft. His dim smile grazes the small screen of the weatherscout radar. No storms tonight. Severe clear. No yellow, no red, no green. The only colors are in the tiny legend grafted on like a medal ribbon at the bottom left-hand corner of the screen. Home free, he murmurs to the stained-glass optics of the dials. Chugging slow as slow can be, he parks and closes down, turns off the master as if saying good-bye to a cathedral.

And he feels his heart go through one of its microbursts. A little wind has blown through it and gone. It is when his heart begins to slow, after the adrenaline ride. Almost a touchdown within the aorta. He thinks like that. In the old days, when he flew, he sometimes envisioned his heart alone in the plane, afloat above the seat, pumping in the midst of zoom, almost as if nothing unusual were going on around it, its blood going faster forward than in going round. *Cavu* he says again in the language of yearning.

There is potash in his eyes. It could be gruel. Vinegar. Silt. Black Minnesota snow a winter old. All that peering has made them bloodshot. Unplugs his headset. Unstraps himself. Unplugs the key. He has been where you increasingly become unfit to go back down. Stock-still on the ground he is still moving at his recent speed. He can talk only to those who answer with *cavu? Hello* would not be much to ask of him, but he does not have it yet, not so much dazed by the vermilion splendor of the sun setting underneath him as by its indifference to his awe. He has peeped. Drawn a mighty, muddled breath, and let it out in praise. He'd like to [fly the local star.]

Here he comes, a balsawood Columbus, half reeling in his walk from his load of charts, radio gear, four heavy reference books the size of *Who's Who* in the larger countries, and the briefcase that holds the travel toothbrush, the paste, the paisley-pattern pajamas, the earplugs, the black satin sleep mask, the filched bobby pins he uses to seal the drapes with in hotels.

He feels left over from the air. Something extruded by a brilliant process he hears rumors of. Back to earth does not cover it. He only feels deprived of the air. He does not so much come down as fly very slow on his feet, yes on the balls of them, castoring rather bumpy until he takes off again. And then it is all right. Each time he goes it is as if, to him, he travels at the speed of light, or failing that of darkness, and his tribe ages vastly while he is gone. So off he takes, a mere boy to them, and outstrips aging with an elixir peculiar to him. The physics is faulty, but his gut obeisance saves his mind through glutted love of speed.

Now he snoozes in front of the test pattern or the weather channel that pours symphonic music through the night. All composers one to him, all symphonies the same. Sleep is that interval of velvet restlessness in which he craves the winds aloft while, in the bright-lit atrium behind the venetians that flank his bed, poinsettias waste their color on dry vacancy. He half sleeps. He roams, tunnels, eggs on his dreams while the TV screen glows all night, a cathode mother giving him the nod.

Outside he counts the trees. Thirty-seven. Eight. Nine. He starts again, he has to have it right even though he has not noticed the weather for years. Only the weather on the screens interests him. Weather as telemetry and tints, not as what he walks out into. The count is thirty-eight as ever once he gets it right.

Now, quivering, he hails Clegg who bears a bag of groceries. Odds and ends, he explains. Call me Rupe not Clegg. Booth is only too glad. He has no idea how to begin this umpteenth beginning. He says the word *Africa*. *Back then*. Ho boy! They laugh. Again Booth tries. Points at the trees. Same number as before, he says. A glitch, Booth says, at his boldest. It was something that went wrong. Kind of a skid. Clegg nods affably. You sure remember it, you sure do. For me it's kind of fading. Some things haunt you when you hold on to them. Otherwise, no. Clegg grins. Some tribe in that same goddamned Africa. Don't count what they don't touch. I mean they'd have to touch each tree in turn if they was you.

Booth feels stuck in clay. You ever been disloyal, Rupe? Sure, what the fuck. Booth advances like a frozen sleepwalker, thinking the first syllable of what he has to say has come into view. Me too. Yeah, really bad. What you never never do, the no of nos. Why, back there in Africa. Clegg stops him with an old expression of his. You sure talk a lot about Africa these days. Is this spring, Booth asks. The end of November, he hears. If Clegg had felled him with the jawbone of an ass he would have talked back sooner. Instead he dwindles to a halt, one hand on Clegg's shoulder while the other arm embraces the eggs, the muffins, the wrapped-up roll of toilet paper, the bottle of seltzer water. He has heard the piled-up wave front of the moment screech toward him and now it decreases mildly away. Wasted. Low-pitched and lost.

What then? Talk with his fingers. Draw in the dirt with a stick? Booth has no idea, but blurts out the one word to do duty for all. *Callous.* The world is full of that Clegg answers and begins to move away, saying something about an oil leak in the Apache. Booth's mind fills with Mooneys.

Soaring and circling like gulls inland on a stormy day. He tells him. Clegg allows as how the FBO has no Mooneys at all. We deal in cheaper planes. These days. Since, well, hell, it was like the Crash of 1930. Ho boy. But as far back for me as George Washington. You got to be un-Africa-ed, Booth, saying the surname with the same casual intimacy as if he's said Barney. And now it is just terse exchanges. The moment has long gone over the lip of the horizon.

Trees, Rupe.

Damn all trees.

It turns into an old flight, their lingo into cockpit talk.

Clear?

Clear, the other laughs.

Have the ball in sight.

Now Clegg is the landing signal officer. Roger ball, Prowler, twenty-eight knots, slightly axial. Don't go high.

Roger, says Booth.

Catch it nice and easy. Catch it now. *Power!*

I went in, Booth says. I ploughed into all them men and planes. Made the wrong play for the deck. I hate the sea.

The desert too, says Clegg, shifting his groceries and privately wondering if what he hears in his head is Sing Sing Sing or Swing Swing Swing. Both by the Benny Goodman orchestra.

Sing Sing, he says and Booth hears.

You gonna send me to jail, Rupe? For a mushy carrier landing in the dark from behind the trees with no power and no and the Bingo field too far away.

No, sir. Nossir. Clegg has had enough. Their lives are full of these marcescent conversations. When what is withered just does not fall off, for unknown reasons.

One day a snowflake landing on Booth's tongue will make him out with it. He'll flinch and blab. He will have said and the other will laugh the whole thing off. Clegg lives on in order to forget while Booth survives a crescendo of remembering in order to get it out of his system once. And for all time. If ever. A shot in the arm might do it, from a forty-five. A jab in the ribs. He is trying to accost a mirage. It does not heed him. It shuntles. Above it the white vultures each with the strength of two hundred horses. Or 210 depending on the model. In his time Booth has flown more types of planes both better and more badly than any pilot in the history of flight. Gourmandizing gourmet. Thinking about one while flying another. Thinking ahead and behind, so he is always flying something not in his hands at any given moment. It might be a definition of immortality in that even when his hands are empty he will be flying the plane of his heart's desire. The one beyond the one beyond the one at hand. Ghostly Booth arranges himself between any pair of vacant wings and steers to his grail. Tongue-tied. Treebound. Breathless at last.

There comes to him now the shiny black Mooney of death, arrayed with scarlet eagle emblems and a thin crimson stripe along the body. Where the face should be at the window only a pelvic bone gaping out. The plane gleams like a wet galosh. Shrinking, it soars in close and enters his nose. No buzz. No float. Not even a slight itch. Deep in a sinus it beds down for the night while, mentally, he rehearses the laws to fly it by. Visibility five miles. Distance from clouds one mile horizontal and a thousand feet above, below. No chance of a disaster in any kind of airspace. He has become the angel of common sense.

So beautiful, he says. Their number is on their tail. All the way to the tiptop of heaven a column of them diminishes with perspective, every cranny in each plugged as if they are already among the dead and have been laid out upward.

Why then such weakness? The word was almost out. Clegg waited for it with his groceries. Any other Booth would have been out with it. *I let you down.* But he sees how Clegg will never believe it anyway, mustering all the convenient phrases from Ho boy to bygones be bygones.

Whenever he leans forward to tell, his shoulder harness holds him back. He cannot rub his face in it. He locks his fingers into one fist. In a trice opens them up to make the steeple and all the people. Blows into his cupped hands to warm them. Toots as into a conch to warn of a strange boat approaching the island. He tries again. Calls after Clegg's long-gone bicycle the one word *November*, phonetic for the N prefix to all the numbers of all planes. No, he has no voice. Just a strand of slime where his voice should be. He blinks Morse but cannot be seen there in the dark in his miscombined overcoats with an anchor on each black button. So he goes back to his screens in search of appalling weather from somewhere in the world. The screens teem with lines.

Everyone else has gone home. Booth hears the slop and creak of imaginary weather on the roof. It snows and rains and blisters and bleaches all at once. He hears the lion grass rattle. The ice pack bangs its gun. Desert sand filters from roof to ceiling. Flames patter against the window glass. He is in his element now. Only to harass himself all over again. He tips a bowl of soup from the machine outside. Snaps two crackers and mouths the flakes. Opens up a chocolate bar and eats it look no hands with little snakelike tilts of the head. Evening comes on and with it the furtive joy he feels when the earth faces away from the sun. His part of it. And the lights come on. Electric. Gas. Paraffin. Carbide. Candle. All the way back to King Alfred and beyond. He dreams that all the amalgamated lights of the darkling world stray into his screens. Hence the sudden flares of color in several, which he taps as if asking them to make up their minds. He hates whiteness, the sea, and salt. Such is now the basis of his days. Air having no hue in his joy, but the faint peppery blur of the propeller has always troubled him as being both more than it seems and less than a solid disk. He has never thought the thought through, though, and he resolves to do so in the spring of some upcoming year. Yawning, he prepares a cup of bollocks to aid him in his vigil as the thunderstorms shift and merge before his eyes. This random menagerie of red weather is his alone and it puts him in touch with all the pilots flying at this time, wherever they are. Heathrow, Shannon, O'Hare, Leonardo da Vinci, but also Blue Grass Field, Lexington, Kentucky, and Cape May County, Wildwood, New Jersey, and Patrick Henry Field, Newport News, Virginia, and Chess Lamberton Field, Franklin, Pennsylvania. But not those only, not only terminals and terminations, but intersecting ocean vectors called Haddock and Plaice and Tuna, and equally invisible points on the approach, such as Heidi, Dresser, and Norway. Bravo Bravo is with you, he whispers into his nightbound terminals. You will never lose him. He will hold your hand even when his hands are cold. I am the undone yearning for the right to do. I am the sunken ship churning about below to attract the attention of salvage vessels. I am the fallen sparrow asking for bed and board until my wing mends. I am the eternal copilot, cap in hand.

He can be heard and spurned in the same breath. But in all these mental forays among those airborne he never once mentions his last line of self-defense, his vehicles of last resort. The model train sets in boxes upstairs and in the unused hangar. Cached against a rainy day in the country of the soul.

Now munching walnuts from a can, he croons the first of his after-hours tunes. Slow and iambic like a badly uttered lullaby it rocks him slightly in front of the screens, which makes the weather move ever so little considering how big it is, how small the colored blotches. Its paw prints.

Blinds closed. Doors locked. He unplugs the phone. He will soon be adrift, capable of sleep in the chair. He licks a hive forming on his wrist. Shoves off his shoes and mates the soles of his feet, the heel of one in the arch of the other. Now the room is dark save for the screens and he plans on not moving again for a couple of hours, when nature will force him. Until then he sails his gaze among the pageant of storms brought in by relay from more than three hundred miles away. The local weather is good, alas for him. His chair creaks and grates. Gently he nods. Off. Tries again. It works.

Waking slurred three hours later, he sees all colors as magenta. Flying through heavy weather not on the screens, he needs lower, he tells them. Or another vector. You got me right in a cell, sir. I'll go anywhere you say. What the controller says next is unintelligible. Vectors around the hole, he pleads. The Trock intersection, sir.

Then, pausing, faltering, humming and hawing, as if to stabilize itself, the other voice comes through again: That's affirmative, uh, you might have to, uh, go around this at your—off your left-hand side, then find a hole that's, uh—I got another aircraft descending through, then go up, uh, it's going to be hard, sir.

Yes, Booth answers, we had a good ride through that other one, we had a descent of four thousand feet a minute. Kind of covered in meteor dust. We're embedded, sir, Bravo Bravo is embedded. We are getting it now, again. It's all tumbling. I can't hold it. We have no up remaining.

Now he seems to hear, as he twirls, the other voice almost stammer: A guy gotta, uh, I got a guy go down abeam, uh, Rapen, I just had a guy go down about abeam of Rapen. Severe weather, so keep them all away from there. On the far side of all that rain. Yeah.

All he sees of that rain is mineshaft lumps amid white thunderheads.

Mouth acid, he is sure he has midaired with something plane or bird. The speed goes from normal to nothing and back, twice in ten seconds. He rides a yo-yo while his blood continues to pool. Silex intersection, he hears. How does he hear? He can hear nothing but weather. There are tigers all around him as he swoops and sinks. He wants vectors for spacing. Get some crossfeeds open. Showing a thousand or better. Get this [deleted] on the ground now. No, we'll get that [deleted] warning thing if we do. Boy, that fuel, his mind says, sure went to hell all of a sudden. Have a good one. Two sets of three clicks. Like advisories, please. Like to start on coming down home. Easy baby, easy baby. Whoo! Deleted. Deleted. Bob? Brace yourself. Hey, baby. Unintelligible. Ma, I love ya.

He does not even move. Asleep again, he has buried the waking dream in the slept nightmare. It is all almost the same to him. To or fro. He is the imaginative one. Clegg dreams of no disasters, but Booth's head is a Roman arena of botched lives, crashed planes, and weather so violent he looks for its volcano. To get through or by while awake he mutters an old motto filched from another air force: *nil nisi carborundum,* fake Latin for don't let the bastards grind you down. Or the weather dump you in the trash.

Sometimes, awake, when his socks have been the color of the floor, he has looked down and seen a gap between his pants bottoms and his shoes. A vacancy without ankles. To anything such he would agree if only the weather would quit his dreams, his days. Weather to him means anything that goes wrong. He has few metaphors, but this is one. It wilts. Sometimes he is all hurt. Bottled up. Wanting to vent his all.

I'm coming to, he says. Your transmitter is very weak and unreadable, he hears. If you're inbound. No, he says, I am nothing but inbound. Key your mike twice, he hears. Breaking up and unreadable. Roger, I'll be looking for you east of the field. Really heavy now, he says in hope. Showers like Niagara.

Am going to try for shoot it. Any price. Even if unintelligible. How do you read? I'm a round robin, homeward bound through deluge rain and, ah, thunderheads like stands of timber split with, ah, there went another one. The tiger blinded me, sir, I cannot see. Vectors, please.

Vectors right around a desk overloaded with weather. He wakes again, wipes away rime ice or tears, blows his nose on rough paper to hand, not even crinkling it up to break the fibers. There is no remedy for morning, he knows that. It has its way with you. Nameless, overbearing, tinted. Tell Clegg on the morrow. A job a day keeps disillusion away. Try to tell him. How many now? Seven hundred tries for not a single success? That many or worse. In the men's room. In the hangar. On phone. At door. On the town. Smashed. Hungover. Stuffed tight. Starving. In summer. Other seasons. This being November, then what about it? He stammers, does not have to answer, rescinds everything, and almost reaches forward to switch off the screens, kill the butterflies. A new color, magenta. Where did that come from? New form of worst? It must be that. He groans a smothered bark. Now he smells bacon and eggs frying. Clegg is bringing him breakfast, but it is only the screens heating up, not bacon and eggs at all but plastic and steel.

Then he sees the Earth in its entirety, as if trapped in an indiscretion, whirling around at over a thousand miles an hour. Rim speed, he thinks. We can fly faster, outstrip the old mother. You could always be someplace before she gets there without you. Peering in the gloom at his hands, which others have read, he wonders at the so-called lines of the surgeon, the healer, wondering what went wrong. The old and the young are alike, he decides, except the old make more apologies. No such thing as fate. There is only what happened and what got deleted.

Half lifting a hand to phone Clegg asleep in his king or queen, he lets the hand droop back to desk surface. Dawn there in ruddy splinters. He can wait. It will be this November day or it will not be ever. He catches himself. It is not November yet. But all months are November to him. All time is Zulu Time. There is no now. There was no then. He dreams feverishly, which is to say he invites a white-hot yearning to lay him waste. Up he stands to pat the faces of the screens. They purr and flicker. One leg is numb from the sit. Stamps it hard, on top of something sharp. Curses. Resumes previous stance of dazed man at window allowing local star to bathe him in surplus light. Feels warmed, encases his own face in the ground effect of his hands. A warm layer. He has used another night to death. As a night waster he rates high. Has undone thousands. Ever since the thing deleted. At the window inhaling he sees the back of his altar, the unpretty rumps of his screens.

Someone arrives at the main door, thumps in, gasping, at once fills the coffeepot, butts head in to ask if Booth wants some and Booth answers. If it is coffee they want him to have even while the first motors of the day are whirring he will drink his portion. Admixed with whatever else they think right.

Now, who is that, he wonders, cannot ident the face, the voice. Suddenly tries to take stock of all those in his employ. Comes up with Weick, Windecker, Thorp, Langewische, Downer, Luscombe, with not a face among them for all their names being so familiar. He pays their wages, foots their bills. Who then he storms in his head are the likes of Ryan,

Wassmer, Lake, Varga, and Nord? Or Mooney? It begins to dawn. The famousness of names well known. The knownness of famous names. He has just hired and fired half the best names in aviation. In relief he turns to other names, hardly the ones he wants, but they make a kind of sense: Moa, Emu, Kiwi are three, he can come up with a couple more flightless birds, he knows that. Now it is Edrich, Verity, Gimblett, Lawton, Mortenson, Hagan, dragging on his mind, as unknown to him as waves of the sea. Has he hired and undone so many? He quaffs the coffee in the tankard, to be polite, prefers his cup of midnight bollocks to this dusty-tasting sap of ebony. His head is full of names, but only Clegg's remains, like Waterloo, Sebastopol, Troy.

He goes to take a leak, almost reels and topples light-headed against the waste can. As if tranced. Broken into tiny round skidding balls of himself. He wobble-slithers to the stall and pours his way to peace. Aims that solitary eye up at his face and peers down at it as if it knows all about the ugliness of God.

In his heart he knows now. Blurt it out. Rehearse by saying whatever to all and sundry. Have you measured it, sir? Does it reek of sherry, ma'am? Do you wipe forward? Do you grab or tear it at the perforations? Once safely in jail he could invite Clegg to the condemned cell and tell him there safe in the knowledge that he'd have no chance of afterthoughts. Tell and be done. Then a fizzy end. Strapped in a chair just like a pilot. He wonders why the chair is not a recliner, go out in style and at your ease. Facing ten or twenty of your favorite screens, with a connoisseur's choice of the last weather. That would be style, he murmurs to the top of the porcelain stall. He yearns for extra layers of clothing. To be clad not only in wool and cotton but tree bark, hides, peat, hunks of lawn, parchment, spiderwebs, frogspawn, lint, and an eiderdown of living doves.

Now he flies the puppet plane of his hand in salute to daybreak. Over what scapes it flies he cannot decide. Craters or deserts, it matters little, whereas he always has to have that close-up, pilot's or stowaway's view of swing-wing articulation, the drop and up-pluck of the wheels, and then the slow boring on of the plane into imprecise infinity.

He glows with sunlight as his hand goes through its paces, drawing his whole body after the plane into virgin airspace. Today, perhaps, someone will come to rent a plane and he will demolish them with questions so hard that no one yet has qualified to rent anything. He stings them, stuns them, with questions of appalling technicality. Letter perfect, he tells them. You have to be that at least. And then.

In a stifled bellow he asks them What information does a Convective Sigmet contain? Tornadoes, he tells them gravely, embedded thunderstorms, and hail—what size hail? You don't know? Three quarters of an inch in diameter or more.

Away they go in bemused despair. Only Clegg will let them qualify, and when Clegg is absent no one does. Booth is happy to sell fuel to the two airlines whose jets arrive here daily and depart, but his own planes are his toys, his mementoes, as if set gently on some gigantic invisible piano that is the FBO. Something no longer available to him, they remain part of his empire. Like Clegg, cherished as only someone you have betrayed can be. Gone the Booth who backslapped. Come the Booth of laconic reserve. Gone their joint dreams of military grandeur. Come their spell of servitude. Gone the glory, come the daily grind. The Booth of old when talking was clipped and terse, and he liked to imagine people saying those words: *clipped* and *terse*. His English was every bit as abrupt and encoded as that of the air traffic controllers, whom an outsider can understand only if knowing what to expect. Now his head swarms with two idioms, the taut civilian one and the more relaxed military one from which he culls, for everyday use, Roger, Roger-Dodger, Wilco, Copy, Over and Out, almost as if evoking some invisible emergency. He belongs with the revulsed deep-sea diver who, in a fit of nostalgic aberration, rams a see-through celestial globe on his head and lives henceforth with the universe for a helmet, hearing only the sounds heard in seashells.

Booth has even been seen on the runway, at dusk, after the control tower shuts down, with two unusably long white walking sticks to which he fastens flashlights, one to each, and on his head a hat five feet in diameter to which he clips a miner's lamp. Thus impeded and lit, he stands inert on the number 14, which represents the compass bearing of 140 degrees at the runway's southeastern end. Then he begins a cumbersome march toward the other end in the northwest. Only when he stands on the ٤Z, for 320, does he halt, gasping, as oblivious of aircraft in the sky above him as of spectators. Seen once, he reappears. Seen again, he becomes part of local lore, almost a myth, eventually so familiar a sight he cannot be seen at all. He makes a spectacle of himself. Booth is roaming again, they say of him. So that is what battle fatigue is like. Africa, they say.

As for Clegg, hearing or seeing this, he tells himself that survivors are forgiving of fellow survivors. Have seen the fire. Far from batty, he concludes, Booth is merely venting the pent-up nervous energy of being a has-been who dreams of drill but walks at a slouch, although nothing like Clegg with his genuine double limp. Cushy job this, Clegg thinks. Hell on Earth to Booth, of course, but Clegg has no idea.

Why, Booth is wondering, is Clegg intent on turning the FBO into a variety store, with a sandwich machine, souvenir postcards of common-place planes, and posters, combs, key rings, decals, transfers, plane kits, even luggage and sunglasses. Who would buy? I have already had to veto his proposal for a novelty machine in which a miniature crane clutched bits of trash from an artificial ocean. His mind moves on, doleful as can be, briefly distracted from itself by the first jet arrival of the day, and the two hostesses walking into the terminal, one an ugly sister to the other as if to flaw the ravishing apparition of her twin. To give hope to those less than beautiful left stranded grounded. I live in the eastward future, he told himself heatedly, soulmate to the ancient Astronomers Royal of Greenwich. It is already afternoon for me. I am already falling toward dusk, I have journeyed along Sierra November, the northernmost route across the North Atlantic. I have my own o'clock.

For a moment he goes close to Clegg. They have yet in common the avi-ator's view of the planet, a view full of the boiling milkiness above corru-gated iron roofs, the cold dense air of morning, the thin depleted air of hot afternoons out West, the fleece puff pastry of clouds pearl or slate. Thun-derheads, wind shear, cyclone and anticyclone. Haze, air pockets, all the named and unnamed winds. We two think about the planet wrapped in its scarf, he tells himself with an almost jaunty shrug. Its brewable broth. Chow-der of spit and muslin, gust and vacuum, lift and loss, vermilion suns and cinder-black thunder. Comes up with the old word *welkin*.

Up we go, he murmurs as the day breaks. Up we go into the thick and thin of it, as in fall slugs and snails creep down from the lowest branches into the fallen leaves beneath, where a harvest of ants and minute spring-tails awaits them. Clegg and he are late-season moths whose coloring blends with that of the flushed leaves: the green and chestnut of the angle-shade, the paler green of the merveille de jour whose wings match the oak trunks' lichen. I tend my pale green model of the mind of God while he flies cargo or executives. We were toppled from the ramparts. Two con-dors now peddling matches and shoelaces at intersections.

As ever, scraps of emergency radio talk blaze through his head like ingots. We're too heavy for a tailwind. Yeah. I put 138.3, the maximum legal. We're going to be a little over that. Yeah, okay. This is where we leave the flaps down. Twenty-five. Thank you. You got the tower over there okay, Jocko? Yeah. I'm looking for that dry wash. The wind blows from the east here.

It hardly matters who is saying what. Or who happens to overhear them. The Doppler shows fifteen miles to down, says one. Flaps fifteen, says the other. No, twenty-five, he says. Got it, says the other. That's the place, he says. That's it, says the other. More like a direct crosswind, he says, than, well, anything else. Okay, Clegg says. Okay, says Booth, just so you know we weigh something like two thousand over gross. Gear down, says Clegg. Thirty with the green, Booth answers. No smoke. On. Beacon. Gravel. Antiskid. Capped five releases. Speed brake. Full forward. Flaps. Thirty, thirty, landing.

They depressurize. Sink five hundred, Booth murmurs into his shirt. Tad low. One-sixty feet. One-twenty. Fifty. Sound of engine-speed reduction. Sound of gear-warning horn. Sound of impact. They have crashed again. They crash other men's crashes as others crash other men's parties.

In Booth's head they do, as if his fate will be incomplete until all that has happened to others has happened to him. And then some. It is what comes upon you, he has persuaded himself, when, far from ordinary speeds of living, a piece of you turns into different metal, is no longer you at all, but thrives in a cold lattice of its own, tuned in to what is remote and heartless, with all of humanity shrunk to statistics on maps, all human motion couched in coordinates, while what is left of you, the quotient, backs away to *The Wall Street Journal,* a bacon and cheese on rye, an air force nurse. Uncanny that interface. Most of you remains a grower of roses who stooges around on weekends in a one-place Citabria, whose name is Airbatic backward. Faust on Staten Island bumming dimes.

He seethes to have survived. It should have been otherwise. Minus the dribs and drabs of his leftover life. No, dribs only, the drabs have gone from him. He sells aviation gasoline to two airlines and that keeps him and Clegg afloat. They own a gas farm.

Then Clegg arrives, takes off for a nearby airport to pick up a new radio. Has to wait all day because it has not arrived. Flies back in the early evening, his mind's eye full of the plane's image as the ground might see it: a clutch of twitchy lights, a red, a green, a strobe, and one big pouring landing light. He taxis all the way into the hangar in the gloom, his mind on Booth, who has not moved all day, except to the men's room twice. Booth has become a human jukebox. Or quietly inhales cocaine. In his wallet, as of old, a homemade microphotograph of his own sperm looking like a wad of deformed fibers, he claims.

Tool kit beneath his arm, Clegg walks out of the hangar toward the FBO, forgetting the automatic arm that guards the parking lot. Activated by the presence of metal, it almost beats him in the head as he blunders past it, his eyes on the lighted window where Booth sits, desking, waiting out the month end. Permanently on final, never touching down.

But touching rough all right, he says. His usual joke. His face pale as fresh sliced mushroom. Like a searchlight in mourning, Clegg answers, trying to say how the airfield looked from the sky, capped with dusk.

Yeah, Booth drones. You could catch rabbits on the runway in your hat. Shotgun the starlings. They'd never see you coming toward them, it is so very dark.

Are there many?

What begins now is a pregnant conversation designed for as few words as can be. Each man glances off the other's implications.

Under the weather.

I have a dread, Clegg says, of late swallows.

Pete, I'm blue.

Up to your ears in meteor dust again?

You got me a real little snowman up here, Booth murmurs, remembering something that not so much happened as goes on being remembered because remembered once. Booth yawns and feels his penis move, then wonders at the connection.

Now, at its purest their exchange is mere tip-tap. They waft toward and away from each other with: Chop? A tad. Well, November . . . Yeah, the ribbon's off. Another year. Looking, Clegg says. I'm looking, I don't see it yet. Like it's eleven o'clock away from us. You bet, says Booth. I go home and dress up in my best suit just to read the goddamned newspaper. Like it was something to live for, like I've come home from a wake.

This is too poignant for Clegg to handle, but Booth with a look of stunned miserableness is moving to another thought, thinking aloud at ground level, on Zulu Time. Yknow, Rupe, the only difference between the old and the young is the old make more apologies. They do more apologizing. See, I even said it wrong.

Clegg pats him on the shoulder as if to pet a broken bone. All he feels is cloth. Booth is no longer in his clothes; for him meaning has become soliloquy, a vague defamation of what once was in the universe as firm as threadbare velvet, but long since gone.

Rupe?

Yes, sir.

Barney.

Your Barneyship?

No. I'm Barney to you.

Only sometimes.

Boyo, Booth sighs. I sure did wrong.

You, sir, Clegg quietly insists, need home and bed, and a warm night drink and one of those easy-to-take Jimmie Lunceford band movies with Sonja Henie or Bing Crosby. To cheer you, sir.

Booth answers as if an air traffic controller has vectored him to another altitude, saying Copy, thank you, sir, Bravo Bravo out of blue for gold.

Have yourself a good one, sir, and thank you. I was in a cell, sir, a real cell. Out of black for bright.

No wonder Clegg thinks evening a good time to approach him, befriend him, and makes a point of dawdling late after a couple of toasted buns with fried fish taken at the greasy spoon next door. Drawn to the man, to the simmering dismay at his core, he finds him hunched there at screens that show the world in its entirety. Or so it seems to Clegg. Not only the weather, but heartbeats, nebulas, green twists of sound rendered in oscillogram. The mundane things they say interrupt the void that roars between them. They talk in echoes and undertones, not really looking at each other, and half recapture what it was like to sit together in that supersonic reconnaissance aircraft with the long nose.

One evening, though, as Clegg approaches Booth in a ploy now become habitual, Booth seems stiller than usual. More slumped than ever, as if the rib cage has given way, the shoulders descended in total dejection. No answer, not even his semigreeting shrug. Clegg advances, holding his breath lest he find a corpse just when things threatened to improve between them. Tapping the shoulder of the jacket, he sees Booth fall away from his touch and, with a light scurry, vanish into the no-man's-land between the chair and the desk. The severed torso lies where it fell, the arms stuffed with newspaper, the hulk wrapped round a shiny black garbage bag inflated to medium pressure. Untouched, he concludes, the effigy would have stayed put all night, a blind superintendent of the screens.

Now he goes after him outside, toward the hangars, in one of which the bloodstained wreck of a crashed sports plane awaits an always postponed next stage of the investigation. Calm as cardboard, Clegg mentally notes something about delaminations of the bonded skin. Like a cornerstone it drops, irrecoverable from the spin. No sign of Booth, so he wanders again through the gloom, flashlight in hand, exploring the reserve hangar, which is empty. Through the connecting door he steals, knowing what he will find, and wishing he had the skills and the ticket to fly it away from here with Booth and him aboard. Squat and low-slung, the Mitsubishi came with the FBO, not exactly rusting, but unused. A lemon, a bear, and on the ground handling like a hog on ice. No one local had ever dared. Someone had flown it in and left it to go to sleep.

Clegg sees his breath mist in the wand of light he snaps on with his thumb. I'll sooner crash a plane than mothball it to death, he vows. I'll fly it yet. Then he sees another light, fuzzy and mellow, in the rear cabin of the Mitsu. A light come newly on, only seconds ago, almost in answer to his flashlight's going out. He tiptoes forward to the low-down hull and sees Booth in shorts and T-shirt doing press-ups in the narrow aisle while a naked woman lolls on the well-upholstered bunk, the sneer of her mouth not deliberate but rather an accidental effect of her top lip's almost touching her septum. Booth is keeping fit in a wasted plane and has a female witness. Clegg's mind blazes, shudders, and shuts down. He gasps in outraged envy as now, with no visible effort, she lifts one leg from horizontal to straight up, seizes Booth by his unmilitary long hair, and guides his face toward the junction. He stays there at the kneel while her leg remains aloft. When it comes down to encircle or trap his head, Clegg moves a step backward in almost a physical blurt, bumping his head on the underside of the wing, which sits atop the fuselage like a long, long wafer. One piece of his mind tries to relate African salt miners to the vision of Booth behaving like an ordinary guy. All the pride and dignity has fallen away from their mutual pain. Back to normal, things are suddenly below normal. Booth is busy coming through, in the faint-lit belly of another plane he cannot fly and refuses to have inspected. For how long? No one has seen her come or go. How many nights a week? Clegg's head buzzes. The scale is wrong. There is no glory after all. No one local has seen how beautifully they flew those missions in the Cyrano. No one ever will. A mere intuiter of other hearts, Clegg backs carelessly away, sits at the phone in the bright-lit FBO, wondering whom to call, what to say, somehow missing the world but unwilling to make further contact with it.

Whose that contracted peevish face? Whose the hand dragging Booth downward to his reward? Like an empress. Is that, he wonders, what I want for myself? Or am I feeling possessive about Booth, hating his being something when he seems so much a zero? Twisted brotherliness, he decides. It happens all the time. I would like to have what he has without his knowing I have it. Yet, surely, you have no right to fuck in what you cannot fly.

No right. He hovers on a giggle. No right to fly in what you cannot fuck. It does not work the other way. His lips feel frayed from biting. Booth has a love nest. A private house of geisha. Lets the weather go to hell for however long he dallies here. Licking. Sniffing. Doing her will, over whom he now roves mentally, from the swollen taper of her jaw to the bold elongation of her eyebrows, the low defiant brow itself, the plucked pout of her upper lip, the commodious fullness of her shortish body, the white puy of her uplifted leg with the clean-shaved Mohawk thatch at its root. *Gam* is the word he mouths, lusting in his own right as never with his casual dates, with whom sex is as optional as soup or butter.

She lives there, he decides. She never goes out. No one swabs the Mitsu down. No one checks it out. One day soon, perhaps, she will be there for all of them, line boys and airline captains, taking on all comers, tugging them netherward to bliss. She does not look the type, but he wonders what the two of them are doing now, whose tongue is where, whose secretions are more copious. Things of the flesh have invaded the sanctum of lift, and he is torn between envy and outrage. Neither he nor I behave like Lammergeyer, screwing all of his female student pilots after screaming at them nonstop in the air.

Booth has been to him like St.-Exupéry, an almost abstract idol whose skills have flowed upward and outward away from him into the ether of myth. Booth's bloodstained medal ribbons, Scotch-taped to the flank of his desk, have warned away the shallow, the facetious, the merely competent. And his long voluntaries, not so much answering an impromptu question as annihilating it, have awed them all, even those unequipped to understand. If the primer button shorted out, Booth is pronouncing, it engaged the system in prime mode, which killed the engine. Now they wire the electric fuel pump to one of your pullout circuit breakers. You can always shut off the pump by pulling the breaker. That's the Turbo Four. In the Three, so help you, you have to dump the pump by shutting off the master switch, and then, ladies and gentlemen, all systems go. The Four is not for short fields. The Three is quieter, smoother. No cowl flaps, so while in the climb you can cool the engine only by boosting forward speed, and that is not to climb at all. Both models hug the temperature redline anyway, no more than a hog's whisker off. Never lean to peak on a warm day at full power. The temperature goes up if you lean the Ee Gee Tee past 50 degrees rich.

Clegg hears Booth's ghost giving seminars aboard the *Raft of the Medusa*, all emergency and bite. No one doubts the man. But Clegg remembers being unable to hear him out. Remembers shutting off as Booth waxed ever more technical, adding footnotes to footnotes because all planes mattered to him. Back then. In the old days. When he was the personification of aerial honor. A bore, to be sure, but an expert one, forever sounding off in a three-button suit and a collapsible buff rain hat.

No, Clegg says, this honcho is a liniment salesman too. No longer on that death-infested plateau. He has truly escaped his memory, as I have not, although what haunts him only nagged at me. He corrects himself. Now it does not even nag at him. He has hit on something else. The screens are just a front. He remembers reading how Christopher Columbus, finding yet another unknown island, said it was like Andalusia in April. And now Booth has Andalusia in April too, someplace to hide and sport. Clegg's head has gone awry. Booth to him is an Oedipus with contact lenses, a paragon turned plague, no longer worthy of what Clegg once called him privately: the Boothsayer, the man who says himself.

Unable to go home and stare at the begonias in the lit-up atrium or plunge into his fisherman's encyclopedia, Clegg stands up from the phone, very nearly clicks his heels on the parquet, and slow-strides back to the hangar, determined to confront them or to be a voyeur again. He will decide at the last moment. The light is even yellower now, less rosy, but all he can see is the woman in the same posture on the couch, with her leg down, and the long wasted-looking Booth like a human splinter nestled alongside her, his cheek on her collarbone, motionless and perhaps asleep. She seems to be talking to the roof of the plane, looking upward with the same disabused expression. The big heavy semiconvex door lets forth no sound. Now he recalls Booth's affable distantness after they flew together, which was a closeness compared to how he is now. Clegg wants to be back in Africa, marooned in the mountains, trying to stay loose. Or in the hospital recuperating among those who wished he'd never been saved. Or even like Booth, hewing salt on the plateau below sea level, wondering if the savages will behead him during the night.

All of a sudden Booth appears to wake, moving his lips to answer her. It is as if a medieval painting of two nudes has come to life. The two pairs of lips flexing like newborn butterflies. Clegg wonders if there were any paintings of nudes in medieval times, but he forgets the idea as Booth rears up, looks at rather than through the window, then sinks back toward a stronger spell than that of air. Clegg wonders if there is anything, anything at all, he would not have done if they had seen him and invited him in to share.

He cannot abide it. The two of them look so settled, so attuned. The glimpse of an exotic domesticity has torn into him there in that cavernous dark whose hush, of flying machines at rest with all surfaces inert and marooned, is denser than any silence of graveyards, gymnasiums, theaters. Whereas his own life is only middlingly good. Good to his ailing mother in Virginia. Less good to his ailing self. Now Booth thrives in brightest Africa, a man for whom Clegg knows he would have given his life at one time. Booth as the more consequential being, he tells himself, wincing, learning at last to hate. If you hate, he wonders, are you obliged to kill? Do you have to do something about it? Or do you just fester away? Is hate enough in itself? He has no experience of such emotions, old as dust-laden spiderwebs. Too young, he is too old. He can add things up without ever reaching their total. Only the beginnings of hate afflict him. Where it ends, culminates, he has no idea.

As you were, he tells himself, military fashion. Two paladins we were. One for all and all for one. Is that right? Is that what we said? He rehearses the years of subordinate givingness. I for you and you for me, but I for you rather than you for me, as the code of military etiquette requires of its knights. He thinks, now, he would have left Booth to live or die among those crazy savages. Had the choice arisen. To hell with chain of command. He knows he would have measured Booth's liver, lungs, heart against his own and found his own the more deserving. His excuse would have been the battering sunlight, the jabbering blacks, the corrosive salt.

Now it is Christmas-clear to him. Whatever his failings, Booth would never have harbored such thoughts about him. This, he punishes himself to say, is why you remain the subordinate officer. Were you not, you would never have subordinated your life to his. What he gives out of conscience has to be commanded from you. A Booth, knowing the mission commander's right to waste a junior for the sake of the mission, backslides gently into fellow feeling, whereas a Clegg backslides into duty. He is more qualified to die than I, he tells himself, but he is also more qualified to waste me than I him.

Now he realizes how old his thinking is. It no longer applies. They are not in Africa, or even in the service. The idol has clay feet. No, the idol has a private life from which all Cleggs have been shut out. That is it. He wonders why he himself has not installed a woman in a white elephant of a plane. His blood sugar miserably low by now, he wonders what it is that Booth has and Clegg has not. Tweak Booth's penis. Will he not squirt? Bang his teeth. Will his gums not bleed? Pee on his sleeping face? Will he not wake and attack? On the point of muttering something final into the cold metal of the fuselage, Clegg recoils as the Mitsu's door opens a crack and then swings right out, just missing his face. Bandanna around her head, the woman shimmies out, her flashlight aimed at the far connecting door, and trips away in sneakers. She sees nothing of Clegg, frozen, who is waiting for Booth to follow. Then he sees him, unable to stand quite erect beneath the curving roof, tugging on his pajamas with a canny smile and seeming to switch on an electric blanket, pale blue on the couch. Clegg taps once, hard, on the fuselage, sees Booth flinch and peer forward to the flight deck, then fast as thought slams the door shut and walks away, bumping into the jamb of the connecting door. As he sees it, he has backed down where he has no right to do anything at all. As with his mother, who wants from him only certain honored phrases such as sleeping well, eating in moderation, avoiding bad women. As with his dates, who want from him only the price of dinner and, at the discos, a better routine cavort than a wounded man can manage. Some of his responses do not belong in anyone else's life. If you respond, he thinks, then your response belongs in the world. It has a right. But he knows this cannot be true. There is no one to tell: only the chance of spying on them again and keeping it all to himself. He could no more blab about Booth than he could knowingly hurt his mother. And now he could no more expect Booth to indulge in ordinary human relationships than he could expect a snow leopard to write its autobiography. Something has changed, he knows. A change is something. Life has not stopped. That much is true at least. And, just like Booth, who has listened to it just as much as Clegg, he hears again bits from that incessant oratorio of the air, in which pilots talk to radar centers and towers, keeping it short and courteous, making the phrases both practical and deferential, mainly because their lives depend on it. But what he hears is not the suave, ongoing tumult of completion, from takeoff to landing with hundreds of thorny miles in between, but the pour of the rain, the rat-a-tat of hail, a faltering conversation ended almost as soon as begun, as if there is nothing left but the Dismal Swamp Reporting Service, who can hardly decipher his transmission.

Romeo Charlie, I'm (unintelligible) to you. He says it again. They seem to hear.

Romeo Charlie, Swamp Service, your transmission weak and unreadable. If you are inbound, Runway something or other, wind One Eight Zero at Two One, altimeter unknown, report turning base or final.

He hears none of this, churning on through cloud and scud, a glutton for punishment.

Romeo Charlie, key your mike twice if inbound. If you read the tower, key your mike, sir.

He sirs them back. Or so it seems. He has not heard them. The sir is wasted. I can just hear you right about here, he calls. Heavy turbulence and thundershowers. I'm busy, sir.

Tower tells him to key his mike twice. If you read.

There ensues a pause of crackling noncommunication. As if to say naught and let things go. Then he talks again. Affirmative, Romeo Charlie, I'm not smiling, sir, I'm real busy with it.

Roger, they tell him. Understand you're southeast and in some showers.

Really heavy at this time, he answers, I am looking for Booth in all this, ah, rain, sir. Do you have him or anyone in sight.

Negative, Romeo Charlie. Understand you are not inbound to the airport.

Oh no, he answers, I'm on hold. Holding short. Like, I can creep around it, not run away from it, sir, but not go through the cell either. It has been waiting for me all this time, and I would like some vectors around it. Romeo Charlie looking. Waiting, sir. Knowing he has become unintelligible, he stops.

Booth sleeps, Booth dreams not about his late-night visitant, but about the flock of fair to middling Mooneys, their twin aerials like white thorns atop the fuselage, all their flying surfaces swept forward in haste like the manes of horses in the friezes of the Parthenon. Not even the black Mooney of death assails him as he walks on their wings upward, along a ladder of stepping stones that tapers to the zenith. Tin gulls, they hover stationary while he climbs.

Clegg decides to write away for details of the Mitsubishi course, intending to return, sneak into the hangar one night, lock the plane's door upon the two of them, and take off while they are in the midst of their most intimate deeds of kind. Already he sees himself taming the monster till it purrs, and even the heavy nosewheel landing thump will have a touch of bird's finesse when he brings them back, after which he flies away never to return. Or he will kidnap Booth's Lady Godiva just to get him back to the desk of screens, where he belongs. Anything, so long as Booth is there to see and sulkily applaud.

He still needs Booth to notice him, as if he were a sailplane skimming over low, all hush and hiss and cantilevered elongation. But Booth, once so observant, is through with noticing him. Booth lives his life by the same method as someone flying through cloud. Head down, aerialist of an invisible wire, the main thing being not to fly Chinese fashion as one of the standard FBO jokes put it: One Wing Low.

To brisken himself up, even as the ground bass of a stereo begins to thump down from the apartment above him and turn his studio into a drum, he lathers and shaves, convinced that for the first time since Africa he has seized unlosable control of his life. Cruise climbing to self-sufficiency at last. I am out of cloud, right at the bottom of it, he decides. I have the rabbit in sight. With two pillows behind him where no board heads his bed, he sights at the weather channel's red-gray-green display on his six-inch color set, and, crossing arms to palm opposite nipples, puts himself into the hands of the autopilot, murmuring toward sleep, a man of mineral tin and light alloy, willing his fame to come, quiet and thin as it will have to be. With that six-inch neglected green sunrise in front of him, he drops off. And off. And off.

Needing release at random, he almost finds it with an air hostess in the airport hotel at his next stop. After lunch she peels his glans and coats it with lipstick, after which he pummels her with it, mottling her with pink until he spills his ache into her mellow throat. For two hours they pleasure each other in almost flickbook ways, making taboo the norm until their nerves give out. They go their separate ways drained and faint, leaving behind them a bottom sheet like manna for a private eye. No one has asked me in three months he hears her saying long afterward. I promised myself I'd say yes to the first. A Deb, this one, but she has not asked his name or what he does, or what has made him horny between planes. He wonders what his mother might think and finds the thought impossible. Before getting into bed, he calls his mother, who always waits after he has left, then watches the electric imitation fire, like a red-hot mountain range with blackened peaks, spinning artificial tongues of flame with little propeller wheels turning out of sight above pieces of wavy shiny foil. He knows how things work.

At the open window in his pajamas, he guesses how he looks. One of the dying, taking a last look at the twentieth century before lowering the blind, unsure if he will wake again to raise it. Or he is an inmate of some asylum staring out at a landscape seen by no one else, all orange feathers and crystal trees.

In the neatly trussed springs of his mattress he hears raucous gulls. In the bray of a donkey in its field he hears the creak of an ancient door. He lives only a few hundred yards from the runway, dotes on the revolving whine, the clotted thunder spewing from the cones under the wings or below the tail. His pageantry. His mind numbs before his eyes close. His hands clench and open on the comforter a dozen times before he drifts off, one straggler part of his mind saying make a course correction before it is too late.

Blundering about with coffee, he shoves knife, fork, and cereal spoon together on the bar-type kitchen counter and, as he yawns at his stool, shuts that image out, determined to have an entire day without pathos, a day, as he says, of No Chancelle. Where the word has come from, he has no idea, but perhaps it comes from the house name dreamed up by a young couple past whose gate he bicycles each morning. Charlie and Nellie have called their home Char-nell. No one has dared to tell them. Or chancelle comes as a variant of the aerobatic maneuver called chandelle, French for candle. Yes, he says, a no-chancelle day is one without inexpert ground reference maneuvers, a day of total accomplishment. Like Booth, who sometimes has his computer print out the longest receipts in living memory, expressing the balance in many currencies, and attaching parenthetical definitions to each word used. A concertina of wallpaper crammed with allusions to weather, geography, navigation, etymology, and world history, the receipt obliterates, smothers, the transaction. Sometimes, for out-of-state flights, Booth lists [the speeds of certain stars] above a certain magnitude, sometimes even multiplying the debt by the speed of the star in kilometers per second. All done in Zulu Time of course. How, Clegg asks himself, can Booth be so bizarre and still in charge? Those erudite monologs. Those roller-coaster bills. Those weather scopes on his desk. The haughty redhead in the Mitsubishi. Booth's way of annihilating time, he sees, is to use the definition of a word instead of the word, then the definitions of the words in the definition, followed, inexhaustibly, by the definitions of the words in the aforementioned definitions of the words in the first definition. Ad infinitum. Is there anything like that for me, he wonders. Any other form of infinite regress, this side of death and short of imbecility?

Then he can think of only a few words. Receivership. Batshit. Africa. It is the low point of his day. All that is left for him is the cultivation of cactuses. He will lick Booth's stamps. Only the Lost and Found will own him.

After this he cheers up. A day is not a dormitory after all. A job is not the Hebrew letter for Jehovah. He begins to wonder if Booth has wondered about him, wondering if Clegg knows anything about Booth that Booth doesn't know he knows. Or even if Booth knows something about Clegg, et cetera. Sometimes the one's life was richer than the other's. And vice versa. Still true, since conjoint lives vary enormously from day to day, entangled as flowers only one of which faces the sun, thanks to almost everything.

Clegg's truth all of a sudden ripens. Booth, he realizes, has been cut from greatness, and he, Clegg, has been cut from what is left. Even Booth's frenzy is born of greatness. His own of being an ordinary guy. Dear Mother, he forms his next letter: Being born with a great madness won't make you a great man. It has to be the other way around. You have to start sane. Then it becomes an open question.

In Boothtime it is eighteen thirty, sometimes nineteen thirty, no less grand than one, but to him one sounds more definite, more pure. His mind stays on the Mitsubishi, though. If it were only betrayal he feels. It is more. Booth has once again outdistanced him, and it is as if, this time around, Booth has left him in the desert. Behind. Marooned. Where in the long run he will come to know not even himself, his name, his rank. Just a mess like mustard on a finished plate.

Outside the FBO, Clegg sees an empty beer can and all of a sudden makes it the source of all his woes. Right foot, then left. Now he jumps on it two-footed, bends it double with his hands, and placekicks it far into the grass. Only, out of some lingering passion for decorum, to go and retrieve it, kicking it back soccer-style until he reaches the outdoor trash bin, into which he flings it with excess force. He has rid himself of something. That is plain. Lighter, clearer, he marches inside with a cramped flourish and goes past Booth to check the board for the day's doings. He marvels how people can come and go, their lives intersect and separate, and nobody is any the wiser. Not ships passing in the night, but ships feeding on the rumor of ships' actually doing that. In Booth's face no vestige of the red-head, in his own he presumes no sign of the air hostess. Or even of his mother. Gross glare of the day all over his face, he pouts at the sky, then at Booth, and, without meaning to, bursts into applause, clapping Booth only an arm's length from his face in a dry untidy crescendo Booth merely nods at. Nonetheless the nothing they now exchange would be said gently were it said at all.

Clegg wonders what Booth might make of his mother. Two beings on the edge. One tottering while she shrinks. The other a savage crouched by a fire and casting quick-change shadows. Clegg loses his mother in almost vengeful reveries about Booth, who gathers up unused bits of human behavior and makes them his own, chaffing or roaring, leering or going blank, as if it no longer matters whose antics are whose. He used to boil over with ways for other people to behave in, but now he is a mere catchment area rather than himself. Daffy but still kind of deep, thinks Clegg, peeling a banana. He used to have a coaxial cable to Lord God Almighty. At least that is how he behaved both in the stratosphere and on the ground. An instant prince who now says yair for yes. He who always said affirmative as if always at altitude, talking to some tower.

He sees Booth's mistress drawing two chalk lines on her pubic bush, which she then clips and shaves into a narrow Mohawk. His mother, as ever, greets him by tapping him gently on the jugular: the touch reserved for those near death. He likes things to dovetail, not to grind on one another. Since a child he has believed in congruity. Still tries to make it or find it. It goes begging in the presence of other lives, he knows. He dotes on the present tense, so eternal and so close to dictionary definition. The past, dried and cut, he cannot knead or fondle. Odd. He is surprised at himself. Instead of reconciling things already hard and fast, he wants to mold them into amity. Godlike, he grins. Hardly Clegglike. There's a bit of Booth even in me. The things he thinks leave bruises behind them in his mind. Scuff the silver sheath of it. All at the same time, he recites as if having intercepted the notion from the airwaves around him, life is gruesome, lovely, raunchy, tragic, daft, manna, barbaric, shit, gentle, genocidal, tame. There are never enough words so long as there are also too many. He knows that does not add up, but he lives with it. One of his halflight paradoxes. He feels pompous amid the flux. Tries to come up with some summary that might be iced on top of a birthday cake, and at last comes up with this.

I do not like the clash. We are not armies. We must be like the sea. Whatever's thrown into it, it accepts.

He is going to blow his stack, he knows it. In his hangdog, faintly miserable way. As if he has come into being only to be a background for Barney Booth. The Barney Booths of this world. But blowing his stack reminds him of falling chimneys filmed and standing up again when the film reverses. Even in a speeding ambulance he needs an audience. In all his days has not been attended to enough. Will even suffer wolves and mambas in the cockpit with him, so long as they notice him, and he swirls into the final spin, his throat torn out, lethal colons all over his face.

Now he sees it. He and Booth are two ghosts haunting a scene where they have committed no crime. But hoping, wishing, harping on it. Asking the crime to come out of the scenery and egg them on. No. The future remains the future, both the future that is to come and the future that can never be. He gives up, goes home, settles down with a toasted muffin and slices of Canadian bacon that slightly overlap the edge. The butter's lip.

From his mother's hoard of second-class mail he has filched a lingerie catalog of which one full-page photograph commands his attention as he munches.

It matches an uncaptured dream. He has to tell. Single-spacing on cream bond, he types a letter to the company, explaining that he wants to be as discreet as possible, lordlove us yes, but the beauty of the three models herein, and their wherewithal, the sumptuous good taste of the setting, and above all the dainty filigree of the underwear underworn, have pleased him, a man of the world, beyond measure, it just so happens a man at present without a regular date, alas, but often much in favor on the distaff side. I am very much in favor of such loveliness, he types. Then, breathing with delicate evenness, he spreads himself, peering hard at the page.

Of the three lovelies on the bed, and all credit to you for a scarlet four-poster, ladies and gentlemen, with really shiny brass knobs that reflect the cream and red satins the ladies have arranged themselves upon, the strawberry blonde in the violet bra seems to be having second thoughts. How young and fresh-faced she looks, almost ingenuous in such a setting. I might even say peachy. Only moments ago, she seems to have done for the first time something she regrets. It shows. Not alone, I mean, but with these others, or with other others. At least with others looking on. She is resting now on her left elbow with the fingers of her right hand touching her cheek and collarbone. Hers is the fairest flesh on view, with just the right tinge of auburn haze, and she would sunburn badly if you took her

outside too much. Her gaze goes into the middle distance. The spit curls
near her eyes look ruffled up, but maybe spit curls are supposed to. Maybe
the other two, who are lovely in the extreme, used their own spit on her
curls. They curled them for her. For all I know, they may have had a spit
party. I worry some because clearly she has been persuaded to look at
something unusual that she did not want to see, or not for very long. Or
she wanted to see it without remembering she wanted to see it. Especially
if she inhaled too deeply nearby. Her briefs barely contain her abundant
hairs, by any other name hardly as sweet, but you might even think there
was a tiny sac hidden away in there. A big tear, or an almighty drop of rain.
A bleb if you like. Not for a moment do I think she peered down at herself
with or without a hand mirror, but it is clear that one of the other two said
Don't waste time looking, you really have an obligation to inhale yourself.
And taste. Imagine first one, then another finger, sliding under the lilac
fabric and through the darkest of the ginger hair easily visible through the
crotch-net, and then one finger, let's have the index doing it, and another,
crooking and gently dipping past her outer defenses and instead of
bridling she liked it and murmured, deeper, deeper. So they would work
about awhile to stir up the maximum, most individual aroma (I would
hardly use such a word as smell about anything so fine). Then there is the
cushion of an index finger just below each nostril and she almost faints
with joy. Musk of the nonmother, you see. When, at last, she tastes, she is
overjoyed. Twenty years of it have already gone to waste. She licks the fingers until they are dull again with that odd metallic flavor of the over-
sucked finger. Now she makes fleeting contact with herself while the
others tug her wide open and she exclaims with pride as she holds her glis-
tening hand up to the light, then draws it to her lips with a moan. As if
deflowered. Do you think this explains her expression? She looks forlorn,
or even hurt, but I think she is brooding on the wasted years, especially
after the other two touched her, then themselves, and then she them, with
soothed-sounding giggles and naughty little dipping scooping motions
done to one another until, really, they were so secretive they were ready
for some heavier traffic not then available on the bed, though I'll warrant
thousands would have walked on their knees from Alabama to Cape Cod
to help them out, yes sir, yours truly included. Only the full hand, I mean
the complete whole thing, or the fist, is enough in that kind of emergency. Making a chair for one another, at least at first, the girl at the back,
I mean the back one of the three, has no pair of hands behind her, but
only one of her own. Can you visualize it? The front girl pleasures herself
left-handed, reaches behind her to the front of the middle girl, who
reaches her left hand forward and her right hand behind her, to Three's

front, who has her own right hand cone-shaped inside her all the way to her cherrystone. Yep. But I got it slightly wrong. They all have the same, and Three would come off badly only if they were using both hands on the girl in front; but One, though held, has nothing to hold, or to push into, and I just wonder which is worse, being felt with nothing to feel at or into, or feeling without being felt. One or Three? The moral of this is always to be in the middle if possible. At least if you are making chairs for one another. When they recombine and really spread themselves, the third party gets left out. The other two are yang and yin, but they can bring her in with fingers if she drapes herself over the zwieback, allots one finger to each butty hole and arranges her three orifices for four hands. The hand left over worries me somewhat, but the two breasts, lovely word in the plural (the lolling cream), I never minded a pair, well, the two of them can be squeezed together into one udder. All this requires timing of course, and practice. Daisy-chaining is one of the neglected arts, but three bright and agile girls could easily end up with a tongue that has no place to go. They should practice with dolls. In fact, I have often thought that little girls are given dolls so they can review all the positions. Three hundred and sixty degrees to every joint. And the famous crying sound when you lay the doll on her back is surely a prelude to the squeak of climax. So that young girls do not frighten themselves to death with the sounds they eventually make. Many a daisy chain has been rehearsed in the nursery. Take three girls. Put the parts of any two together like two mated tuning forks and you have two mouths for the third girl's pleasure. The one known as Three. Imagine the sound track and the heaving threesome, marking the satin while the four gold knobs reflect it all in curvy focus! But I am neglecting the other two, one of whom has one hand behind her head while she kneels up near, but not in any way against, the satin cushions with a spray of small red flowers off right. A nice touch. Surely, though, her knees are on One's bottom. At least they touch a tad. These two have the same lilac underwear, no doubt sopping wet by now, or sodden, but the brunette has a haughty pout, and her look tells you that she has just gotten rid of a tension, or a pressure, she was becoming mighty impatient, kind of looking out to sea. That was good, she is saying to herself. When do we start again and really get into it this time? One of your small-boned Latinas, I wouldn't doubt, in real life that is, and a little square, metaphorically speaking, for my own tastes, whereas the little strawberry blonde with her elbow resting on the upper part of her own belly while the rest of her belly sags a bit, invitingly, to the coverlet, she almost looks willing to try anything even if only once. I know, your redhead or your blonde is flighty and vivacious. Effusive. Maybe she feels she somehow is not solid enough and has to compensate for that. Your brunette has brains, they say, and doesn't need to go to sexual extremes. In between you find those mousy ones, and you think these women are bound to be moderate. Not flashy, not noticed when they enter a room. They have no scruples at all. They will lick, eat, allow, anything, and they do not care how much damage they sustain. They are as insatiable as spaniels. This one here, for instance, in a strapless bra, garter belt, and G-string, she is wearing white and that sets off the thickness of haunch and pelvis I have always been partial to, even while recovering from wounds. So she has stockings on as well, and her entire lower tropic is a mantrap. Twang those elastic suspenders. Let the briefs smack back in place after you pluck them away for a peep. So agonizing just to look. She is smooth as oiled liver. You could slide off her as easy as stay. She has the aroma of straw, sour cream, bananas, and her face tells you that, although she is done up in those brand-new undies crisp and fragrant from the tissue in the box, her entire mind is on what is behind them, pleat and slit and thatch and twig and thimble, all of it as wet and hot as Quito in Ecuador, with the tiny nerves wound up like hair springs ready to go. There is nothing she has not done and will not do again. Nothing too off-beat, stale, oversized, with man or woman or animal. The heat in this bint (she does have that Arab touch) comes off her at you like a weather front. She has exhausted the other two. This is the first time her legs have been together in hours. She glistens with completeness, not only Jell-O slick and ready to whisper the words no human has heard, but looking at you with blank but somehow surly eyes that say I know what you're thinking, I have oil, cream, rubber, leather, needles, bulldog clips, razor blades, tweezers, carrots, mice, archer fish, and hair dryers.

I am a tower of technique. So although she looks swollen and aloof, her gaze is full of dare you to. How long can you hold your breath, buster? Does she go for blood? The eyes will tell you all. Butter would not melt in this one's mouth. She looks so healthy. She has that slight overdevelopment of the total physique that tells the connoisseur her juices flow nonstop. Just notice that slight tolerant depravity in her expression. What she does she does in no boudoir like the one depicted, but on a ten-foot square of gleaming stainless steel with runnels built in like the blood gutters on a good quality bayonet, and she always has a pulmonary resuscitation kit by her. She always gives the kiss of life in the wrong place, though, greedily puffing into the fundament or elsewhere. Nor does she easily or readily give up her dead, having in her something of the morticians who distinguished ancient Egypt, whom newly dead flesh turned on in the pyramids. Sometimes the steel becomes so slick she'd skid right off, so it has flip-up sides as in hospital cribs. Her still waters run deep and are always piping hot. Trudy I would call her. Something German there. Ginger is the strawberry blonde, and the other is Latina. How do I make a reservation for an afternoon with all three, at the same time? While I am about it, please send me one dozen of what Trudy has on. Demi-cup strapless with front closure. 36D. Lacy bikini with nylon spandex back and comfortable cotton panel, large, and champagne garter belt, large. I am quoting from your catalog, of course. Please have Trudy plan all the afternoon's activities. I have been in the service, an aviator. I know how important a flight plan is. I hope this finds you as it leaves me, in a state of enthusiastic excitement only slightly this side of madness. Yours gratefully.

Clegg's body has fallen in love.

When he reads the letter through, he finds it more exciting to keep by him than to send. So this is what he is like deep down. Not a hero at all. Yet why fret? He and Booth land on the Danakili plain by helicopter, hand out food, clothing, bubble gum, shaving foam, Polaroid cameras, and transistor radios. Then, after speeches, they whirl away again, the debt discharged into the milk of human kindness. His knees do not knock. His lips do not quiver. His hands do not pluck the coverlet. What it says somewhere about the impairment of his moral fiber (as if he were a bread) has long since vanished into more slanted language that says of him accelerated attrition initiative shortfall, otherwise known as the dreaded Aaisfall, said as assfall. He has come to terms. These are the terms he has come to. And soared beyond. Termless now, he is less operatic than Booth, but they both are singing the same aria. The medium pressure of enormous pressure's aftermath has driven them to visual song. To aural graffito. The in-between modes are theirs. The next to the last straw included.

Two men. One song. Two voices. One fate. Now they share what other humans have no idea that humans can ever possess. Clegg and Booth way out beyond themselves are groping for another planet to belong to. Like the men of the Middle Ages, they do not know they are of the Middle Ages. Beyond the pale, yes. In their suffering they hate all sufferers. Booth would love to have for the first time in years a clear head, and to be no sex at all. Clegg, mimicking his mother's rhythmic wheeze, wants a jailbait nymphet to play with, in skintight jeans flaunting the basin of her mound. Doing his bidding.

The trouble with sex, Clegg decides, is this: It is what you do while waiting for sex to deliver something new. Yair, says Booth in his mind's ear. Sex is the only barbaric thing left to those who do not kill. They need an equivalent to risking their lives.

Clegg folds his letter into three, firming the creases with a knife handle as if to help it fit an envelope, but he slips it into an inside pocket, thinking he must make a copy, lend it to Booth, maybe, to read aloud to his woman in the Mitsubishi. Make contact with her. Contact of any kind. Say hello, then. Or hi. Brush against her next time she leaves and say something profound. It'll rain or go dark before morning. Offered with a jolly grin. She goes away thinking what a good egg he is, less demanding than the other one. The gent of the two. The Laurel, the Harpo, the Jekyll. She is not so much well read as well screened.

They are wheeling a yellow Mooney into a hangar. He follows, waits until they leave. He wants to be alone enough to savor the frosty magic of the air.

It is always November. The only month. He listens to the hangar structure creak and ache inside the outside of the wind. He taps a finger on cool flimsy metal wings. On the less cool doped fabric of a rebuilt biplane. Caught in two minds, he wonders at the bulky slightness of planes. Here at a dead halt, with all their commotion somehow turned to stuff. On a whim he enters the next hangar, but, bypassing the Mitsubishi, skirts the crash remains strewn in one corner, and begins to poke about among the debris. Nothing. But under a sheet of plastic draped over the Mitsu's high wing, he espies Booth's enormous sombrero. Tugs at the corner of the plastic. The hat crowns the plane like a radar dome. Down it comes with a soft scrape. Dove gray in that impeded light. Made from some airworthy plastic, cardboard, and balsa wood, he thinks. The very latest. He gets it down without breaking it. No one hears. At least, no one comes to see. It could double as a kite, but the chin strap is a thick elastic. In an area big enough, he tries it on, inhaling Booth's brilliantine of cloves and heather. It settles on the bridge of his nose. Urgently casting around, with the hat off, he finds a bundle of old shirts, some oily, some not, and stuffs one into the hat, then tries it on again. Now he can see and, weirdly off-balance, begins his march to the hangar doors. He removes the hat again, standing it up against the wall, and sees the two long white poles carefully aligned with the bottom of the wall almost like two heating pipes. Shoving hard, he gets one hangar door to move a foot, then all the way. He goes inside again, first assumes the hat, but not before arranging a pole convenient for either hand, and then makes his rigid march, feeling oddly barbaric.

Out in the open, with the last wasps failing in clumsy flight, he stands still, not so much an apparition as another kind of flying machine. A saucer with legs. Now he extends the poles sideways until their weight restores them to the macadam. There he poses, in the unsteady breeze, his chin strap taut, facing the tower, like some disfigured lunar lander. Unmoving, waiting to be noticed, distantly telling himself the poles should be strapped to his arms so he can wield them. Five, ten minutes he waits in front of the open hangar door, and then begins to walk, letting the poles drag on the ground. Birds flutter around his face, land on the hat's brim, squirting white lime and hopping about, but on he trudges, not that easily, unable to dismiss the thought that he might lift off into the air. Right to the FBO he goes, amazing the passengers and crew of a waiting jet just beginning to taxi away from the terminal. They see not a man but an outsize party favor. A macrocephalic cripple going fishing.

Rapt at his desk, Booth sees something he dare not identify, a clone of himself arriving to haunt, and then Clegg's expressionless face. They all jostle outside to look and Clegg tells them he is peddling shade. Flipped, says Lammergeyer. And then there were two. Booth remains silent, but he hears someone, maybe Ratito, saying very quietly: Would you look at that. Clegg confronts them in a joyous daze. The gallery parts. Booth walks forward as if advancing to be recognized by a sentry. The jet takes off, some of those aboard craning their necks as Booth raises his arms to sight the shotgun at the birds tripping to and fro on the hatbrim. He hates birds as much as he hates the sea. Still he has not pulled the trigger, but there he looms in his suit and green eyeshade, waiting no doubt for the glint on the foresight to fade. Yair, he murmurs, and sends the salvo high over the hat. Clegg does not budge, but he says: You going to kill us all with barrel two?

Booth cocks the second hammer and takes aim at the crown. He will blind me, Clegg decides, and makes a cumbersome turn in order to march away with the poles dragging after him. As he recedes toward the first taxiway, he seems enclosed in a V-shape. His feet are inaudible, even to him. When Booth fires again, Clegg hears the bang only in the abstract, and then the whistle-seethe of the pellets as they soar over him, just another noise of little birds. Always Booth haunts the airfield, on foot or in a jeep, to fell crows or sparrows. Sometimes he hides in the vegetation, then, after shooting birds on their nests, emerges with the stately self-consciousness of one who has put a dying elephant out of its misery. He knows, better than most, that only half a mile away Sapsipper Woods, the bird sanctuary, feeds him his prey, and he stores up the vicious dream of sneaking in there and murdering the birds at source. All varieties. Clegg's view of birds is different. In his FBO locker he keeps a selection of rubber snakes to drape on parked planes' noses or on the engine nacelles. No bird comes near when the snakes are in place, but Clegg forgets to bring them indoors. They blow off, they rot, they get kicked aside.

Use real snakes, Booth has told him with his overbearing grin. That'll work. You don't want to stay at dildo level all your days. Rattlers and mambas first.

This is the exchange that comes back to Clegg as he advances toward the runway, taxiing from the shooter behind him, still hearing the echo as loud, as faint, as the shot itself. If Booth reloads, he muses. If. The poles are heavy, he lets them drop, making a right angle aimed north so as to keep his bearings, and stands inside the apex to read his still uncopied letter, his mind lofted ahead to the three lovelies on the bed, who can be the first hostesses on Clegg Airways. A high-wing single pauses on the taxiway to inspect him and lights from the tower dither at him, urgently flashing. He is in the way.

Clear, he whispers to the churning engine of the single. All clear. I am monitoring the taxiway. He begins to read his letter aloud in the imperfect light of midafternoon, but is too lost in his scarecrow role to find it provocative. He is one of the grandees today, in headdress and plumes, for once a Clegg writ large. He resolves from now on to wear his military decorations sewn on his breast, and to hell with the line boys, Ratito, Moa, and the rest. His left thumb feels out of place on his hand. He pulls at it, it clicks back into position, and he blames the pole. Yes, what Booth fastens to his desk, he can fasten to his breast pocket. They both have medals galore. All he needs is a plane of his own, something to dote on and fix up. To stooge around in. Altogether his. In which, yet again, he will feel the slight knee-trembling, the lip-twitching effect of adrenaline squandered. The cool suction that empties the wrist and leaves them with the coffee-shakes. He does not need a huge hat and two poles, he sees that now. He decides to look for fresh fields, fresh women, fresh machines, fresh ways of enduring his mother's final years.

The best way to return the hat and poles, he decides, is to wear the hat and tow the poles behind him. He does. No one interferes, but the gallery has not dispersed. It awaits the rest of his performance. No Booth sprays shot. All the birds have fled. Finish the letter and mail it. He sees his life opening up again. All he has to do is touch other lives. He can be ample and radiant as in his youth. He will play polo and shoot arrows into targets stuffed with straw. Ski cross-country. He is going to live in a house with a separate room for each activity. His mother will be downstairs to save her legs, and the three models will be up in the bedrooms. Giggling and wobbling as they run up and down the hallways in scanties, playing tag.

He stows the hat back on top of the Mitsubishi, redrapes it with the plastic, and lays the poles along the foot of the wall, too preoccupied with his future to check for pellet holes, of which there are four in the crown.

Lucky. He hears Booth wholly out of character saying So you still want to be really happy, Rupe.

Such the eye of the hurricane that's the usual Barney Booth. Clegg looks on the bright side, forgets the bad Booth for the good, and so has a hopelessly skewed view of the man. Booth the affectionate, the expansive, the selfless. And to borrow Booth's disguises is not to meddle with Booth at all. That he knows. Walking around the low fat nose of the Mitsubishi, and feeling oddly grateful to be alive in a world of wings and propellers, rudders and flaps, he almost bumps into Booth's woman, sheathed in jeans and a black sweater, just coming out. The fine-cut sneer has not disappeared and her eyes are just as haughty, but he notices most of all the color of her face. Bright orange, not from a false suntan, or one revived by ultraviolet, but stained with stage makeup. Her mouth is purple, squeezed and tugged upward until the inside of the upper lip shows. Then the whole shape splits wide open for a voice of mellow, purring resonance. She presumes he is Rupert Clegg, thus far unintroduced. He says a yair. All the time, he joshes. She is almost tall.

That she has a name amazes him. Bellanca Cruisemaster. A nickname only, but she chooses to go by it. He says it aloud, almost smirking. Has she seen him in the hat? She has. She advises him not to taunt Barney Booth. Clegg stares at her orange face, the thick wavy hair that springs and bounces, the narrow simmering green eyes. Now they talk again.

Call me Rupe. I'm no stranger, ma'am.

Certainly not. You are a very strange stranger indeed.

Rupert, then. You're no stranger to me.

Ah, she sighs, my fame has preceded me.

Clegg is staring at where the Mohawk haircut nestles within her cling-film jeans. He dreams he can see the very outline. Belle, if he likes, she is telling him, but Belly never. She hates houses. Birds nest in any part of a plane they can get into. She likes to come and think in the Mitsu. He knows. She is not telling the whole truth. He dares not mention the rest of it. She also uses a room above the FBO. He cracks his thumb again. She says the Madonna of the Sleeping Cars. She lived in trains. He has no idea what she is talking about. She likes how the interiors of planes smell. The vinyl, the leather.

Now she tells him that he, Clegg, is very much on Booth's mind. Talks of him nonstop. The two of them have been through hell together. And alone, Clegg adds. Booth desks and Clegg flies. Barney minds the store, he says, and I fly the charters. Anywhere you need to go, night or day, and I'm your man. She has a man already, she cautions him. And there is nowhere she needs to go.

Clegg, she sees, has one of those wide-line Australian mouths, a little sucked in, but with the gift of ready smiling, wry, and she wonders what his life is like. After so much, and with so little now. She knows how much Booth wants to make a clean breast of it, brother to cousin, or cousin to brother, she cannot untangle exactly what the relationship between them is.

She cites her father, in optical equipment in Fort Lauderdale, far from the beach, with no pool. Her sister spoke eight languages and drowned in the Amazon. A nurse. She, Bellanca or Belle, never tries too hard. Almost forty. From the primrose path to the psychopath. Clegg blinks, taken unawares. She jokes. She looks at him with skeptical rigor, as if preparing to bargain. She tells him that Barney Booth is flickering like an electric lightbulb just before it quits. She hurries away, leaving convection currents of perfume behind, dark and feline with a bitter tang.

Buenas dias, thumblickers, he says after she has gone, his mood one of bleak exhilaration. Something has happened, but he knows not what. Buenas, he says again, dropping into a formula used when the bogey was dead center in his gun sight. The afternoon hangar echoes, then goes still again. If Bellanca Cruisemaster has a son, does she save his discarded cigar boxes? Out of mingled love and practicality. Or, like his mother again, does she wear an undergarment inside her bra mainly because she feels something indelicate in her bosom's touching the satin inside the cups?

Is he dreaming? Every now and then he gets the feeling that events are tuning him up for a life both richer and more daring. Downtown with his umbrella, pausing in the rain at the plate glass door of a shopping mall, he feels the vibrations of cars' engines in the thin stem and the upside-down shepherd's crook of the handle. Telling him what? To be ready for the summons to do, to be, to go. Phrases idly intercepted from newspapers or radio take root in his head and unfurl their hints. He hears about a job at, he thinks, London University. A Readership. All the lucky occupant has to do is read, night and day. He never sleeps, he never eats. Before him sits an ever-bigger stack of books that will kill him in the end. First go the eyes, then the mind. It sounds like a punishment. The Reader reads for all who no longer read. He reads himself to death. Clegg will not mind when the phone informs him that he has been appointed to the job. Perhaps it will be not in London at all but in an open university. Another phrase that has wandered into his range. No walls, no rooms, no lecture halls, but the wind and the rain evenhandedly mauling everything, books and papers, desks and chairs. At any rate it will be roofless though it may have walls. He puts the walls back into his image of the place and sees legions of Readers crouched at their vigil, knocking the snow off the page in front of them, anxiously checking their progress by the nearest sundial half the year useless. It reminds him of Monino, the Russian air force's open-air aviation museum outside Moscow. It is very special, high-class, but it has no walls. Yes, he has put the walls back in, he has just done that. Alumnus of a large state university, he now creates a Stonehenge in the Ivy League, beaming with sly satisfaction. Druids are the Readers. The books are massive as flagstones. From time to time the readers grab a handful of snow for breakfast. Thinner by the week, they read until the death rattle halts them. Now he shifts the scene to any of the well-known deserts, siting his open university in tents of silk or rather mazes of it, open to the sun. Now the readers lick the salt from their arms. It will kill them just as soon as the snow. At least they have lush rugs to squat on. He tires of the game, embodies the whole thing in one image of a reader, the best-read reader of all, chained to a lectern whose shelf is the brass back of an eagle, whose book is gigantic, whose pages do not turn. This reader reads again and again the same words incised by lightning. All ye need to know on earth, he muses, and walks into the mall to buy his monthly ration of aviation magazines, usually four, with a military one making five.

And there, with coffee in Styrofoam beaker, he sits reading on a bench by the ersatz fountain into whose pool children toss pennies. Even as he reads, a few of them make tiny splashes. Oblivious, he is Rodin's Reader, his tall form skewed vinelike, his head racing with how other men fly their planes, what kinds of planes they buy new or used, why they have crashed or flown nonstop to South Africa with their wings crammed full of fuel. He is a lover of the cockpit, yes.

Savors that word. It will do. Feet first he climbs in, but with penis second. It is a fuller sensation than he gets from boudoir models in scant satins or air hostesses dubbed Deb in airport motels. These monthly magazines are his manna, his fix, his aerial pageant. Booth has his storm scopes and Bellanca Cruisemaster, his assignations in the unused Mitsubishi, but Clegg has what he sometimes calls his reading matter, not just magazines, but the matter in them springing out like the fourth dimension from a tesseract. He still flies, of course, but humdrum stuff, whereas his reading matter lets him ferry light twins all the way across the Atlantic, win the Schneider Trophy in a seaplane back in the nineteen thirties. The China Clipper is his, stolen from the hands of Alan Ladd, or someone similar. He does not, however, even in his overloaded head, fly the Cyrano, that dark blue dart crashed into the desert so long ago. Too much pain. Flying Cyrano was less flying a plane than departing from the species altogether, each man his own guided missile. So fast, so high, so pure. It lurks in his memory somewhere behind the Dark Ages, a corpse of rapture, its useful load how many thousand pounds? He cannot bear the thought. What, then, is the useful load of a head, before it bleeds open at the seams or through all the fine knitting on the bone of the skull? He thinks he is approaching overload. His monthly reading matter fills him up until he forgets it bit by bit, the better to take in next month's flying news. An anemic child, he has not grown into an anemic man, but he remembers as if yesterday his mother explaining how she cooks in an iron pan, just for him, and thrusts long nails into his apples beforehand. He eats iron. No, Mamma, he hears a little Clegg insisting, I will eat aluminum. His mind is on planes as young as that. He eats his iron, though, but dreams its filings fly through him to a big fat magnet at his core. Somehow he flies. He flies anyhow. In his dithers and his dreams and on the potty and at the table and while buying a corsage for his date at the prom. And at his desk too, prematurely Boothlike. The thought arrives. He dwells on it. He makes it go away. Not yet is he mad enough or thwarted enough, nor has he been reckless enough, to fly a desk. Certainly, doing charters, he is Hercules snapping a toothpick, but never mind, he goes up, he soars, he comes down full of drunken longing. All the rest of his days is an in-between, even here by the fountain next door to the pattern of pennies in the six-inch water. The fountain plays and so does he, his ears become sharply elfin in the imaginary slipstream, his feet on the rudder pedals of his shoes, his hands holding the magazines tilting the ship with slight adjustments of page corners until, as the lingo has it, he trues out at such and such a speed, trimmed right, cruise-climbing to an unthinkable height above the glossy pages. And now, as if on earth at the time for lighting of lamps, it is the time to breathe oxygen from a mask, leaving humankind far beneath him, making the very condors jealous, nudging his way through the purple zone into the black of an airless weatherless otherwhere.

A small boy is reading over his shoulder right beside him, snaffling up a bit of this big man's private dream. A Clegg minor who is going to be a major in some as yet undevised air force. Clegg smiles at him, points at a Mooney 231. Fast, he says. See how clean and streamlined. Sometimes hard to slow them when you land. When the wheels are down the spats that cover them almost touch the ground. You get scratches in no time. Rock strikes chip the paint away. You will find it a tad nose-heavy, son, if you're accustomed to the 201. And no short fields. Be careful. No Mooneys in the boonies. The boy sidles away to start up his three-thousand-pound pipe dream while Clegg resumes, holding all the magazines in one wad, supporting one with four, as if afraid to let them go, which to him is like abandoning control of the yoke.

Back to his lair he drives, having bought some rolls of mints, a bag of potato chips, a stack of muffins, and a pound of butter. Toast, he thinks, as always in November, in tune with the embers of the year. It is Saturday, with a ceiling so low the street lights are on at three in the afternoon. By the cheery glow of the news channel, his fire, he reads and reads, head above the clouds.

Organ music, faint but calm and ecclesiastical, comes from the speaker next to the screen. He can never quite turn the volume to zero without switching the whole thing down. He gets up, pours bleach into the wash-basin and dilutes it to receive two sets of shorts and two shirts, all of which he presses into the liquid with the bottom of the plastic mouthwash bottle. Soon everything is underwater to whiten evenly. That he can take such care not to bleach his hands amazes him. Does their faint tan mean so much? The tan of the seasoned pilot after thousands of hours with the sun drilling him through the canopy. Yes, he thinks, I should have told that kid about the dark glare shield above the 231's cowl. When you go that high, the sun is a factor. What amazes him more, though, is the cross-warp of his being, at once lewd and vulgar and crude, but also tender and finicking and sensitive. *Easily hurt,* he feigns with his mouth. Willing to be brutal too. How can any human be such a mess of contradictions, even if on the way to a better self, at which he will arrive by seventy, seventy-five, eighty, then, surely not with his last gasp? The childlike side of him has always been something he treasures. Proof that he is no monster, no dragon of maturity.

He will never get old, but only become an older child, his face crease-less to the end and full of slightly marred naïveté. Even now, none of his hair falls, none of it droops into gray. Heartbeat a touch faster, yes. His wounds affecting his gait. Of course. Eye muscles perhaps a millimeter slower than when he was hot stuff, murmuring *Buenas dias,* thumblick-ers, over he has almost forgotten which chunk of an Oriental sea. If not in the pink, at least in the vermilion, he somehow has to get through until his mother is no more, and beyond that has made no plans, perhaps infected by her desire to have him cease with her. If he survives her, he will go back to school to study astronomy, anthropology, or literature. Things will open out, he will sow seed in his mind, and then a harvest will come. He almost fits Bellanca Cruisemaster into this scenario, as if she is his already. It might not be so hard, he broods, to wean her from the down but not out Booth, whose misery threatens to choke him like a swallowed cactus. When Booth flips, he muses, will be just the time. Or even before, if she so much as drops a hint.

And so, he resumes, then halts. His mind will not work. Has it ever? He tries to figure out what his mind has ever done. If instead of working it has come up with clumsy little buzzes masquerading as thought. His entire life has been a series of salutes, as inappropriate for a human as a draft horse in the New York Public Library, awaiting its turn at the daily paper. He has acquired rigmaroles and routines, but he doubts he has ever learned to think. At least to think as Booth thinks, with bite and flair. Never groping for the right word, able to divide speed into distance mentally and have the answer before Clegg has even formulated the problem. Whenever Booth flew, he seemed to shade over into being the part-inventor of the plane itself. Handling it, he found the ideas that brought it into being and then brought them back to life as hunches. Even at the desk, he encounters the first designer of desks and thinks up the notion of one solid leaf across two pedestals.

But a Clegg just might know better how to cope with a lion in an airport lounge. He rams the rod for opening high windows down the lion's throat and shoves until it comes out the other end, at which point he and another coolie carry the still heaving beast away between them. Brave. Picturesque. Foul. Booth is more metallurgical, Clegg is more down home. Men going mad need leisure in which to do it. Words, he decides, are the outpatients of a mind diseased. Glory be, he has begun to think again, not as well as Booth, but up to his own standards.

He turns the organ music up loud, nods amiably at the vision of God he discerns behind the news on the screen. It is one of an ancient, mahogany-skinned, blue-haired organist with calipers for hands and ectoplasm pouring from his mouth all over the keys. Not an Ancient but a Recent of Days, like Bellanca Cruisemaster moving to music no watcher can hear. Something defiant in her name, something racy too, sets his newly awoken mind pondering her real name, possibly Ellen Wulfric. It can be any other name too. He knows her true name will never figure in his dealings with her. Sheathed in her alias, she will take him far even though she sounds like a motheaten goddess of war. Truth told, she names herself after a plane that Clegg knows well, and he is more than willing to go along. The Ellens, the Debs, even the Marjes, the Maes, the Kittys, godhelphim even the Winnies, have taken their toll of him, and now he wants nothing to be for real. The man in love with Booth's woman will always have to keep a hunting knife handy, not to quell Booth with, but to save himself from her most abandoned caresses. An also-ran, he strikes himself as a belated winner, as of old when he and Booth passed their women to and fro, even during the same afternoon, no more than biologically diverted to be riding where the other's semen had only recently spilled. If this was akin to a bond of blood-brotherliness, it augured a sharing to come. If we have indeed grown apart, he reasons, then this is how to bring us back together. He avoids me, but not all the time. Pain has made him shy. He wonders if, in those days, any of the other man's sperm had swum up the other man's urethra, to a deader end than any woman could provide. Booth's senior to his own, of course. They soon got washed out again, into the arena, on the other's tide. He remembers how Booth, telling his tale in the lecherous vivid present, recounts having seen a woman prone and stitch-naked on a towel on a North African beach. Her thighs parted, says Booth, screened from the shore by a small rectangular strip of sail or parachute silk. I approach, I kneel, I make initial contact, wondering how soon I will be arrested, and enter her, and she does not even look behind her, nor does she turn her head when he withdraws and wordlessly walks away, tugging up his shorts. Like all Booth's tales, it makes Clegg tingle. The life he wants has always been over the other side of the hill. He is more likely to buy Leonardo da Vinci an ice cream cone. Had he been on that beach instead of Booth, the woman would have melted into a desert mirage and the police would have been ready for him, concealed in a foxhole under the top sand.

He swallows his breath to seize control. What he thinks was overture has been his entire life. Downhill from here, he tells himself, for me and the charter game. Nameless things or thingless names are all he wants. Only do. No more done. A brave code at his age, but he faces his decline nimbly. Bellanca Cruisemaster is teaching him to be himself. To swoon, if he must, among the silks and sherbets of any given red-lamp district. Cairo. Delhi. Istanbul. He corrects the bits about sherbets but lets the silk stand. If his day has not come to him, at least he is going to it.

The small meal begins. Broccoli, small whole potatoes, one wedge of lightly battered tempura. Not the low-residue meal of Cyrano days, but enough to get him to Africa should the need arise. Human life, he has almost been on the point of telling his mother, reduces itself to buying food in one alcove, consuming it in another, disposing of it in yet another. With the destroyer of all delight peering over the wall at you, as unforgiving as the air. That temporary cooperation from a lethal thing, he dotes on that. No boss to please. No influence to peddle. No praise or blame. Just the ax on the neck or not. Wind shear or gall bladder, it is the same to him. Because it kills you does not mean it dislikes you.

So, he reminds himself, nibbling a thin mint coated with chocolate, when I fly home empty after a charter and fly upside down on one engine, just to vary things a little, the air does not take offense. Has no opinion of me. Luck and the laws decide it all. Booth holds on to me as if I were a souvenir. Were I Barney Booth, I would be rid of me, I'd rid myself of

Clegg. So what is the link? Why am I any longer important to his well-being? As a butt? A pet? A toy? Just because it always seems to be November, today being November the 309th? Not as his mother needs him. Staring into his eyes that stare into hers, she knows what he has seen. He has seen awareness pondering its own end, the look that forecasts the end of all seeing. This is the dire, drab knack of having a mind at all. Peer and see yourself in another's fading. Hers the stoop, the lunging but girlish lurches on standing up straight, the dozes and the hand tremors, but these are his too, dealt him by blood and time.

Barney Booth, Clegg finds, as he does the dishes one-handedly, sterilizing them rather than washing them under a scalding stream, Barney Booth knows all the how. Want a Western omelette, a free tube of brushless shaving cream, a glass of Strega, and a Spanish porno magazine, en route cabin class from Keflavík to Cozumel? Then Barney will tell you which flight to take on which airline. So to speak. But that is all. He knows nothing durably olden. He has only added up the horsepower of all the aircraft engines ever built and worked out its ratio to all the energy in the known stars, arriving at a number so forlorn and enormous he simply calls it B's b for Barney's batch or Booth's byte. Booth has abolished the discreet and handy art of abbreviation, not referring you to *Moby-Dick* but saying the entire book aloud rather than refer to it in insufficient form. Thus Clegg lies to himself, distorting Booth's bizarre behavior into an antic easier to manage. Thus he believes that Booth wants, as soon as possible, a wholly unmanageable world, with all systems foundering. Booth to him is Samson, pulling the pillars down on top of himself. Clegg, as is plain for all to see, pulls him clear at the last instant. Out of kindness, gentle-heartedness. Out of do as you would be done by. Do unto Booth as, unless ragingly insane, Booth will do unto Clegg.

Now he is close to it. It sounds right, but he knows it is wrong. Booth is not Clegg. Booth's sanity is not Clegg's. And their insanity when it blooms will be different as two artichokes. As when his mother mishandles something with rheumatic hands, each time setting off a wholly different chain of circumstances. Writing a check, she tugs a sheet of spare paper from under a vase, so smashing it and cutting her finger, then getting blood in her eye from rubbing it, next dropping the glass eyebath in the washbasin, and wearing herself out as she searches for every last splinter of glass. Next time she tugs a sheet of paper free it will paper-cut her finger. She cannons on from day to day, wishing she were with him in the realm of utter cloudlessness, where the temperature is more or less stable. A climb of from five to eleven miles, depending on whether you are over the pole or the equator, and she is there, in ultraheaven, not quite in orbit but smooth as a feather afloat on cream. Vacancy, sameness, violet, quiet, are what they have been trained for, Booth and Clegg, but these are what Clegg's mother likes as well, not knowing their slang word for them. Isodrome. The place where all things are equal. In his mind, he flies all charters away up there, tempted to take a leaf from Booth's book and use Zulu Time as well. A few bumps, though, and the illusion sags, but when he says high-minded he says it with slow-motion reverence. If that Mitsubishi is his Trojan Horse, then the isodrome is my monastery. He says it. Believes it. Knows that believing it makes it real as a laburnum, a tomato, a wren.

Four mugfuls of strong sweet tea laced with top-of-the-milk cream. Enough tannin in there, he thinks, to cure the leather for a shoe or two. Into T-shirt and shorts for the baked heat of the apartment. Fondling his letter, he wonders how to get it to Bellanca Cruisemaster, and already thinks ahead to the next stage of their acquaintanceship. A what-you-are-like breakfast. Booth's of caviar, burned toast, seared sausages, olives, black beans, and black coffee. Black napkins made of leather. Booth is insulted. Clegg's is runny-yolked fried eggs, white bread poached in milk, butter-soaked toast, mousse, pâté, and Bavarian cream cake. Eggnog to drink.

He shrugs at the contrasts. He does not even know her, and here he is rehearsing party games. But all of a sudden he knows how and yells aloud. Yair, he yells, crying aloud the word that Booth whispers.

Unseen so far, this time she ministers to Booth in the Mitsubishi. He lies on his back as if counting stars while she, at a slight diagonal away from him, continues what she has done before. She reads to him something of her own choosing. She is well into it, this thing she thinks he needs. Now she declaims, now she whispers. She halts on one word and lengthens it out the better to dwell on it. Hair-ah-arld, she says *herald*, and clar-ree-own *clarion*. Booth has never heard anything like it except in her readings to him. It comes fusty and dim from a darkness preceding any ancestors. Or so he thinks in his tumbling, green fashion, never a reader of poetry or even someone who gave it the time of day alongside pepper, ammunition, or old cognac. Out come the swords as bright as silver, she says, up spring the spears as high as twenty feet. They hew and cut the helmets all to pieces. Out runs the blood in smoky streams. Down go one or two horses. One rider rolls under his horse just like a ball.

Booth drifts off, hears talk of rest and drink, then something about a tiger in the vale of Gargaphia, name he does not know. She, or what she is reading from the chestnut-brown limp book in her hands, waxes pensive, and he knows he might have heard this before, this about there being an end sometime for every action. The sun goes down, but still the swords bite flesh, and some hero has to be cut out of his armor and put to bed with gentle fussing, with clucks and cooing hushes, until he cries out for his loved one. Who can she be? He will not die. Oh no, but he will never be as good again. And Booth asks her to go back, away from the field of honor, to that stuff, at least a day ago in Zulu Time, about the putting on of goldsmith's work, steel and embroidery, coats of mail, coats of arms, buckles, straps, rings, and thongs. Yes, he says, say that part about the golden bridles and the herald who blows an O on his trumpet. That's my meat.

You asked for it, she says, and without the book says mine is the prison in the dark hut, mine the strangling and the hanging by the throat, and he sighs, moves his mouth as if to resume where she leaves off, but makes instead a gentle puff without the smoke. He is calming. He is trying to calm down. She reads his comfort to him, but what the verses tell is far from balm. The wounded man begins to swell, the blood clotted goes bad, the bleeding and the cupping do not help, and no herb works its magic on him, nor vomiting nor, as the line goes, laxative downward.

Now she resumes, appearing to skip with almost random precision, and mopping something that stings her eye. With my cousin Palamon here I have had strife and rancor for much past time. The lines jar him, but he whispers aloud the last few words, drenching his mind in much past time. Then says no. He does not like the phrase. Then, no, he means it isn't true. Then, yes, it could be true, but he doesn't like the phrase that much. She reads fast. He has heard it before. There is a watershed between end and beginning, between farewell and onset, but she ignores it, merging the last words in the first, but he knows when, like a cable channel being switched at source, the live thing spills into the other's wake, when she says: *this fair company, Amen. Once upon a time,* and he sites a mental slash mark between Amen and Once. He has learned. He plays her like a phonograph record. She knows it by heart, but pretends to read it. Less strain on her. He likes to see it in her hand, a hymnal maybe. It is a mental leech. A poultice. A swab. It eggs him on and does him in. It lures him back into bits of himself long forgotten. They warm as if deluged with unvarying sunlight, and his mind warms at them. He dotes on the colors, the bravery, the clatter of gear, the snorting horses, but he hates the parts about the lover howling in his tower, the love triangle behind the heraldry. He tries to tell her what upsets him. Stirring a dream of glory, the tale is full of blood. Blood of friends. Friends at odds. Too close to home, but will anything farther from home get through to you? She asks this, but his answer is a wave. He has to wait it out. He has to chomp a bitter pill. Won't let her read anything else. Wants this radiant nightmare as familiar as no-man's-land, through which he crawls, memorizing it inch by inch. The day will come when. He never says the final bit. As if he's answered a why with a *because*.

Fired, he tells her, yet again, about the Cyrano, embellishing just a little. Dagger point. Beaver tail. Huge engine pods. It squats. Burnished metal cylinders enclose the wheels in flight. To keep them from melting. He coos. They are always torn and scarred anyway. Look at them, full of nitrogen. Air is no good. Now the two cones of the engines. Just like two tits from the Congo. He laughs. It is as far ago as the Middle Ages. He refuses to say long ago.

They never fly them full throttle, he tells her. I mean those who fly them now. I am no longer part of any they.

She tells him he is part of a we. To hell with theys. They is, well, remote, almost nobody at all.

He needs to hear such things. She says them because she feels sorry for him in an almost scholarly way, as if he is a rained-on text, a shrapnel-torn bit of the Bayeux tapestry. Booth has been something he will never be again, and its tremors linger.

He is talking again. Titanium. Steel. Special paint, he says, absorbs the light. She does not, he adds, meaning the Cyrano, paint on radar. The leading edge of the wing, she learns, is smeared with tarlike goop, which at night glows like St. Elmo's fire. She begins to disbelieve him, even more when, with jerky vehemence, he says it helps the plane to sweat its fuel vapor out. The thing is sheathed in tiny plates, just like some forms of armor, see, and the tarry stuff helps it to breathe. It is full of fuel.

If, he says, getting homely, you wash your shorts in the bathroom basin, wring them out, and then forget to put them on a hanger to dry, but leave them on the porcelain, they will make an exact damp print of themselves, and so the plane. A wet bear on sand. You would think it had to be super polished, but they leave it rough. It does not so much fly through air as through high heat. Once there were thirty of them. Twenty-five, say. Maybe a dozen now. I'm out of touch. Sixty-odd ground crew to each plane. Those were not the days, those were the years. Far ago. To and fro. He bites home a sob and fishes behind him as if for a pistol to end it all.

But he drags it on without even getting up, a royal blue jumpsuit with, on one shoulder, the emblem to beat all. This, he tells her, triumphantly tender with his own memory, is the patch. Plan view of the Cyrano. The view from on high.

He points at where it says 3+ in white on black. Three times sound, he whispers, and then some.

And this, he says in the same whisper, pointing to what she cannot see, is the Habu sign. Japanese for a snake like a cobra. How we struck without ever striking. All we ever did was reconnoiter. They called it that on Okinawa. The name stuck. The patch sticks. When a man becomes a skeleton, if he has flown the Cyrano, the patch holds on to his very bone. Jesus, Bell', the new ones go so fast you get a 6+ on the patch. Six plus. Which will get you to Greenwich from here in twenty-four minutes. That is what cousin Clegg dreams about. Reads about. What we still share. Not that he wants to go to Greenwich. He wants to go so high he won't come back. Now, why, in such a giving universe, would I ever think poor enough of such as him as to kill him off inside my head? As if he never mattered. Like he was a blade of dry grass. I truly think I wanted him dead so's I could get out of there and not look back. Or have to get him out as well. Selfish. Self-ish.

He drones into it again, accusing himself in curt asides, airing the wound, tapping the scab that peels away, dabbing the seep. He has no power over this acid doldrum. He finds himself wanting, even so long after, and she hears him out, thinking you give a child a spoon to play with, a rusk, a paper gnome. Now quit, she says. I've heard it. Let it go. It is not you. That was another. He went away with that year. You think it's guilt but it's nothing but fucking vanity. I humor you. Then you humor me. Out of your system with it and into the trash. Life does not so much go on as never leave off. *Barney.* She pleads but he prevails, wondering why her profile never seems to match her seen full face. He gets up, still in the royal blue jacket. They come and go, lugging and tugging, even to the point of gasp and puff. Into each vacant seat in the Mitsubishi they fit naked plastic mannequins, taken by night from the horn of plenty over the FBO, behind the whitewashed windows, where he stores the model trains, the Erector sets, the scrubbed-out churns, the folded-up hot-air balloons, the lecterns, the searchlights, the six-foot teddy bears, the swords, the steel helmets, the spurs, the saddles, the suits of armor, the hogsheads of acid, the trouser presses, the man-sized sponges, the diving suits, the ten-foot mahogany templates once used for designing the hulls of oceangoing ships. It is as if, and this her thought, he has been a looting army that has brought everything home with him, meaning one day to devise a plan that will bring it all into active relationship in the light. Instead, he has gathered it up from junk shops mainly in the area, stowing it upstairs at night, each month adding a lock or changing one. You know how fatso Göring glommed onto all the art in World War Two? Well, he sometimes tells her, even though she knows differently, I have Göring himself locked up in there, in sawdust, in a hippo box, kept alive on offal and onions against a rainy day. You'll see.

If it's a shelter against nuclear fallout, she says, sometimes entering into the spirit of things, why isn't it underground? And then —

Things will never come to that, he says. I'm just keeping my stuff by me for when I decide to spread myself. In another country, say. When my ship comes in. They sometimes do. Then you unpack.

Inexplicably hushed among the figurines in the seats, they tap the wood and plastic of the hands, the shoulders, the neuter faces. Deathless passengers, these, prey to no flaw in the Mitsubishi, with no spleens to rupture, no hearts to break. He likes them. They are his idea. She would like to paint mustaches on them, dress them in something old, something new. Adopt them as props. Air them in a garden. Let the birds drop lime on them. Wet them. But no, he pulls the faded drapes upon them, checks each window from the outside, and nods.

Them's my dead, he says.

Speak English, speak American.

When *they* do, I will.

Wood and plastic, she says. They're duds.

They won't be, he exclaims, once I get this bluebird out of here, up where she belongs. These are mine. It must be true. Honest, where the oxygen begins to give out, that's the place they'll come to life.

No, he is not mad, she decides, but just a doodling hobbyist who can't believe his shrines don't hold a deity. Humor him, he'll get bored, and then we'll go to bed again, right here on the bunk, as before. He has his ways and I have mine. I go by a nickname. He goes by a nicklife. I'll take eccentrics any day before another bloody dentist with his golf, his stocks, his dermatitis hands.

Something pure sweeps through her as if she has plunged her hands through a sunset. What she feels for Barney Booth is really what she feels for people at large. He the peg for it. Sad for folk, but willing to be deliciously consternated, she fixes on him. His oddity stands for human oddity at large. What was wrong at Troy and Thebes is wrong with him. A man she generalizes into Man. And she is no longer bored.

Neither, at the curtained window, is Clegg, woolgathering in the gloom while his feet steer him hangarward. He cannot hear, he cannot see. He wriggles, he can see a bit. Booth gets louder and Clegg can hear the wind-throttled moan of his officerly voice. Clegg sees Booth addressing a group of nudists, on his face a look of dredged-up sewer cheapness. His eyes are taut.

You can understand, he says, why it matters to someplace like Numbskullville to beat Assholetown at baseball two to one, because they can all as it were shimmy down into the game, lost or won, I mean squirm down into it like into a sock. Outside there is only something awful like [plates of glass a thousand miles square,] not on the human scale at all. No wonder we get into little victories. You have to look away. You have to shrink the scale. There have to be small things to care a lot about because our big emotions are not big enough for what truly dwarfs us. Well?

She does not answer, but cranks a hand at him, meaning he should go on. Frowning, Clegg has heard only a few words such as *baseball, glass,* and *scale.* It isn't fair. He'll put it right. Knock on the fuselage?

Who else is there? They don't do much. Dummies, of course. The woman nude, Booth in that Cyrano jacket whereas Clegg has never worn his own since Africa. Booth pantsless. No, Clegg thinks dismally, I never intrude on the nude. Booth's hand rises as he seems to incantate, then falls to a dummy's shoulder. Gifted folk in a lousy world, he's saying, give the world the crap it wants. But that will not wash, Bell', at highest altitude. Only the best. Nearer to God, who I firmly do not believe fraternizes with caterpillars, roaches, and worms of the Earth. In the end, whether you march up the runway in a gigantic hat with two fishing poles, or jump out of a biplane without a parachute, you are out of scale. Your death is just too trivial. It harms only those whose deaths are trivial too. If this sounds unhinged, it cannot possibly be so; I was never hinged. None of us is. But, when you're right on top, way above the very tops of the clouds, and there is nothing much between you and the sun and it is pouring in on you like murder water, then you feel in scale. You are doing something so damned outrageous that you kind of fatten up mentally. You are quite alone. You own it. It obeys you. You grind over the world in a rapture of the heights.

Move back to Clegg the loveless. He loves his mother, but that is not what loveless means. Alone in the FBO after an all-day charter, he scratches his head, tugs away a small scab, and flicks it off his nail onto the tabletop. Eyes it closely. Picks his teeth with an amber-colored toothpick split from a rack of them in something like a matchbook. Eyes the morsel too. Bits of him are coming together apart from him. He picks up the scab by pressing the morsel upon it with watchmaker delicacy, then ports the toothpick across the room to the trash can, walking with stealth. He knows what to do next. It is no longer a matter of inventing little projects to kill the time when he isn't flying. All he has to do is pick a moment and go. If he can only be patient, things will come his way.

Nonetheless he goes home and slides little magnetic planes across the cool white of the refrigerator door, changing the formation from this to that. Line astern, when they are all behind one another. He scoffs. When they are all in a forward-flying line, anyway. Then they fly forward abreast of one another. The next formation he makes a V, which becomes a miss-ing-man formation with a gap for where the dead man used to fly. This one moves him. Whom is the gap for? One of the two of them, to be sure. No, his mother is nearest to that vacancy. Now he arranges them to fly into one another like arrows into a bull's-eye. Rearranged yet again, they all fly from the same center to different points of the compass. He feels he has discovered [infinity.] Stand there long enough at the refrigerator, not even opening it for a slice of ham to keep him from going faint, and he will exhaust the combinations. Never: there is always one more to do, forced into being by the one before. So, instead, he distributes the little planes around the apartment, attaching them to anything metallic, and the tiny see-through plastic disks of the whirling propellers fan him into some sort of peace. Were this Lilliput, the local sky would be aroar with aero engines, and the white foam earplugs he uses to save his hearing when aloft, and to guard his sleep, would have another use. He marvels at how much of his day he wears them. Seven hours' sleep plus six hours' fly-ing equals almost half a day. This is why everything, even the fountain in the mall, feels too loud. He recalls with a wan, stunted grin the old avia-tors' joke about hearing. How come you haven't gone deaf, flying all your life without earplugs? What? What did you say? It can still fish a grin from him. Without humor, how daunting the vastness of the unknowable world would be. He types it on a slip of paper as if preparing a speech for some coming occasion. When he has fifty, he will make his speech. As he types, he looks up, switches off the On-Off wheel, caressing its knurl, and grins again; each time he switches it off or on, the TV screen crackles and the image does a little jump, almost a sprint into nowhere. Not quite. He tries again. It happens only when he switches off, and a small oblong of white light soars away sideways like a calling card jettisoned in space.

He is close now to some imperfect serenity, the cool intact closeness he needs before attempting something big. He has to settle down within himself. He has to come free in the mind. It is almost like self-hypnosis. The little magnet planes watch over him, watched over in their turn by cut-out pictures of planes from magazines. But he never mutilates his per-fect series of back issues. If he finds a photograph he likes, and wants to mount on white cardboard, he buys another copy to cut it from. So the first half hour with a new magazine is mainly a scouting expedition to see if he needs a duplicate. This month, no, he already has the ones he likes. The magazines repeat themselves, alas. His apartment is full of planes. Even the nondescript mass-produced pictures that his rent includes have gone, blocked out by planes Scotch-taped over them. The walls fly. They teem with wings and tails, cabins and sharp noses. Only the ceiling is left, and he will turn to that soon. In maybe a year he will have to use the floor, leaving tracks to walk on. And then the inside of the refrigerator, the swollen hips of the toilet pedestal, the insides of the drawers in his desk, the other drawers that hold his clothes. And then the walls of the shower? No, that would require waterproof reproductions, which are nowhere sold. In another life, another time, even that might be possible, but he knows the limits of the world he lives in. After death, though, he sees himself in a small round room papered with planes the world will never see, and flying a small paper plane in endless circles from his right hand past his mother who sits opposite him, in a rocker of crystal and gold leaf, to his left hand, from which he transfers it to launch again.

Now he is utterly calm. It is night. Out to the FBO he goes, bicycling lampless by moonlight. If only, he dreams, they won't be there. Now he treads gently from point to point, arrives at the hangar, sidles in, breathing in little gulps. He knows how to do it. Like a Boy Scout, he is prepared. He is going to come full circle, given a bit of luck. At the Mitsubishi, to which he knows his way blindfolded by now, he can hardly bear to look. The cheap-looking drapes are still drawn. He peers inside. No Booth, no Bellanca Cruisemaster. They must be having a night off, at the movies, or they are midnight boating on the lake. Anything romantic. The nudes are still there, though, and Clegg bristles with delight, enters, lifts one up and carries it into the far corner of the hangar, where he wraps it in an old tarpaulin sheet. Back, he strips naked, stuffs his clothes neatly folded under the seat, and takes up position, humming a mild military march. With a long wait to come, he ought to have brought something to read. No. He will be too busy. How light the plastic nude was. He has not even noted its sex. Now he applies light brown makeup to his face, his neck, his chest, to all of him, glad he has never been hairy. Soon done, he stows the tube and waits, casting sideways glances at the other figures. He cannot figure why Booth has left them there to give the game away. If the pair of them want to be private and secret, then why leave the mannequins in place?

He has no idea, but something firm swims through him: the certainty of having exerted himself in a gesture. It is almost enough. He can go home now and wash off. Vowing, though, to give up a few hours, having gone this far, he gets comfortable and begins to muse, delightedly aware of having done something he has never done before, something whose consequences are wholly unknown. Even if no one comes, he will still have accomplished one thing. A decisive blank. This is his vigil. He sits there stained and chilly, not quite at the Lourdes of aviation, but half expecting a miracle. If he were they, and they found him, he would be pleased, full of mingled delight and envy. After all, he is one of them, one of the team. He has shown willing. The rest is up to them. His thoughts come and go like the windblown tatters of a crashed plane, motes of fabric wafted about. Motes is too small, though. He settles for scraps, wisps, tads.

Almost two hours later, someone arrives. There are voices, little taps on the fuselage, the scuff of shoes. Clegg suddenly thinks an awful thought: he is the only one of the figurines with genitals. He should have taken care of that, painted his shorts light brown. *Anything.* Through a crack in his left eye he sees the door open, Booth scramble in, reeling from liquor or fatigue. One quick look and he is gone, but he has uttered something, not to the unseen Clegg, but to the plane's interior. Booth has checked to see if everything's in place. No more than that. It is. He goes, grumbling to her. Even with his flashlight, Booth has not seen the daubed-up Clegg, who either wants to be noticed or doesn't. He just doesn't wish to be walked away from.

They are far away, however, when Clegg decides what to do. His grand move has petered out, but his imagination has not quit. Blundering forward naked, he eases into the cockpit and locates the master switch, gets light, and plumps into the left-hand seat, wondering if he just might have a stab at it. He does, and the left-hand Garrett coughs into life right there in the hangar, blasting everything loose into orbit behind it, but too enclosed to reach Booth already far away. A faint engine noise reaches him, and he shrugs, envious of course but too sloshed and jaded to care that much. All the way to maximum revs goes Clegg, with a truant schoolboy feeling from many years ago. He has never flown it, but he could. He would have to go away for a week to learn, and then return in triumph. Then they could all go up, the dud and the living both. Naked or clothed.

Enclosed in the engine's storm, he knows no other world, only vaguely remembering Booth has told him the engines will not start. One does, he knows, but he does not start the other. This is enough. There is no night watchman here. Booth is too cheap. How long, he wonders, has this fuel sat in the tanks? Surely it goes off. Surely water forms in it. After a five-minute run he shuts the engine down, appalled by the sudden silence amid which he hears the insectlike clicks of parts cooling. Another Clegg would have started up the other engine and blasted his way through the hangar wall, at some risk, of course. This Clegg works in a lower register of the dramatic. Slowly he leaves the cockpit after shutting off the master, slow-gaits into the cabin and finds his clothes in that neat pile under the seat. He closes the door with a gentle nudge and walks away without a thought for the mannequin under the tarp in the hangar's far corner. As content as Booth to let things be, to be found or not, he inhales the evening air as if he has never breathed before. He does not relish going back to the apartment and the thump-thump of stereos played loud into the atrium through open windows. Only once has he retaliated, turning his own up full and leaving the building for an hour with all his windows wide open behind him. As far as he can tell, no one noticed, or if they did they liked the noise. He has reported the noise once too often for security to care.

Were an aero engine to run in his apartment all day, he would not mind. Such racket is manna to him, the manger of an aerial miracle, whereas drums and double bass hurt his sinuses and make him sweat.

Opening asparagus, he bends the can's lid back on a tiny flange upon which he sets bits of fiber he cannot chew. This is his way. He uses what is at hand and modifies it with practical sweetness. His mind thrills with what he has just done, a thing far deeper than marching on the runway in Booth's big hat. This time he was inventive. Next time he will be better. Nothing dangerous, but impossible not to notice. Where is he headed to, he asks himself. He does not know. Mere motion must suffice. Opening a bag of potato chips, he smells the aroma of someone who has lain too long in bed. Nothing is wrong, the chips are fresh and crisp, but their bouquet has been trapped in too small a space. Two seconds and it clears, yet not before he has wondered if there might be, somewhere in town, someone who smells precisely this way. Not he, of that he is certain. Cleggmusk has peppermint in it, a touch of honeysuckle sap, a breath of heather to drive the girls crazy.

Now he wonders about Booth's belle, wonders why, at a distance of only twelve paces, her mouth and nostrils seem to form one splotch, not unattractive by any means, but merged. A pad to kiss. Why, that is duelling distance, he thinks. Twelve paces. They march six apiece, then turn and fire. In the old days, when you never lasted long enough in the military to be pensioned off. Or out. Airman again, he thinks about the Mitsubishi, worth a pretty penny still. Why does Booth use it as an igloo? Why not sell it? Why fill it with fake humans from shopwindows? Booth has reminded him of the dummies used in tests of car or plane, but these dummies are not even strapped in. No, there can be no test afoot, but maybe Booth is experimenting with seating arrangements for the long-postponed day on which he will take the Mitsu to the air, just a quick tour around the pattern, then home to a summons from the government agency that has banned him. It will be worth it, Clegg decides: I'll help him, come what may. Even if we have to serve time together. It isn't airworthy. We are not current in it. I have not been away for a week to learn. I just might, though, given enough encouragement. He plans tomorrow's brunch at Arthur's, exhilarated by the afterwave of prankish joy. Eggs Benedict from eleven in the morning on.

His cuticles are ragged, his eyes feel crusted, his scalp itches, and he has a slight shaving rash under the chin, but all this falls away from what he thinks his feat. He deems it that, unearthing an old word of sufficient heft and ripeness. *Deem*, he says aloud: I judge it so. When he drifts into this mellow vein, even Africa comes back as something fabulous. Booth saved him. No, Booth was saved at much the same time. Booth had nothing to do with the fluke that saved them both. That other crash. He means forced landing. A one in ten thousand chance or better. Now, in mind's eye, he enters a sports supply store and knows what he is looking for. He should have thought of it before. It is just as well that Booth did not look close when he came aboard tonight. Next time, a more conversant Clegg will be ready for him. *Be prepared.*

And so he is. And so it turns out. In light brown satin panties the exact hue of his body, he sits again in the Mitsubishi in the same seat, on his face and head the off-white mask of a hockey goalie, quite dehumanizing him into something between what sits in an electric chair and someone in a sinusitis helmet. He even feels inhuman. He thrills with a shiver at how uncouth he looks, at how demure. They do not come. He waits an hour, then two. They must be trysting in Greenland. And still they do not come, but a mechanic sent by Booth, who telephones, actually enters, gapes at the dummies in the gloom, and heads for the cockpit, where he tests the master, the magnetos, and in general fiddles about without switching an engine on. Nothing so vast for him. In ten minutes he is done, brushing past Clegg's shoulder on his way out. He will wonder later about that faint brown stain. Someone, Booth says, has meddled with the Mitsu. The engine ran. Now, who? A gremlin, they all tell him. Barney Booth is imagining things again, just when they thought he was partly calming down: the bonkers boss. Booth insists. No engine switches on itself. It cannot happen. Some tampering oaf.

Whom he will behead with the four-bladed propeller if he catches him.

What's in there? Like sculptures, the mechanic says. He is starting up an art gallery in there. A new gimmick. Them's the only kind of passengers Barney Booth'll get in there. The dead, the dumb, the daft, the doomed. Not that they don't amount to a sizable population.

Tempted to cough or speak, Clegg keeps mum, of course. It is no use scaring the man to death, or even Booth and his doxy. In his mask and briefs he wants to eavesdrop on their lovemaking, of whatever quality, and

rear up at them from his seat like one of the living dead in the exact middle of their whitest fit. Something like, when passion's gasp and blather
turns to good-humored astonishment at having such merry company.
And then they all join in. Three musketeers. Clegg dreams with style. He
does not hedge or fidget. He waits well, and with seething purpose. During his mother's naps, he has sat thus for an hour, afraid to move and wake
her with a creak, a rubbing noise. So this is as nothing to him. He finds
the book. He reads. The flashlight fails. He rummages for another, finds
one. Continues reading that softbound book of hers, nodding as he does at
poetry, especially of an antique sort, and at last begins to doze, wondering
what he has read, it meant so little, he not having realized that the left-
hand page was English medieval, the right-hand English modern. He has
gone from left to left, for some reason omitting the twentieth century,
which means he must have been following some of it because the words
run on from one page to the next: *unto the stake. / And in the rescous . . .
gan to turne,* he reads, *and leep asyde.* Not even the police have come to
get him. Does he wish them to? He has just decided yes when the pair of
them arrive, enter, take no heed of him, and without unclothing fall to it,
or something very like, right there on the bunk. He halts his breath and
makes a brick of it within his chest. All very lovey-dovey, Clegg decides.
Nothing fierce in this at all. The kisses cluck. The sighs achieve a higher
pitch. The gasps become impetuous. The endearments fly. Then the velvet roars of true togetherness and Clegg has become a voyeur, aurally at
least. No longer that virginity for him. He sighs, he has to let it out. Booth
hears, then shrugs. Who is he to know?

Up gets Booth, still trembling, unsure if he is furious or glad. At last
Clegg has gone too far. Booth scans the dummies, easily picks out Clegg,
and, while she calls faintly after him, prods the top of his shoulder with his
forefinger. No response. Then the Adam's apple. A gulp. Booth prods
again, then taps an eye, at which Clegg flinches. Got you now, Booth
says. Then he loudly tells her that a friend has come to call on them.

Stripped for action too, says Booth.

How quaint, she says. In drag.

Well, Clegg, he says: How did we do? How do we do when we think
we're being private?

Clegg has nothing to say, but he fidgets some.

Now Booth seizes his arm and shakes him hard, but Clegg goes on
looking straight ahead, his mind on the boudoir beauties to whom he
thinks he wrote a fan letter.

Hell, says Booth, isn't that a jerk-off kind of thing to do?

Not in the old days, it wouldn't have been then.

Oh no?

You know, Clegg tells him. You remember. We shared more then. It's a fact.

Clegg has no idea how fabulous he looks in that dim light, a waxwork talking while staring ahead into the cockpit. He sticks to his line.

We used to share. Clegg at his humblest.

Not everything, Booth says. Not *this*.

We did so. Clegg with a touch of whine.

Then not like this. Booth faltering a bit.

We could still. Clegg getting eager.

Are you propositioning us both? No, Clegg says, being friendly in the best way he knows how. Honest. Hey, Barney.

I'll tell you what, says Booth, with mouth of steel. I'll give you something. How about a mouthful of meat, Rupie-boy? That your dish? No, you weren't thinking of that.

Something else, Clegg says wanly. Not Algerian.

How's about something Baghdad then?

Oh no, Clegg says, I've made a mistake. I'll be going. Sorry I butted in.

You don't butt out so easy, Booth says in a grinding tone. Now you're here you can help.

Clegg is shivering, eager to dress, but Booth hauls him up and toward the cockpit, plants him hard, goes away, comes back, starts up one engine and then the other, slow-taxis the plane out of the hangar in a whirligig of thunder. All Clegg can think of is the checklist, the preflight check, the bar on Booth's flying anything at all, the low state of the fuel, the sheer unworthiness of the Mitsubishi to take to the air. Then he relaxes. Booth is only showing off, as ever. He means nothing serious. They move forward into a blinding fan of light, Booth in the left seat, Clegg in the right, and Bellanca Cruisemaster crouched naked behind them in heedless fascination.

Clegg refuses to give up his seat. Only that way can he make certain Booth stays on the ground. She goes to sit where she came from, looking out at gray vacancy. This is for Booth, not for her, and Clegg is the only one of the three with a stitch of clothing on. Everyone should have come running, such is the noise, but the tower is closed, the flying club next door has shut up shop, the terminal is void, the police will not make their rounds until three and a half hours hence. The air is theirs to maul. The land too. No harness. No run-up of the engines. No checks of any kind. Maybe, Clegg thinks, Booth is going to pull up the wheels beneath them and so strand them on the taxiway. But, instead, Booth steers for the lights at the runway's far end, half tempted to attempt the most illegal takeoff of his life.

All he does, though, is speed up and then abort with banshee brakes. To and fro, back and forth, gunning the engines, then abruptly cutting back. As if dithering. As if always finding a cloud of birds in front of him. As if hoping to burn a channel in the macadam. As if swimming lengths in the Mitsu. After half an hour, she pleads with Booth to end it, and she palms her breasts with her hands, although Clegg has seen all by now, and all through Booth's exertions he has had a halfway erection from the combined excitements.

What happens next amazes him. How he got into this prank in the first place, he isn't sure, but now Booth has dared him to stand at the runway's end, almost naked, and help him play chicken. The Mitsu is a wad of light and noise as it comes toward him, seeming to slow as it speeds up, and to speed up as Booth cuts back the power and applies the brakes. The plane sighs to a halt a yard from him, fanning him with its slow double spin. He has braved it out. He would like to be home now, saying the commercials aloud as the TV plays them.

Or wandering through the tomato patch with an old salt shaker, dusting the plants with almost any helpful powder. Eating ripe fruit right off the vine.

But Booth goes back and Clegg waits, wondering why he lets himself do anything a former colonel commands. *Sir*, he says, and does as told.

He wills the Mitsubishi not to impale him with its nose. It leaps toward him, but he stares it down and makes his mind command it back. Only just in time: Booth, surpassing himself, has brought the nose past Clegg this time, and Clegg's body fits into the space between the whirling tip of the propeller and the cabin side. He dare not move. His ears are numb. Booth gestures at him to get out of the way. Go backward. He freezes, fanned silly. Then, glueing himself to the fuselage, inches noseward, away from the blades, his mind on nothing else. He walks away, heading for the FBO, but Booth catches up with him, goes past, rolls down the gentle slope at an extra five miles per hour, and expertly swerves the plane through the hangar doorway. Booth is as good at this as a pickpocket. He puts away his stolen toy. When Clegg arrives, they are both dressed, awaiting him with grins as if they have sat reading the evening paper while he washes his hands. He dons his clothes, asks about the Mitsu master switch, hears Booth's guffaw, followed by the maddest Boothism yet. They will all three play airplane polo on the airfield, each taxiing a plane, the object of the sport being to pop an outsize balloon.

Thus discovering, says Booth at his weirdest, the ugliness of God. I'll provide the balloon, and the planes. A daylight game, of course. It'll be easier that way.

Clegg chooses a word: *flabbergast*. Then *dumbfound*. Adds the *-ed* of the past participle, putting his insane world together scrap by scrap. Booth is rapidly going over the great waterfall from which no one returns. That much is clear. Yet to him it is sport. He is as unoffendable as the sun vomiting light.

Cycling past them, he calls good night, as if saying *Eureka* to two polar bears looking for gold. They belong together, she and he. Clegg is not the third. He does not come from the same planet. Yet he lets Booth order him about, lets him play chicken on the runway with his doxy in the right-hand seat.

Home, he checks his notepad, noting that his mother has almost run out of vitamins. He monitors her supply, mails them to her in small padded bags. She cannot get them where she lives. So he counts them off, one hundred after another. Capsules blue and white link her to her son and the healthy life. If she only knew. It would kill her, like the motel sex, and what really happened in Africa. And that letter he never mailed. Vaguely he is still trying to please her without being in the least a mamma's boy. Yes. He is allowed to love. It does not say that in the Constitution, or anywhere else; but he can, he knows. Like anyone. If there have been witnesses to this night's doings, they will all three end in jail.

Clegg flicks on the news channel, which, a recent bonus on the cable, pours away twenty-four hours a day, informative mainly in its tone, its frisky smugness, its constant whir of background activity. He does not need the news. He needs the rhythm of its up-to-the-minute fakery. He needs the world in his living room, but at that precise distance. At that distance, he could accept Booth, sealed in the cathode-ray tube, an agitated leprechaun.

No, Booth is more serious than that. Booth just happens to be some form of revenge on legs. An atrocity waiting to happen. Clegg vows to find a new job at once, a new boss, a new woman to eye.

He might as well. He is going to stay behind to mature. Through some barbaric caprice of his creator, which he will attribute to heaven's weariness or from his having risen on the shoulders of ogres, he will be obliged to dedicate himself all over again to the privacy of life, aiming low. He will be the poor Roman who fetches sand from Egypt with which to mop up the blood in the arena, year after year, along with thousands of others just like him. Later on, he will be the poor dogsbody who, since depth charges have not yet been invented, leaps from a motorboat and puts a black bag over the periscope of the surfaced submarine, blinding it with a condom. He will report life on Earth, little knowing that the novel is not a program for reform or a handbook to devout living, but a wild growth breathing in its own right. Our man on Terra Nostra. Our growth, spawned by a crystal, beloved by an inventor. It will always be he, should he ever regain the heroic life he once knew, who slithers out onto the carrier deck and props up the sagging arrester wires with rolls of toilet paper: sturdy enough to support them, flimsy enough to yield when struck.

FIVE

Shane

LET US CONCEDE THEN ILLUSTRIOUS COLLEAGUES THAT THE EXPERIMENT OF EARTHING OURSELVES IN THE GUISE OF SO-CALLED ANGELS MUTATIVE IN FORM ALL THE WAY FROM BILLY GRAHAM TO OLIVIER MESSIAEN IS A WASTE OF TIME WE FOUL UP THE TIME SCHEME WE MISINTERPRET FRAGMENTS TORN FROM GREAT OR TRIVIAL POETS WE ACHIEVE AN ALMOST PALPABLE REALISM IN OUR HOMUNCULES BUT WE GET THINGS WRONG FROM SIMPLE LACK OF FAMILIARITY THE LEARNEDLY ACQUIRED IS NOT THE LIVED AMONG WE SHOULD SEND NO MORE FABRICATING WORKING MODELS FROM FILCHED IMAGES UNTIL WE HAVE A SOLID PREMISE WE SHOULD DESIST LEST WE AGAIN NOT QUITE KNOW WHAT WE ARE DOING THE FOREGOING GALLIMAUFRY IMPRESSES US AS NO MORE THAN A XYLOPHONETIC OR WHAT THE AFOREMENTIONED MESSIAEN CALLED AN ECLAIR TO HIM AN ILLUMINATION OF THE BEYOND TO MANY EARTH BEINGS A CREAM AND CHOCOLATE PASTRY WE ARE NOT IN THE BUSINESS OF BAKING ECLAIRS TRUE WE WERE LOOKING FOR A GLIMPSE OF LIFE OR HEROISM ON ANOTHER WORLD BUT ALL WE FOUND WAS HUMANKIND LOOKING AT ITSELF WE FOUND A KIND OF INTELLIGENCE BUT NO EVIDENCE OF AN ALMIGHTY BEING THOUGH MANY GUESSES WE MUST AWAIT FURTHER WITNESS FROM THE HUGE LITERATURE-GATHERERS ON MOUNT JERJ THEY HAVE NOT WORKED TOO WELL SO FAR OR CAPTURED ANYTHING COMPLETE SOMETHING WENT WRONG WE SHOULD HAVE SENT OUR MEN TO THE LIBRARIES YOU DO NOT SEND US ONLY HEROISM AND FOOTBALL BASEBALL STAND UP COMEDIANS BUT WHAT ABOUT MILTON I ASK I WHO GOT BUMPED AND BUMBLED AROUND IN AN OBSCENE BODY JUST TO KEEP A NARRATORIAL EYE ON OUR WAYFARERS WE WERE RIGHT IN ONLY ONE THING IF YOU WISH TO BE IGNORED ON EARTH BE PITIFUL BE A MERSA FATMA THEY HAD NO IDEA WHAT I WAS I THE PREFECT OF INTUITION OUR CELESTIAL MARKSMANSHIP WAS SUPERB WAS IT NOT WHEN WE PLANTED BOOTH

AND CLEGG AND SUNDRY OTHERS IN THEIR SO-CALLED
FAMILY BUT OUR NARRATION ERRS IN MANY PLACES AND
WITNESS BOOTHS AHOY WE ARE NOT SKILLED IN PRETEND
NARRATION WHICH WE COULD GLEAN FROM YOU THE
TELLING OF WHAT DID NOT OCCUR BEGUILING AS THE
GIST MAY BE WE GO ON PRACTICING NOW THE ACTORS ARE
BACK IN STORAGE WHOEVER TOLD YOU THE FIRST SEV-
ERAL HUNDRED PAGES HAS NOW BEEN DEMOTED TO
CRATER INSPECTOR HAVING IMPOSED ON THE TEXT CER-
TAIN HINTS OF HIS ORIGIN SEE LATER THE HEARER READER
IS ENCOURAGED TO DELETE ALL MANNER OF THINGS AS
SMOOTHLY AS POSSIBLE WE DO NOT DO THIS EVERY EON
HOW WAS IT WE WONDERED TO BE HUMAN SO WE ENGI-
NEERED AND SENT OUR SEMI HEROES WHO QUICKLY
LEARNED THE WAYS OF HUMANS ALAS WHAT CAME BACK
GOT SCRAMBLED IN TRANSIT AND THEN WE HAD CLEGG
SILENT BOOTH RAVING THE WHOLE TRANSMITTED AS ONE
WORD IMAGINE THAT IN A HUGE GULP OF WELL AIMED
LIGHT SHOULD KEEP SCHOLARS BUSY FOR YEARS HUNTING
MINUTE ERRORS WHAT IS BUBBLEGUM FOR WHOM IS
ELMERS GLUE NAMED NAMED WHAT IS A CHURCH KEY I AM
SORRY THESE PUZZLES WILL KEEP US MOANING FOREVER
NO ONE TALKS BACK TO US WE COULD COULD DO THE
EXPERIMENT ALL OVER AGAIN OF COURSE SENDING SO TO
SPEAK A MALE AND A FEMALE TO THE CALLING OF LIBRARI-
ANSHIP ABOUT WHICH WE KNOW A LITTLE WE HOPE THIS
FINDS YOU AS IT LEAVES US OR SOMETHING LIKE THAT
LADIES AND GENTLEMEN COME OUT AND SEE US SOME-
TIME WE ARE WHOLLY PEACEFUL BUT MONSTROUSLY
INQUISITIVE WHAT FOLLOWS IS BY WAY OF MERSA FAT-
MANA SHOWING THAT WE BURN TO EXCEL EVEN WHEN IN
DISGUISE CRITICIZE US ALL YOU WANT BUT PLEASE SEND
US YOUR COMMENTS AS IF WE WERE AN EARTH HOTEL AND
IT STAYED WITH YOU WE DO NOT DIE BY THE WAY WHO WAS
ROSA CHANCEL WHAT DOES SHE DO YOU NEED NOT RUSH
BUT PLEASE INDULGE OUR DODDERING CURIOSITY BLESS
YOU KINDLY THE READERS WE ALL ARE

AS FOR [SOLAR FLARES] PAGE NINETEEN BOOTH AND
CLEGG SHOULD HAVE BEEN USED TO THEM BUT IN THE
PROCESS OF FABRICATION THEY LOST SOME OF THE FAMIL-

IAR IN ORDER TO ACCOMMODATE THE NEW OR RATHER
WERE MADE TO THIS COULD BE ONE OF OUR LITTLE SLIPS
IT CERTAINLY WOULD BE IF AN INSPECTOR GENERAL WERE
INVESTIGATING OUR TEXT AND ASKING WAS THIS STUFF
CONCOCTED OR BASED ON SOMETHING THAT ACTUALLY
TOOK PLACE STARTING BOOTH AND CLEGG AND COMPANY
AS ORPHANS LONG AGO WAS ALL VERY WELL BUT GRAFT-
ING THEM INTO EPHEMERAL HUMANITY WAS ONEROUS WE
KEEP GETTING THINGS WRONG AS YOU WOULD ABOUT US

REGARDING [A THIRD PERSON] PAGE TWENTY KINDLY
MAKE UP YOUR OWN MINDS ABOUT WHETHER OR NOT I
WAS ABOARD THE CYRANO IF SO WHERE

[GO BACK HOME] THEY SAY ON PAGE TWENTY-ONE AND I
ADD ONLY THAT SOMETIMES MAINLY FOR DRAMATIC
EFFECT UNPARDONABLE I KNOW I HAVE THEM SAYING
THINGS NOT TRULY SENT FROM HOME OR FOUND ON
EARTH SAVE AS METAPHORS WHAT CAN YOU DO WHEN
ABUNDANT IMAGINATION RIDES HIGH

SPEAKING OF WHICH WE WONDER IF YOU DETECT HUMOR
IN THE COLLOCATION OF THE PHRASE PULLING SO MANY
GS AND THE MENTION OF A G STRING AND THE G MISSING
FROM CLEGGS NAME IS THIS HOW LITERATURE BUILDS UP
ONE CAN SEE HOW BOETHIUSS CONSOLATION BUILDS UP
MANY TEXTS COME TO US IN A STATE FAR FROM ENTIRETY
BUT WE DOTE ON THE TITLES OR FRAGMENTS WE HAVE AS
DO YOU WITH STICKY SAPPHO AND THOSE OTHER INCOM-
PLETE GREEKS EDITED BY DILIGENT PROFESSORS OH YES
WE HAD HEARD SOME COUNTRY HAD BANNED THE WORD
SUNSET WE HAVE TWO SUNS AND MAKE A DIFFERENT HUM
WITH EITHER LIP SPEAK DOUBLY ALWAYS TWO THINGS AT
ONCE WE LOVE ALL BOOKS TO DO WITH SEASONS FICTION
TO US

THAT WAS PAGE THIRTY-TWO NOW TO THIRTY-FIVE AND
[THE ONARY] ACTUALLY WE KNOW MORE OF DICTIONARIES
THAN OF LITERATURE WE KNOW ENOUGH OF THEM TO
RELISH ONE THAT IS INCOMPLETE NOTE THE RACY MAN-
NERISM OF OUR COLLOQUIAL MODE PLEASE CORRECT

ANYTHING AND SEND IT ON USING THE SUPERBOWL SIG-
NAL YOUR STRONGEST EVEN IF YOU HAVE TO WAIT FOR
DECEMBER IF THAT IS THE ONE AFTER NOVEMBER ABOUT
WHICH WE GET SO CONFUSED OR DID

NOW TO PAGE THIRTY-EIGHT AND TWO REFERENCES TO
[UNIVERSE] IN FEEBLE ANTHROPOMORPHIC ANALOGIES
ATTRIBUTED TO EARTH ALPHAS OUT OF WEARINESS AND
MALICE NOT EVEN THE STATEMENT NO STATEMENT
ABOUT THE UNIVERSE IS ACCURATE IS ACCURATE

IN RE [HAROLD ROBINS TO TROTSKY] ON SIXTY-SIX SPLIN-
TERS MY DEARS WHAT A STORY [INERT CARGO] FOUND ON
SEVENTY-FIVE EXACTLY WHAT BOOTH AND CLEGG WERE
DURING EARTH TRANSIT OUR ENTIRE STOCK OF EARTHEN
LITERATURE PIPED INTO THEIR EARS MUSIC TOO DURING
VOYAGE HARDLY ANYONE AT HOME READS OR KNOWS OF
THEIR ADVENTURE

MAYBE [AN ANIMAL] ON SEVENTY-NINE PROMPTS ME TO SAY
GOOD EVENING MEET YOUR MAKER NOTICE IN WHAT SOR-
DID WISE I MAKE MY ENTRANCE HOPING TO PASS UNNO-
TICED AS

FROM EIGHTY-NINE YOU WILL GLEAN MY NOTION OF A
DEATH SENTENCE TERRESTRIAL PUN

[MERSA FATMA] NINETY-THREE I WOULD HAVE RATHER BEEN
RIGEL KENT BUT I HAD THINGS TURN OUT OTHERWISE I AM
JUST WONDERING IF THE OMNIPOTENT DEITY SOTUQ-
NANGU IN ANOTHER NOVEL HAD AS MUCH POWER OR WAS
CONTROLLED BY A HUMAN WITH DIVINE PRETENSIONS

[MIRACLE] IT SAYS ON ONE HUNDRED TEN BUT THE AUTHEN-
TIC MIRACLE IS THAT THEY WANGLED THEIR WAY INTO
AMERICAN SOCIETY SOMETIME BEFORE THE VIET NAM WAR
AND WENT UNDETECTED ALTHOUGH FREQUENTLY AROUS-
ING WONDER OR DISMAY WITH THEIR IGNORANCE OF TRIV-
IAL THINGS THEIR PRESCIENT SCIENCE A MOTHER A SISTER
HELPED OF COURSE AND A GIRLFRIEND

WHERE IT SAYS [KNOW HIM ALREADY] ON ONE HUNDRED TWELVE WE SEE BOOTHS FAMOUS INTUITION AT WORK WAS HE A MAN WHO THOUGHT HE WAS A CHARACTER WHEN ALL THE TIME HE WAS A MAN OR WAS HE A CHARACTER WHO THOUGHT HE WAS A MAN WHEN ALL THE TIME HE WAS A CHANGELING HOW IS THE READER EVER TO KNOW OR THE OVERHEARER ALL ACCOUNTS OF BEINGS ARE IMAGINATIVE EXCEPT THOSE PROVIDED BY DOCTORS AND ACTUARIES AND SOME OF THOSE WRONG

AS FOR ONE HUNDRED TWELVE WHERE IT SAYS [NOWHERE TO BE SEEN] YOU SHOULD UNDERSTAND VISIBLE TO SOME, THE BELIEVERS

AND ON ONE HUNDRED SEVENTEEN AS FOR [ICONS] UNDERSTAND A MOMENT THERE OF TRUE CONTRIBUTIVE MYSTICISM

TURN NOW TO THE [LOVING GOD] ON ONE HUNDRED EIGHTEEN CLEGG BEING ENTITLED TO HIS COMPARISONS THOUGH I THINK HE HAS SOME DISTANCE TO GO INDISTINGUISHING AUTHOR FROM FIRST CAUSE SOMETIMES MY BRACKETS MISLEAD AS MUCH AS OUR NOTION OF NOVEMBER

AS ON ONE HUNDRED TWENTY-TWO NOT STRESSING THE TRANSLATION BUT SINGLING IT OUT AS NOW TO MAKE THIS MERELY PROCEDURAL POINT

AND SO TO ONE HUNDRED THIRTY-SEVEN [WALKING ON WATER] A MUCH DESPISED WEEKEND PRACTICE ON OUR HOME PLANET THE TECHNIQUE ONCE LEARNED CALLOW

WHEREAS ON ONE HUNDRED FORTY-EIGHT IN [HEART BEAT] YOU HAVE NOUN AND VERB SORRY

ON ONE HUNDRED FIFTY-THREE NOTE THE NONVERB [ENTHUSE] ODD HOW THE PREROGATIVE OF GODS HAS BECOME INNER DIRECTED AT LEAST IN IDIOM

BUT WHAT THE HELL WHEN YOU REACH ONE HUNDRED FIFTY-EIGHT AND [WHO HE REALLY WAS] QUITE OFTEN WE FOUND IN OUR EARLY RESEARCHES ADVERTISING WILL DECLARE A CERTAIN ACTOR IS HE REALLY IS THE PART HE PLAYS AND CHARLIE CHAPLIN IS HE REALLY IS BELT IT OUT THE GREAT DICTATOR WHICH MEANS HE ASSUMES HIS ROLE UTTERLY WITH NO PART OF HIMSELF UNUSED THUS CREATING AN IMPRESSION THAT THE GREAT DICTATOR COULD BE ENACTED BY NONE OTHER THAN CHAPLIN CIVILIZATION SO CALLED ON EARTH THRIVES ON SUCH LOOSELY INSPECTED CONCEITS THAT GAVE US ENORMOUS PROBLEMS IN THE PLANNING PHASE MUCH MORE SAY THAN CLEGGS INTERNALIZED PARAMOUR AQUA REGIA FOR WHOM WE HAD TO EXERT OURSELVES TO GAIN CLEARANCE

ALAS ONE HUNDRED FIFTY-EIGHT SPEAKING OF FEMALE APPARITIONS OUR SULFUR BOGS HAVE NO NAUSICAAS NOR EVER WILL

AGAIN TO AQUA REGIA ONE HUNDRED SIXTY-ONE THE KIND OF INTERNAL PARAMOUR OFTEN MINTED BY OUR RACE SOME BEING BETTER THAN OTHERS AT THIS PASTIME ON TO ONE HUNDRED SIXTY-TWO THAT SAYS [HE HAD NEVER WANTED SIBLING] WE FORCED THEM ON HIM FOR COPIOUSNESS OF ILLUSION A COUPLE OF AUTO WRECKS PROVIDED THE RIGHT LAUNCHING PAD AND THE ORPHAN MYTH CAME INTO ITS OWN PLIED BY THE LOST MEMORY FIX

JUST ANOTHER OF EARTHS UNSOLVED MYSTERIES COMING OUT TO US FOR AGES NOW ALTHOUGH CLEGG DID NOT SEE MUCH OF THE SHOW HERE HE SAW THOSE REPEATS ALL WRITTEN BY SALLY HOWELL WHOM WE HAD THOUGHT OF KIDNAPPING EXCEPT THAT WE DO NO SUCH THING NOT EVEN ON PAGE ONE HUNDRED SIXTY-TWO

WE HAVE NO IDEA WHY WE KEEP MENTIONING AQUA REGIA BUT IT MUST BE THAT WE FANCY HER FOR OURSELVES IN OUR DIPSY DOODLE WAY TO CONSOLE US IN OUR BUNGLINGS WE HAVE LEARNED THAT YOU HUMANS TRY TO AMASS ENOUGH ECSTASY TO MAKE DEATH WORTH-

WHILE YOU TRY TO BALANCE THINGS OUT HOPING TO AMASS ENOUGH BEFORE THE COUP DE GRACE COMES EVEN WE KNOW THIS WHO HAVE WORKED YOU OUT FROM MOVIES RATHER THAN FROM LITERATURE WELL ON ONE HUNDRED SIXTY-SIX IT IS HAIL AND FAREWELL TO [PARENTS] THE EXPENDABLES

AND ON ONE HUNDRED NINETY-EIGHT THE REFERENCE TO [BABETTE] REMINDS ME THAT SHE WAS AN EXPORT LIKE OUR TWO ORPHAN PILOTS AND SHE RETURNED WITH THEM REDUCED TO SOMETHING YOU WOULD CALL AN AGATE PRISM THE SIZE OF A CABBAGE WHITES EYE

[MICROCOSMS] ON TWO HUNDRED FOUR INSPIRES ME TO THINK HE IS GOOD HERE ISNT HE GIVEN HIS LIMITED FREE WILL

TWO HUNDRED EIGHT [ALCUBIERRE DRIVE] SOUNDING LIKE AN ADDRESS IS NOT DO NOT FRET ABOUT IT IT IS DECADES AFTER YOUR TIME

WHEREAS [BETA PICTORIS] TWO HUNDRED NINE PROVES HIS MIND IS WANDERING

AND THAT REFERENCE TO [ANOTHER STAR] ON TWO HUNDRED NINE MEANS MERELY WOOPS HERE THEY ARE FRESH FROM YOU KNOW WHERE

ALTHOUGH SEE TWO HUNDRED ELEVEN [TRAVEL BETWEEN STARS] BECAUSE AS EARTHLINGS THEY HAD NO IDEA THEY HAD ALREADY ACCOMPLISHED IT SOMEWHERE YOUR BLOOD SPITTING KEATS WRITES OF A MAN WHO IS TO BE MURDERED AS A MURDERED MAN EVEN CROPPING A SYLLABLE AS IN MURDRD PROLEPSIS THAT BOOTH AND CLEGG HAD DONE IT BEFORE THEY KNEW ABOUT IT

TWO HUNDRED NINETEEN [IF SHE WERE AN ANGEL] THE TROUBLE BEING THAT OUR IDEA OF AN ANGEL IS SOMEBODY COMPULSIVELY TRAVELING FIRST CLASS AND ALWAYS QUOTING

[I CAN BE ANYTHING] IT SAYS ON TWO HUNDRED NINETEEN COURTESY OF YOU KNOW WHOM WE DONT ALLOW JUST ANYTHING BUT WE ARE VERY PERMISSIVE

TWO HUNDRED TWENTY-EIGHT TELLS YOU [MERSA FATMA HAD VANISHED] QUITE RIDICULOUS BUT SO IT GOES WHEN YOU ARE NARRATING SOMEONE ELSES THOUGHTS

THE JULY MUDDLE SHOWS UP ON TWO HUNDRED TWENTY-NINE ALL AMERICAN AIRCRAFT BEAR THE LETTER N WHICH STANDS FOR NORTH AMERICA AND NOVEMBER HAPPENS TO BE THE WORD CHOSEN TO REPRESENT N SO IN A SENSE IT IS ALWAYS NOVEMBER IN THE AIR AND FOR AMERICAN AIRMEN WHO SOMETIMES REGARD JULY AS NOVEMBER SAY WHATEVER THE WEATHER ONLY FOR THIRTY DAYS A YEAR ARE THEY IN TUNE WITH NATURE I COULD HAVE REPAIRED THIS MESS GIVEN MORE TIME BUT ALL I HEARD WAS GET IT DOWN TO THEM THEY HAVE BEEN AGES WAITING SO I DID YOU CAN SEE THE PROBLEM AS WITH ZULU OR GREEN-WICH TIME ANOTHER CRAZED HUMAN ILLUSION OUR OWN PLANETS AXIS DOES NOT TILT

IT IS ALWAYS NOVEMBER IN OUR HEARTS

SO ON TWO HUNDRED THIRTY YOU READ [WAS JULY] GOD HELP US ENCORE UNE FOIS SORRY YOU CAN SEE MY PROB-LEM SOMETIMES I NEED IT THE WEATHER TO VARY A BIT AS IN CHAUCER WHO HAS A DAY OF UNUSUAL HEAT SOME OTHER POET RAN OFF WITH IT

PERHAPS TO PAGE TWO HUNDRED SIXTY-SEVEN WHERE IT SAYS [IF INDEED UFOS WERE TAKING SAMPLES AT RANDOM AS SOME RETURNED ABDUCTEES CLAIMED] NOT ONE OF OUR HABITS I AM GLAD TO SAY WE MAY GRAFT AND IMPER-SONATE BUT WE DO NOT KIDNAP WHO THAT READS MINDS AT COLOSSAL DISTANCES NEEDS TO

THEN ON THREE HUNDRED FIVE YOU HAVE TO DEAL WITH THE PHRASE [HARDLY AT HOME ON HIS HOME PLANET] AND I ADD THAT THERE HE HAS NO NAME BUT IS NAMED FOR AN ABSTRUSE WAVELENGTH EVER A FIDGET A GADABOUT AN

EVADER BUT REMEMBER DOMESTICALLY VISIBLE ONLY AS
A LATTICE OF BLUE AND AMBER LIGHT ALTHOUGH YOU NO
DOUBT THINK I AM LYING BUT ONLY ON TERRA FIRMA AS
WE CALL YOU DID HE HAVE A FACE AND THE REST AS FOR
OUR HOME PLANET AS YOU YOURSELVES MAY NOT CALL IT
ITS NAME BEST TRANSLATED GOES *SALMON ILLUSTRIOUS
CODICIL* MAKE WHAT YOU CAN OF IT

AH THREE HUNDRED SIX IT SAYS [PROXIMA CENTAURI]
MEANING ALPHA AMOUNTING TO A BIT OF SUBURBAN GOS-
SIP EQUIVALENT TO THE SIGHT IN A SEEDY SUBURB OF A
STRETCH LIMO OUTPOURING MESSIAEN

ALAS THREE HUNDRED SEVEN THAT [THE RHESUS CON-
DOR RIFT] AND ENVIRONS ARE NOW SPRINKLED WITH VUL-
GARIAN MOTELS

[SOME PLANET OR OTHER] SAYS THREE HUNDRED ELEVEN
AND I AM IMPOSING ON HIM AGAIN PLEASE REMEMBER WE
ARE NEW TO THE PRETEND MODE AND UNUSED TO TAK-
ING THE BLAME FOR WHAT WE HAVE FUDGED UP

THAT [WHITE FLASH AMONG TIN SWALLOWS] I RATE AS ONE
OF MY BETTER CAMEOS WHEREAS [LIKE AN ALIEN] REFERS
YOU TO THE ONLY ALIENS WE KNOW WHO INDEED ARE
TINY AND CAN BE INHALED ALL THE TIME LIKE GERMS
THREE HUNDRED THIRTEEN–FOURTEEN

A JOKE ON THREE HUNDRED FIFTEEN [FLY THE LOCAL
STAR] PARDON MY EXUBERANCE AKIN I HOPE TO THAT IN
THE WILD APPENDED NOTES TO TSELIOT WHOM WE PRO-
NOUNCE TZEELATH PLEASE NOTE THE HEADY REASSIGN-
MENT FOR A PILOT TAKING CHARGE OF IT NOT SPINNING
ALONG THE RIND

OF COURSE ONLY ON EARTH IS HE A PILOT

THREE HUNDRED THIRTY-FOUR HAS [THE SPEEDS OF CER-
TAIN STARS] ONE OF OUR MAIN PREOCCUPATIONS THIS
RATHER LIKE EARTH ENTERTAINMENT BUT TEMPERAMEN-
TALLY WE ARE CLOSEST THE NORWEGIANS WHO HAVE NO

TV AND BOAST ONE RADIO STATION TRANSMITTING
ENTIRELY IN LATIN MUCH TO OUR MOOD THAT WE ARE A
GLUM CREW IN THE MAIN

AS YOU CAN TELL WHEN I SAY THREE HUNDRED FIFTY-
EIGHT [PLATES OF GLASS A THOUSAND MILES SQUARE] SIG-
NIFYING PURE HOMESICKNESS DISGUISED AS HYPERBOLE

AND SO TO BED WITH [INFINITY] ON THREE HUNDRED
FIFTY-NINE IN OUR WORLD AN OBSCENITY TANTAMOUNT
TO MOTHERFUCKER WE ALWAYS SPEAK OF FINITY INSTEAD

TO WHICH I MUST ADD THAT EVEN AT A SPEED OF ONE
HUNDRED MILES PER SECOND THE TRIP FROM YOU TO US
WOULD TAKE SOME FIFTEEN THOUSAND YEARS SO IF YOUR
SHIP STARTED OUT IN THE TIME OF ABRAHAM IT WOULD BE
ONLY SLIGHTLY MORE THAN HALFWAY EVEN NOW HENCE
THIS ROMANCE SENT YOU TO DISPLAY OUR PACES
WHEREAS YOUR TRANSMISSIONS REACH US IN FOUR AND A
HALF YEARS WHY DONT YOU BUCK UP AND WE NOW WON-
DER WHY WE BOTHERED SENDING ENTITIES WHEN
WORDS WOULD HAVE DONE JUST AS WELL JUDGE FOR
YOURSELVES THE RESULTS ARE YOURS DEDICATED WITH-
OUT PERMISSION LIKE VAUGHAN WILLIAMSS FIFTH SYM-
PHONY TO JEAN SIBELIUS WITH THE SINCEREST FLATTERY
YOUR GREAT EXAMPLE IS WORTHY OF IMITATION SIGNED
YOUR APPROXIMATES IN CENTAURUS AS YOU CALL US
WHEREAS OUR NAME FOR THE CONSTELLATION IS FOUXGY
NAL THE PATTERN OF A CERTAIN BIFURCATING VEIN IN
OUR LEGS SORRY AGAIN ABOUT ALL THE LITTLE SLIPS YOU
CAN BRACE YOURSELVES FOR REVISIONIST POSTSCRIPTS
ALL WE ASK IN RETURN ANOTHER SERIES COMPARABLE TO
WINGS OF THE LUFTWAFFE NOW COMING THROUGH IN
DRABS AND DRIBS MY CORRECT NAME SHOULD YOU NEED
IT FOLLOWS THIS DE RIGUEUR PAUSE AND SPACE

ONE EIGHTH HUMBLY